ABOUT THE AUTHOR

alex:g is the stage name of ALEX J GEAIRNS. In 1981, his school heralded him as a science-fiction author in its silver jubilee year, splashed all over the local newspaper, and it's taken until now to live up to that hype. He achieved a degree of notoriety on Sky television for his year as the presenter and producer of *On the Edge* for Edge Media's Controversial TV channel.

He helmed the annual Cult TV Festivals from 1994 to 2007 (www.cult.tv), and was the creator, producer and presenter of *Behind the Sofa*, a DVD/Blu-ray review show, again for Edge Media Television.

For a decade he wrote for *Satellite Times*, and was the TV and Video Review Editor for "lad-mag" *Front* during its debut year.

Alex wrote the English version of *The Avengers Companion*, originally published in French, detailing the adventures of Steed alongside Mrs Peel and fellow partners. He was a DJ for the whole of the 1980s, including a nightclub residency and a diary filled with personal appearances.

He current produces and presents alternative current affairs show *Doomwatch* (www.doomwatch.com) on community radio station Peterborough FM, and is available as a lecturer, giving presentations on the facts in screen fiction.

Alex is a member of the National Union of Journalists, Equity and the Chartered Institute of Marketing, and can even be found in Spotlight. His official website is at www.alexg.com

MINDFUL

alex:g

Matador
9 Priory Business Park
Kibworth Beauchamp
Leicestershire LE8 0RX, UK
Tel: (+44) 116 279 2299
Fax: (+44) 116 279 2277
Email: books@troubador.co.uk
Web: www.troubador.co.uk/matador

ISBN 978-1784621-346

*Extract of lyrics: "(We don't need this) Fascist Groove Thang" (Gregory/Marsh/Ware) is published by Virgin Music
Publishers Ltd/Sound Diagrams, and used with the permission of Heaven 17 – thanks guys!*

British Library Cataloguing in Publication Data.
A catalogue record for this book is available from the British Library.

Printed and bound by CPI Group (UK) Ltd, Croydon, CR0 4YY
Typeset in 11pt Bembo by Troubador Publishing Ltd, Leicester, UK

Matador is an imprint of Troubador Publishing Ltd

MINDFUL

* * *

Limited Edition
First Hardback Printing
Number

00625

of 1,000

DEAD HEAT

Late again. It wasn't an attribute appreciated in a Prime Minister, but Ray Grady had made it acceptable. And he certainly knew how to make an entrance, although this wasn't a baying pack you'd want to keep waiting.

There was that feeling of something Earth-shattering about to happen. A tightening of expectation. Like those shivers up the spine experienced as a teenager; would the target of your affections say yes or no to your offer of a date? Butterflies beating their rhythm, swarming in the stomach.

Tony Pearce was feeling all that and more. Time had wound down to a snail's pace. Beads of sweat formed on his forehead. After a casual dabbing, as well as swabbing his chunky cheeks, courtesy of a monogrammed handkerchief, he felt somewhat repaired. It helped to keep up appearances. Deep breaths were his way to settle his blood pressure. His doctor blamed that on all those custard doughnuts. In terms of vices, that was the only one he still allowed himself.

But no, this wasn't a date. There was a lot more riding on this meeting than a romantic entanglement. Would his boss deliver a quality performance? Tony knew he was quite capable, but still he was tense.

He looked around the meeting room. No external windows cranked up that feeling of claustrophobia. Pristine cream walls on three sides, clinical in a way you'd associate with a hospital ward rather than the Stock Exchange. Talk about striding into the lion's den to deliver bad news.

The front of the auditorium was just undergoing the final stages of set-up. The bulky speaker's lectern was bathed in a harsh spotlight, the big screen at the back of the stage all ready to induce "death by Powerpoint".

Suddenly the logo of the House of Commons appeared on the canvas, almost an anachronism given what had happened in the last few weeks. Joey the technician, clearly the top dog, was ushering his colleagues around, demanding pace and accuracy at the same time. He stopped centre stage, to provide an unwelcome pose for a photographer who was trying to get a march on setting his focal lengths.

Tony picked out the buxom power dresser striding from the stage area towards him. Her shoulder-length brunette hair was bouncing in time with her steps. They'd only known each other a couple of months. Why they hadn't crossed paths before was anyone's guess. Tony exhaled a couple of sharp breaths to try and gain a little more composure. Georgie fixed eye contact with him, and smiled.

'All set,' she almost whispered, pointing back to the stage to emphasise her point. Tony forced a smile.

'Any minute now. One big jungle. One hell of a rumble,' he replied tensely. Georgie felt the vibration of her Blackberry and retrieved it from her pocket.

'You'd think they'd know by now. We have the best hunter of them all,' she commented, while clicking keys on her mobile.

Tony snorted. 'Unifying a country on the brink of civil war, putting some faith back into politicians.' He looked down at the back of his hand, fingers out-stretched. His nails were finally beginning to grow back again. 'Curbing bankers? A piece of cake.'

He didn't get to see Georgie as much as he wanted to. She was in charge over at the Home Office, something that just a few months ago would have been considered too onerous a task for a thirty-four-year-old. Georgie was so much more, well, *likable*, than previous incumbents such as Theresa May. As far as Georgie was concerned these were women pretending to be men. And doing so very badly.

Tony jumped with a shudder. A strong hand had clasped his shoulder. He looked around to see their head of security, Carl Meddings. Tall, cool and dark, wireless headset in place, a chunky mobile phone in his free hand. Tony sighed with relief, his eyes staring lasers at Meddings, silently suggesting "please don't do that again".

Meddings raised an eyebrow. 'All set?' he enquired.

Tony unconsciously wiped his hands together. 'Let battle commence,' he intoned, with a theatrical flourish. Meddings nodded sagely, and strode off towards the double entrance doors, Tony and Georgie watching him go. Neither of them quite understood his military mind, and the cold detachment that seemed to go with it.

Tony looked up at the control room booth, in the ceiling at the back of the auditorium, only too conscious of it being a frenzied hive of activity. The shadows within were hyperactive, no doubt adjusting lighting, checking sound levels, and getting a focus on their camera feeds. If they only knew this was the lull before the storm.

Georgie was using her Blackberry to make note of those who were joining the congregation. The venue was beginning to fill up ever-faster now. Word of mouth had made this the place to be, regardless of any previous commitments. From oligarchs to middle managers, some of the biggest wheels in finance were here, the atmosphere so close it almost felt like they were attending their own execution.

Tony had given up trying to hide his smugness. 'Wait until they hear what Ray has to say. Stampede with the emphasis on "stamp".' Georgie kept looking up and around, adding more and more ticks to her list of invited guests.

'Anyone with any sense has long been out of the markets,' she confirmed. The irony of staging the forthcoming announcement right above the Stock Exchange trading floor wasn't lost on either of them. Give Ray Grady his dues, this was a Prime Minister media-savvy enough to know what would grab the headlines, even if the subject matter was a little dry for most tastes.

The hustle and bustle for some reason ceased. A short pause of complete silence. Without warning, the double entrance doors at the back of the auditorium were flung open, Meddings crashing through at the front, with his operatives Dougan and Kindon either side of him to hold the doors open. As Meddings carved a gangway through the massing reporters, nonchalantly behind him strode the Prime Minister of just over fourteen weeks, Ray Grady.

Hands initially in pockets, he wore a knowing but self-effacing smile. He was remarkably casual in fashion choices, light brown jacket, turquoise trousers, and a distinct lack of a tie. With his hair ever so slightly disturbed, people always said he looked shorter in real life than "on the box".

You could almost smell the media-savvy aspects of his personality, looking younger than he really was, with the sort of demeanour which gave away his former career as a long-running "Television Personality". All done without

3

the help of a surgeon's knife, just clean living from only consuming food and drink which helped his body prosper. Well, most of the time anyway.

Following him into the venue were his entourage, a balanced mix of half a dozen male and female civil servants, united by all being very much in the "smart casual" bracket. They too looked younger than the type you'd have expected to inhabit the corridors of Whitehall, a nod to the civilised revolution which had so recently occurred in the United Kingdom.

Flashbulbs were heavily illuminating proceedings, throwing the carefully balanced lighting into disarray. The noise level was reaching a crescendo, with every member of the press acting like a spoiled child demanding attention.

Meddings was doing a fine job of keeping the gangway clear. With door duty no longer required, the burley Dougan and Kindon were ensuring the waves of journalists and cameramen didn't overwhelm the passageway. All, that is, except for one.

Ray knew Phil Conway very well indeed. They had scratched each other's backs for years. The thirty-one-year-old Phil had been an entertainment correspondent, who often made connections for Ray. That way, Ray could poach the cream of the celebrity fraternity for his ratings-juggernaut of a chat show. Phil had become disillusioned and set up on his own, just before Ray had realised what was really going on, behind the scenes, in the once "Great" Britain. Suddenly they found each other working together again, hand-in-glove, behind the scenes.

Phil darted under Kindon's arm, giving the security man a surreptitious wink. With a top of the range micro-audio recorder in hand Phil caught Ray's eye, just as they began to walk side by side, down the auditorium aisle. They both knew their acting had to be impeccable.

'Prime Minister,' Phil barked at Ray. Ray feigned slight annoyance.

'It's Ray. You know we don't stand on ceremony, Phil,' replied the PM, as he shifted a photographer out of his direct path. They were going to make this bit of business look good.

'Some worried faces amongst these bankers,' Phil intoned, pressing the recorder nearer to Ray's mouth.

'*Bank-sters*,' corrected Ray. 'Like gangsters, creating a ghost town, except not enough fighting on the dance floor.' Ray hoped he wouldn't have to pay royalties to the 1980s band The Specials for quoting them in his impromptu mash-up.

The best-laid-plan was usurped by another reporter, who had used the bustle surrounding the duo to dart through the only possible gap. He was now right in front of them. Judging by his looks, you wouldn't have been surprised if his nickname was "Weasel".

'Mister Grady!' he almost whistled. 'What effect will your announcement have on stock prices?'

Ray cleared his throat, indicating a considerable degree of annoyance. 'Hold on! I haven't said anything yet!' The weasel visibly took a step back as Ray barked at him again. 'Besides, it's the effect that it has on ordinary people that's important.'

Moving the weasel to one side, Ray left Phil with the rest of the pack as he reached the auditorium stage. His step up was more like a bounce, the stupidity of the weasel being enough to prepare the ground for Ray to be ready for a fight.

Some of the pack found places on whatever seats had been left available, with others having to stand around the sides. This was now a packed house. Phil found himself standing next to Dougan, and had a quiet word. Dougan laughed, and Phil smiled back, shrugging his shoulders.

Meddings looked at his watch, and carefully made his way out of the room. The tedium of presentations was something he was never comfortable with enduring, and he always told anyone who listened that he had something else to do.

Camera crews were panning around the auditorium for shots of the crowd. They were ready to crash-zoom in on anyone showing the slightest hint of a yawn. They had their orders as to how this event was going to be portrayed on the evening news, and they all wanted to be the one who got the "money shot".

Ray readied himself at the lectern. He went to straighten his tie but then realised he wasn't wearing one. The habits of a lifetime are sometimes hard to break. The stage technician whispered gently into a headset microphone, which was enough to make the house lights dim. The room was enveloped in silence, as the stage became the centre of attention.

Ray glanced aside to Joey the technician, who with a very slight nod gave the cue to begin. Ray paused briefly, cleared his throat, every action cranking up the expectation.

'Lords, ladies, gentlemen, thieves, wastrels…' Ray's beguiling venom increased with each word. It helped to test the mettle of his audience. 'As I am finding to my cost, civil servants have great difficulty keeping a still tongue. So, you may think you know what I am going to announce today.'

Amongst the oligarchs in the room, those with the contacts, the "inside tracks", there was a lot of staring into space. Their arrogance permeated the room like the smell of molten vomit.

'Our beloved television and radio networks are present,' Ray continued, not pleased with how the Fourth Estate had been treating his government. 'En masse. This speech has to go out live if they want to talk to me later. Franklin D. Roosevelt-style. Like his "fireside chats". So my words aren't filtered by selective editing.' Ray was overwhelmed by mock indignation. 'Not that they'd do anything like that. Surely not!'

Deafening silence from the media representatives. Those who had been around long enough knew those who had put the truth before their own careers. None of them were here today, as they had long-since been moved sideways, sacked, or pensioned-off. From those outside of the mainstream juggernaut, there was a knowing, muted laughter. It was not a well-kept secret anymore as to how much the news had become a propaganda machine. Not for the government, oh no. The corporate interests behind the media machinery had been exposed to the light of publicity. Mainly during Ray's lightning-fast election campaign.

The PM was soaking up the uncomfortable atmosphere. Cheerfully, he continued, 'This is an anniversary, of election victory. Our first one hundred days. Just over one-fifty since our alliance of independent candidates was formed.' He never tired of spelling it out. 'We have an appeal to what we call "political atheists". We keep things simple. Good solutions usually are.' Yes, he knew he was gloating, but the majority in the audience had written off his chances before he had even started. And they still didn't believe what had happened on "Election Night".

'So, as announced in our manifesto, we will honour the pledge to ban the gambling elements of the share markets. The "put options". And encourage greater worker ownership of shares.'

That was as popular as Jeremy Clarkson at a Greenpeace rally. Nervous shuffling. "Squeaky bum time" for those who appreciated their annual incomes had just fallen off a cliff. Looking to the sides of the room, and towards the back, Ray saw a few smiles amongst those not so benefitted by such lucrative career add-ons.

Ray knew it was time to turn up the heat. The cameras would be zooming in on him now, after all. 'Money is not the God. Social responsibility, in its truest sense, should be. You, me, everyone, will be in charge of our own lives and actions.'

It was as if he had lifted the fear from those further down the pecking order. They applauded, stopping only when they realised they had identified themselves to their seniors.

Ray could make out Tony and Georgie, standing to the side of the stage, and joining in with the appreciation. Tony nodded supportively, which Ray picked up on. Tony continued the applause, before turning to Georgie and giving her a brief, underplayed wink.

Realising it might now be time to stop, Tony put his hands awkwardly to his side, cleared his throat, before straightening his tie. In a whisper he addressed Georgie. 'Hold on to something solid.' Georgie overplayed looking around for something appropriate, before playfully gripping Tony's arm.

Ray was now into unexplored territory as far as the audience was concerned. 'The manufacture of goods is the key to restoring the sovereignty and independence of the United Kingdom. But where will the money come from for this?' Cheekily, with a tint of meerkat, he chimed, 'Simples.' His supporters chuckled nervously. 'As of today, I am ordering an audit of the Bank of England.'

If they still used such things, you could imagine the journalists in the room breaking their pencils. There was a cloud of bluster and indignation sweating out of the oligarchs.

Ray was on his soapbox, well and truly. 'No-one actually knows who their shareholders are! Much like the Federal Reserve in the USA.' He could feel his fists clenching as he continued, almost unable to control his rage. 'I have also informed the lunatics in charge at the International Monetary Fund that we are reneging on further interest payments. Our country's debt has been paid off many times over.' The next bit was purely for the broadcast cameras, and others in the room who knew the truth only too well. 'The only reason Britain still owes money is the exorbitant interest rates we have been charged. Enough is enough!'

More of those from the "coal face" began to break ranks. Applause came from some of the middle managers as well now, and to hell with what the oligarchs thought of them for doing so.

Ray was enjoying himself far too much. And the show was far from over.

'We will bring derivative trading to an end. There will be no more betting on companies and businesses failing. How do you win in that game?' Ray paused for dramatic effect. 'By making those interests fail. If you control the system, you can engineer the outcome, and that will stop...' Again he cranked up the tension, and slowed his speech right down: '...as of now.'

He sought out the positions of the broadcast cameras again. Ray's media experience meant he knew he would be staring right down the barrels of the lenses, directly at the audiences at home. 'Want to play that game with businesses? Go elsewhere. This honey pot is officially closed.'

All around the venue, there was silence, quickly replaced by a buzz of amazement. On the sidelines, Tony checked his nails again, palms outward, beaming an almost luminescent smile. Georgie breathed out slowly and turned to Tony.

'Is that the FT One Hundred I hear jumping out of the window?' she whispered, in mock outrage.

Ray realised the audience was expecting more. And boy, he was going to give it to them. Both barrels. 'Our Government is not going to underwrite any more bailouts. Please don't hold a gun to your own heads anymore...' He paused yet again, knowing his audience was hanging on his every word. 'I'll only tell you to shoot. Society no longer cares if banks disintegrate ...' This was an unspoken truth that the entire financial industry knew.

'Go ahead, go to the wall.' Ray wasn't joking. 'The UK will ensure its money is backed by something tangible, not magiked out of thin air.' Again it was time to elaborate further for the video cameras. 'We are at the rebirth of the civil society. The key to celebration of British culture. And "British" will no longer be a dirty word, hidden behind the "straw man" of alleged racism. There are three corners to our society. State and marketplace being two. We have all forgotten the third... The people!'

Some enthusiastic applause punctuated the occasion. Ray raised an arm in grateful appreciation. It was like his election rallies all over again. Only those who thought themselves still in power were notable by their staying in their seats, stony-faced and ashen.

What sounded like a car backfiring, twice, caused the crowd to spontaneously mute. There was no way to hear noise from the streets surrounding them, so there was a reason that everyone should be just a little bit puzzled. Someone on the front row, a mousy secretary, saw it first. Her scream was enough to focus everyone back to the lectern. They didn't see Ray standing where he had been. Eyes were drawn to the floor of the stage.

Panic immediately hit the audience like a tidal wave. Some immediately theorised it was a heart attack. Tony and Georgie were the first out of the blocks to dash to the body, closely followed by a pair of smartly dressed medics, and then Meddings. From the back of the room, Dougan and Kindon paced swiftly to the front of the stage, like a cross between tanks and hovercrafts, looking from side to side to watch for any behaviour you wouldn't associate with what had just happened.

It was Kindon who noticed the dishevelled, short-sleeved hunched figure of Chris Bowden. As everyone else rushed to the exits, or sought some sort of explanation, this gawky thirty-something stared blankly at the stage, breathing far too heavily for someone who had been sat down for several minutes. It was the eyes that really gave it away to Kindon. Lights on, nobody home.

The crowd was beginning to piece it together, and that ramped up their hysteria. Those were shots being fired. Could anyone tell where they had come from? Was the Prime Minister okay? Was there a hitman with a gun in here with them? A whisper went across the room, as one by one the unflinching stance of Chris Bowden drew the attention of many of those around him. They all stepped back, creating a vacuum that made him the centre of attention. Everyone could see him sweating, still not moving, with his dark, greasy hair getting wetter by the second.

Kindon caught Dougan's eye, and highlighted his intentions. With stealth they approached their target from two angles, one still mesmerised by the single point on stage.

Suddenly, breaking from the third corner of a triangle made with his operatives, Meddings dived onto the statue that was Chris Bowden. Kindon and Dougan quickly responded, ensuring there was no place to go. The quarry was toppled, like a Saddam Hussein monolith crashing to the ground, and limbs were grabbed. For such a slight man, Bowden put up one hell of a fight.

On the stage, Tony and Georgie were ensuring the handful of reporters and cameramen trying to get close to Ray were intercepted. The pair of medics toiled, doing their best to patch things up. Tony's mobile phone rang, not entirely appropriate as the music was the chase scene from *The Italian Job*.

He nodded in response, and shouted down to the medics. 'We have our ambulance to take him away. Can you get him ready to be carried out through the kitchens?'

The medics looked at each other. Clearly not the suggestion they would have made. Their concentration was again broken by the commotion from down in front of the stage. Chairs had been hurled out of the way as a baying pack assembled around Bowden and his captors. Bowden had something to say, and he was shouting it out loud.

'Stop these madmen! Stop these corrupt politicians! Stop these madmen! Stop these corrupt politicians!' If these security types worried about such things, they might have been suspecting rabies as the cause. Dougan and Kindon were somehow managing, with a little help from Meddings, to slap cuffs on Bowden's wrists and ankles. The way his limbs were flaying they might well have had every suspicion they were dealing with an octopus rather than a human being.

Bowden chanted his mantra again. 'Stop these madmen! Stop these corrupt politicians! Stop these madmen! Stop these corrupt politicians!' As he got into the swing of chanting his chorus a third time, Meddings hit him with the sweetest right uppercut those surrounding them would ever see. The struggle was over. Dougan grabbed the legs, Kindon the arms.

'Gangway please,' barked Meddings. Those assembled came to brisk attention, half-marvelling at the quality of the knockout punch, half-fearing they might be next if they didn't move on.

As Bowden and his captors left the room, so did the majority of the delegates. Rubber-necking was not something people did much of on foot. Back at Ray's felled body, there were several grimaces being shared by the medics.

Georgie bit her lip as she looked on. Tony reached for his hankie to dab off his brow. Neither wanted to really look at what had happened. They were united in hating the sight of blood. Although there weren't huge pools of it, there was enough to cause great concern. Bandages were already applied, which meant there was nothing much an onlooker could be able to work out from what was still on display.

Georgie was always level-headed, and other matters now concerned her. She encouraged Tony to move away from being tempted to look at what was happening. Under her breath, she quizzed Tony. 'Where did those medics come from?'

Tony's first reaction was to roll his eyes. Georgie was well into her conspiracy stuff. He then remembered that, most of the time, when she found something which didn't add up, she was on the money in terms of there being an issue. His brow furrowed as he tried to think back. Subconsciously, he was shaking his head.

Their deliberations were broken up by the sounds of their Prime Minister, their friend, gasping for air. By now, the room had cleared, save for some of the venue's own security personnel.

Ray was surprised at how calm he found himself. He had been shot, God-dammit, in an assassination attempt. No doubt part of a coup. They say that these moments near death were the same for most people. Highs and lows of your life zooming past your eyes, like the ultimate motion picture trailer.

He recalled his early days as a television sports reporter. He smiled, both at the fun of it all, and his naivety at the time. He knew that, even with the benefit of hindsight, he would have done everything the same. He might have got the hang of his late night talk show a little earlier, but there's no substitute for getting it wrong, so that you never make the same mistakes again.

He had always been good at that. Learning quickly, analysing his performances and correcting them. He fast-forwarded to his recent election campaign. The struggle for a breakthrough. Turning the tide in a corrupt political system, rigged against newcomers. That sinking feeling, and then the elation when everything came together.

As he suspected, of course, it wasn't long until he saw the smiling face of Alicia, his second wife. And the two wonderful children she had brought into this world, with just a little bit of help from him. Alison and Ryan. Alicia had good reasons for their names, but he had long forgotten what those were.

That was the thing, in general your near-death showreel spinned backwards, forwards, and backwards again. Nothing linear, and that made everything a jumble. It was no surprise that his first wife soon came into the frame. He had forgotten how much they were soul-mates. They'd said it at the time, all the time, and Ray winced at how he'd somehow managed to let that memory fade, if only for a few seconds a day.

Ray wasn't prepared for what happened next. He felt himself lifting off the ground, parallel to what was below, as if he was in some corny magic trick. As long as there were no lions or tigers – he drew the line at caging animals like that for such trifling entertainment.

He began to rotate to a standing position, aware that from behind him a bright luminescent white light was bathing him. He looked down into the shadow he was casting, and saw what he suddenly appreciated was his own body below. There was Tony and Georgie, hugging each other for support, and looking on. Two figures dressed in medical fatigues packing away their tools. He smiled as he thought it wasn't like him to be laid there, so still. One thing he could never do. Even on holiday. And why did Americans call a holiday a "vacation"?

His eyes were drawn to what he was now wearing. Which costume designer had come up with this, then? A suit, shirt and tie all in white? Blimey, had these numpties just got out of college and been given the box set of *Randall and Hopkirk (Deceased)*? Whilst he had always admired Kenneth Cope in the Marty Hopkirk role, he was going to write a memo about this in the morning.

Now what? The techie boys were certainly over-doing the dry ice. Strangely, it wasn't choking him as it normally did. Perhaps it must be some new formula they were using?

Ray suddenly felt a reassuring hand on his shoulder. Someone else must have joined him on this gantry above the stage. Only, very strange, he couldn't make out the rigging. It was marvellous what they could do with technology these days.

He calmly looked over his shoulder. He had to do a double-take, and found he had to quickly spin around and face the person behind him, head-on. It was Anna, looking just as he remembered her all those years ago. But this was her at twenty-five years of age, looking svelte in flowing white gowns. Her red hair was in a 1980's style bouffant. Her eyes the so-memorable, piercing diamond-blue he could never look away from.

Reality suddenly kicked in. This could not be. 'Anna?' he mouthed, failing to find any volume in his voice.

His first wife half-laughed, and half-snorted. 'Who else would be looking out for you?' She half-giggled, and placed her hand on Ray's shoulder. He touched the back of her hand, to qualify that she was actually here with him. It was then that guilt jumped on his back.

'You know I remarried?' he said, sheepishly. So much for being wed to each other, and no-one else, for life. Anna scolded him, not for any sort of disloyalty, but more for his poor taste.

'That was never the problem. Who you chose to marry was.' Ray raised an eyebrow, channelling his very best Roger Moore impression, bemused by the revelation, before making the obvious realisation.

'My late wife has a jealous streak?' There was an embarrassing pause, and then simultaneously both of them laughed. Always the impeccable time manager, Ray decided to move things on, realising now exactly what was going on. 'Are you here to usher me through the pearly gates?'

In a way, Ray was a little disappointed when Anna shook her head. 'This isn't your time,' she noted, as sad saying it as he was to hear it. Ray suddenly recalled the tragedy that had befallen her. Moving quickly on, his mind started to try and connect the dots.

'So, I'll survive?' The hesitation from his late wife meant he wasn't going to like what came next. He looked around and surveyed their backdrop. They were in the clouds. He was almost disappointed that no musicians were sitting on the adjacent balls of cotton wool, a chorus of harps banging out a rendition of "Bohemian Rhapsody".

'There's been a complication,' Anna said, apologising. Ray wondered how any omnipotent force could not quite be in control of proceedings. And then considered what might be the worst thing that could have happened.

'Paralysed?' he enquired.

Anna gently shook her head. 'Brain dead.' Ray's sharp intake of breath was well-known to Anna. She well knew the way he handled disappointment.

'No problem. I'll still be able to function perfectly as a politician.'

Anna pulled up the sleeves of her voluminous gown, preferring to not look him in the eyes. 'You still don't take anything seriously.'

Ray felt the need to define his attitude. 'Gallows humour,' he offered, clearing his throat to try and suggest they both advance the conversation. Anna was good at taking his cues.

'I had to fight hard to become your guardian angel, your spirit guide.' This change of topic still didn't manoeuvre Ray away from the facetious.

'And what a perfect couple we'll be. "May I introduce you to the moronic Prime Minister, and his Missus the ghost?" Jeremy Kyle will love it.' Ray raised an eyebrow again. This quip failed to get a reaction from Anna. Stuff like that normally hit the spot. The penny suddenly dropped that Kyle would have been off her radar. 'Sorry. After your time. Think Robert Kilroy-Silk without the fake tan.'

Anna steered the chat into a more practical arena. 'Ray, you have some wonderful friends. They are going to come up with an amazing solution.' Ray's knee-jerk reaction would have usually been to ask a follow-up question. Get his interviewee on-the-hook for top-drawer celebrity tittle-tattle. This was far more important a scenario, though. He realised people should never know too much about their own destiny. Where that morsel came from he had no clue, but thought better than to question it. For some reason he was reassured, and smiled at Anna.

'Bring it on.'

2

BLUE TOUCHPAPER

Charles Raymond Grady was born in the later Summer of 1957 to keen tennis fans Don and Pat. He was named after Raymond Tuckey, an English-born Wimbledon doubles champion of 1936. This inspiration for a name had also been famous for partnering his mother, Agnes, who had herself been a Wimbledon winner in 1913. And so it was, early on in his career, 1931 and 1932 to be precise, that they teamed up in the tournament's mixed doubles competition.

Home for little Ray was a quiet road in Darlington, County Durham, halfway between the River Tees and the train station. There were bigger houses all around them, and in some respects their compact dwelling meant it was a blessing that Ray was to be an only child.

Father Don liked trivia, such as that about tennis stars, and was a legendary encyclopaedia. He honed his knowledge to a level which never left him stumped for a way to strike up conversations on his sales calls. He loved his movies, was keen on a range of sports, and was a whiz at all-things historical. Whilst not quite good enough to be a professional tennis player (never enough time to practice), he hoped his son would carry the torch for him.

Mother Pat felt the same – she was a careerist homemaker, and her own love of the court meant Ray was never without a partner for a knockabout. In their own little way, Pat and Ray were a re-enactment of Ray and Agnes.

It was all going so well. Ray was popular at school, but not with his tutors. He could easily talk his way out of fights, and was never short of female admirers. When he should have been doing homework, he was on the tennis circuit, working his way up the ladder. He quickly climbed from local to regional to national tournaments. Pat would escort Ray on those train trips, going all over the country, but mainly to London.

He walked out at Wimbledon in his early teenage years, making a name for himself as a very fast serve-and-volley player. He was quickly the talk of the pavilions, in far but hushed tones, touted as a prospective British number one. Coaches were queuing up to work with him, confident that they would be able to ride along on the shoelaces of his success.

He left school as soon as he could, aged fifteen, in the summer of 1972 without any qualifications. Ray was confident that he was never going to need any, and his timing was impeccable. From September of the same year, the mandatory leaving age was raised to sixteen. As far as he was concerned he was once again in the right place, at the right time, and in this case the right age!

Anyone who met Ray knew he was desperate for success. He realised how much his parents wanted to see him become a tennis champion, which meant he trained night and day. He broke into the men's singles tournaments at the age of sixteen, even reaching the quarter finals of the French Open, the *Roland Garros*, when a few major players were unexpectedly knocked out by other upcoming talents.

Unfortunately, this was to be too much for too long, and too soon. He began to suffer repeated stress fractures of his lower back. Serving in tennis requires a combination of spinal bending back, together with rotation and side bending of the trunk. Serving was, to put it mildly, the "ace" in Ray's game.

His service may have been hard and fast, but it put repeated pressure on an area of the vertebra called the *Pars Interarticularis*. That's where the stress fracture kept happening, again and again. He'd miss a couple of tournaments at a time, before hitting the road again. And then he'd be injured again for another few weeks. There was no way he was going to be able to continue as a professional player without doing himself permanent damage, especially with the way he played the game.

It was a nightmare for Ray when the specialist revealed this uncomfortable reality. Father Don had got time off work to be there with his wife and son. Part of him wished he hadn't bothered. He was always at a loss when Pat shed tears. She was normally so strong, and hysterics hardly ever happened. He was so glad she was not like this all the time, like the wives his work colleagues would tittle-tattle about. He envisioned them like jellyfish in smocks.

Don wished he could just say the right things to calm all three of them down. But the only trinkets in his mind were snippets of trivia about famous sporting injuries.

And so, at the age of nineteen, Ray found himself retired from the game, and from the only job he knew.

He had youth on his side, and his enthusiasm. Despite having no O levels, or even CSEs for that matter, he picked things up quickly. A tennis commentator had given him a tour of BBC Television Centre at some point, during one of Ray's numerous periods of convalescence. Ray had been amazed with the technology on display, the camaraderie amongst the tension and pressure of the live broadcasts. You had only one chance to get things right.

It reminded him of the same buzz he got playing tennis.

He wasted little time in cashing in on the sympathy for his tragedy. When he was asked to take part in a live show on the pressures within sport, he didn't even need to consider an answer. He just asked what time they wanted him at the studio.

Those witty skills from the playground days were the foundations for his performance. The audience laughed with him, his fellow guests applauded him, and the camera constantly picked up the cheeky twinkle in his eyes. Following the show, the researchers asked what his other interests were. All that boring travel time had been consumed with an insatiable desire to read.

Not just the newspapers and magazines left on the trains and planes, but a well-thought-out reading list prepared as a concerted effort to catch up on lost time. Political history, the geography of ancient monuments, even the basics of quantum physics (which he readily admitted was a little bit of a "stretch"). And yes, of course, he was familiar with the better recent television and film productions, the celebrities to talk to and those to avoid.

The researchers were impressed. They took his contact details, all a little surprised that he didn't have an agent. Ray didn't think it appropriate to say that, during the time on the tennis circuit, his mother had filled that role. This broadcast stuff was far removed from her area of expertise, and he didn't think it appropriate to continue to burden her.

The next few years were a blur, as he became a well-travelled sports reporter, covering all manner of events. They started him off doing some of the fun inserts at horse race meetings, often quizzing the bookies over their latest triumphs, as well as their disasters. All while getting some very astute tips, and supplementing his income very nicely indeed.

He would find himself at second-string first division football games, carrying out many of the pitch-side exchanges, as well as the post-match interrogations in the depths of the changing areas. He managed to smile every time he was sprayed in champagne following a memorable victory. Equally, he could pick himself up and dust himself down when he caught the fall-out of altercations between the players, both at half time and the final whistle.

Ray was most at home when they got him to cover the tennis, and he would try to interview the stars of the time on-court, while exchanging rallies with them. John McEnroe was impressed by the service deliveries, but Ray felt the twinges for several days after each of these action-packed rallies. Still, it impressed the producers, and wowed the viewers.

He didn't mind all the travelling, but relished the chance to be the Saturday afternoon sports anchor when the opportunity was presented. The "top floor" had liked Ray's ability to think on his feet, despite whatever disaster unfolded in front of him. The person at the helm had to be able to juggle several inputs of information at the same time, taking decisions on what happened next, adjusting running orders in a split second.

Ray's first Saturday in the spotlight saw all sorts of chaos unfolding, right behind him. A wildcat strike meant they had to film their sports results on the breakfast show set. It was a comfy enough sofa, but unfortunately no-one mentioned the set builders had "downed tools" halfway through a major revision of the layout.

Backdrop slats suddenly began to cascade to the floor, one by one, with loud bangs punctuating the afternoon. Ray quipped that the sound was just that of a starting pistol, a method dreamed up by the studio floor manager to get him to move on to the next item.

Several months went by, and Ray was now considered the headline talent in the sports department. Once more, chance was to deal a splendid card. He had stayed on at the studios, following the Saturday sports show, mainly to try and engineer a meeting with Anna, one of the team of young producers on the late night talk show. By the time they went on air, the producers would watch what went out in the green room, their role in the proceedings having effectively finished for the night. That was the time when the techies came into their own, and the rest of production team looked on from a vantage point which had its own drinks bar.

Sooner than Ray expected, he got his chance to interact with Anna. He was in the canteen, taking the chance to grab dinner. Steak on a Saturday, a special, and remarkably well-cooked, perfectly medium-rare as he had asked. And the subsidised rates meant he could eat like a king for less than the price of a bag of fish and chips on the way home.

Ray recognised that look on Anna's face. Someone had cancelled. He'd seen it before. About two months ago. Still, they couldn't call on him again? Mind you, if he was the producer, he'd send the person best equipped to persuade him, and that would be Anna. That was how they had first met. A C-list guest was a little worse for wear, thanks to that well-stocked bar, and they needed someone to fill in. He was ready, available, and hadn't drunk the entire contents of a bottle of vodka. Mum later told him he had done very well on that show.

Ray watched Anna stop to look around. Her gaze passed him by, and then she did something of a double take. It didn't look like he was her first choice. Still, he could understand the logic: being a repeat guest, just a few weeks' apart, was probably not good for the show's reputation. She smiled, gave a small wave, her fingers gyrating like a captured spider, before skipping on over.

He was besotted by her long red hair. It was a natural shade, too, bouncing around like the "Farrah Fawcett" had never gone out of fashion. Whatever she was going to ask, he wasn't going to turn her down. She slid into the chair across from him. Ray thought better of savouring any more of the steak just yet.

'Ray, I'm so glad to see you,' she trembled, out of breath, and trying not to put him off what was coming next. Ray did his best to reassure her.

'And me you. Too,' he stumbled. So much for his glowing reputation of always being in control. Ray did manage to show the necessary amount of concern, though. 'Looks like you've got a bit of a panic on?'

Anna huffed, halfway between panic and fear. 'You could say that. They've just taken Derek to hospital.'

Ray's eyes darted from side to side, processing the bombshell. Derek

Green was the host of Anna's show, the interviewer everyone made time for on a Saturday night. His guest lists were positively galactic. Almost robotically, Ray enquired, 'What's happened?'

'Acute peritonitis,' she blurted, almost apologetic for poor Derek's condition. Ray was trying to get to grips with the ramifications.

'So, he won't be able to do tonight's show?'

Anna furrowed her brow. She thought Ray had a considerable intelligence, although he seemed to be a beat behind the action at the moment. 'You're not drunk, are you?' she frostily enquired.

'No, well, no, not really.' Ray tried to stop himself from glancing at the half bottle of claret on the table in front of him, and coughed. 'I still have to drive home.' He changed the subject. 'So, what's the plan?'

'We can't get hold of any of the standbys,' she confessed. 'Here we are, at the centre of British television broadcasting, and no-one's about.'

'It's a Saturday night,' Ray blurted. He realised stating the obvious was not going to be appreciated. 'That's the problem when you don't have anyone kept on a retainer.' It hadn't taken him long to understand the cost-cutting nature of the organisation. It was only at rare times like this they got caught out.

Anna requisitioned a wine glass from a table opposite, and drained what remained from the half-bottle. She took a gulp to steady herself, before fixing Ray's gaze. 'You could do it.'

For Ray, this entire encounter was rolling by in slow motion. Here he was, sat opposite the only girl he would want to be in the company of at a weekend, or any other time in fact, and Anna was handing him an opportunity which would put him forever in her debt. He tried to inject some reality into proceedings. 'Surely your exec will have to approve your choice?'

'No one can find him,' she shrieked. The disturbance rattled some of the other diners, who she acknowledge and mouthed 'Sorry' to. 'Can't find the show's intern, either,' she whispered. 'Make of that what you will.'

Ray subconsciously drummed the table with his fingers. He couldn't quite grasp that, at the humble age of twenty-five, he was getting a break like this. Or that he was being given it by someone fresh out of university, albeit so highly commended.

Anna looked pointedly at her watch. 'Well?'

That was enough to jolt Ray out of his trance. His stomach was churning, but he knew this was something he wanted to do. 'I assume there's time for a camera rehearsal?'

Anna held her hand out, and when Ray responded he found himself almost pulled out of his seat. 'If we hurry, you might even have time to prep a little with tonight's guests.'

Almost dragging him behind her, Anna led the way to the studio. 'Who's on the show tonight?' he enquired. If Anna had been in Ray's shoes, this would have been the first question she would have asked.

'James Stewart, Alan Whicker and Kenny Everett,' she announced, off-hand. No women. Not a good balance, but a stellar line-up.

'Okay. A quiet week, then.' Stewart would need answers teased out of him. Whicker would be a mine of follow-up anecdotes based on whatever Stewart came up with. And anything could happen with Everett. Ray was already working out how he would shape the conversations.

Anna, herself making things up as she went along, was almost telepathic in her teamwork with Ray during the show. She was the one on talkback with him, guiding him to where he should be positioned, which camera to turn to next, and suggesting questions when necessary. The production team around them realised this was the beginning of what would be an indomitable double act.

The studio audience loved it all. Everett was gentle on Ray, realising it wouldn't be fair to do his usual style of outrage with him. Whicker was the erudite professional, helping to steer the conversations into more expansive areas. And James Stewart did everything you would expect of someone who rightfully was described as a Hollywood icon. The critics loved it, and said so in the Monday papers.

Derek Green survived his health scare, but was unable to return to his show for an entire month. Ray, having been an instant hit, got to do another three editions, cementing his skyrocketing profile.

Green returned to his show post-op, but within weeks gave it up to get involved with the set-up of Channel 4, then just about to launch. Everyone thought that Ray was going to be handed Green's show, but those higher up decided he was too young for a regular gig.

Anna was outraged by Ray being passed over, and her fiery temper meant she quit without a second thought. The tabloids had a field day when Ray declared he would not be negotiating a new contract for his sports role. Anna persuaded him that the two of them could form their own production company. Between them, she was confident they would be able to do anything they wanted.

It was obvious to everyone that this was the perfect couple. They had a bond which meant they knew what each other was thinking, and both felt their lives were complete. Marriage and a child swiftly followed. Little Bonnie took after her mother, and Ray and Anna shared the parenting chores.

The next big break came from an unexpected source. Derek Green had landed the role of commissioning editor at Channel 4, and could see that Ray had everything necessary to make late night Saturdays his own. When Anna pitched a new format to the station, a chat show mixing up more quirky guests, upcoming musicians and bands, and a centrepiece of one hard-hitting piece of journalism every week, Green hit the green light immediately.

Anna had studied *That Was the Week That Was* at university, the 1960s television phenomenon which changed the way politics was viewed in Britain. She knew the current Conservative government under Thatcher was very divisive, and satire dressed up in a variety of trappings could catch on again. She didn't just want to make a television show. She wanted to challenge the audience every week. Supply a "Trojan Horse", with hard-hitting social commentary within. A suitable title was needed. They decided on *The Saturday Soup*, although neither could ever explain why.

Ray's profile allowed them to do virtually whatever they wanted. His credentials had gone international, thanks to various chat show appearances in all the main television markets. Everyone knew who he was, which as a consequence made booking talent very easy.

Most would have thought the 11.00pm Saturday slot was not going to bring in the ratings, but the couple knew what they were looking for – the "post-pub demographic", as they coined it. Their celebrity guests would give their informed point of view on the news of the week. The bands booked would play an appropriate song. And within all the fun and merriment, Anna's team of journalists would deliver one bombshell of a story every week. Reputations were tarnished, businesses almost closed down every night, and politicians and officials exposed. If audiences didn't tune in, they certainly heard about happenings in the papers the following week.

Their audience began small, but loyal, and the right sort of demographic for those oh-so-valuable advertisers. Despite its timeslot, it became one of the most profitable shows on the schedules.

The Independent Broadcasting Authority found they were getting complaints about the series, not from members of the public, but various organisations. Luckily, these weren't the sort who would promote their wares on commercial television, so Channel 4 just shrugged their collective shoulders, mainly at Derek Green's insistence. None of the complaints were upheld, every single incident being judged as "fair comment".

Ray and Anna soon clocked up over a hundred episodes together, and their investigations were always a talking point. Those just wanting to be entertained were prepared to put up with these five-to-ten minute intrusions into the frivolity that permeated the rest of the show. Aside from taking a few weeks off in the summer, and over other holidays where they'd package up "Best of" shows, they were residents in the schedules. They both loved their jobs, and Channel 4 was happy for them to broadcast as much as they liked.

Everything changed in November 1985. London was at its coldest since 1952. Heavy frosts had hit the entire country. Anna had been away all day, keeping her hand in with a big story she was working on. It was past 11.30pm at night when Ray got the call.

They called it "black ice". She had wanted to get back at a sensible time, as it was going to be Bonnie's second birthday the following morning. That may have accounted for the speed she was travelling. Ordinarily she was a very safe driver. Hated breaking the speed limits, one of the only pillars of authority she had any time for. The goods lorry she crashed into hardly had a mark on it. Her little car, a bright red Datsun 280ZX, was mangled beyond recognition, having ignited in a spectacular fireball.

There was no way to identify the body. The number plate was the only clue as to who was driving.

Ray knew Anna would have wanted him to carry on, but no show was broadcast that weekend. In fact, there were no more shows on Channel 4 ever again. The couple were inseparable, and that meant he couldn't see any way to carry on alone.

He devoted the next part of his life to bringing up Bonnie. Every time he looked into her eyes, Ray could see the exact same twinkle that Anna always carried with her. This was the project he wanted to work on for the next few years.

Ray would keep his profile in the public spotlight, making appearances on various shows, even *A Question of Sport* a couple of times. He felt something of a con artist doing so. You could hardly say his sporting career had been prolific.

It was a satisfying combination that brought in enough money to live a comfortable life. The appearances were limited to a couple per month, which meant he could give Bonnie all the attention he wanted to.

In 1995, Channel 4 decided to do a retrospective documentary about *The Saturday Soup*. Ray had insisted on no repeats, or recycling of clips, up until that point. A lunch with Derek Green saw the old hand persuade the now not-so-young Turk that the time to face his ghosts had come. Ray initially said "no", but Green found he had an ally. Little Bonnie.

Bonnie had asked how Ray's day had been. He explained who he'd met, and that it was about Mommy and Daddy's old TV show. Bonnie was fascinated, as Ray had downplayed their work together up until that point. Bonnie was about to go to secondary school, and had yet to suffer from the teasing of other children about her father's profession. She wanted to be proud of him. She told him so, and asked to see some of the episodes.

Ray dusted down some old VHS copies he'd got recorded off air. It was the first time in a decade he had watched them. Bonnie was a bright girl, and understood almost all of the adult references. Some parents would have been concerned at this, but Ray admired her appreciation of the world. Better to learn now, than be shocked later on down the line.

Bonnie helped Ray see the show through fresh eyes. Even ten years on, the format was as fresh as ever. The political jokes may have had a different cast of characters, but the themes were exactly the same. Corruption. Insider dealing. The lack of empathy shown within politicians for fellow human beings.

Derek Green put his best independent crew onto the documentary. The young director was a fan of *The Saturday Soup*, and even told Ray it was one of the reasons he had wanted to work in television. Ray initially thought this was flattery, until he was presented with an encyclopaedic knowledge of virtually every episode.

Bonnie made an appearance in the documentary. She had very little memory of her mother, but showed steel in her answers, coming across as measured, vibrant and intelligent. She gave Ray the strength he needed to talk about Anna, this being the first time ever, and put her importance to the show in perspective.

They called it *Bring Back The Saturday Soup*. The ratings were remarkably good for a retro documentary of this sort. Celebrity guests who were on the show, some of them right at the start of their fame, were falling over themselves to be featured. It was like the whole country had been in a state of amnesia about the series for the last ten years, and had suddenly awoken from their collective trance.

Ray and Anna had been astute in their contractual negotiations. They had kept all rights tied up to the concept, including merchandising. The documentary was quickly repeated. Derek Green begged for the opportunity to rescreen episodes, with Ray doing introductions that set the context for the current affairs content of the week, and also giving anecdotes about some of the guests. This was the right level of respect for the "product", so Ray agreed.

Under Ray's control, the rebroadcast of what was branded *Saturday Soup Re-canned* saw a glut of tie-in merchandise hit the shops. T-shirts. Badges. Mugs. Ties. Can openers. And yes, even a line of soups.

Despite all this, Ray resisted going back to helming a chat show, despite Derek Green's extremely lucrative proposals.

And then, in 1998, the fledgling Channel 5 came knocking on Ray's door. They had been on air less than a year, and it was an offer he couldn't refuse financially, again with Bonnie being his adviser. Taking on *Parkinson* on a Saturday night, who had just returned to the BBC. There would again be no constraints on whom, how or what he could broadcast. He would hire his own team, and take it in whatever direction he wanted.

Things went well initially, but soon the squeeze was put on the budget. The ratings were satisfying for the channel, but not for Ray. Channel 5 had become something of a backwater, save for its American drama imports, and the channel was simply trying to gear programme expenditure to the advertising revenue it could generate.

By 2001, Ray decided enough was enough, and refused to renew his contract. He spent the next three years writing and researching, trying to work out what the magic ingredient was which had been the lightning in a bottle that was *The Saturday Soup*.

Michael Parkinson once again became a driving force in Ray's career. In

April 2004, "Parky" had announced he was leaving the BBC for ITV, as he believed Premiership football highlights would be taking his usual slot. In a fit of pique, the BBC decided they wanted to take their turn at pitching Ray against Parkinson. This was an offer Ray initially refused, even though the salary was now positively stratospheric.

BBC1 Director of Programming Benedict Stone, a hard-nosed entrepreneur brought to the channel to justify the licence fee with increased ratings, wasn't used to people declining his offers. Being aware of Ray's background, Benedict decided to bring his own nineteen-year-old daughter into play.

Alicia Stone was one of the darlings of the showbiz pages. She epitomised the concept of nepotism. Benedict had hired her as a producer for youth programming, arguing that if they were going to cater for a teen audience, then they needed someone in that age group, to tap into what was going to be the magnet for such an audience.

Unlike other sons and daughters who were elevated to such positions of power, there was one thing which set Alicia apart from the rest.

She was bloody good at her job.

Alicia was born in the same year *The Saturday Soup* had concluded. She fast-talked her way into getting an appointment with Ray, going direct, as even then he still didn't have an agent. Bonnie was off at university, just about to start on her Masters' degree, so Ray was honest enough with himself that he could do with a new project. Despite him realising only too well that he was letting himself in for a "hard sell", he was intrigued by the bravado of someone so young.

She suggested The Ivy in West Street as a venue. That showed some class. Ray arrived to find her seated at a discrete table towards the back of the main dining area. Matters didn't get off to a good start. Up and coming stars, as well as gossip journalists, formed a constant train of bodies who, one-by-one, took the chance to interact with Alicia. She was tiring of the constant attention as much as Ray was, so beckoned the maitre d' over.

Almost instantaneously they were guided into a private dining area. The staff were all so attentive to her, and she was gracious back to them. Ray had seen so many of her type in the past, which were just so damned rude to those around them. Power in the hands of those so young can have that effect. But not Alicia. Ray was impressed.

She knew her wines, too. The waiter brought a Paloma Merlot Spring Mountain District, vintage 2001, to the table. A Californian tipple, not ridiculously expensive but extremely well thought of.

The two of them danced around the subject they knew they were there to discuss. She had a very deep laugh, which had her apologising on more than one occasion. Ray liked her attitude, and she had done her homework on him. He had been told by many in the business that getting a commission these days had many strings attached, and contractual loopholes by the bucket-load. Alicia knew that Ray would want carte blanche, and nothing she said suggested he would have any restrictions.

Ray was absorbed in her life story. She went against the family wishes in not going to university. There was a drive in her application which made Ray both elated and depressed at the same time. The last time he had encountered this level of commitment was in another lady whose name began with the letter "A". Yes, Alicia reminded him so much of Anna.

Her blonde hair had echoes of Anna's redhead stylings. It was almost spooky in terms of the similarity. Alicia had the same type of piercing blue eyes, too. He tried to kid himself that the feelings stirring in him were paternal. After all, there was over a quarter-century difference in their ages. He was old enough to be her father. In fact, she was younger than his own daughter.

What would Bonnie think? That helped him focus on keeping the discussion business-like, although if he didn't know any better he was sure Alicia was flirting. He found her staring at him a little longer than she should on more than one occasion.

The finer points of the deal were agreed, and they clinked glasses to confirm their intention to work together. Ray was sure he would find a problem in the small print, but when the paperwork was pushed through his letterbox, everything was as discussed. No turning back now, he was going to be helming a show in prime time once more.

They offered him the slot directly before the late evening news and *Match of the Day*, starting a few minutes before Parkinson's show on ITV. The irony was that both formats were given better scheduling than if Parkinson had stayed with the BBC. Such details were not lost on media commentators. Whilst "Parky" pulled in an average of six million viewers, Ray's new format, called *Grady and Guests*, (he had vetoed "The Grady Bunch") was pitched at a younger audience, and matched the ratings of his senior. Both had carved their own niche.

And this time the driving force behind Ray's success was a lady called Alicia. She took on the production chores for the series with no small amount of glee. She could have delegated the role, but she wanted this project all to herself.

It was over a year before the two of them would start formally dating. Alicia wanted to keep their relationship out of the gossip columns, mainly as she knew her father would not approve of the huge age gap between them. Ray, in the meantime, hadn't quite worked out how to tell his daughter about the two of them being an "item". That was made a little easier when Bonnie went to work in the States. She had a doctorate now, in various medical disciplines. Bonnie certainly hadn't followed in the family's footsteps, although she was quite an accomplished tennis player.

The couple's privacy was smashed in 2007 when Alicia became pregnant. Ray was bemused, as they had always been so careful. Many said their marriage was made down the barrel of a shotgun, but both were sure it was what they wanted. The show's production team were able to fill in for Alicia, and father Benedict Stone's rage was soon diminished when he realised he was going to be a grandfather. Bonnie, meanwhile, was stoic in her response. Ray had been "on his own" for nearly twenty years, and Bonnie thought it best that both of them took the chance to move on.

That didn't diminish the fact that Bonnie absolutely hated Alicia. There was just something about her that seemed to be so false.

Alicia, on the other side of the coin, was impressed with how Bonnie had turned out. Bonnie did such a good job of hiding her true feelings from her, so Alicia never twigged what was going on in her step-daughter's head. One night, around eight months into the pregnancy, Alicia made a suggestion to Ray. She wanted to be a proper mother. No juggling work and rearing for her. The show had carried on without her, without any drop in standards.

Initially, whilst Ray thought the suggestion very noble, he didn't want Alicia to feel trapped. She was very persuasive, so he succumbed to her charms. Internal promotions within the team meant the series kept its feel of being a family.

Daughter Alison was born in 2008. Son Ryan followed in 2010. Ray joked he would be the "point four" which would make up the 2.4 children that

Alicia would be looking after. There was no *OK! Magazine* spreads for the family, they kept themselves to themselves.

Grady and Guests became a fixture of Saturday nights as much as *Doctor Who* and the National Lottery draws. The show settled in to a routine, where many said it didn't quite have the teeth and influence that had been the trademark of *The Saturday Soup* all those years before.

By 2015, the show was still as popular as ever, even though the BBC was a little battered by what had gone down with the Dr David Kelly affair. The production team were vetted more than ever on any tricky issues, and on occasion found their prospective content censored. Ray felt himself saying "whatever" more and more. He had turned into part of the establishment, part of the furniture, and was only too aware he was prepared to do most things to maintain a quiet life.

A couple of weeks after that year's spring general election, suddenly Ray found himself in possession of the hottest of stories. It excited him in a way that he hadn't known for nearly three decades.

It had been just another Saturday night, an average show, where they were taking swipes at the new government's bizarre policy about-turns. As the audience cleared, and he unhooked his radio microphone and pack, Ray noticed a nervous, slim figure of a man at the side of the stage.

He had that look of a civil servant, and was dressed far too smartly compared to the rest of those who had come to see the recording.

'Autograph?' enquired Ray of the man, not really believing this was such a fan. The man shook his head, nervously.

'Are you still interested in the truth?' the man enquired of Ray.

'You're not a regular viewer, are you,' Ray replied, quite dismissively.

It was at that moment that the quiet, nervous man thrust a large manila envelope into Ray's hands.

'You aren't going to believe this. If you open this up, your life is going to change, as will the course of history.'

Ray laughed, although he stopped when he saw the quiet man was for real. He had encountered whistleblowers before, albeit a very long time ago. There was something about them that was very haunting, almost tragic. He recognised the signs. 'Perhaps we should find somewhere quiet to talk,' Ray eulogised, as he led the quiet man to his dressing room…

3

DARKNESS BEFORE DAWN

Ray had done many an interview with people who spoke of days that changed their lives. They said you knew straight away that everything was about to transform. As he was driven back home by his company-provided chauffeur, the folder on his lap weighed heavy. He patted it as he stared out of the rear passenger window of the Mercedes, the dancing cascades of street lights suggesting there was much to see beyond their glow. Sometimes your moment of revelation was related to something you always suspected didn't quite ring true. How poignant that was in this case.

The family home was quiet. Alicia had long got out of the habit of waiting up for him. The children weren't allowed to stay up, but they'd get to see a recording of the show in the morning. Nothing egotistical here, they demanded to see their father at work. Ray clicked on the reading lamp in his lounge, the room now matching his mood, illumination in a fog of darkness.

He looked over the paperwork, all carefully copied. He believed every paragraph to be genuine. He hoped something would be different, but every detail was the same as he recalled from an hour earlier. Part of him wished he had misread the documents, picked up the wrong inferences, or could find something that would preserve the status quo in his universe. The second reading made things worse, actually sending shivers down his spine.

The quiet man made it clear there had been previous attempts to get this explosive information out into the mainstream. Independent bloggers who had tried to reveal the details soon found their websites closed down, their contents being reclassified as "hate speech". The quiet man had scoffed at the suggestion that a major outlet would surely cover it. They had all been approached, even the more "substantial" production offices within Ray's own broadcaster, but all had turned down the opportunity to run with this exclusive.

The staff had all said there was not enough evidence. Ray scratched his head. The facts were all there – names, dates, locations, even pictures. He could easily get the information checked before he proceeded. Why couldn't they? It wasn't as if such current affairs were his specialist area. Far from it. But he knew enough to get by.

The clocks had just gone forward, and the general election in the UK had taken place a couple of weeks previously. The coalition had not left it to the very last moment, as had been expected, but it had still been the best part of five years since the country last went to the polls.

In the run-up, there had been talk of people voting for change, moving away from the three major political parties. There had been a handful of prospective alternatives that were expected to benefit, even in the devolved environs of Scotland, Wales and Northern Ireland. UKIP had already been derailed by dirty tricks a-plenty. Their dawn never edged past the grasp of twilight.

In the end, despite great promise from the opinion polls, it was the same as it had been for the last couple of decades. The general public voted only for the parties they thought had a chance of winning. Put to one side were all the broken promises. Everything forgotten, the past failures sidelined, even though the key players in all three "top dog" parties were despised or completely anonymous. The media put it down to the lack of experience of the alternatives, forgetting how much they had crowed that all these new contenders were "unelectable".

These confidential documents brought into focus why there had been such a gulf between what the opinion polls had forecast, and the final declared election results. Ray found himself subconsciously rubbing his eyes. It was the biggest story of his career. Of anyone's career. Of the century. If true, that is. He couldn't sleep, despite the long day behind him. The paperwork continued to transfix him.

The following day, Ray called in favours from some of the investigative journalists he knew. He asked each one to investigate part of the jigsaw of the alleged deception. These experienced writers were each of the same mindset: what had been committed to paper simply could not be true. However, the more they delved into the scenario presented to them, the more the accusations were substantiated.

A couple more days passed, and briefing after briefing confirmed everything as legitimate. Ray realised what he had in his hands. Putting this out in the open would change the country. It would probably change the world. It was a perfect centrepiece for next week's show. However, he surmised that advertising the content beforehand, even making an allusion to it, would get the edition pulled from the airwaves. He knew the level of influence within those he was going up against. He would need an enticing piece of bait to get as many people watching as possible.

He had to announce a combination of special guests that would add up to "appointment television". Ray looked through his smart phone's address book, flicking through the names. That was the best thing about putting yourself out there for people all the time – when you needed something they would come to your aid, a favour for a favour.

Hugh Jackman. Gemma Arterton. Russell Brand. Music from Adele. Something for everyone. He informed the PR team immediately, insisting on speaking to the head of department. Even she was blown away by the combination that he'd put together. Ray told her just occasionally you get the breaks like this. He hadn't lied, just not said precisely what the "breaks" were which he was talking about.

Ray kept the actual running order of the show privy to a very tight group of people. In fact, the only person on the studio floor he brought into his confidence was Joey, the technical director. Joey was a Scotsman, keen on his single malts, but an old-school professional. He was one of those people who had a propensity of brown fat in his body; he could eat like a trucker, and never put any weight on, always being slight of build.

Joey had learned to trust Ray's sixth sense on all sorts of matters. When Ray arrived in Joey's lair at the studios, armed with a bottle of Dalmour Highland Cigar Malt, the audio-visual guy knew a "big ask" was coming. Two whisky glasses came out from a locker, quickly filled with ice from a mini fridge-freezer. The Scotsman poured the liquid nectar and interrogated his benefactor.

'So, the scripted content will under-run by fifteen minutes, and you want the transmission to continue, regardless of what the top brass demand?' Joey summarised.

Ray sniffed deeply on his glass of Dalmour. 'I don't want anyone to get in trouble but me. This is really big, and the fallout should keep me gainfully employed for years to come.'

'Your confidence borders on arrogance, you know,' declared Joey. He slapped his lips together, half savouring the whisky, half contemplating how to accomplish Ray's request. His eyes widened as a plan formed. 'About eight months ago, on an edition of *Watchdog* I believe. I hear they couldn't break away from the studio back to channel continuity. Part of the software had frozen, so they had to fill in for a few minutes before there was a reboot.'

Ray smiled. 'Terrible if that was to happen again. On a live show. Such as ours.'

Joey put his glass down, and picked up a pen and large flowery notepad. He started scribbling notes down with relish. As he did so, his glass was refilled without question.

Saturday arrived, and Ray realised he hadn't even told Alicia. There had never been the right time over the last few days. Perhaps it was for the best. He trusted her with everything else, and never had any reason not to.

Eight years together, now united by their two children – Alison, seven years old, and Ryan, a real chip off the old block, even at just five years of age. Alicia would undoubtedly call him, straight away, after the show. She tended to do that if the night had been particularly good, or more often particularly bad. What she would make of something which could potentially be "career suicide" was anyone's guess. Besides, she wouldn't be able to talk him out of this. In his gut, it almost felt like a pre-ordained date with destiny.

For some reason, Ray didn't even think if there would be any consequences for their relationship from such non-disclosure.

The show's dress rehearsal was remarkably uneventful, and Ray did get the chance to take all three of the stars, separately, to one side. He explained they would be asked to walk off set several minutes before the end of the show. He smiled wryly, and suggested they might like to hang around and watch a little bit of history in the making. Top line talent sometimes really does respond to enigmatic teasing, and Hugh, Gemma, Russell and Ms Adkins especially so in this case.

Joey took the chance to let Ray know he had a "feeling" a technical issue might arise, which would mean they would stay on air to the end of their allotted transmission time. 'Longer if needed,' he slyly concluded.

The show began on schedule. They had been late for two of the last three weeks due to live events running over in the slot before them. The audience was very responsive. It's funny how those watching lift their game when the guests they get to see are beyond A-list. They book their night out, unaware of who will be entertaining them. Tickets might be free, but they knew that tonight they would be priceless.

The banter was electric, and everyone was taken through the entire spectrum of emotions. Hilarity, revelations, and honesty were all in the mix. The Twitterati were already saying "Best Show – ever".

Ray looked to one side of the stage where he knew Joey held court. A gentle nod from the Scotsman was all that Ray needed. He thanked his guests, who took their cue to leave the stage, sending the production gallery into some confusion. A few restrained words from Joey over his headset calmed them down, telling them on one hand he didn't know what was happening, but on the other to trust their presenter.

Some of the audience looked at their watches, immediately realising this was a diversion from what had been advertised. Ray moved to the front of the stage, looked down to compose himself, and coughed to clear his throat.

'Ladies and gentlemen, there are no more guests this evening, but it's not the end of the show. We've saved the biggest talking point until last.'

Ray could do that. Add gravity to a situation with just a few well-chosen words. The audience were now hanging on his every syllable. 'When I took on this show, it was with the understanding that we could tackle tough subjects. As well as entertain you. I've taken this next story to reporter friends of mine, but they have been blocked from running it.'

It was no surprise that Phil the reporter was there, uncomfortable at his failures being pointed out. Ray had the good grace not to name names.

'Two weeks ago, we had a general election. You already know about the scandals that enveloped UKIP just before it. We saw that party derailed from any hope of election success. Like it was planned. Yes, I am talking conspiracy. And then there was the little matter of using brand new electronic voting machines.'

Some in the audience were a little exasperated at this. They hated the "c" word, and disliked anyone who dared to use it. Ray picked up a folder from the chat show stage table, and waved it above his head. 'I have conclusive proof that those machines were rigged!'

This locked the attention of the entire audience back into what Ray was saying. Conspiracy theory or not, this was something pretty big for Ray to be talking about. 'You will hear the gory details, and I hope we get to stay on air, so our viewers at home can hear the evidence, too.'

Ray looked to the side of the stage. Joey chose not to give him any further signals. Ray consulted the folder, and read a line aloud, word for word. 'The introduced bias was significant enough to preserve the three-party status quo.'

Phil realised the story was going to break, and was well-placed to sell an "inside track" with all the evidence at his fingertips. He started to type on his mini-computer, thinly disguised as a phone.

Ray pulled up a high chair from the side of the set, and made himself comfortable. He hoped the audience didn't begin to think this was a Dave Allen routine with a funny punchline. 'You have been constantly told that a vote for anyone but the Lib-Lab-Con was a wasted vote. Now we know why! Had things played out as they should have done, it would have meant, for the first time, more people would have voted for other candidates than those of the "big three" combined.'

Ray pulled a small remote control from his pocket, and suddenly the screens around the studio all started to show a Powerpoint presentation to support his words. It was high-tech but amusing at the same time. You don't normally get many laughs from explaining the election voting system and introduced anomalies, but somehow he managed to.

'This is how it works. You key in your choice. If you voted outside the "big three", the machine allocates it to whichever main party candidate it has been programmed to prefer. We also have documented evidence of postal ballot anomalies. Your vote is counted only if it swings a result the chosen way. And then there are "ghost voters", the registering of non-existent constituents. And believe me, these are not the only reasons to get mad.'

By now, those in the studio were hanging on to his every word. 'Guess who's a major shareholder, and board member, of the company that makes these voting machines?'

Ray rifles through the folder, and pulls out a 10" x 8" picture of the new

Prime Minister, installed just a fortnight ago. Ray showed the image around to the audience, supported by the zoom in of one of the broadcast cameras. Everyone could recognise the face that was on their nearest monitor. Ray's audience were always well-informed compared to others who sometimes occupied their seats.

'That's right. Your own, our very own, Prime Minister. You'd expect this to be listed in the register of Members' interests, now wouldn't you? But no, that wouldn't be in the "national interest".' Ray took a dramatic pause, and in a deep voice continued, 'Guess who's also a board member of the same company?'

He went to the folder again, and pulled out another head-and-shoulders, this time an opposition politician, and held it up to the nearest broadcast camera. 'That's right, the former Home Office Minister before the election, and now the Shadow Chancellor. Guess who divvied out the contracts for those very same voting machines, when at the Home Office?'

The wave of rage began to build. Only a few queried the research, but if Ray believed it, they believed it. His face began to reflect the mood of those in the room – anger in every furrow. 'Are you getting the picture? They really are "in this together"!'

Even with such a tsunami of anger, Ray could still break the mood. The politicians would not like it. They were being laughed at. Ray ushered the audience to calm down, with a downward motion of his hands. This was his chance to play Howard Beale from *Network* for real.

'Ladies and gentlemen, let's make this clear. As one fictitious broadcaster once said "I'm as mad as hell and I'm not going to take it anymore"!'

The crowd arose in unison – a shockwave of cheering and applause. Ray took this as a cue to applaud them back. As he looked around, Joey caught his eye. The technical director shook his head and made the action of slitting his own throat. They'd got the message out, but only just.

And this was when the "fun" really started.

Aside from the supportive piece, which Phil only managed to get published on his own "Monty Cristoe" blog, almost the entire press pack were hostile to the story. Despite the evidence being conclusive, they attacked the person, not the details. The dictionary would describe it as an *ad hominem* attack – against the person. For some reason it was seen as right to defend the status quo, to try and keep things as they were.

Ray had seen this before, from a distance, on other stories. As a young reporter, he knew there were exclusives which even hardened hacks would not touch. His own stories on his first television series never quite pressed the buttons in such a way as to be pulled or challenged. All soft targets, in the grand scheme of things.

This was different. He knew it would be, but he had gone ahead anyhow. The story was no longer about political corruption. He himself was the story. Everywhere he went, he was mobbed by paparazzi and the most bottom-feeding of journalists. He took to wearing sunglasses, even at night, so harsh were the flashbulbs of the cameras.

Alicia and the children weren't immune from these attentions, either. But Alicia understood the high stakes, and why Ray had to do what he had done. As a consequence, she went out without the children, and in heavy disguise. She was amazed how easily she got away with it.

Ray was approached by Georgie, an agent who he had dealt with in securing various top-line talents for his shows. She never saw problems, just opportunities. Over what they hoped would be a quiet dinner, she pitched her services to him. Ray needed someone to help fight his corner. They seemed like the perfect combination. A deal was made on the spot, just before the flashbulbs caught up with them. The vermin even hinted in by-lines that the pair might be having an affair.

He wasn't going to hide. It was still a free country, in a manner of speaking. It was at quieter times of the day, early morning, and between the rush hours, where he started to notice the mood of the general public was far different to how it was being portrayed in the papers. People would give him the thumbs up, or take the opportunity to shake his hand. It was almost as if words weren't needed.

One individual put it all into perspective. A beanpole of a postman came up to him, and furtively checked around to see there were no onlookers. He whispered in Ray's ear, 'Go get 'em,' before darting off to continue his round.

Maybe there were just a few who understood, then. Hardly a vindication, though. It was the call from Leonard White which helped reframe the reality that was behind the headlines.

White was one of the last of the old-fashioned media moguls. His *News First* tabloid had tried to take a genuinely different view of world affairs. Sales weren't huge, but the customer base was passionate and loyal. He wasn't the biggest of players, but was shrewd in his dealings. He differed from the others in that he was fair to everyone. Reasonable deals, which were mutually beneficial. He certainly was a throwback to better times. He suggested to Ray that they meet up.

Ray went to White's newspaper offices, and was swiftly shown to a meeting room off from the main reception. Several minutes later, White appeared. This was a man who would never retire, although the most recent round of allegations of corruption against him had worn him around the edges. He was rotund, with a hangdog expression inherited from his days covering the big stories on the front line.

White took a coffee from the impressive automatic machine on one of the tables against the wall. 'I guess you're black coffee at the moment?' he enquired. Ray nodded, as White played butler and dispensed a second brew. 'How do you think things are going?' he asked.

'The system is closing ranks,' Ray replied as he took hold of the cup he had been handed. 'There seems to be a few people who understand what's happened. But only a handful.'

White snorted. 'You know what they say. Don't believe what you read in the papers,' he grunted while being able to guffaw at the same time. 'We've had to change the emphasis of what we write, due to the "feedback" we've been receiving. No doubt you will have seen that in the last couple of days?'

Ray was non-committal in his response. He didn't want to admit *News First* wasn't on his reading list.

'I'll admit a vested interest,' White confided. 'I've seen how the system operates, and now it's coming after me. As such, you and I have a mutual enemy.'

Ray blew on his coffee. Although not boiling, it was still the wrong side of hot. 'Things not going well with that case Stateside?'

White rocked nervously in his chair. 'The extradition requests keep on coming. Some big corporations are at work in the shadows.' White leaned across the table towards Ray. 'What I am trying to say is, whatever your next move, count on my support.'

At that moment, the door burst open, and a greasy stump of a reporter, with recorder in hand, and a burly chip-chomping photographer with a camera even bigger than his frame rushed towards the duo.

'Are they with you?' Ray enquired, as he bolted upwards.

White was far too long in the tooth to move with such speed. 'Never seen them before,' he confirmed.

The reporter started spouting off, 'Mister White! Mister White! Marc Croft, *Daily Post*. Is it true you leaked this made-up story to Ray Grady?'

White was just so cool, Ray observed. He firmly picked up the white phone in front of him and barked, 'Security! Room one zero one.'

* * *

Later in the day, reporter Phil was on the scene with some more information. Not trusting the telecoms to be free of wiretaps, the two met up, in person. In what appeared to be an empty street, a manila A4 packet was thrust into Ray's hands by Phil. Ray wanted a bit more detail, but suddenly from nowhere a pair of paparazzi revealed themselves with a succession of flashbulbs.

Ray was starting to get just a little paranoid. How did they know exactly where he was going to be, all the time? The photos with Phil appeared the following day, suggesting that Ray was accepting bribes from extremists for trying to unstable the country. All via a plain brown envelope.

The fact that Phil was a reporter, and a well-known one at that, and was the one allegedly handing over such bounty, was glossed over. The suggestion was that he was some sort of Aryan terrorist. Evil-doers could have any colour of skin, these days. That is, if you were to believe the narrative the press was putting over.

In reality, this was in fact market research material Phil had gathered. There really was more popular support for Ray than what was being reflected in media coverage. People were afraid to speak up for him, as they thought they were in the minority. How wrong they were.

A phone call later in the day came as no surprise. Ray had been sacked, his television presentation services no longer required. Ray got on to Tony Pearce, who looked after some of his business affairs, to ensure that as a counter-measure he withdrew the show's format from the broadcaster. He wasn't going to let someone else be brought in to take on his role. Tony had some good contacts in entertainment law, who would relish such challenges.

All of which just fanned the flames. The mainstream media tried to smear Ray with even more outrageous and unfounded allegations. And again Tony got to work, getting solicitors geared up to seek significant damages. Time and again, whenever Ray was asked for a comment, he tried to get them talking about the revelations of the political scandal, but these *press-titutes* sidestepped the elephant in the room. Instead, they preferred to intimate he was cavorting with whores, getting involved with dodgy business deals, and taking even more bungs.

Ray was at the point of just wanting to retire to a desert island. What encouraged him was the start of approaches from smaller broadcasters and weekly papers. The polite name for them in the circles he used to frequent was "the alternative media". There was always the impetus to marginalise them, to assume they were irrelevant. And if it looked like they had an exclusive on a story, to immediately claim it was a hoax, or a misrepresentation of the facts.

Not that what they were saying was ever investigated. How could they possibly find things out that the hugely-resourced mainstream had missed?

Any platform was better than no platform. So it was that Ray found himself on the phone with a smart young thing called Tina. He doubted it was her real name. Certainly, he didn't believe for a moment that her surname was "Truth". She admitted to being twenty-four years old, but she sounded much more mature than that.

Tina had a voice like sour treacle. A perfect timbre for broadcasting, he could easily think of her on late-night radio. Come up to Birmingham, she said. Chat through with us what happened to you, she said. They couldn't afford a fee, but they'd pay for his train, she said. Ray hadn't been to the second city for years, and with no paying work to get in the way, he certainly had no good reason to decline.

As he pulled in to New Street station, he immediately picked her out on the platform. Tall, waif-like, gothic make-up, a shrunken dress. She hadn't described what she looked like, but that combination was like a beacon. He knew for sure this was who was meeting him. As he got off the train, his hunch was proven correct. She glided over to him and held out her long-fingered hand to introduce herself.

They squeezed in to her battered black Volkswagen Beetle. A graduation gift from her parents, he discovered. Very unlikely that it came with the psychedelic paint job it now had. The family was surely well-to-do, and deeply understanding of their offspring's inability to get a paying job in broadcasting. Ray was genuinely interested in Tina's life story. A Masters' in Media Studies, counter-cultural enough to impress her tutors, but far too much of a live wire to do as she was told for any major station.

She was honest enough to describe how a former boyfriend had introduced her to conspiracy theories. Ray bit his lip repeatedly, as he was told that 9/11 was an inside job, that money wasn't real and just a fraud perpetuated by high-ranking bankers, and that the pharmaceutical industries saw people as revenue streams rather than patients needing a cure.

Ray was getting anxious. He really should have investigated Truth Media TV first, before agreeing to take part in a live interview. Tina was very perceptive, and sensed his nervousness. She changed the subject, and soon had Ray revealing everything that had happened to him in the last couple of weeks. Before he knew it, he was relaxed and fired-up at the same time. She was good at prepping guests. He'd hire her in an instant. If he still had a career in TV production.

They reached their destination. A fairly anonymous industrial unit on the outskirts of the conurbation. No signage to reveal what was within. Access was through some heavy fire doors, a flunky giving access following Tina's orchestrated loud tapping pattern on them. There wasn't a suspended ceiling, so you could look up to the high rafters above. A pod table of four work stations was the centre of operations, staffed by young graduates around the same age as Tina.

'Don't worry about any grunting you might hear from that side of the building,' Tina urged. 'It's what helps underwrite the operation.' Ray knew that being free-to-air on the Sky channels and Freesat wouldn't be cheap. He estimated something like £40,000 per month before you even turned the lights on. He noticed that one of the work-stationers was updating the Electronic Programme Guide, which gave him a chance to see what their type of output was.

A cursory scan made him realise this was not the sort of content which would appeal to large corporate advertisers. Alternative health practitioners, no doubt with on-screen disclaimers to satisfy Ofcom. Proponents of "lightworking", a way to contact other spiritual dimensions, really "out there" stuff. And Tina's show, *Truth Injection*, with recent guests which included ex-MI5-er David Shayler, rebel botanist David Bellamy, and the excitable financial analyst Max Keiser.

Tina led Ray through to the studio, at which point he was won over to the merits of the station. Whoever was bank-rolling the operation hadn't cut too many corners, not if first glances were to be believed. The set was small, but easily capable of a range of options. The equipment was broadcast quality, but around ten years old. He could see it had been jerry-rigged with more domestic modern computer technology to make everything function for a social-media-inspired audience.

The bottom line was that they could handle everything from the one room. It was really quite ingenious. The gallery, where the production personnel sat, could seat just two people. A bearded guy with a dark ponytail was in one of the seats, a petite blonde in the other. Both dressed in a cascade of leather, hers mostly reds, his quite naturally all black.

'So, where do the rest of the crew sit?' enquired Ray, wondering how the live show would run.

'This is it. One on sound, that's Rachel. One on vision, that's Gareth. And me, presenting.'

'Who's the producer?' Ray asked.

'I am,' Tina replied confidently. 'Gareth acts as director, given that he controls which camera goes to air. We get texts and emails in, and there's a camera on Rachel who reads the repeatable ones out.'

Ray was still struggling to get his head around the lack of staff. 'Cameramen?'

'All automatic. Controlled from the gallery.' Ray nodded, having realised the unions would be up-in-arms about how these shows were being made. Tina walked over to a fridge and took out a litre glass bottle of mineral water. She filled the two cut-glass tumblers on the desk at the centre of the action, and beckoned Ray over. He saw the brand, Waiakea, from Hawaii, and raised an eyebrow.

'Never cut corners on what you put into your body,' confided Tina. Ray smirked. 'Stop being smutty,' she chastised. 'Is it going to be one of *those* interviews?'

'Sorry,' said a suitably repentant Ray.

Tina was right, though. It certainly was "one of those interviews", but for all the right reasons. She charmingly disarmed Ray right from the start, with a suitable amount of respect and praise for his accomplishments. They talked of his early life and career, before tackling, head-on, the level of corruption that had been uncovered. Ray continued to protect his sources, and Tina knew not to drive too hard on this point.

This was the Ray Grady the country remembered, not the grotesque caricature that had recently been painted in the press. He came over as a man of principle, standing up for the population at large. The channel's guerrilla tactics in getting the news of Ray's appearance on the show paid dividends. Without a mention in any major media outlets, social media had gone berserk in driving people to the show that night.

For the first time ever, the overnight ratings put the show's audience at over a million. When the consolidated ratings came out a few days later, that figure was down to 10,000. Apparently the system had been victim of a glitch, and had put the decimal point in the wrong place. Or so everyone was told.

Tina was immediately courted by major production companies, but she refused all offers. She knew that something big was about to happen, and she wanted to have the freedom to cover it in her own way. Being Hoovered-up by a big corporate broadcaster was a standard trick in sidelining those who challenged authority. That wasn't for her. Besides, she was now on Ray's speed-dial, and vice versa.

With a mainstream news blackout on the show, Ray had no idea what real impact his appearance had commanded. Tony Pearce called the following day, and said there was someone he ought to meet. A business contact of his had made the connections.

She was a former official in the European Parliament. Her name was Dawn Blunt, and she had news of corruption at the highest levels in Brussels. She had seen Ray on Truth Media TV, and had to meet him. One of the 10,000, obviously. Dawn had a suggestion as to how they could do something constructive about transforming their country. Weed out all the corruption.

Ray sensed this was more than just another whistleblower. He asked Tony to make the arrangements, and as quickly as possible.

4

TRAIL BLAZING

Dawn Blunt impressed Ray with her savvy in politics. She'd travelled the corridors of Westminster since leaving sixth form. She'd not been one for going to university, and had been lucky enough to get a job in the expansive House of Commons post room. She learned quickly, and was noticed for her efficiency. Time and again, one high ranking civil servant after another suggested she apply for a promotion here, or a sideways move there. She interviewed well, and steadily worked her way up the ladder.

It was becoming more and more difficult for Ray to find places to meet with people. His house wasn't practical, as he knew the gossip-mongers would burn up some mileage from anyone visiting him there. Equally, Ray felt the need to impress any potential new ally, and this was particularly true in Dawn's case. As a consequence, he pulled strings to get access to the Post Office Tower's defunct rotating restaurant.

They met in the reception. Ray smiled at the security guard, who pointed to the doors of one of the high-speed lifts. As the doors opened, he beckoned Dawn through.

'We'll be at the top in thirty seconds,' Ray informed, pressing the button for the thirty-fourth floor. 'Seven metres per second. Nearly sixteen miles per hour.'

The restaurant was what they would probably call a "work in progress". The plan had been to reopen it in time for the 2012 Olympics, but that project had been quietly shelved. Ray wasn't sure of the background, but he didn't believe the official explanation of the costs being too hefty.

He knew an Act of Parliament had to be passed, upon its original opening in 1966, to vary fire regulations. That was so the building could be evacuated by using the lifts, unlike every other structure then or since. He'd marvelled at its use in a William Hartnell *Doctor Who* story when he was just eight years old. His infatuation with the building never stopped from that point on.

With it having been the victim of a small I.R.A. bomb back in 1971, he could see where the logic had probably gone on this. It wasn't closed to the public until 1981, the year after the lease for the restaurant expired, which had been in the possession of holiday camp merchants Butlin's. In terms of a re-opening, no doubt B.T. came up against loads of red-tape, all "terrorist related", which quashed their visionary plans for this particular floor of the structure.

How Ray would love to get the place functioning again. Perhaps that would be his next venture. Screw broadcasting, take on a restaurant. Dawn could see Ray's childlike adoration as he stared out at the vista of London, which was nothing short of breathtaking. She was also aware of the exposed wiring, the piles of rubble, and the tired furniture all around. You would almost think they hadn't cleaned up after that I.R.A. incident.

'It's almost a landmark to more innocent days,' she opined to Ray, wondering if she'd left it long enough to break the silence.

Ray puzzled over her comment. 'That's the thing. The world hasn't really changed that much, just our perception of it.' He pulled up a couple of chairs, unique by not being covered in dust, and placed them so they could both continue to watch the view slowly passing by.

'It revolves once every twenty-two minutes,' he remarked. 'The length of an American half-hour sitcom these days.'

Dawn chuckled. 'How would I ever know you were a broadcaster?'

'*Was* a broadcaster,' Ray corrected. 'I don't think those doors are open to me anymore.'

'I know that feeling,' Dawn said, supportively. 'Sometimes you just have to stand up for what you believe in.'

'You know my story, so what's yours?' Ray enquired. He had done a little homework on her, but wanted to hear it direct.

'It all came to a head last November,' she replied, staring out at the skyline. 'That was when the European Union auditors once again rejected the accounts. Twenty years in a row. And here was I, head of their media relations department, once again having to spin it.' Her despair was very evident. 'Press releases with the same by-lines as we'd run in previous years. Headlines like "Another clean bill of health for EU accounts, auditors find improvements in many payment areas". I was sick of it, so I didn't go back in on the Monday morning.'

Ray finally took the chance to size up the lady in front of him. He thought her to be in her early fifties. She was slim, and power-dressed in a shiny black suit, offering almost no contrast to her dark skin. He couldn't quite place the material of her garb. It wasn't leather, but it had a similar sheen. 'And from everything I have read about you, global governance seems to have been one of your passions.'

'I suppose I look on that as idealism these days,' Dawn commented, a little exasperated at herself. 'Seemed like such a good idea. Stop all wars by having everyone on the same side. But that plays in to the hands of corporatism, maybe even fascism.'

'You think there's a difference?' Ray suggested, looking at her as if peering over invisible spectacles.

'What I do know is that if there is a one-world government, then whoever has an opinion different from those in power is labelled part of the "Axis of Evil". Historical scholars know this only too well.'

Ray realised that both of them had travelled very different paths to reach the same conclusion. It allowed them to cut through to the nitty-gritty.

Dawn made her pitch. 'You know the public aren't buying the stories about you?' To this, Ray nodded, but only very slightly, if not quite believing it. 'You are seen as a man of principle, standing up for what you believe in. The kind of man they would support in a general election.'

Ray was a little taken aback. This wasn't even a wild fantasy in the far reaches of his mind. 'But I'm just one man,' he reacted, 'how on Earth am I going to get support across six hundred constituencies? I'm certainly not going to be taken on by any of the major parties.'

Dawn had it all figured out. 'Less than two thirds of people voted last time. That gives you one in three people who are looking for a genuine alternative. And within that, plenty of people who will be prepared to stand as an independent candidate, under a generic umbrella which you could be the figurehead for.'

Ray stopped himself from stroking an imaginary beard. He was trying to filter all the reasons as to why this was a bad idea. 'But it will be five years until the next election,' he declared, seeing this as one of the biggest stumbling blocks.

'You've not been following the fallout from your actions,' chided Dawn. 'You've seen the civil unrest. People have been cornering their MPs. Demanding they all stand down due to the fixing.' Ray looked deep into her eyes, raising a mischievous eyebrow. Yes, of course he'd seen the odd small riot here and there. From what Dawn was saying, it sounded like much of the dissent had been suppressed. 'There's going to be a vote of "no confidence" in the government tomorrow. In the Commons. The Prime Minister has refused to resign, as has the Shadow Chancellor. The backbenchers want blood.'

'And no doubt want to do anything to save their own seats. Separating themselves from what has happened.' Ray was running through the calendar of events in his head. 'Hang on, that could mean another general election in around six weeks' time. If it goes through.' Dawn nodded, confirming Ray's calculations. 'How on Earth are we going to get all this ready to roll with such a short run-in?'

Dawn was keen to sell the benefits of the short timetable. 'They won't know what has hit them. Every alternative party which has been set up in the last few decades has been infiltrated, demeaned and sidelined. There won't be any time to react to what we are doing. With no control grid on our side of things, they won't be able to halt the momentum. Any of our candidates who utter something out of place, we simply note they are independent from everyone else.'

Ray was catching on. 'And that gives us the chance to demonise all the parties, for their "three line whips", their approved selection lists, and everything else which stops individual MPs from following their hearts, rather than what their parties tell them.'

Dawn smiled. This was an easy sales pitch. 'Besides, what's the worst that can happen? As they say, "The most dangerous creation of any society is the man who has nothing to lose". I think that might well be you.'

* * *

The following evening, the House of Commons was full to capacity. The recent reduction in the number of constituencies, down by over fifty with numerous boundary changes, had little effect on the buzz coming from what was once described as the mother of all parliaments. The Prime Minister and the Shadow Chancellor had been advised to keep a low profile.

The Environment Secretary, Duncan Hurst, was trying to rally the troops, to suggest that passing a no-confidence vote was the very last thing the country needed "at this most difficult of times". Parliamentary Members who no-one had ever seen before were suddenly demanding the right to speak, having been told in no uncertain terms by their constituents that they would be watching, and seeing how they handled themselves. And, of course, they were going to check how they voted. They were going to be made accountable, whether they liked it or not.

The mainstream media was trying to paint a no-confidence vote like turkeys voting for Christmas. They might have had a case, but their underlying message was that going to the polls again was a bad thing. The whips of all three parties were trying to encourage the politicians to vote against the motion. After all, this was going to taint all of them in one way or another, and no-one was sure from the opinion polls how this would be reflected in another election.

In the end, there were thirty-three votes in it. The motion of no-confidence was passed. And that led to the next stage, or "Division" as they haughtily liked to call it. The motion for a general election. More of the MPs now had the courage to defy their whips. Four hundred and fifty-one votes for, one hundred and forty-five against. That was the two-thirds majority which was needed. Bedlam infused the room with a mixture of fear and outrage. The race was on.

Ray Grady suddenly found himself with a mission. His back room team picked itself, led by Dawn and supported by Tony and Georgie. All three of them were confident that, even if they didn't win, they could give all the parties a run for their money, with Ray at the helm. They could see it all being rather fun, whatever the result.

The day after the no-confidence vote, Dawn called a press conference. They shouldn't get drowned out of coverage, as their story would run the day after all the kerfuffle. She didn't pick a venue that was too big, as she hand-picked the small contingent of the "press pack" to invite. Luckily, she had plenty of friends in the media, who respected her for her fairness with them when she was over in Brussels.

Dawn hooked them in by stating that a new political movement was about to take the country by storm, led by a famous face. She intrigued them with her pitch. They cleared their diaries to be there.

The grapevine responded to the mystery. Although the room booked would hold twenty-five people comfortably, before they even began it was edging towards forty. The video crews took up an unexpectedly large amount of floor space. Dawn wasn't expecting them to be that interested. She hoped no-one mentioned "fire limits" to the venue.

She called the meeting to order from a modest lectern at the front of the room. She was amazed at the number of microphones being thrust her way. 'Good afternoon. It is not often that we are able to talk about a new concept in British politics. But don't let that put you off,' she smirked. There was a rumble of amusement. 'Many have said a new approach is needed, to address the one third of our citizens who do not vote. And within the two thirds that do, they tend to vote for the lesser of two or three evils. That is not a very positive outlook. Vote to keep someone else out, rather than put someone specific in. To explain more, may I invite you to listen to the leader of a brand new political alignment. Ladies and gentleman, Ray Grady.'

A couple of people made puzzled grunts, before the rest gave up light applause. Underwhelming was the word that came to mind, as Ray went up to the lectern, giving Dawn leave to stand to one side. He looked at those before him, and smiled. 'No need to be a tough audience. I won't keep you long,' he joked.

Ray looked at his notes, but realised he didn't really need them. 'It's not often that you can say you were there at the start of a new dawn in politics. It's my delight to announce "We The People". Some of you may point to the S.D.P in 1981 as the last time this happened. That wasn't the same. You see, all our members will be united by one thing. They never wanted to be Members of Parliament. Which makes them far more suitable than any of the shower we currently have at Westminster.'

Making the most notes of all was Phil Conway. This was certainly a departure for Ray, and was going to help Phil move away from his rather unsatisfying "entertainment" brief, where he had been pigeonholed in his career. Ray continued.

'First off, we are delighted that our Parliamentarians have done the right thing, and dissolved the Commons so that we can run in a new general election. However, the method of voting must not be tainted. Let's get back to tradition. Votes only allowed at polling stations. Counted by hand. Off paper forms. We don't want any possibility of what happened last time to happen again.' Ray then made it look like a wrinkle in the plan had arisen. 'Sorry Mister Dimbleby, you're on call for another long night on election day!'

He was winning the audience around. Certainly he had created a talking point which was bound to be popular with editors. The days of voting machines had come and gone.

'So, what can you expect from us? "We The People" will field a network of truly independent candidates. Chosen locally, they will contest every seat. We believe a well-organised minority can beat a disorganised majority. We are already getting extremely organised, and it will not take much for us to make a breakthrough.'

The best laid plans, as they say. Ray got coverage the following day, but it was all for his demand for voting machines to be outlawed. The new alignment of independent candidates was an afterthought, if it was mentioned at all.

Ray and his "three musketeers" – as he had nicknamed them – began to accumulate frustration in trying to get the word out about their new kind of politics. There was considerable resistance to giving them any coverage, but that just meant their efforts could be put into other areas. Ray and Dawn didn't quite understand the importance of social media, but Georgie certainly did. She had, for a long time, known how to raise the profile of her celebrity clients via her agency.

These skills were indispensable in getting the interest of potential candidates. Georgie knew the right tags to put into messages, and where to get them placed to intrigue the type of people they were looking for. They ended up with at least a handful of volunteers in each constituency, and between them those groups decided who to put forward as parliamentary candidates. It all happened in a matter of days.

Dawn was sure that this time they had a message which could not be ignored. "We The People" now had a full suite of candidates for every Westminster seat. Not only that, but it was a true "grass roots" movement, as each group had raised the money themselves to pay the deposit to enter the race for each constituency. All good talking points for the press to get hold of.

Except that no mainstream outlets bought any of it. Ray, Georgie, Dawn and Tony each took a list of journalists to call to find out what had happened. Every single one of them was evasive as to why the stories weren't running. Eventually, when pressed, it turned out that the decision had already been made that this "Party" wasn't going anywhere, so they weren't going to waste time with such a "distraction".

Ray was still convinced more guerrilla-style tactics, in the mainstream, were the order of the day. Linking in with contacts he'd made across all six of the major British television broadcasters, he was tipped off as to where camera crews would be, who were going to be broadcasting live.

And where better to start than the lawn outside of Westminster? The usual hang-out for news crews on so many occasions. It was Lord Argram's secretary who had given away his location and activities. Argram wanted the chance to try and defend the use of voting machines, even despite the fact he was known to be a shareholder of the firm who had received the contract for them.

His timing wasn't all it could have been. Public opinion had again swayed the politicians into a debate in Parliament, and a vote. The machines were being thrown out. It made Argram's participation rather pointless, but there was still an angle to quiz him on.

It was a sunny late afternoon, perfect for outside broadcasts. Nicholas was a young presenter, sharp-suited and hair dolloped with a little too much gel. His cameraman and boom mic girl were far too relaxed to advance their careers any time soon. They were all waiting for the signal from the studio that they were going live.

Argram had that smug attitude which made so many people want to punch him. Despite his unlimited wealth, he could never get a suit which didn't hang off him like crude oil off a pelican.

With a five second countdown underway, suddenly Nicholas pulled Argram towards him for a tighter shot, and found himself live, broadcasting to the nation.

'We are already a week into the election, and it's looking like a two-horse race.' Turning to his interviewee, Nicholas took on the sort of delivery style which suggested he was talking to someone not quite "with it". 'Lord Argram, it seems that the Liberal Democrat vote is flaccid once more?'

Argram harrumphed. 'It's too early to write us off,' he opined, trying to ignore that their support was now at a low, single digit percentage. Even the Green Party were doing better than them now.

Nicholas was a little uncomfortable, as he was aware of a commotion approaching from some way off. Argram was too self-absorbed to be aware of anything that would unsettle him. 'You have to understand that both Conservative and Labour supporters are yet to be satisfied by the claims that this was just a couple of bad eggs undermining the system,' droned Argram.

The background agitation was getting louder now, picked up over her headphones by the boom mic girl. She was a little frustrated that their "big moment" was being spoiled by noise pollution.

Nicholas decided to continue. 'Do you think any of the minor parties might be in with a chance? Perhaps their time having come?'

Nicholas was wondering whether a UKIP mention would be forthcoming, but there was none of it. And now it was the cameraman's turn to be annoyed that his art was being subverted. Through his lens he saw a group of young protestors, wearing balaclavas, baseball hats, sunglasses and pink and orange T-shirts emblazoned with the phrase "We the People". They carried banners, a multitude of statements fighting for attention, including "Don't ignore WE THE PEOPLE", "Red – Yellow – Blue – You Can Fade to Black" and "Ray Grady CAN handle the Truth".

Through all this, Argram was on autopilot. 'UKIP self-destructed, as will any of these Johnny-come-lately groups.' Nicholas had the quote he wanted, but Argram was suddenly aware he was having his thunder stolen. 'And it certainly won't be this lot!'

It was very reminiscent of the "flower power" era of the late 1960s. These protestors were happy, having a great time, and having fun at rattling cages. Argram decided he would try to demean them. 'These are the sort of oafs who try to stifle free speech. This disrespectful behaviour is nothing short of the anarchy we can expect if they ever get their way.'

The camera was something of a plaything for the protestors, who were changing the emphasis of the broadcast image. Through the melee, Ray made his way to the front, standing centre shot between Argram and Nicholas. His smile was broad, and everyone's eyes couldn't help be drawn to the large orange and pink rosette he was wearing. In the centre of it, the wording announced "WE THE PEOPLE".

'That's rich, Lord Argram,' Ray launched into the member of the landed gentry beside him. 'Your media chums have ensured there's no coverage of the grass-roots support for "We The People". Why is that?'

The cameraman found it difficult to frame his shot as those around him tried to redirect his choice of image. Nicholas was frenetic, and a little out of his depth, as he stated the obvious. 'We appear to be in the midst of a large disturbance! Help!'

Ray took his opportunity as the camera aimed straight at him. 'Hello, United Kingdom. You know "We The People" is gaining massive support. These clowns are trying to make you believe we are on a hiding to nothing.'

Ray was aware the camera was moving away from him, and looked around to see what the problem was. Flanking him were two police officers. They put their hands on his shoulders and began trying to march him off.

This was unfortunate, as Ray hadn't finished his piece to the camera. Shouting from what was now a distance he urged, 'Look it up on the internet! Search for "We The People"! Find out what's really going on!'

The studio programme editor chose that point to cut away from the feed. He was new to the job, and believed he'd been part of a piece of event television. That wasn't a view those "at the top" agreed with. He found himself consigned to what they described as "gardening leave", until after the election at the very earliest.

Ray's visit to the police station was not as brief as it could have been. Not that he was mistreated in any way. He found that he had allies in the force. They fed him the latest intelligence information. The word from "on high" was that they were to clamp down on any unlicensed political gatherings. Ray asked how one acquired a licence. He shouldn't have been surprised when he was told he couldn't. Only the major parties would be able to do that, and no-one else would be recognised as legitimate.

Ray found himself signing autographs, and off-the-record he was told he was making an impact, even without any national coverage. He had the inkling of this from the crowd who had responded to one of Georgie's tweets. She'd asked for supporters to gather at Ronnie Scott's for a peaceful demonstration march. Over fifty appeared from all over, some travelling from the far reaches of the London Underground to join in the fun at short notice. And that was what had landed Ray in the local police station. It would be the first of many such "flash gang" gatherings.

They had the necessary impact, although the picture was painted that these "flower people" were dangerous, maybe even armed. This was clearly ridiculous to anyone who saw the often-repeated footage. Once again, the general public had been taken for mugs, and were again proving there was a lot more nous about them.

Another tip-off took Ray and a group of volunteers to a shopping centre. It was a brand new build, open air in places, and at the time was packed with shoppers, most of which hadn't been told there was a huge recession continuing to eat away at the value of their money.

In charge of his "pack" was Emily, an eighteen-year-old gothic redhead taking a gap year. She had brought a handful of her friends with her. Together they looked like super-villain escorts rather than a band of canvassers. Their smiles were radiant enough to cut through any objections as they handed out leaflets.

The weather was continuing to be unreasonably warm, even for late July. Ray looked up to the sky, shielding his eyes from the sun's brightness, but only too aware of the pattern being carved in the clear blue above his head. It was gradually being cross-hatched with patterns of well-defined white trails. Some would insist that these were simply contrails, condensation out of the back of plane engines. Ray knew that wasn't strictly true.

For these were chemtrails. Seeding of the atmosphere by persons unknown. Purpose unknown. Everyone would eventually realise they were part of some ghastly experiment, from which no good was ever going to come. Ray shook his head in annoyance. Perhaps this was yet another reason why the stakes at this re-run of the election were far higher than anyone realised.

Everywhere Ray went it was the same. He could be talking to women with pushchairs in front of them and a couple of older children pulling them in all directions. Or the local teenage unemployed, with nothing to do but intimidate people who responded to their baiting. Or the abundance of local shop owners who still weren't sure whether trying to make a living was actually worth it.

The quintet then saw their quarry. A local television news crew. The public they had spoken to, on this day and many others, all wanted to know the same thing. Why weren't they hearing about "We The People" on the telly? Ray knew that it was going to be easier to get coverage on regional news programmes. They weren't going to be so strict about what got on air.

While Ray and the others continued to spread the word, Emily was given the task of keeping tabs on what the crew was doing. She reported back that these particular news gatherers were so starved of engaging interviewees they were now getting desperate.

Those who they hadn't recorded, but kept on one side for live broadcast, were milling around. Many were looking at their watches, wanting to get home. The crew then spotted Ray, as he had hoped, and saw a story. A hysterical message back to the studio and they got the authority. They gambolled towards Ray and the students.

'Mister Grady, can we have a word?' enquired the presenter.

'Are you live?' Ray requested, almost off-hand.

'We will be, in half a minute. *London Tonight*. Any good?' came the reply.

Ray had trouble suppressing a wry smile, and in a deadpan retort said, 'Oh, very well. Welcome to the campaign trail.'

The presenter put his hand to his ear, so that he heard the message through talkback correctly. He nodded, so the studio could see on the camera feed that he was ready. 'Ray Grady, our viewers have just seen some interviews with local people. They all seem to be voting for the major parties. Not long left for your "revolution" to ignite?'

Ray tried not to be dismissive. 'Yes, I saw you do those "vox pops" earlier. Good work, good work.'

The presenter was almost taken aback by the flattery. 'Thank you,' he graciously replied.

Ray wasn't finished there. 'How many interviews did you broadcast?'

The presenter looked around for assistance. He was given the answer through his earpiece. 'I think it was four.'

Ray could sense blood. 'And how many interviews did you actually carry out?'

'I'm not sure,' hesitated the presenter. Ray ushered Emily into the shot, who was sporting a brightly-coloured clipboard.

'Thirty-seven in this shopping precinct alone,' Emily boldly stated. Ray nods sagely, looks down to compose himself before staring directly into the camera. A task made easier by Emily's friends ensuring, by stealth, that the cameraman keeps his attentions on Ray.

'So there you are, Ladies and Gentlemen, you heard from four people out of thirty-seven. Getting the big picture yet? Here, let me show you.' Ray beckoned everyone to follow. 'Emily, the camera. And studio, be aware if you cut transmission, people will know you're hiding the truth!'

Emily and her team confiscated the camera and the boom microphone. In the studio gallery, initially the director went along with Ray's analysis. Beside which, they were short on content, and this would at least take them to the commercial break with little creativity required. The internal phone rang. Those on high wanted the feed cut. The director barked at the put-upon vision mixer. 'Kill it, for Christ's sake,' he demanded.

The vision mixer flapped at the myriad of buttons in front of him. 'I can't. Some sort of over-ride. Up the line.'

The director flapped his arms in the air, stamped his foot, before turning tail and storming out of the room. The vision mixer looked at the trainee producer next to him, and winked at her. She smiled, cottoning on. The vision mixer leant back in his chair, now also smiling, and put his hands over the back of his head.

Back at the shopping centre, Ray was making best use of the short time he knew would be available to him. Emily and the gang were doing a superb job of capturing the manic activity. He stopped at a mother with a baby buggy. 'Excuse me, can I ask who you will be voting for?'

The mother was initially annoyed at being disturbed, until she recognised Ray Grady. She beamed at being addressed directly by him. 'Well, Ray, it has to be "We The People".'

'Thanks for your support,' Ray shouted over his shoulder, quickly moving on to his next targets. On a wall, half-sitting, half reclined, a quintet of young Asian men, dressed in mixed cultural garb, worshipping the music coming from their compact ghetto-blaster. 'Hey there! Have you ever voted?'

The trio guffaw. Half mocking. Half laughing. 'Never had the chance,' said the one who was obviously the alpha male.

Ray wasn't going to try and be "hip", knowing how wrong that would look on camera. 'Who's on your radar?' he enquired.

The alpha male deliberately paused, then smiled. '"We the People".' Most of his posse backed him up on this. All except one.

'Hate your show,' he hissed, pleased with himself for the attention he was getting. He might have been the smallest of the group, but he had the biggest attitude. 'And as for "We the People",' he began, smacking his lips together, '…real slammin'.'

Ray took a moment to evaluate the answer. 'Is that good?' he enquired.

'Righteous,' was the reply, with lots of shaking of hands, as if trying to dry them off after a chemical spill. Ray decided to conclude the interaction with a "thumbs up" gesture, hoping it to be sufficiently timeless not to be seen as a fashion faux pas.

It was a tradesman next, in Ray's short tour of as many types of people as he could reach out to. The guy was a glazier, fitting a new window to a shop that had seen some hostility. 'Can you spare a moment? Local telly?'

The tradesman placed the pencil he was using behind his ear. 'Go on,' he said, folding his arms.

'Who will you be voting for,' Ray asked, cautiously.

'Been Labour all my life,' came the robust reply.

Ray hoped he could turn things around. 'Final answer?'

The tradesman winked at Ray. 'Won't be fooled again. Voting for your lot!' With that, Ray reckoned he had made his point. He again addressed the camera directly.

'See what you're not getting on the national news? This isn't just happening here. It's happening everywhere. Look us up. "We the People"! Tell your friends. Be part of the peaceful revolution. Remember, no matter who…'

It was at that point the programme went into the pre-planned commercial break. When they watched the output again that night, the team's verdict was that there was enough context presented for people to understand the point being made. The public was being manipulated, but the scam was beginning to unravel. The citizens were proving they really weren't that stupid.

Not all the media battles were tough. Ray felt obliged to accept Tina Truth's second invitation on to her show. This was going to be a pleasure, not a pain.

Truth Media Television's profile had jumped in surges. Clips from Ray Grady's first interview had been requested by all the major channels. The station only allowed their footage to be used on other media if there was a constant on-screen credit. That intrigued the viewers who had never heard of them. Those with satellite dialled through the channels to find them. And Ray knew he could rely on Tina to get the word out about him being on her programme again.

So here they were, once more cramped and intimate. The countdown to live broadcast began. Before Ray knew it, the duo were sparring just like before.

'Ray Grady, thanks for taking the time to join us on Truth Media Television once more,' gushed Tina, a little nervous, knowing this would easily be her biggest-ever audience.

Ray took a sip of water. 'A pleasure, and my thanks to your station for bucking the trend.'

Tina checked her notes for a split second. 'Our broadcasting licence says that we must be impartial, but as no other channel is honouring that, we thought we'd see if anyone cares to challenge us.'

Ray laughed at Tina's bravado. 'I like your style.'

Tina half confided, half informed, 'We're making this interview free to view on the internet. I know our supporters will help it go viral.'

Ray was thoughtful. 'As long as you're not a vaccine. We know how useless they are.'

Tina realised she had to move on from formalities, despite Ray putting out an obvious talking point. 'Since we last met, things have changed drastically for you. You have become a career politician.' Ray laughed. 'I gather you have a problem with the latest opinion polls?'

Ray put on his serious, focused demeanour. 'Absolutely. When we're out campaigning, I know that we've got more than single digit support.'

Tina found herself tapping her pen on the desk. 'I'm struggling to find anyone who's voting for the three dinosaurs.'

Ray nods sagely. 'A good description. There's this daft idea people only want to vote for winners. Being able to say you selected the victorious side. All that jazz. Seriously thinking choosing anyone outside the "big three" is a wasted vote.'

Tina qualified Ray's statement. 'In many constituencies it was the big two.'

Ray remembered the head points he wanted to get across. 'I think we've brought the underdog back into fashion. You're too young to remember the Grateful Dead?'

Tina is almost annoyed at such a question. 'No-one is too young for the Grateful Dead. That Jerry Garcia quote?'

'Precisely,' Ray commended, knowing he should have given her more credit. Together they find themselves reciting the line together. 'Constantly choosing the lesser of two evils is still choosing evil.' They giggled, almost childlike, at their spontaneity.

Tina gets to the meat of her questioning. 'How's it feel to be excluded from the televised Prime Ministerial debates?'

Ray rocked a little on his chair and deepened the tone of his voice, ever so slightly. 'That's the galling thing. We know the polls are wrong. They give us 8.5%. For heaven's sake! But that's what they'll do to keep us out.'

Tina knew her supporters would want practical solutions, not just pitiful bleating. 'How can people help?'

Ray suggested a course of action, knowing even by saying it he would be declared an idealist by certain media pundits. 'Simply tell other people what's happening. Go to every rival candidate's hustings. Demand justice. Call them cowards, cheats, whatever it takes.'

Tina continued to be methodical in her probing. 'Say we get you in on the debate. Isn't that just the beginning?'

Ray realised he had to dangle a carrot to get the audience working for him. 'Through this show, I want to challenge everyone.' He worked out which camera was the close-up on him, and addressed the viewers. 'Vote with your heart. Vote for what you believe in. More than anything, if we get a level playing field, we can make a difference. Get me in to those debates!'

The camera remained on Ray as Tina asked, 'Do you have a message for your Prime Ministerial challengers?'

Ray turned up the sincerity and purpose. 'Yes, Tina. Labour. Conservative. Liberal Democrat. Debate me if you dare! Running away is not something the people of Britain have ever admired.' He then appealed to the communal sense of logic. 'Look at the odds. It's three of you against one of me. Are you that scared of "We the People"? If our policies don't stack up, you'll be able to dispose of our challenge once and for all.'

A commercial break provided a brief respite, before questions were taken by text message from those watching. Some of them were so vitriolic and complete nonsense that Ray scored one point after another. It was a faultless advertisement for the movement.

So much so, that the major news outlets could not ignore what was happening any longer. A particularly vicious "media darling" was top news anchor Zena Carsley, a twenty-six-year-old exotic high flyer with an acidic, snide streak. She had modelled her style on the American current affairs hawk Michelle Malkin, but with the benefit of what could be a very soothing Scottish accent. Against her wishes, Zena found she had to cover "We the People", but she didn't do so with good grace.

At the top of her news channel show she declared, 'Ray Grady is getting desperate. The pitiful display in the polls of his "We the People" movement has seen him resorting to bleating to anyone who will listen.' She continued in a ludicrously childish tone. '"That's so unfair", he mewled on Truth Media Television last night. That's an obscure satellite channel watched by the tin-foil-hat brigade, by the way.'

The production team were ready to support her "hit piece". A hardly flattering image of Ray, tongue out, hair dishevelled, was superimposed opposite her head in the screen shot's composition.

Zena was getting more fervent in her execution. 'Asking for help from nut-jobs who believe Elvis runs a colony on the Moon. That holding crystals works better than prescription drugs, and that the Easter Bunny crash-landed on Earth from Planet Skaro. These are the only sort of supporters he has. The man is delusional.'

Zena decided it was time to address her target directly, via the camera lens. 'Hey Ray! Get some help, you washed-out has-been! Nobody was watching your show anymore! This is a pathetic way of trying to get yourself a new job!'

Unfortunately for those pulling the strings, this only drew more attention to "We the People". The prospective Prime Ministerial debates were a hot topic, discussed on radio phone-ins at both local and national level. The momentum was building, and every other call turned out to be a demand for this new movement to be represented.

The stations all tried to screen the calls and kill such discussions. Unfortunately for them, Georgie widely circulated the etiquette of how to get "on air". She permeated the methodology throughout the social networks. They were to say they wanted to discuss one thing, and then turn the tables once on air. Followers were only too eager to participate.

A rogue opinion poll was put out. Well, "rogue" as far as the establishment was concerned. It demonstrated an incredible 80% of people considered it only fair to allow "We the People" into the debate. But still there was no progress in getting a route into what would be the showcase television spectacle of the general election. The musketeers realised something more was needed. Some way to put bait down, to guarantee a response to a challenge, even if it was only along the lines of the Farage-Clegg European set-to.

Dawn got a tip-off from one of her friends in the civil service. Conservative leader Duncan Hurst was scheduled to attend the launch of a new railway station as part of the East London line extension. It was going to be a security nightmare, not something which in the scheme of things you would have expected an MP of Hurst's cautious nature to have even entertained. The PR gurus had an angle on a good story though, and persuaded him to take part.

They could build on the Tories bringing in the twenty-four-hour Tube services at weekends. Show they could achieve things which real people wanted. The question as to why something like this had taken so long, given it was a necessity with the around-the-clock nature of the shops and cultures of modern Britain, was always glossed over.

And Hurst could demonstrate how the Conservatives had planned this new station by re-opening sections of disused railway line, and converting track, signalling, line-side signage and other systems to mainline standards. *Making good use of everyday things that had been left behind*, thought Ray, when Dawn told him what was going on. He just couldn't get the image of Hurst surrounded by Wombles out of his head.

This wasn't Wimbledon, though. It was on the branch from Surrey Quays to Clapham Junction. The station was called Surrey Canal Road, an essential cog in a new development which would eventually host around 2,500 new homes. These would be serviced by new shops, offices, restaurants, and sport and leisure facilities. Even Ray had to admit it was impressive, but there had been some bad blood with the local Millwall football club. There was talk of the station not having the minimum number of people using it during the week to make it viable. *Plenty of loopholes to exploit*, Ray mused.

Blending in to the crowds which had assembled for the opening ceremony was easy. Ray and Georgie had joined the throng of party workers who fancied a chance to pop Hurst's bubble. Ray wore heavy sunglasses, and a beanie on his head, disguising himself perfectly. Georgie had decided on a long-haired redhead wig, and sported horn-rimmed spectacles which gave

61

her a makeover of mystery. Or a place in a *Scooby Doo* tribute act. All the banners the congregation carried with them were folded away out of sight, thus none of the Conservative Party workers at the scene suspected any skulduggery.

It was as open a gathering as Dawn suggested it would be. The train service might now be calling in regularly, but there was still a lot of building work to be done outside the public throughways. Temporary panelling hid the areas not yet ready for the eyes of onlookers, but also gave Cluedo-style shortcuts to allow you to turn up in areas where you would not be expected.

This was now very much the case, as Ray had spoken to some disgruntled construction workers who had released padlocks which would hinder progress "backstage". He smirked as he recalled Sir Roger Moore saying that he 'had a face which could open doors.' This was evidence of this in the most literal sense.

The police presence was in the right places. All located where they might expect the protestors to be, that is. Members of the public congregated on the platform where the incoming train was not making a stop, and looked across to a podium fronted by a litter of channel-branded microphones. Those assembling had to compete with television news crews for the best vantage points, as the media insisted space be made for them, so they could deliver Hurst's attention-grabbing stunt to their editors. The gurus had decided to time it so that it could go out live on the lunchtime news bulletins. And they had pulled strings to ensure they got the necessary coverage.

Ray peaked out from behind the sealed-off enclosure at the end of the platform. His footing was a little shaky on the debris beneath his feet. It was easy to understand why the health and safety bods would have such an issue with what they were doing. He was going to challenge Hurst to a duel of words, at a venue and time of his rival's choice, but he wasn't sure what the irresistible bait was going to be.

Behind Ray, his dozens of volunteers were getting excited, and were trying their best to not make any noise. There was so much pent-up energy. The force of feeling was tangible. Ray saw Hurst's party of hangers-on appear at the top of the steps down to the platform. He turned around to signal an even greater level of quiet. As Hurst appeared, and began his descent to the platform, Ray felt a tap on his shoulder.

He had to do a double-take. In front of him, wearing low-slung leggings, a bright tracksuit top and ridiculously dark, shiny sunglasses was Tony. The baseball hat worn the wrong way round was perhaps an accessory too far. Slung over his shoulder was an incredibly large ghetto-blaster. The sort that didn't need a separate sound system, able to compete with the roar of a small plane taking off. Tony raised his sunglasses to his brow, and smiled. 'Party time!' he hissed.

Ray tried to whisper back to Tony in an even quieter voice. 'Didn't think you liked these guerrilla marketing exercises?'

'I've got bait for your hook,' he confided. 'Trust me. This will do it.'

Ray looked back to proceedings. Hurst was approaching the podium. Georgie crouched down to look through the gap at proceedings, head beneath Ray's at their vantage point. She'd noted to Ray that Hurst's whole stunt was flawed, as the news crews wouldn't see Hurst board the train from where they had been placed. What was to their benefit was the train couldn't approach the platform until they were given the signal that Hurst had finished speaking, and then there would be a delay of several seconds. That would be time enough to issue the challenge before Hurst could dash away. All on live television, and it would be too much of a spectacle to cut away from.

A hush descended on the audience as Hurst made ready. 'My thanks to you all for coming to see this historic occasion,' he began. 'We in the Conservative Party have campaigned tirelessly for urban regeneration, and this is yet another example of that policy in action.'

Ray barged Hurst off the microphone. With the stealth of ninjas, the assembled protestors had, within a split second, "kettled" the legitimate occupiers of the platform, totally surrounding Hurst, and giving him nowhere to run. 'Your lot weren't prepared to support this project at all, until private enterprise stepped up to intervene. And here you are, taking all the credit for it.'

Tony stepped forward with the ghetto-blaster in front of his chest, posing his index finger ready to hit the play button. He explained. 'To show willing, demonstrating the alleged frugality of your party, you came here in a taxi,' he noted. 'Now here's where your anti-terrorist measures come back to bite you. You see, snooping works both ways.'

Ray smiled at Tony, as eager to hear what was coming as anyone else. Tony pressed "play". Booming out all around was a deep voice, and within just a few words clearly identifiable as Hurst. 'What's this lunchtime engagement? Surrey Canal Road? I thought we'd decided against it? Good God, no!' Hurst made a lunge towards the ghetto-blaster, Tony lofted it high, almost out of reach, as a pair of Ray's contingent intercepted him.

A husky female voice replied on the recording, 'You need this, Duncan. To win the election you are going to have to mobilise different segments of the population.'

A loud snort of derision blasted out of the speakers. Ray pretended to clean out his ear with an index finger as a reaction, much to the amusement of the public looking on across the platforms. 'I know your specialism is public relations, but you know nothing about politics.' Hurst was looking more and more uncomfortable.

Hurst's aides continued to remain "kettled" away from him, including a lady power-dresser who was becoming particularly agitated. No doubt she was the one on the recording. 'This is an invasion of privacy!' she squealed.

'Public interest!' Tony hooted back.

Hurst continued on the recording. 'The only person who had the right idea about that area of London was Hitler during "The Blitz".' Gasps from those assembled, even a number within Hurst's contingent. 'That area is full of the sort which give democracy a bad name. Don't play any part in deciding who rules over them, but are the first to complain. If you want a dictionary definition of "plebs", that'll be it!'

Tony stopped the recording, and took to the myriad of microphones at the lectern. 'Recorded this morning. Three hours ago.'

'Taken totally out of context!' Hurst bellowed, loud enough to be heard over the audio system, even though he was a couple of feet away from the lectern.

Ray intervened, 'Out of context, Duncan? Sounds more like you're out of touch!' It was a line designed to get a round of applause. It succeeded.

Hurst rose to the bait. 'Someone needs to take you down a peg or two!' he exploded. The effect was palpable. The trap had been sprung. The PR gurus backed off from the "kettling" line, collective heads in hands.

'Tell you what, if you reckon your finger really is "on the pulse", and mine is not, why not debate me about it on live television?' Ray looked Hurst right in the eyes. Hurst licked his lips, realising the figurative landmine he had just stepped on. 'After all, what could possibly go wrong? Frightened that people will see what you really are, just before the general election?'

The build-up of bile from Hurst's mouth gushed into Ray's face. 'Why on Earth would I give you the credibility you lust for? Politics isn't a game. It's serious. I am not having you turning it into a circus!'

The crowd jeered with menace. 'You've taken their bread, Mr Hurst,' Ray opined, 'at this time they'll take their circuses to compensate!' And now the crowd cheered and applauded. Ray had no idea where that line had come from, but he wondered whether Winston Churchill might have just whispered in his ear.

Hurst had turned from black to a very dark purple. 'Name the time and the place.'

Ray jumped in like a prosecution lawyer who had just witnessed a defendant being felled by a heart attack. 'And the channel?' he enquired.

'Whichever of your "chums" wants to run it!' Hurst hissed.

The reaction of the audience was like a goal had been scored from forty yards, and against the run of play. Hooting, apoplexy, shaking of fists in celebration, rejoicing on both platforms. In the commotion, the expected train appeared, and very quickly Hurst and his party scuttled onto it and away.

With the tracks between the platforms clear again, Ray waved across to the onlookers. It really was like the final whistle of the World Cup Final 1966 all over again. Behind one of the news cameras, he wasn't at all surprised to see his old pal Joey, who slowly nodded to Ray and gave him the "thumbs up". The message had got out to the TV audiences watching at home, and could not now be ignored.

One target bagged. Ray wasn't sure how they were going to ensnare the other leaders to debate him. This was a trick they could only play once.

The subsequent media coverage appreciated the entertainment value in this potential "sideshow". The polls demonstrated there wasn't going to be any sort of breakthrough for "We the People", regardless of what might happen in the debate. What harm could it do to encourage it? And the spin doctors made it look like Duncan Hurst was being very statesmanlike in tackling such a challenge head-on.

It was past ten o'clock the following evening when Ray got the call.

Would he make himself available for the prospective debate?

And would he find it acceptable if the leaders of the Labour Party and Liberal Democrats also took part?

Dawn reasoned it out. The other two parties were frightened of being accused of ducking the challenge. They too were left with no choice but to enter the fray.

Ray smiled. They had been given an opportunity. From nowhere they had been provided with the catalyst they needed. Maybe they had friends in much higher places than they could ever imagine...

5

HUSTING LIKE HELL

There was no greater sense of irony when Ray saw the studio once used for *The Ray Grady Show* would be the location of the Prime Ministerial debate. It had always been a busy production hub, so the significance was only felt by Ray himself.

He knew its every nook and cranny. Joey the technical manager was still part of the team at the complex, despite a rap on the knuckles concerning the final *Ray Grady Show*. As punishment he'd been pushed onto some outside broadcasts, as Ray had seen.

Joey was one of the fixtures and fittings. You hired this studio, you got Joey's expertise thrown in as part of the deal. He gave Ray a subtle nod as the "We the People" candidate entered the room, not wanting too many people to be reminded of their connections.

The frenetic activity meant Ray was anonymous in the room. Joined by his musketeers of Dawn, Tony and Georgie, as well as intern Emily, they had to fight hard to get their invitations.

Fire safety numbers they said. Massively over-subscribed they insisted. Having to fit in an extra speaking place already, they pontificated. Ray could do without the aggro, so spoke to those in charge of front-of-house. He acquired four of the emergency V.I.P. allocation, always kept to one side. Okay, they weren't technically visiting dignitaries, but it all proved it's never what you know, but who you can cajole.

Four lecterns had been placed across the central area of the stage, with a large panoramic video screen behind them, swamping the entire set.

Ray looked around the audience as they filtered in. They were a lot smarter in attire than the folk who used to frequent his show. He realised they had all been "hand-picked" from the plethora of ticket requests that had been received. No-one with militant tendencies ("terrorists" as they were now described). No constitutional experts. Just the rank and file who believed what they were told in the papers. That grumble aside, every race, colour, creed and social class were represented.

Studio hands were being watched like a hawk by Joey, ensuring they were wiring up the right things in the right places. Ray's colleagues dispersed themselves amongst the audience, as if they wanted to have every exit covered. With the final details being checked, the floor manager, a new face which Ray didn't recognise, stepped forward to calm the crowd. They were very compliant to his simple action of putting his index finger up to his mouth.

It was time to get the show on the road. He shouted out, 'Places everyone! Audience stand by! We are live in ten seconds!' The excitement was tangible. The pompous theme music began, as opening credits played out over the studio monitors, their images scattered amongst the audience. A set of fresh-faced rookie "associate producers" escorted the four candidates to their respective lecterns, as the introduction continued, which tried to summarise the concept of democracy in forty-five seconds.

Taking his place at the first lectern was Richard Devine. He was the recently-installed fresh-faced leader of the Liberal Democrats, rebuilding their support after their tragic dance with death in a parliamentary coalition. His finely manicured hands gave away that he had never done any blue-collar work in his life. The suit was tailor-made, making him look like a malnourished model in a catalogue, except such a mannequin would have managed a more believable smile. Ray winced at Devine's acknowledgement of the audience. His wave came over as if he was mimicking Queen Elizabeth.

Next to him was clumsy Alice Kavanagh, playing the card of being down-to-Earth. Her school-matronly approach to being leader of the Labour Party came across, to many, as deeply patronising. Her fashion sense was stuck in the 1950s, her figure as short as it was wide. She wanted to be a remodelled Margaret Thatcher of the left, but came over more as Margo Leadbetter from *The Good Life*. Ray was distracted by thinking of this analogy, recalling the trivia that the show was transformed into *Good Neighbors* in the States, with that wrong spelling inflicted on it as well.

Then came the bookies' favourite, despite all that had happened. Duncan Hurst, the leader of the Conservative Party. His Afro-Caribbean roots meant he was trying to be a British Obama, even despite how that former President's reign had been hastily concluded. Ray reminded himself that poor old Barack was the perfect example of how you can go from people's choice to people's pariah, within just a few short months.

Ray took a couple of seconds before allowing himself to be guided onstage, pretending to quickly look at a text message on his mobile. His rookie producer didn't have the heart to hurry him along, but what it meant was that when the audience saw him taking to the podium, there was a huge surge in applause. Even some cheers from certain sections of the congregation. That short pause had put both a physical and emotional distance between him and the other candidates.

Ray milked the situation, going to the front of the stage, with a confident wave to the audience. He could see that this wasn't a feeling of adulation shared by everyone, but the significant minority were making sure that the other candidates understood what was in front of them. A partisan crowd. With hands now in pockets, Ray skipped toward the final lectern, giving a broad false smile to the other participants.

As the music faded, a booming voice came over the sound system. Ray recognised it as Seth. If only the audience could see him, as their mind's-eye impression would be completely different to what he was like in real life. Ray was never sure if the guy washed his T-shirts. Ever. And a smell of burning rubber. Pungent. 'Welcome to the Prime Ministerial debate for this general election. Here is your host, Zena Carsley.'

Ray wasn't expecting her as the referee. He anticipated it would be one of the "old guard" fronting the programme. No doubt this would be touted as some nod to trying to entice younger voters to the polling booths. He'd never met Zena before. There was no reason in his pre-politics days as to why he should have done. And given her hostility to his campaign, there was no reason why Zena's producers would have wanted to get Ray on her show.

As Zena strode on to the stage, taking her place at her adjudicator's desk, the audience in general were polite in their applause, if not exactly enthusiastic. She was facing the candidates now, upright and tense, the onlookers almost mesmerised in the view over her shoulders. Her eyes gave her away, too deep-set and intense, betraying that success was everything to her, no matter how it was achieved. Ray also noticed she had upped her power-dressing a notch, and was a little surprised that such a psycho could really look a little nervous. As the music faded, she began her carefully co-ordinated performance.

'Welcome to this first appointment debate with the potential new hands on the levers of power. Tonight, we have four candidates who want to take up residence in Number Ten. First, I will introduce to you the Liberal Democrat prospect, Richard Devine.'

Devine revelled in his close-up. Another unhelpful smirk, something the spin doctors could not get him out of doing. As he stared at Zena, the expression was that of a schoolboy in love. 'Good evening Zena, good evening United Kingdom,' he minced, looking at the camera exactly as he had been taught.

Zena moved on swiftly. 'Leader of the Labour Party, Alice Kavanagh.' Her image consultants had also failed to round off the edges.

'Hello,' she giggled, ridiculously out of her depth.

Ray had the first inkling of a migraine. Zena was trying desperately to add gravity to the situation, as she felt the oxygen being sucked out of the room. 'Acting Leader of the Conservative Party, and temporary Prime Minister, Duncan Hurst.'

Hurst was clearly much better coached than the other career politicians on display. If there was a toxicity meter for measuring schmaltz, it was rocketing off the scale. 'Delighted to be here, Zena.'

Zena was a little taken aback by the undertone of flirtation coming from Hurst. It reminded her of that uncomfortable TV interview that old artist and entertainer had given, where he was flirting with the female host, young enough to be his granddaughter. Briefly, Zena looked like a bulldog chewing on the ear of a Chihuahua. Concluding the introductions, and oh-so-begrudgingly, Zena barked, 'And finally, representing the umbrella brand of "We the People", Ray Grady.' The intonation of the word "umbrella" was decidedly strained.

Whether by accident or by design, the director made it look like he had not been prepared for a fourth candidate in this debate, a wild crash zoom taking in an extreme close-up of the hairs in Ray's nostrils, before settling back to a more respectable mid-shot of his head and shoulders. With a smile which indicated he was taking the gathering seriously, he announced, 'A pleasure to be here, and my thanks to Duncan Hurst for making it all possible.'

Zena had her first chance to turn up the heat on Ray. Consulting her notes, she jumped in. 'If I may challenge you on that, Mister Grady?' She had Ray's full attention, as he quizzically raised one of his eyebrows. Zena's follow up was laced with vitriol. 'You find yourself here, when quite rightly the SNP and Plaid also wanted to be included. That doesn't show much respect for them.'

Ray smiled, and subconsciously shook his head. 'As you know, Ms Carsley, it was my learned colleague from the Conservatives who responded to my challenge. I think he thought he was being invited on to my former chat show. Not that I am suggesting he is out of touch with events, of course.'

The audience who understood the reference giggled. Ray brought them to order again. 'The nationalist parties have been denied the right to take part in these debates in previous elections. Yes, that's wrong, but I will make myself available to debate them on their own terms, too. All they have to do is ask. And if this lot don't want to take part,' he waved offhandedly at his rivals at the other podiums, 'well, we'll have a lot more fun and get a lot more done.' Sections of the audience laughed, and politely applauded. 'Oh, and my thanks to everyone who jammed the switchboards of television and radio stations, the lines to offices of Members of Parliament, newspapers, and local councils to demand our inclusion here tonight. Who says there's no "people power" anymore?'

And so, the questions began. The topics were exactly what Ray was expecting. It was almost a template which had been adhered to in similar debates over the years. Unemployment. The National Health Service. Education. Law and order. Ray was amazed that a question on defence spending was almost brushed aside. He quizzed the candidates as to why, as sitting MPs, they had allowed Britain's capability in this area, to be dismantled. 'The British military has more than 500 horses but fewer than 230 tanks,' he noted. No-one challenged the figures, which concerned many of the yet-to-be-converted in the audience.

It was the European Union where he gained a lot more support. The trio all made their usual arguments that the UK's balance of trade would be hit severely if they were to leave Europe. Ray pointed out there was still a Commonwealth to trade with, and the latest figures showed that the UK was doing progressively more trade with the rest of the world.

The bad press around UKIP saw everyone hammering home their belief that the debate over EU membership was over. Ray made up a huge amount of ground in this arena, demanding to know why they thought it acceptable to still be part of a body that hadn't had its accounts signed off in twenty years. He shook his head as he noted, 'Self-employed people know that if they'd done that for just two years in a row, they'd find themselves behind bars.' As Ray had surmised, debating on the issues left all the three major parties spectacularly exposed.

Lib-Dem Devine was becoming more like a nuclear-powered windmill, waving his hands around in imperious motions every time he spoke. Labour Kavanagh was, in turn, limited in her motions, getting into the habit of putting her hands together, always expressing contraction and austerity. Tory Hurst was getting very rattled, jabbing an accusing finger furiously in Ray's direction with every sentence. Ray looked pointedly at the audience and shrugged his shoulders in response every time, causing a degree of amusement.

Zena was getting into the swing of things, initially revelling in trying to keep order. Someone in the props store had fished out a judge's gavel and block for her, and she relished every thump she made with it on her desk.

She took great exception to Ray making the shape of a "gabbling beak" with his right hand as Hurst spoke up on immigration. The audience were warming to Ray's antics with every passing minute, and responded with laughter.

Kavanagh was nervously taking a sip of water from a glass under her lectern when Ray pushed a question in her direction. The ensuing spluttering delighted his supporters.

Zena wasn't keen on the way Ray was winning the congregation over. As he tried to make a statement on beer duty, she cut him off on a spurious point of order. The audience jeered, and Ray folded his arms. On another occasion, Ray was panned away from in mid-flow by the cameraman, who instead focused on Hurst, surprised to be the centre of attention and trying to work out what his facial reaction should be to what Ray was saying. Ray broke with tradition, carried on speaking and stood behind Hurst so the audience at home could still see him. Ray had to stand on tip-toe, such was Hurst's relative height to him. Stepping to Hurst's side, Ray pointedly looked at Hurst's notes. He then looked directly at the camera, pointing down at the paperwork, took in a sharp intake of breath, before shaking his head in disbelief.

Devine was first up at the section where candidates summarised their particular party's position. He didn't seem aware of how hard he was banging his fist on his lectern. It led to distortion on the microphone, meaning much of what he said could not be heard clearly.

In turn, Kavanagh and Hurst made summaries that were so soporific there was nothing memorable for any of the viewing journalists to take a bite into. Phil Conway was in the press section, and looked around to see if everyone else was as stumped as he was as to how to sum up this candidate. There was a lot of subconscious shaking of heads.

The hacks had their instructions to portray it as a neck-and-neck contest, but even the "hard of thinking" in the audience were aware of what was going on. Ray's media training and straight talking were allowing his platform to emerge through the fog of negative propaganda.

With her vitriol hardly hidden, Zena almost choked on her next bit of script. 'Finally, to round off his party, er, umbrella brand's position … Ray Grady. You have two minutes.'

Ray thought to comment on the lack of time limitations on the three candidates that had preceded him, but realised he would only be robbing himself of available seconds. He adjusted his tie, and cleared his throat. A quick sharp smile was followed by sombreness.

'Nice to get a word in edgeways.' A knowing ripple of laughter came from the audience in response. 'I am sure that my fellow party leaders will agree with what I am about to say. You've seen tonight how politics works in our once United Kingdom.' Ray pointed out his three rivals. 'It's about divide and rule, not what is best.'

Ray walked away from his lectern, knowing his Lavalier radio microphone would allow him to wander amongst the audience. He passed Zena and her desk on the way, and winked at her. She was not sure whether she should try and stop him going walkabout, but couldn't work out exactly how she could do that gracefully.

'We are paying twice as much for membership of the European Union than we were just a couple of years ago. We can't have governance at a local level if everything is fed down from a central decision-making junta. One we have no control over. One that remains unaudited in two decades.'

As the nationalist parties had been mentioned, Ray decided it was time to engage those citizens specifically. 'The Scottish and Welsh people are intelligent enough to realise that replacing Westminster rule with Brussels bureaucracy is not progress. English and Northern Irish citizens also understand this.'

Ray was close to a camera on the wings of the audience, and walked towards it slowly. He knew this particular cameraman, and surmised the guy would be able to give it a sufficiently *Reservoir Dogs* style to captivate the viewers. 'Labour. Liberal Democrat. Conservative. It's very difficult to believe in any sort of conspiracy when you trust the establishment. I say to you now: question everything! Remember, if you tell a lie big enough and keep repeating it, people will eventually come to believe it.'

Ray thought he needed to explain further. 'Know who said that? Joseph Goebbels, the Nazi minister of propaganda, 1933 to 1945.' Mentioning that period of German history always made any audience uncomfortable.

He allowed himself a brief moment of amusement. 'As a particular broadcasting friend of mine always says in his catchphrase... "They wouldn't do that... Would they?"'

The relevance was lost on the majority. Ray whispered. 'Yes... they *would*.'

Ray spotted a bespectacled slither of a man wearing a yellow and black rosette. He addressed him directly. 'None of these three parties have the answer. How can they have, when they themselves are part of the problem?' Ray reckoned it was time for another question for the audience, 'How many times tonight have you heard these three utter the word "change"?'

Right across those assembled, there was a mumble of part-realisation, part-agreement. It seemed to have been the word of the evening. Ray turned back to face the roving cameraman who had appeared from nowhere. Someone in the gallery had realised this would add to the visual impact of Ray's invasion of the audience's perimeters. 'The one question none of you asked. Is this going to be a change for the better?'

That was the cue that Georgie, Tony, Dawn and Emily had been waiting for. They sailed through the audience with wads of papers in hand. Georgie approached Ray, and gave half of her much larger pile to him. Tony approached the journalist area of the studio, and pointedly gave his first copy to Phil, whose compliance and enthusiasm encouraged the others to readily accept what they were being offered.

Ray continued talking as he handed out his own supply of papers. 'These are some figures you won't see in the mainstream media.' At that, Joey the technician took his cue, surprising fellow staff by him knowing what was coming next. The lights faded as the musketeers continued to distribute their wares amongst the audience.

A headline flashed up on the main screen, and was quickly relayed to all the monitors around the studio. The words sent a tremor through those connected to the main three political groupings. "Party Donations".

Ray addressed Joey directly, 'Put them up on the big screen.' It was a moment of revelation for Ray. 'Always wanted to say that. A "Captain Kirk" moment.' Knowing laughter glided through the proud geeks within the audience.

Everyone in the studio saw the same company names coming up for all three parties. Raydima – the pharmaceutical giant. Nordstrome Fleischer – agricultural heavyweights, big in genetic modification. Maclarstic Inc – manufacturers of aircraft, arms and one of the biggest winners of military contracts. Lorecarn Ltd – transport and infrastructure giants, who made their fortune re-equipping countries torn apart by the wars fought over many decades.

The list of corporation names went on and on, common across all three columns, one for each party, coloured blue, red and yellow to hammer the point home. The figures revealed hefty donations, in the low millions, to each of the parties. Conservatives got the most, Labour just a little less, and the Liberal Democrats were given enough to be getting along with.

By this point, the programme director was realising the Earth-shattering importance of the information on display, and decided to throw what had been a tightly orchestrated "tone briefing" out of the window. Devine, Kavanagh and Hurst were not happy, they were clearly looking for someone to intervene. Each of them tried to usher their campaign managers to try and stop the paper distribution. As they did so, many audience members got up and offered to help spread the paperwork more quickly. In what seemed like a couple of seconds, everyone had been package-dropped.

A trio of campaign managers bustled their way to Joey's mixing desk, but were swiftly blocked by Dougan, Kindon and another security guard. Nobody needed to say anything. The rules of engagement had suddenly changed. And Joey had made sure there was no way transmission could be cut. You'd have thought they would have learned what he could do by now, where his loyalties actually resided.

Ray knew he was going to go over his allotted time. 'See how it works? These guys donate to all the parties. If you want to win a game, control all sides. All the teams.' Ray took on a thoroughly sarcastic tone. 'But there's nothing to worry about. No impropriety here.'

Ray cupped his hands around his mouth, and shouted out into the audience. 'Nothing to see here! Move along!' Ray again spoke directly to the roving camera following him, 'Tomorrow, they'll tell you this is all made up. They'll fail to mention the facts which support what I've just said.'

Ray held up a copy of the document he had helped to hand out. He waved it around above his head. 'They'll tell you that this didn't contain anything not already in the public domain. They'd be right. But, did you actually know about it?' Ray was met by an uncomfortable silence. 'Of course you didn't. Whilst you have trust in the establishment, it's very difficult to consider a "conspiracy" as anything but "theory" when the facts are concealed.'

Ray continued to talk directly to the roving camera as he walked back towards the stage, machine-gunning the delivery of his speech, realising his time must surely be almost up. 'Think of this tonight, if nothing else. If all those who did not vote in the last general election did so this time, and chose us, then "We the People" would win. Without anyone else changing the way they vote. Tells you everything you need to know about our broken system. All parties start Election Day with the same number of votes. Zero.'

Ray stopped in his tracks, dead centre stage, directly facing Zena, and the camera that was over her shoulder looking at him. He made his closing remark very pointed. 'Don't you dare tell me that you cannot make a difference.'

With that, Ray turned away and walked back to his lectern. There was a slight pause. Suddenly, the audience erupted in unison, hectic applause, with a mixture of cheering and screaming in support. It made the venue seem ten times larger than it actually was.

By this point, the programme director had been yanked from his post, replaced by a "Senior Producer", keen to keep up the payments on his massive mansion and multiple villas around the world.

Desperate to get the broadcast back "on message", the focus was not on Ray any more, but instead an extreme close-up of Zena. The sound mixer faded down the commotion in the background, its impact being limited to what Zena's microphone was picking up.

Unfortunately, even with the camera almost up Zena's nose, it was clear what was happening behind her. The vision mixer was forced to matte in a "news studio" background behind Zena, not an easy task without a green screen. The effect looked like something from a 1970's edition of *Top of the Pops*.

Zena was told via her earpiece to read off her autocue. She had no choice but to shout over the revellers behind her. 'That is all we have time for. Join us on Thursday for the second of these debates, thankfully this time with just the prospective Chancellors from the three major parties.'

With that, the studio broadcast was cut, an unconvincing jump to the late evening news replacing what the viewers at home were previously seeing.

* * *

Ray arrived home to find Alicia still up. She'd realised how crucial his performance was going to be to the task-at-hand, and wanted to tell him what a great job he had done. After all, he was risking not only his reputation, but the ongoing prosperity of the family. The system never liked to be challenged, and would find a way to cause a comeuppance to anyone who dared to stand up for what they believed in. And that was especially true for anyone who should be grateful for how far they had progressed within the "matrix". It made the night something special for both of them. They made love with ferocity and urgency, something which hadn't happened since the children arrived on the scene.

The following morning, Ray and the musketeers got an idea of how difficult their task was going to be. The newspapers had headlines about riots in the television studio, caused by the audience's violent objections to the performance of Ray Grady. Half of them called the policies of "We the People" blatant Nazi-orientated fascism. The others described their manifesto as pure undiluted Communism. Ray managed to see the funny side to this polarisation within the reporting.

For those who had dared to help Ray, the resulting fallout was brutal. Joey the technician was suspended, politely described as "gardening leave", and was informed his contract would not be renewed the following spring. Dougan and Kindon also found their compliant behaviour on security detail unappreciated. The company they worked for immediately dispensed with their services. Kindon phoned Ray to tell him what had happened, and that the two of them wouldn't have changed the way they had handled things for anything.

The call came through just as Ray was finishing up his second cup of coffee of the morning. He was staring out of the kitchen window, down to the bottom of his home's driveway in Coombe, Kingston-upon-Thames. Yes, he'd done well for himself, but it was also a case of making sound investments. This was certainly a plush area of the outer London conurbation, but less than five miles from the underground network, and a mile from a rail station.

Ray noticed there were journalists and photographers encamped outside the main gates. His family were now not going to be able to go about their business without a significant amount of intrusion, if not hostile barracking. The serendipity of the call wasn't lost on Ray. He asked what was now the most obvious of questions. How would Kindon and Dougan like to come and work directly for him?

Kindon relayed the job offer to Dougan. As both of them had reported to work together, and had been fired in unison, it was natural that both of them would be sat down in the same hearty transport cafe. The offer was considered for a nanosecond. They reckoned they could report for duty within half an hour.

Alicia came to look at the assemblage way down their driveway. She stared pointedly at her watch. 'I'm still going to have to leave in about half an hour, to get the kids to school,' she pleaded.

Ray smiled. 'Not to worry,' he reassured. 'I've got you a pair of "minders" on the way, neither of which is Dennis Waterman.'

'That's a shame,' mocked Alicia, 'I'm sure I could have taught him some "new tricks".' She stroked Ray's face, realising the stakes were now going to be raised by the day, if not the hour.

Dougan and Kindon were as good as their word. They arrived in Kindon's own black Cadillac limousine, betraying his hobby of being a classic car aficionado. The paparazzi thought better than to take pictures of them entering the grounds of the house, probably concerned as to where their cameras might end up if either of these guys ever got hold of them.

A few polite introductions, and Dougan and Kindon escorted Alicia, along with Alison, the eldest at seven years old, and Ryan, a quite mature five, to the waiting vehicle. The security duo applied their regulation dark sunglasses for the rest of the journey. Remarkably, the press corps made short shrift of getting off the road, of the mind that Kindon wasn't going to be stopping for anything.

Ray was to learn later that there was a separate press entourage waiting at the gates to the children's school. Despite Dougan and Kindon making a very respectable corridor from the car for Alicia, Alison and Ryan to navigate through, it didn't stop the insistent camera flashes, or the barrage of questions.

'Mrs Grady, Mrs Grady,' one frazzled witch of a hack caterwauled, 'what do your friends think about your husband planning to tax women's magazines?'

Alicia wasn't in the mood. 'Read the news release,' she spat, dismissively. 'Or didn't they teach you to read?'

The witch wasn't done. She knew how to throw a red rag. 'Doesn't it show you're elitist?'

Regrettably, that was the sort of bait which Alicia always found herself rising to. It was her militant friends who had instilled that in her. 'It's any lifestyle magazines which concentrate on distractions. Celebrity culture, for instance, rather than what's important.'

A second alleged journalist, this one a great friend to fast food, all zits and wobble, took up the baton. 'It's still a tax on knowledge, reading, education.'

Alicia knew enough about this policy to defend it. 'The release says, quite clearly, academic works or magazines dealing with serious issues will be exempt.'

Another journalist, so nondescript as to almost blend into the pavement, decided to do some prodding. 'I'm from *Heat*. If Will-I-Am talks about Soviet existentialism, then we avoid the tax?'

Alicia stopped in her tracks. She was trying to picture the rapper stringing together something so esoteric, and snorted amusement. 'If you get him to do that, you'd deserve to!'

With that, Alicia and the children reached the school gates, curtly closed behind them by the dishevelled security man, who also doubled as a caretaker. Dougan and Kindon, themselves with no media currency, were able to make it swiftly back to the limo.

Ray had some interesting business to carry out to fill in his day. At the crack of dawn, he had received a call from media mogul Leonard White. The guy was old-school, one of those business folk who got a lot done before anyone else's working day had even started. He'd seen Ray in action on the television, and had decided it was time to provide some of the promised support he had spoken about. And it had to be done right now, so that he could lend a hand before his potential deportation to the States on corruption charges. This wasn't the sort of thing he could delegate.

White's idea was simple. He'd set aside his printing presses, and provide his tabloid's editorial team, who would produce a special edition of their paper, and publish it overnight. The following morning it would be distributed for free by every network they could tap into. A short, sharp, countermeasure to all the negative spin Ray and his party were enduring. Cut out the middlemen, get the message straight to the people. Even go to the expense of getting it delivered to every front door across the nation. A donation to the Royal Mail staff benevolent fund would hopefully smooth over any objections from the postal workers. After all, if Murdoch could do it with *The Sun* just before the World Cup 2014, then imitation would become the sincerest form of theft.

When he revealed the plan to them, the musketeers dropped everything and hurried over to the newspaper offices to support Ray. Luckily, Georgie knew you had to have all your messages and materials ready in a variety of formats, and had found both Tony and Dawn to be excellent copy editors, knowing exactly how to write for different audiences. Working with the paper's editorial staff, together they crafted a manifesto document disguised as a "red-top", with a reading age of nine years old.

Ray found himself involved in several impromptu photo calls, all designed to help illustrate a particular policy line. The in-house photographers traversed a fine line, balancing humour with getting the message across. Ray in a Sou'wester, holding a prime cod by the tail, helped to explain their policy bravado on fishing quotas. Ray with chalk and blackboard, on which was scribbled "Assist in understanding, not just retaining facts". Ray in a police helmet, about to drop a taser into a large rubbish bin. As has always been said, these pictures were each worth a thousand words.

Section by section, the paper hit the presses, finally being combined and spat out by 10.00pm that night. Ray had asked Tina and her cameraman boyfriend from Truth Media TV to come and cover the event. He didn't understand what Tina saw in the lens man, but mentally shook himself for getting so paternal about her.

Leonard White was with Ray for the occasion. Tina arranged for the usual sort of footage demanded of such a "broadcast package": paper rollers turning at speed; finished newspapers folded on racks and being bundled; and, of course, Ray and White pulling copies off the production line to examine the content. These copies of *News First* couldn't help but hit you between the eyes. The front page headline, "WE THE PEOPLE: THE TRUTH", sufficiently neutral to ensure that readers of all political colours would investigate further.

Tina moved Ray and White together, so her cameraman could film a bold close-up of the duo. It was in fact a necessity, so they would be able to hear them above the din of the machines in the background. Such was the shoestring nature of the operation that Tina herself held the boom microphone down low, just out of camera shot.

'Leonard White, what made you decide to help Ray Grady?' she enquired.

White found Tina's style a blessed relief. His media encounters of late had simply been cruel interrogations. 'He's been very vocal in not accepting any kind of campaign donations, so I wanted to contribute "in kind", so to speak.'

Tina continued, knowing they would get fill-in close-up shots of her, nodding responses, a little later. 'Ray, the mainstream will take issue with Leonard White, the claims against him, and this publicity. Is it wise to accept his assistance?'

Ray was pleased that Tina knew exactly the lines of attack the mainstream would use against the party in the morning, when they became aware of the newspaper being circulated. 'We have nothing to hide. This is about open government. We are starting as we mean to go on.'

With that, Ray held up a copy of *News First*, headline facing the camera. The man behind the lens knew to zoom in on the paper's headline.

'This edition will be given out free at supermarkets, rail stations, shopping centres, as well as copies through your front door,' he continued. 'We've reached as many people as we can through the internet. We had to find a way to cast our net wider.'

Again, Tina helped pour water on the ammo expected from big media counterparts. 'Will you be helping Mister White out with his court case, if you become Prime Minister?'

Ray couldn't hide his delight at being asked about this potential stick to be beaten with. 'Leonard is big enough, and ugly enough, to fight his own battles.'

White decided it was time to jump in. 'Let me be clear. I'm supporting Ray Grady and "We the People" because it's the right thing to do.'

As Leonard had made himself the subject of the close-up at this point, Tina asked the final line of retaliation which was expected from the opposition forces. 'What about the stipulation that all newspapers should be balanced in their election coverage?'

White laughed heartily, and with a steely glint in his eyes said: 'If you find one that is, drop me a line.'

Both men knew this was one hell of a gamble. What they didn't know was they had just lit the blue touch-paper on a dramatic change of course in their party's election fortunes…

6

RISE AND FALL

Damian knew he had acquired Darby Island on the cheap. Nestled in a very discrete part of the Bahamas, he had a varied choice of pure white sandy beaches to frequent, all matching the colour and texture of his hair. He had immediately developed the island's own 5,000 feet runway, at the estate agent's suggestion. After all, if you collect jet planes, you want to make it as easy as possible to fly them.

The island spanned over 500 acres, was less than a hundred miles from Nassau, and a mere 250 miles from Miami. He had always admired the Exuma Cays. Magician David Copperfield was his nearest neighbour. That had appeal, less so that Johnny Depp and Nicolas Cage also had islands in the vicinity.

He was now the Lord of a 7,000-square-foot castle. It had been built on the island by an Englishman, Sir Baxter Darby, and completed in 1938. Baxter had allegedly played a less than glorious part in World War II, by allowing Nazi submarines to refuel in his substantial harbour. Many of the royals of the time very much approved and often called by. Damian liked properties with history, and especially any with even the remotest of connections to his pals, the *Sachsen-Coburg und Gothas*.

The castle would have been a nightmare for most prospective owners, but as money was no object he made the most of the existing mahogany floors and original furniture. The minor problem of acquiring electricity, running water and a sewage system was easily solved, by giving the developers a blank cheque. Some of the solutions were very environment-friendly, but that was never one of his priorities.

Damian kept himself fit. This meant he could continue to look sharp in the finest designer labels. Today, his air shuttle had brought his sommelier to visit. She was a voluptuous redhead who had inherited the family business and voluminous cellars, in every sense of the phrase.

As he admired the view from his mountain top, watching the sun set, he turned to browse along a line of vintage champagnes. Breaking him out of his trance, admiring what was on offer, the familiar sound of a phone broke the mood. Modern satellite technology was a blessing and a curse. Making his apologies to his merchant, Damian placed a 1970's style red Trimphone handset to his ear, adapted to be a very 21st Century cordless phone.

'Who's there?' he demanded as he walked along the line of bottles. He had long since mastered how to multi-task. One step behind him followed the sommelier, taking notes based on Damian's very subtle hand movements towards each of the three dozen bottles.

Damian stopped in his tracks, miffed by what he was being told. 'I am a little concerned that you seem to be leaving this all to chance. We don't have the electronic voting machines this time around.' He continued to listen, tucking the Trimphone between his head and shoulder, freeing both hands to dust off a particularly vintage label. He turned his nose up at what he found beneath the cobwebs. Again, his deliberations were distracted by his caller.

'So, you are telling me that, when it comes to it, the public will not vote for Grady? Somewhere between their front doors and the polling booths they will all get cold feet?' Damian's demeanour was helped by finding a particularly pleasing 1976 Krug Brut, which got a "thumbs up".

'Your market research trumps the conventional reports, then? Very well. For your sake, you'd better be right.' With that, Damian terminated the call. His attention was drawn to an Armand de Brignac "Ace of Spades" Rose. He looked at his sommelier. 'How appropriate,' he grinned. It was perfectly chilled, too.

Within seconds, his well-manicured fingers had cracked the bottle open, the sommelier holding two old-fashioned saucer glasses ready to catch the golden liquid. What a wonderful world it was, when from the other side of the Atlantic he could have such a controlling interest in affairs of state.

* * *

Back in the United Kingdom, it was sunrise, and the newspapers were spilling out into every outlet imaginable. The postal workers around the nation could have been very grouchy about the extra workload, but most were circumspect as to where this might all lead.

There weren't any disastrous typos, although Tony Pearce found enough to add to his niggled demeanour. If anyone needed at least six hours' kip, it was him, although he didn't necessarily sleep at night. He could doze when time allowed, even in a hurricane. Dawn did her best to placate him, noting that the majority of readers wouldn't pick up on the handful of errors causing him such distress.

Georgie's phone didn't stop ringing all morning. Her talent agency pals were passing on the good news. Their clients had seen the television appearance, and now the copy of *News First*. They'd like to help. Was there anything they could do?

Georgie put Dawn and Tony in touch with a camera crew she knew, sending them out to grab the celebrities interviews. All good stuff to put on the internet, seeding each clip to go viral on appropriate social media channels. The wider the range of personalities on-tap, the greater the range this fishing net would be cast.

Musician and singer Jerry Helm decided to throw his cap into the ring. He had been mocked by the mainstream media for befriending David Icke, and the devil-may-care attitude of Ray Grady was something he could empathise with. His interest in football of the distinctly British variety was well-known, and he wanted to go on record about the latest lunacy coming out from Brussels.

Jerry invited them to dash up to London Road, the home of Peterborough United. He was a major shareholder, so getting filming permissions was as easy as a wave of the hand. As he sat in the stands, the camera crew got some wonderful footage of him giving his views on many an issue. 'I'm not keen on this idea of any European being able to play for England in the national football team.' He used his rock star video training for all it was worth, picking the right facial angle to match the required mood for each sound-bite. 'Regardless of parentage or birthplace. It was getting stupid with the rule on grandparents! Only "We the People" are making a stand on this. Brussels has gone mad.'

Next up on the whistle-stop tour was bespectacled comedian Max

Sandling. They caught up with him in a coffee bar in central Birmingham. Another victim of press attacks, he was only too pleased to bring his views to the table. 'Legalise drugs. Legalise prostitution. That sounds like my kind of party!' he joked, delving into the new grouping's more controversial manifesto bullet points. 'Seriously, they should do this, and target anything else that allows those involved in crime to profit.' Max looked straight into the camera, grinning. 'And they'll collect tax on all this stuff. We all benefit!'

Friend of the Gurkhas, actress Gemma Ferris, was next up. Georgie booked a private room in the London Library in St James's Square. Gemma got right into the part, stylish glasses perched on the end of her nose, reading from a particularly cumbersome tome. 'The liberty of a democracy is not safe if the people tolerate the growth of private power to a point where it becomes stronger than their democratic State itself. That, in essence, is fascism – ownership of government by an individual, by a group or by any controlling private power.' Ms Ferris put the book down, took off her glasses, and looked right down the lens. 'Franklin D Roosevelt. Now you know the type of statesman that influences Ray Grady.'

The video testimonials weren't limited to British shores. The word had reached former pro wrestler, and ex-Governor of Minnesota, Jesse Ventura. The informant found him surfing in Mexico, and must have driven all night, video camera in hand, to get something that "We the People" could use.

A few set-up questions, and away Jesse went, the quotable words rolling off his tongue at the same rate as the waves crashed on the shore in the background. 'I like what you guys are doing over there, with the suggestion of a return to "common law". It's a simple premise: "do no wrong". Currently you're moving towards Napoleonic law, where everything is illegal, unless it is specifically noted in statute to be allowed.' Mr Ventura scoffed at this. 'That's crazy. "We the People" seem to be a crater of sanity on this crooked planet!'

This first quartet of testimonials were loaded on to websites by the end of the following day. Viewing figures went stratospheric. Success begets success, and the celebrity circles no longer sat on the fence. More and more well-known faces, from the big screen, television, sports and even the literary world, made their own video statements. All of them bypassing the mainstream, circulated and watched by millions. The established media simply couldn't keep up. The odd "soft target" on the celebrity roll call was singled out for derision, but this was a tidal wave of support. To a certain extent, this was also safety in numbers.

This made the opinion polls even more baffling than anything previously. Every single one highlighted a decrease in support for "We the People". Ray and the team wondered if the general public had decided they were perhaps too much of a good thing to believe in.

Before they could rethink their strategies, Election Day had arrived. For better or for worse, they knew they had all given it their best shot.

As is the tradition, the potential Prime Ministers and their homes were staked out by news crews, hoping to catch a glimpse of them on their way to their respective polling stations. For some reason, Ray had been given the "honour" of being on the call sheet for the BBC, Sky, Channel 4 and ITN. This was perhaps a clue that the stations sensed blood. Ray called some of his contacts at the various outlets. It transpired they were there to gloat, and not because they sensed victory. All the opinion polls suggested a humiliating performance for Ray and his candidates lay ahead. These media "tools" weren't going to be anything but savage in their mauling of the new party. You could guarantee it would be so, when the election results came out later in the evening.

With Dougan and Kindon waiting nearby, in a more family-friendly nifty metallic blue Land Rover Discovery, it was time to say hello to the press corps. Ray, Alicia, and the children made their way out of the front door, and walked down the drive to their entrance gate. The weather was being kind. It was a bright sunshiny day, just a little breeze which drastically reduced the temperature. Or perhaps, Ray mused, the cooling came from the weather manipulation being caused by the obvious chemtrails overhead? The main road's verges were clogged with boxy satellite vans, ready to instantly relay transmissions.

Ray summoned up a positive demeanour. 'Good morning! Bit chilly today?' He rubbed his hands together to emphasise the point. The journalists weren't really interested in this sort of forecast.

'Mister Grady, what do you make of the polls?' chirped up a young, pushy, prissy little lady.

'You mean next week's Fish and Chip Shop paper?' he replied. A kinder audience may have given a polite giggle, but Ray was met with stony silence. It was time to hand out a contextual sound-bite. 'That is, if the EU hadn't banned it being used in that way. To quote one famous philosopher, I forget his name, "All truth passes through three stages. First, it is ridiculed. Second, it is violently opposed. Third, it is accepted as being self-evident".'

'Arthur Schopenhauer,' piped up another of the reporters, almost stereotypical in his now dated David-Tennant-Doctor-Who-style glasses, beaming with his command of such trivia. He had missed the point that Ray was being modest in his level of knowledge.

'Very good,' noted Ray, trying desperately not to be patronising. 'And as dear old Arthur also said, "Noise is the most impertinent of all forms of interruption. It is not only an interruption, but is also a disruption of thought".' It was an inspired put-down. The reporter shyly looked down at his notes. Ray had the good grace to swiftly carry on.

'Whether we win or not, from this day forward, politicians will forever have their feet held to the fire by their electorate. If nothing else, that makes everything worthwhile.' In hindsight, Ray thought he could have put that over much better. It sounded like he was admitting defeat.

A greasy-haired elderly hack ploughed on with another query. 'Zena Carsley implied you were a racist on her show.' What was it with this woman? Was she forever going to haunt him? Her comments about Ray got more airtime than those made by his Prime Ministerial rivals.

'For wanting "out" of Europe?' Ray responded, addressing the real issue directly. 'It's about conservation of our culture. By that, I don't mean just us, but every nation. We should celebrate diversity, just as we do in the natural world.' Perhaps he was over-complicating his answer. 'Plants, animals, habitats. We don't want to become one homogenous mass, completely the same around the globe. Infinite dimensions. Infinite diversity.'

The prissy little lady jumped in again, 'Your campaign seems to have faltered in the last couple of days?'

Ray could have questioned the use of the word "faltered", but instead took a bite on the bait. 'And you're surprised? Given that any websites promoting "We the People" have been closed down? By either the Internet Service Providers or the police. All described as "hate sites". But that's kind-of backfired, hasn't it? People noticed, they're not stupid.' Ray knew that, in fact, people hadn't noticed. But if they played his quote on television, the general public would then actually realise something nasty was happening.

Ray looked at his watch, knowing that the day was already racing away with itself. 'Now, if you'll excuse me, my wife and I have votes to cast.' He decided to pre-empt the dumb question that usually followed on occasions like this. 'And don't ask me who I'll be voting for. It's a secret!'

With that, and despite the begging for more photos and answers to more questions, the family walked over to the Discovery, with Dougan and Kindon marshalling them into their seats.

More camera crews were waiting at the polling station, a St John Ambulance base, which had got the call this time to be the local home for the booths of democracy. A couple of members of the Women's Institute were trying to gather exit poll data from those who had cast their votes. Despite Ray doing his most cheeky of approaches to them, they were very cagey about the information they held. Perhaps it was for the best he didn't know. On their way back to the Discovery, Ray enquired of Alicia who she had voted for.

She smiled, and coyly said, 'It's a secret, between me and the ballot box.' Ray raised an eyebrow, which caused Alicia to laugh, perhaps a little too deeply.

The rest of the day welled over with the feeling that there was nothing else that could be done. Ray went around some of the local shopping centres within his ward, and was amazed with the good feeling he was getting from people. Every other person who came up to speak to him would reach out to him. Either shake his hand, or give a consoling pat on the shoulder. They were in the minority, they would suggest, but offered that they had voted for him anyway.

Ray mused that this was a self-selecting sample. It must have been just his supporters who would dare to approach him. Still, at least it wasn't going to be the total humiliation that had been predicted.

That night, Ray and Alicia sat down together in their expansive lounge, watching their huge flat-screen TV. Tony had suggested Ray watch the results with the rest of the team. Ray wasn't keen. He had never been able to handle defeat well.

At 10.55pm, the election coverage announced the first result as it came in. Labour had held Houghton and Sunderland South. Many constituencies would again take until the early hours to declare, now that they'd thrown out the electronic voting machines of the previous election a couple of months before.

Ray decided that was all he needed to know. It was one seat they expected to do well in, as there was no real rival to Labour, who had a huge majority. He suggested to Alicia their time could be better spent in bed, the suggestion coming with a knowing wink. Alicia preferred to carry on with her cross-stitch, a hobby she was channelling all her passions into.

Ray wished sometimes that she wouldn't be so cold towards him, but he hoped it was just a tricky patch the two of them were going through.

Ray did try to sleep, the queen-sized waterbed usually making such a task very easy. Just after midnight, the phone rang. Ray annoyingly wondered why he hadn't bothered to turn off his mobile. It was Tony, unsurprisingly. Had Ray changed his mind? No, he hadn't, and the land of nod was still beckoning. This time he did turn off his phone, and on any other day he would have been concerned as to why his wife still hadn't come to bed.

Alicia did finally make it into the bedroom. He felt her hand on his shoulder, gently shaking him. He squinted at the bedside digital clock, its bright orange display reading 2.00am. 'Come on, you need to get up. Tony's here.'

Ray knew how Tony's mind worked. He would have gathered all the team so as to thank them for their efforts. And Tony loved a party. He was right, of course. They had all done their best, but the giant monolith of the establishment was simply not going to let them stroll into its citadel and change things. Going for the smart-casual look, T-shirt – with the wording "Just Pull It – World Trade Center Building 7" on it, mingling with a rip-off Nike- swoosh – sports jacket and black jeans, he descended the stairs to hear a commotion coming from the television.

Tony and Alicia were standing up, his arm draped across her shoulders, almost but not quite jumping up and down, gawping at the screen. Georgie and Dawn were also in the room, also excited, each with opened large bottles of Babycham in hand. Heaven help them if the press ever got images of the pair looking like that. Tony had obviously come mob-handed, not taking any chances in trying to drag Ray along to the planned wake.

Perhaps it was having just been woken up which made Ray so slow on the uptake. 'What are you all so happy for?' he enquired, unable to comprehend the facts and figures whirling across the television screen.

'We won, Ray. We bloody well won!' screamed Tony. 'Or should I say, we won "Prime Minister"?'

'A landslide,' Dawn echoed. 'We've already got over two thirds of the seats.'

Ray looked at Georgie, and all she could do was nod her head frantically. Alicia unhanded herself from Tony and jump-hugged Ray. Tony, Dawn and Georgie joined in, one huge mass of people bouncing up and down, as if they had won the lottery.

'I take it this moment has been prepared for?' Ray enquired.

Tony looked at Alicia. 'Can Ray come out to play at the O2?' he jokingly enquired.

Alicia laughed. 'As long as you look after him.'

Ray snorted. 'Fox in charge of the hen house,' he responded, as the quartet prepared to make their way to the celebrations. 'Shouldn't I be getting a congratulatory call from the opposition?'

It was Tony's turn to snort. 'Are you bloody-well joking? You've just thrown the rulebook out of the window. They'll follow suit!'

Dougan and Kindon had quietly entered the room, standing by the door, as Ray checked he had everything he might need. That new Discovery was going to have repaid its price-tag very quickly, judging by this turn of events.

"Ostentatious" probably wasn't quite the right word. Invitations to the gathering at the O2 had been quietly circulated amongst the constituency groups. Almost everyone who was part of the movement's structure had made time to be there, journeying from all the corners of the UK. In their thousands.

Ray could not help but be impressed. The half-hour to get there had been eventful. Even at such a godforsaken hour of the early morning, there were revellers on the streets. At every turn. And this wasn't all fuelled by drink. It was a surge of adrenalin, a release of tension. The totally unexpected had happened. The opinion polls had been so very, very wrong. The voters hadn't "bottled", they had actually sided with what they believed in. Ray's constant unswerving message on this theme had sunk in.

A buzz went through the audience as they realised Ray had arrived. Tony picked up a bottle of champagne as they passed by a catering table, removing the foil and cage from its top as the two of them walked through a sea of revellers, which parted for them as they progressed. As he popped the cork, Georgie and Dawn joined them with a quartet of glass flutes, the cascading nectar bubbling over within all of them. Tony smiled at a contingent from his own constituency, carefully managing a hug with a couple of the middle-aged ladies. Victory was sweet for all of them.

Ray, Tony, Dawn and Georgie reached the front of the venue's stage. Staring up at the raised podium in front of them, Emily made an appearance, an array of synthesizers and drum kits behind her. 'Ladies and gentlemen, your new Prime Minister, Ray Grady,' she hollered into a microphone, whipping the audience up into frenzy. Ray and the musketeers climbed the stairs, applause and cheering of a magnitude like a teen-idol concert. Ray turned to face the audience and waved with both his hands above his head, being careful not to spill the champagne. The screams, a thunderous meeting of hands, it was invigorating. Ray took it in turns to raise the arms of Tony, Dawn and Georgie, so they could each get their own separate appreciation.

Emily was made for playing a host like this. 'And now, get your dancing shoes in order, as we welcome the first band of the evening. Ladies and gentlemen... Heaven 17!'

Ray approved. Glenn Gregory bounded onto the stage, absorbing the zealous reaction, as Martyn Ware and the rest of the band took their places at their banks of instruments.

There could only be one song from this band to start off the festivities. The opening ambient chords of "Temptation" filled the auditorium, before launching into the excited main body of the song. Ray and the team began dancing with decidedly new-romantic stylings, giving away their music era of choice, while also being very careful not to spill any champagne. The rest of the audience followed their lead in their hectic swaying.

Reporter Phil Conway was on a balcony, laughing and joking with Dougan and Kindon. Ray saw him, and they exchanged smiles and nods. Phil lifted up his bottle of "Freedom Beer" to toast Ray, and Ray reciprocated with his champagne flute. It was terrific that a British brewery had decided to celebrate "We the People" in such a way, whatever the outcome of the election.

It was 3.30am when Ray was ushered into a quiet side room. Finally he was to receive a phone call from the acting Prime Minister, Duncan Hurst. Conceding defeat, and having great difficulty in having good grace about it.

The call was made even more difficult for the former PM as his wife had lost her seat. Like his own, it was supposed to be one of the safest in the country. The victory there was for the indomitable Dalston Kingsland, a quite amazingly eloquent bohemian, who had changed his name by deed pole to that of the London Overground station. Kingsland was, of course, an independent candidate aligned to "We the People".

Shortly after, Emily took to the stage again. 'Ladies and Gentlemen, your attention please. Mr Grady has just heard from the Prime Minister, who has conceded defeat. The next United Kingdom Government will be formed by... "We the People"!'

Ray, Tony, Georgie and Dawn were now lined up near the back of the auditorium, hogging the front of the crowd safety railings. A few independent reporters had found the location of the celebration, and were "blagging" themselves into getting access and accompanying story. They surrounded the quartet, but everyone was struggling to be heard over the music and the revellers.

Straight away a young freelance got into Ray's face. 'Prime Minister...' he began. Ray quickly jumped in.

'Call me Ray. You know I don't stand on ceremony,' he chided. The reporter was having none of it.

'Prime Minister, you must have been confident of your success, judging by this party having been organised weeks ago?' smarmed the reporter.

Ray smiled. 'All Tony's idea,' he declared, quickly pulling Tony to the front of the group. Tony was a little reluctant to take the praise. Ray ushered him to speak.

'Everyone's worked so hard. There was always going to be plenty to celebrate tonight, even if it had turned into a wake!'

A second reporter, an Amazonian lady with a sharp suit, wanted a piece of the action. With her cameraman and boom microphone operator close behind, she immediately betrayed her music journalism roots. 'An interesting choice for entertainment at the moment. Heaven 17?'

Dawn, slightly slurring her words, jumped in. 'From when music had a message,' she speculated, wishing she was more accustomed to alcohol.

Ray sensed it was time to give out his own message. 'This is the end of the straitjacket of "political correctness". These guys behind me... their song was banned by the BBC when it was released.' He looked to Georgie for clarification. '1981?'

Almost astounded that she had to answer such simple trivia, Georgie confirmed, 'Made its chart debut on 21st March.'

Ray continued. 'As the song says, "We Don't Need This Fascist Groove Thang!" Presumably banned as it upset all the fascists. Political correctness is fascism in all but name.'

Ray was being enticed by the music again, and the quartet danced once more, but still with style rather than a "Prescott way". Georgie even took one of the male reporters by the hands and encouraged him to join in. Some of the journalists were put off by this abandon, and sidled off. Glenn Gregory's rendition of the lyrics really helped quantify what they all believed they had been fighting.

'Hitler proves that funky stuff — Is not for you and me girl — Europe's an unhappy land — They've had their Fascist Groove Thang'.

Meddings arrived at the party, realising that he had a new boss to get familiar with. That is, of course, if he was allowed to remain in charge of the Prime Ministerial security detail. The door staff were not that discriminating as to whom they were letting in, as the now-Leader of the Opposition Duncan Hurst had wanted to gatecrash, hence Meddings being there. This was obviously where the action was. Hurst was surprised to see the freelance reporters and camera crews present, as it meant they would be asking him for his views. He was sufficiently narcissistic as to never turn down such an opportunity.

* * *

The main TV networks didn't want to cover what was now a victory party. Zena Carsley's handlers decided their only option was to cast doubt on what had happened. She sternly spoke to camera at her forlorn television studio. 'We are getting reports of riots on the streets of London, Glasgow, Cardiff, Manchester, Birmingham and Edinburgh.'

With no such footage in existence, the clip producers opted for library footage of exuberant revellers, acquired from coverage of a previous New Year's Eve, with an overdubbing of the sounds of rioting. A lame attempt to give a different impression of the nature of the scenes, and a ruse they would later think should never be repeated.

Zena again continued to try and reframe reality. 'Not everyone is happy with the results of the general election. The United Nations has been alerted to the possibility of election fraud. The result in favour of "We the People" was unlike anything predicted by the pre-election polls.' She tried to cast doubt on the ability of the new party to answer its critics. 'No-one from "We the People" is available for comment, apparently having gone-to-ground at a private function somewhere in the capital.'

Many people took to Twitter to pick up on Zena's dead eyes. That look, they reckoned, couldn't have come from just working long hours.

* * *

Nobody was quite sure exactly when the party finished. The clean-up operation took up most of the following day, and putting that next to the fact that Muse were booked in for a couple of dates, beginning that evening, made "We the People" none too popular with the venue. The clean-up crew themselves were glad of the overtime, and took the chance to "bag" some souvenirs.

In the weeks that followed, the UK population was buoyant, despite the stock market crashing worldwide. As one European country after another announced trade embargos with Britain, so other more far-flung nation states wanted to do deals instead. The new government wasn't going to be as disastrous as the citizens had been led to believe, but still the mainstream media tried to paint the situation as being unacceptable.

This was a replay of what had been the case in the former Soviet Union many years previously. The informed public were no longer paying attention to what they were being told via the major news outlets. They sought out alternative sources. Some independent businesses, not tied to global corporations, supported the outlets who were reporting the real news. Truth Media Television was able to expand its operation at a rate of knots, thanks to such advertising support.

The pharmaceutical industries were hit hard. Their patents on everything were ripped up by Ray's government. Natural remedies were given the financial backing to be subject to major clinical trials, which of course would take a few years to report back their findings.

The major political parties tried their best to regain support, but instead found many of their local branches being wound up. The irony was how the better appointed buildings, particularly former "Conservative Clubs", were quickly turned into "We the People" societies.

Parliament was quickly overhauled, so that Bills could become Acts of Law in record time. The Parliamentary majority meant "We the People" was able to be true to their word on their manifesto commitments sooner rather than later.

People were happy again. The welfare system was quickly reformed, ironed out so that hard work would be rewarded, but those who had fallen on hard times were encouraged and supported. Public improvement schemes, from roads to housing stock, nature conservation initiatives to hospital staffing expansions, all were put into action, financed by reneging on repayments of international loans, which had been the subject of ludicrous interest rates from the corporate bankers responsible.

Unemployment figures decreased as people found a fair day's work was rewarded by fair pay via these new ways to help improve the country's infrastructure and services. All of it financed by a return to the Bradbury Pound, a scheme put into place just before the first World War, where government rather than the banks printed and issued the money, and as a consequence no interest had to be paid to such bankers.

It all proved there could be enough money in the system to oil the wheels of progress, provided it was spent in the right places. So much was already underway by the end of the first one hundred days of "We the People" coming into office.

The overarching objective was reforming the financial and banking systems, and it appeared that those behind the scenes took great exception to what Ray had in mind.

And now, here he was, fighting for life in the back of an ambulance.

This medical team, different to the pair who had first taken care of Ray as he hit the floor of the stage, wanted to be able to say they were the ones that had saved Ray. The ambulance zipped through the streets, lights flashing urgently, stopping for no-one. A quartet of motorcycle cops sat imperiously astride their bikes, guarding all four corners of the ambulance, ploughing a speedy furrow along the road ahead. Police cars cordoned off many of the side roads along the route, allowing the ambulance an even smoother free passage.

Inside, Ray's spirit sat just out of the way of the action, and looked over his body on the crash cart. His long-dead wife Anna was there beside him, shielding her eyes from some of the procedures the crew were administering to the empty husk, which somehow was still breathing.

Ray was circumspect. 'None of this looks promising, now does it?' he suggested, as shock paddles were again applied to his host body's chest. He recoiled slightly as his body's back arched brutally with the arc of electricity.

Anna, for no reason she could explain, licked her lips. 'All I know is that your future isn't written yet, but it doesn't end here.'

'Don't suppose you've got any horse racing tips?' Ray quipped. 'You know, ones with actual names, times, dates and on which course?'

Anna raised a curt eyebrow. 'You're in a difficult place. I realise this. It's always a little embarrassing, this limbo thing.'

Ray shook his head indignantly. 'Yeah, I know. Never could get under those low poles.' The attempted humour was interrupted by another electric shock to his body, laid opposite. 'Can't you give me any guidance on what I should do?'

'You never could "go with the flow", could you?' Anna remarked. 'Just be satisfied that you still have a role to play in this life, although it will probably not be as "centre stage" as you have been used to.'

Ray was half annoyed, half frustrated. 'That's very obtuse.'

Anna responded to what she saw as childishness. 'You remember *Back to the Future*?' she chided. Ray nodded. 'What was it Emmett Brown said? "No-one should know too much about their own destiny"?'

'Why not get me a flux capacitor, and I'll show you a way to make none of this ever happen?' countered Ray, never to be outdone on trivia.

Anna shook her head. 'Call yourself a *Doctor Who* fan? You know you can never cross your own time stream!' With that, the ambulance screeched to a halt. They had arrived at the hospital, but judging by the excessive length of the journey, this certainly wasn't one in central London.

* * *

In another direction, over two hundred miles away, in a cramped laboratory, Vernon Snow was watching the latest news. He was concerned that the coverage hadn't stuck with the ambulance. It was almost like the driver had deliberately given those following the vehicle the slip. That sort of behaviour always concerned Vernon, as it was usually for an ulterior motive, one where skulduggery was in the air.

His scientific mind wasn't so left-brained as to not be creative on the possibilities. Maybe Ray Grady had been kidnapped by a foreign power? Or this was all a cover so Ray could retire from public life, having made the impression he had wanted to? Or perhaps they were taking him off to make sure he really was dead, never to come back? That sort of thing had happened in the past, even to royalty, so why not again now?

Vernon's hair was half wild, half missing, with bald patches in places he really wanted to tackle with some follicle surgery. Sure, he knew the best people for this, but to do it right would take far too much out of his busy schedule.

He could make time, of course, but it was difficult changing the habit of a lifetime. In what seemed like all of his thirty-nine years to date, he had to constantly try and affirm his status as "boy genius". He'd hated being called "Joe 90" at school, which meant that as soon as possible he had his eyes fixed, so he was no longer adorned with cumbersome spectacles.

Vernon found himself sucking hard on a pencil, and stopped himself. His doodles on the pad in front of him had been getting more and more manic. For no good reason he took the pencil in his mouth again and broke it in half with one swift downward movement of his hand. What annoyed him was that he had spent all that time composing a letter to Ray Grady. Ray, for sure, recognised men of vision. Men keen to underwrite his next round of experiments, if only he could have an audience with them. Men who were intrigued by the cutting-edge nature of what he would get them involved with.

Vernon's efforts would now be all for nothing. He couldn't surmise how anyone could have survived such an assault of bullets, even though details on the news had been sketchy at best. Vernon could have spent the time he wasted on that letter having some of his hair fixed. He knew he shouldn't have bothered. The non-response suggested it must have come over as too insincere, too much like begging.

Vernon's attention was drawn back to the television. First reports were coming out of violence on the streets. Riots. Cars and shops firebombed. Police attacked as they cowered behind barricades, their stations being the most obvious pillars of "the establishment".

These weren't mocked-up pieces of footage this time. These were real. And these frantic and confused initial stories suggested it was all "kicking off" due to the attempted assassination of Ray Grady.

The people suspected foul play. And they would rather burn down this "new Rome" than let the dark forces win through again.

Vernon wondered who he could call. Maybe he could help after all…

7

WHO KNOWS WHODUNNIT?

They called it the "Operations Room", although originally it was designated as a "Drawing Room". Ray had changed the name so as to avoid confusion with other areas with the same description across the building. Number 10 Downing Street was the workplace for dozens of civil servants, some with their own offices, but in this new era "Ops", as it was nicknamed, was a hive of "hot desking". Staff would be assigned a workstation when they were attached to specific projects. Ray wanted to call it the "Marvel Bullpen", but Dawn insisted that would have other connotations without the required "gravitas".

Ray had trimmed the number of staff working at Number 10. Prime Ministers Wilson and Callaghan had kept the numbers to just a few dozen. Thatcher increased it to between sixty and seventy. Major to between ninety and one hundred. And Blair went completely spin-crazy, peaking at 225 "administrative" staff. Ray trimmed it back to a maximum of fifty. They could then hire specialists for particular projects. It was an approach he had stolen mercilessly from business guru Tom Peters.

"Ops" had been decked-out in a mix of classical affluence and high technology. The room was dominated by a picture of the House of Commons at night. Previously, past Prime Ministers had graced the position, or even royalty. That was unlikely to happen during this parliament. Ray's opening gambit, when he went to see the Queen to ask for permission to form a government, saw him being far too honest. He noted he would be seeking the people's thoughts, via a referendum, on the UK becoming a republic. The S.N.P. and Plaid had suggested such a vote to him, and he considered their request a fair point to explore.

Besides, the nationalists would take the flack if the majority of people had a problem with such a constitutional change in their nations.

Ordinarily, "Ops" was a bright and buzzing location. Ideas would be bounced around, flip charts always adorned with the results of the latest brainstorming, with no suggestions being considered too wild. It was hub of creativity, a happy place.

Now, it was awash with stunned waves of murmurings. Those present spoke in hushed tones, not wishing to break the sombre mood. Most had been given their new jobs personally by Ray. One or two exceptions had talked their way into being kept on the payroll.

One such was the head of security, Carl Meddings. He had carried out the same role for the previous administration, and Ray appreciated his inside knowledge would be crucial. He would add an extra dimension to making sure their collective backs were being covered, with consideration for every loophole.

Ray didn't know much about him, aside from the confidential CV stating he was a former M.I.5. officer. Everyone Ray spoke to about him gave glowing references. He was seen as a safe and calm pair of hands in every circumstance. Some of the harshest comments noted he wasn't the brightest bulb in the set, something of an "open book", but his loyalty to his country was unquestioned. Many of the female staff spoke about him with an unconscious smile on their faces. Ray was in-touch enough with his "feminine side" to understand what the appeal was. And it all came from the reptilian, lower part of the brain.

In one of the corners of the room, leading deeper into Number 10, Meddings was touching base with Dougan, Kindon and other security operatives, working out a plan for where to station themselves across the building. Ray had appointed Dougan and Kindon second-in-commands to Meddings, but still having the majority of their duties as looking after Alicia and the children. Meddings decided they should go and keep permanent watch on the family, for a couple of days at least. Who knew what would happen next after this terrible tragedy? They could well be targets, depending on the mindset of the perpetrators.

Over by the main window in "Ops", the command desk was in an unsightly state. Newspaper cuttings. Confidential file notes. Scribbled thoughts on who might have been responsible.

Tony, Georgie and Dawn had been fielding calls all day, and making their own, initially to ensure Ray was safe and out of the public gaze. They had even misled Meddings with a decoy, so as to decrease the chance of any leaks.

As Dawn was the Foreign Office Minister, she had been receiving calls from governments around the world. They all tried to sound concerned, but in many of those countries, often considered more "civilised", she was sure she heard part relief, part gloating. How she remained polite was beyond her comprehension, her mood now as black as her patent leather ankle boots.

Georgie, being the Home Office Minister, was making several appearances on camera for the sake of the baying media. In her previous career as a talent agent, she often spoke up for her clients in very difficult situations. In some cases she would defend them, help get them off the hook, and then quietly drop them from her books when attention had been diverted elsewhere.

She found it very difficult to find enough ways to confirm she had no idea who was responsible for the shooting. Each reporter would ask which terrorist groups she had her suspicions about. The hacks suggested it would not be any contingents from overseas, as it would be home-grown agitators most likely to have sufficient grievances. Georgie found herself saying "nonsense" on far too many occasions. Later, some "wag" put the various instances of her uttering the word to music, and promptly received thousands of hits on YouTube.

Tony was handling the situation the worst of all. As Chancellor of the Exchequer, he found himself now the temporary Prime Minister. He'd only ever seen himself as a right-hand man, so this was new territory for him. He and Ray had never discussed the possibility that Tony would one day have to be the centre of attention. It had been enough for him to sort out the budgets and finance of the country, having to explain the nature of money to one civil servant after another.

Luckily, he had a knack with such administrators. Long ago he had been a lobbyist, pacing the corridors of Whitehall and the Commons. He had worked for a big agricultural corporation, doing their bidding by ensuring no detrimental policies in that arena got onto the statute books. It was the problems with genetic modification which finally saw his conscience come to the fore. He began to question his company's in-house scientists, who simply wouldn't admit the irregularities in their own data. None of them had any comprehension of why what he was being asked to lobby about would impinge on civil liberties.

A round of redundancies loomed, the corporation cutting back on its UK operation, moving instead to Brussels. Tony took the chance to quit the city. He bought a modest farm in Norfolk, and used his knowledge to ensure he was at the forefront of organic non-GMO agriculture.

It was all going "great guns" until sales of organic foods collapsed. In 2012 alone, there was a 12.7% reduction in land conversion to organic production, and a 7.4% reduction in the total amount of land classified as "organic". Land dedicated to organic vegetables fell by 21.8%, cereals by 8.8%, and other arable crops by 10.4%. And don't even get Tony started on the drop in organic farm animals. All against a backdrop of a dilution of what could be considered "organic". The way things were going, soon the term would be meaningless.

This decline in all things organic was partly due to ludicrous accusations, suggesting there was no benefit in its outputs over what "Big Farmer" was producing. Even the Soil Association attacked the "findings" as ridiculous. By the time they had their say, it was too late to avoid the negative impact.

Tony found himself having to sell up, part of the 6.4% drop in the numbers of organic farmers that year. And those numbers had fallen over several successive years. He ended up making a huge loss, which wiped out most of his redundancy payment.

Tony had known Ray ever since an episode he put out the previous year. Ray had been covering GMO technology, and had asked for evidence of malpractice from those against the marked expansion of its use. As Tony noted to Ray when they met up, the most dangerous man is the one with nothing left to lose. So it was that Tony revealed where all the metaphorical skeletons were in the vast cupboards of GMO.

The research, particularly from French scientists, was damning. The "Big Agriculture" corporations tried to spin away the criticisms. Not big enough samples to be relevant, they said; went against the findings of their own research, they spouted; conclusions from scientists who had been discredited, they insisted.

It didn't help that the mainstream media decided to side with the corporations, completely ignoring the revelations. Still, those who made their own investigations realised who they should be listening to. Plans to ban native crop varieties, as well as stopping citizens growing their own, had to be put on hold, such was the small but intense public reaction.

Tony managed a smile as he considered what they had achieved, even though at the time it just looked like a temporary reprieve. He gawped around the office, seeing interns rushing around, answering phones, surfing the web for news stories, passing papers here and there. Multi-tasking at its best. He went back to looking through some printouts of news report transcripts.

Dawn tried to focus everyone on the realities of the situation. 'There was always a chance this would happen,' she confided.

Tony summarised what he was reading in front of him. 'Big surprise for the media, judging by the reports they're filing.'

Georgie decided to stand up, rather than continue fidgeting in her chair. 'Why did we think we could beat this system?' she huffed, wondering at what point such an insanity had overtaken her.

Tony tapped his highlighter pen on the desk. 'Doing nothing was no longer an option.' He turned to Dawn. 'How's it playing overseas?'

Dawn subconsciously shook her head as she summarised. 'Top dogs offer their "full support in these most difficult of times". They are probably popping corks right now.'

Georgie made her way over to the window, to look at the bewildered press corps standing around below. 'And how about those wonderful financial markets?'

Dawn had been checking the stats on her Blackberry. 'Share prices have gone through the roof.'

Tony laughed heartily. 'Marvellous to be appreciated!'

Georgie was picking up the wrong signals from Tony. 'You expected that?' she enquired.

Dawn stepped in. 'They expect our era to be over already. That's their vote of confidence in forthcoming change.'

Tony was sucking on the highlighter. In between puffs, he noted, 'Like most promises of change, it ends up being business as usual.'

Georgie returned to staring out of the window, the magnitude of what had happened progressively sinking in. She was still niggled at the content of the press interviews she had carried out. Meddings marched over to the group, just as Georgie decided to pipe up again. 'Do you know, I even had one of the red-tops ask if I thought this was all the work of some Jewish cabal.'

Meddings snorted. 'You ought to see some of the websites which keep that idea going. Distasteful.'

Georgie felt like letting off some steam. 'Look, I'm Jewish. Okay, lapsed Jewish, and I've heard all of that stuff before. The trouble is they all confuse the Jewish faith with Zionism.' Dawn knew what was coming, and decided to be distracted again by her Blackberry.

'I didn't realise there was a difference,' remarked Meddings, not appreciating he was putting his head in the mouth of a lion.

'You don't have to be Jewish to be a Zionist. Look at former Vice-President Joe Biden. Not Jewish, but a self-declared Zionist,' explained Georgie. Meddings shrugged his shoulders. 'Okay, let me nail this for you. There are many sects to the religion of Judaism. I am, or was, Naturei Karta, the "guardians of the city". We originated in Jerusalem, and oppose Zionism. We'd like a peaceful winding down of Israel, as we are forbidden to have our own state until the coming of our Messiah.'

Meddings tried to make light of the ambush he had walked into. 'And what if your "Messiah" turns out to be a very naughty boy?' Georgie fixed him with a piercing stare, but was now conscious that her cultural lesson was coming across as ranting. She decided not to complicate things further by mentioning her former sect's take on things was hardly universal amongst the faith.

Tony looked at both of them, and calmly enquired, 'What has this to do with the Prime Minister having been shot?'

Meddings took this as his cue to quiz the assembled. 'My team lost the convoy. I assume you know where he is?'

Tony thought it time to brief their Head of Security. 'They've taken Ray to a military hospital. Less chance of prying reporters…'

Dawn jumped in with, 'Or nurses who can be bribed to give access.'

Georgie was taken aback by the statement. Even at thirty-four years of age, and her revolt against her own religion being a decade ago, she was still a little naive. 'Someone with an axe to grind in the military?' As they'd put their faith in a Brigadier to get Ray under deep cover, she thought the question logical.

Tony wasn't keen on letting Meddings hear anything further of the "inner cabinet" discussions. Even though his loyalty was unquestioned, Tony didn't like the way the guy would take their conversations into a cul-de-sac. 'Meddings, apologies for all the cloak-and-dagger. Now, make sure Ray's got the best team on his watch.' Tony tried not to sound ironic.

Taking his cue, Meddings sternly replied, 'Count on it.' He stomped off to make a few phone calls from his desk. Tony looked at his watch.

Dawn leaned in to Tony, and whispered, 'You're not letting him know?'

Tony replied quietly, 'That our beloved leader is deader than a hammer? And not where he thinks he is? Not a chance.'

Georgie was circumspect. 'We have to pick our moment. Now isn't it.'

Dawn tried to remind the group of their principles. 'What happened to being the fair, open and honest government?'

Georgie sniffed. 'We have to think of the greater good,' making it sound like she was quoting a briefing note.

Dawn, in the absence of any leadership from Tony, decided to set the agenda. 'Get this wrong, and we'll look as bad as everything that went before.'

Tony again glanced at his watch. 'One minute to six o'clock. Fireworks time.' He walked over to the fifty inch plasma screen, hung on a wall in the nearest corner of the room. He ushered Georgie and Dawn to follow. Tony grabbed the remote control, and turned up the sound on the news bulletin's opening graphics, which were dancing around in front of them.

Zena Carsley was acting like she was on amphetamines, lapping up the chance to narrate the dreadful events to her audience. Across the country, people were on the streets, police keeping out of their way, as the peaceful protests clogged up the high streets of every major city. Thousands upon thousands of distraught and angry civilians, awakened to the reality of how their country was really being run. The more vocal were making comparisons with the assassinations of John F. Kennedy, Martin Luther King and Bobby Kennedy. All now shown as being state sponsored, thanks to Ray releasing the relevant confidential files. Every single one of those killings took people out for upsetting the establishment.

In Birmingham, they were just starting to wake up from their slumber, Ray having immediately sanctioned removal of hydrofluorosilicic acid from the local water supplies. With their pituitary glands beginning to respond to the cessation of medication, New Street was clogged from end to end.

There was no smashing of shop fronts, just a peaceful vigil which was intense in its sincerity. Hastily-made banners were held up proudly, scattered amongst this gathering. They were daubed with texts such as "Death to Bankster Hitmen", "Grady Lives or the System Dies", "Liberty Must Survive" and "We the People know who's Responsible".

Being this was Zena's show, you wouldn't expect the editors to play nicely. In amongst this genuine reportage, they dropped in stock footage of rioters taking on the police, petrol bombs being thrown, and shops being looted. The impact ramped up with the overlay of the most horrific sounds of mankind, portrayed in its worst demeanour.

Tony, Georgie and Dawn were dismayed at the scenes, mainly by the obvious fakery. Dawn knew what could be expected later. 'Guarantee they've got their agent provocateurs in amongst that lot. They might not have any footage now, but they'll make sure they will later.'

No sooner did she say that, and the scenes in Birmingham turned gruesome. A small group started causing trouble, smashing in the windows of one of the banks, desperate to get inside. Tony got as close to the screen as he could, a palm's width away, and used the television's live pause on the remote control, freezing the image.

The picture was of a yob with a megaphone, standing on an indented transit van roof, bawling out his messages. Tony rewinded the scene a little, and pressed play. The yob is making his feelings known, whether anyone wanted to hear them or not. 'I tell ya, I told you so! You voted for individuals rather than parties.' He looked around, as if asking for permission to continue. He licked his lips and kicked off again. 'No structure! Time to bring down this system! Rip it up! Start again!' Tony paused the image again.

Even though Dawn knew the worst of the actions were being staged, she couldn't help but be frustrated. 'And here we were, thinking by immediately banning psychotropic drugs it would mean we'd no longer have lunatics "going postal" all over the place.'

'Say "agent provocateur" to most people and they think sexy underwear.' Tony couldn't help sneering. 'Which is more than can be said for this dildo.'

Georgie read between Tony's lines. 'Recognise him?' Tony checked the screen again. He only wished he hadn't.

'M.I.6. – I met him at some junket in Chipping Norton. Thought he was there for a conference about weapons, but they'd booked him into the wrong event.' Tony exhaled sharply. 'Didn't want to miss the opportunity of a freebie though, so he stayed on. Man after my own heart.'

Dawn was amazed. 'They're a bit cocksure,' she ventured.

Georgie wasn't surprised. 'When you've got the media on your side? Who's going to believe us? Even if we got someone to report it.' Tony clicked the remote control to go back to real time on the screen. The protests and riots were now interspersed with the usual news clichés of presenters and talking heads. Tony turned the volume down, exasperated.

'Ray would make them listen,' Tony offered.

Georgie was formulating responses on-the-fly. 'We need another word for it. Not "Agent Provocateur".'

'Oh, the corruption of our upstanding Queen's English!' Tony mocked.

Dawn went into her school ma'am mode. 'It's a French term.'

Georgie went off at a tangent. 'Do you remember when *Big Brother* didn't mean talentless wannabes?'

Dawn felt it necessary to issue another call to action. 'We have to do something. Now. Too many ways this could get leaked.' They could try keeping this to be all about Ray, but the last thing they wanted was to be accused of dishonesty, given their policy stances. Tony felt it an opportune time to blow a raspberry. Georgie tried to bring him to order.

'Dawn's right. The opposition can use this as a "straw man" to bring us down.' Tony still had no answers, other than to turn up the volume on the television again.

Violence was breaking out everywhere, or so it would seem. The common denominator was that it was led by just a handful in each city, diverting the peaceful vigils of the majority. Footage from the cameras on mobile phones was quickly being uploaded into the hands of the major media outlets.

'It's been a long time since we've seen immediate news coverage like this,' remarked Georgie.

'Partly our fault,' noted Tony. 'After all, we were the ones who ordered the deactivation of that phone function. You know, the one which allowed cameras to be switched off remotely, in whichever geographical area the establishment wanted to. I wonder if Steve Jobs really did know how he was helping to bring in the Police State? Surely the top man would have been in-the-loop on something like that?'

Tony flipped through the channels, hoping to see a different news angle. It was frustrating to see every programme adopting the same template. On one channel, Piers Morgan had been brought in to front a show.

'Bloody hell,' exclaimed Dawn. 'He gets thrown out of the United States, and rather than disappear with his tail between his legs, he has the gall to be in our primetime once more!'

Tony shook his head in despair. He surfed back to the channel he had started on.

Zena was in TV heaven. At just twenty-six years of age, her exotic looks had helped her do well, but they hid a vicious streak, applied once someone had outlived their usefulness to her. For some reason, her usually soft Scottish accent was remarkably broad this evening.

'Ray Grady, so-called prophet of the "new way" in British politics, is in a critical condition tonight. There is no doubt his so-called "We the People" alliance of independent candidates will wither on the vine without him.'

Dawn wasn't keen on the level of perception Zena was showing. 'Bitch might be right.'

'His bid to try what Abraham Lincoln and John F. Kennedy had in mind during their American Presidencies was not without flaws. Taking the printing of money out of the hands of the Bank of England has pros and cons.'

Tony was gritting his teeth, almost making a scratching sound. 'Tell us the cons, you pro.'

'Now, Ray Grady clings for life, a target of an assassination attempt.' Zena tried to aim for sincerity, but missed pitifully. 'Let's hope his fate is not the same as the two Americans who inspired his vision,' she offered, before changing the direction of her glance, to a camera at her side. 'Their lives ended for even considering such a move away from safe finance.'

Tony was getting increasingly sarcastic. 'This is a meaning of "safe" I'm not aware of?'

'Ray Grady turned British politics into a farce. A laughing stock on the global stage. We became an island nation once more, cut off from the rest of the world.'

Georgie's perception was ignited. 'Here it comes…'

'Whilst I would not wish this of anyone…'

Tony was getting gruffer by the second. 'Oh, really?'

'Perhaps Grady's expected death will not be in vain.' Zena was excited by the prospect. 'We could see people back to treating politics with the seriousness and respect that it deserves.'

Tony had heard enough, and muted the sound once more. He directly addressed the screen. 'Cheers, Zena.' He turned to Georgie and Dawn. 'Sidestep the Bank of England. The government prints money at zero interest. No debts mount up. Used to be called the "Bradbury Pound".'

Georgie felt the need to be supportive. 'That's why Ray made you Chancellor.'

Dawn tried to add to the positivity. 'Don't tell anyone but Thatcher wanted to try the same idea.' Such clarification was something of a misfire.

'And that's why they kicked her out,' Tony replied. 'Quad Erat Demonstrandum.' He was amazed he was being met with blank stares. 'That which has been proven,' he qualified.

Georgie felt she had to address what had become the elephant in the operations room. 'Is she right? Are we only viable with Ray at the helm?'

Tony, even now, was still trying to come to terms with it all. 'For now. Leaves us in a bit of a pickle.'

Dawn harrumphed. 'Hardly the time for understatements, Tony.'

Something suddenly clicked within Tony. He realised that he was supposed to be the one taking the lead. So, that was what he was going to do. He took out his mobile and began pushing buttons. 'First things first. We need to know who was behind this hit.' He pressed the receiver to his ear.

Dawn realised this was to be no easy task. 'Pick from a long list,' she exclaimed. They needed to run the country in Ray's absence, and without those more militant of the population going after the elite. They also had to expose who was really behind the assassination, to at least allow those citizens so motivated to channel their hatred.

* * *

Across the city in Soho, down a side-street away from the commotion, The Posada Pub was counting its blessings for once. It was just enough off the beaten track to not be suffering from any of the national angst engulfing the major streets around it. Recently renamed, recently renovated, it had set out to be a place for those who appreciated their real ale. Bucking national chains, they instead had a network of micro-breweries supplying them, from the whole of the South-East. With people staying out of the capital, tonight it was almost empty.

Phil Conway liked his beer. Not in a heavy consumption way, but he certainly made the most of his membership of the Campaign for Real Ale. He'd find some magazine or local paper to underwrite his numerous real ale festival visits across the country. They'd get features fit for the connoisseur, as well as adding a travelogue aspect to the national commissions.

Now a freelancer, he was unshackled from having to follow journalistic uniform so much. The most striking element to his look was the thin tie, top half red, with a diagonal separation in the middle to a bright blue at the end. A sharp dark suit with black shirt made him look like a member of Gary Numan's 1979 backing band. He was sat at the high level bar, leaning over it on a tall bar stool.

Phil had lost track of which beer this one was. It was a golden colour, bitter with a subtle backbite of honey. He looked at the pint glass, noting it was the esteemed twenty-three ounces in size, a white stamp near the top noting the fill line for twenty fluid ounces. Your good old-fashioned British pint. No-one got short-changed on their measures at The Posada.

Up above the bar, mounted on the wall was a flat-screen television, which usually showed around-the-clock sport. It was still on the usual channel, but there were images of football, rugby and cricket matches having been called off, punctuated by Ray Grady's face and muted grim reportage.

Phil shook his head, before taking another sip of the brew. Ray had given Phil the idea for his blogging website. Take a look at the work of Guido Fawkes online, he said. "Of plots, rumours and conspiracy" was the subtitle of that particular blog.

Choose your own historical character, fact or fiction, to base your own alter-ego on, Ray suggested. Phil immediately thought of *The Count of Monte Cristo*. He had always liked the Dumas novel as a child. No, he hadn't spent time in prison, but that was how he had felt sometimes, writing for the mainstream media.

Now he was free of such shackles, not totally anonymous admittedly, but his sources were a well-protected secret. And he ever so slightly amended the name, so as to avoid confusion with the fictional character. He was Monty Cristoe.

The closing theme from the original version of *The Italian Job* movie suddenly provided welcome, if inappropriate, relief from the dark clouds spilling from the TV. This was Phil's mobile phone. An old man nearby, adorned with a flat cap, smiled. The first movement on his face he had managed all day.

Phil looked at the smartphone screen to see who was calling. Getting his priorities in order, downing-in-one the remnants of the drink in front of him, he then waved his hand to summon the barmaid. The only employee he could see in the entire place. A tall, svelte, long blonde-haired student, immaculately dressed in white blouse and short black skirt. He should tell her she could be a model, but knowing the surrounding area she was probably on someone's books already, or would be offended by the suggestion.

'Same again please, Harry,' he chirped. Harry took his glass from him in order to oblige. Phil wondered what the reaction would be if he was to say he was dating someone called Harry. Given her age, once his friends got the idea he was talking about a woman, they'd then have more ammo by mocking the age difference, no doubt calling him a "dirty old man". These days, perhaps it would be something even worse.

Phil clicked his mobile phone and answered the call, with insincere surprise. 'Tony! Fancy hearing from you! Bit of a slow day all round, eh?'

Tony decided to join in with the charade. 'Well, you know how it is. Hunting season for politicians.'

Phil suddenly realised this was in bad taste, and sobered up. 'I know. I was there.' He looked up at the big screen. 'Have you seen the telly?'

Of course Tony was looking at the television. It was the only way of being sure this wasn't some bad dream. The scenes had changed their emphasis now. Late night masses, candles being lit by the assembled congregations. A communal prayer for hope, begging for intervention, fear that the country would spontaneously combust. 'Only time to catch a few bits and pieces. Busy, busy, busy,' Tony lied. Perhaps small-talk would do the trick. 'How's the new-found freedom of freelancing?'

Harry brought over Phil's freshly-pulled pint. He had found watching her carry out the task strangely compelling, awkwardly erotic. Phil flicked a twenty pound note across the bar, and pointed at Harry to indicate she should have a drink too. She smiled in appreciation. 'Happier but poorer,' Phil noted to Tony. He looked up at some programme information spilling out onto the TV screen. 'You know they've cancelled *Eastenders* tonight? The storyline had a shooting.'

'Call it collateral damage,' Tony proclaimed.

'No wonder there are riots on the streets,' Phil concluded, indignantly. He lowered his tone again. 'I'm sure this isn't a social call.'

Tony cut to the chase. 'I need some help with the blogosphere. Maybe some legwork?'

Phil kept his eye on the deal. 'I assume there's some exclusivity out of this?'

Tony felt chided that the question had even been asked. 'As usual. We need names. And reasons.'

Phil had already been making his own discreet enquiries. Now having a paymaster would make further work feel less of a chore. 'Leave it with me. I'll get back to you as soon as I can.'

Finishing the call, he put his phone in his jacket pocket, and noticed Harry staring at him. She had a half pint in her hand, and from the colour the same drink as Phil was enjoying. She raised her class in appreciation, and smiled. Phil reciprocated, wondering whether he was brave enough, or could set aside the necessary time, to follow up on this opportunity. He smiled back at her. To hell with what anybody thought.

∗ ∗ ∗

Over on Darby Island, Damian was entertaining. Ashley Mellons called herself a model, although the industry described her as a pornographic actress. She was an acquired taste, long straight mousy-brown hair with saucer-shaped eyes to match. Her stage name was filled with irony, as her bra size of 30AA meant she was constantly being thought of as "underage".

Her website made making contact with her easy enough, and despite her rules on such things, she couldn't resist the deal on offer for visiting a desert island for a couple of days. Damian was introducing her to what he considered the finest of the finest. Foie gras.

They were standing by a high serving plinth, bejewelled with a range of foods, a bottle of champagne already cracked open in an ice-filled cooler bucket, and two flutes filled to the brim. Ashley couldn't help but be hypnotised by the enchanting view of the sandy beach beyond the expansive balcony, with the crystal clear ocean beyond.

The phone rang, which allowed Damian to once more demonstrate how well he could multi-task. He picked up the receiver. 'Hold on a moment,' he said to the caller, while keeping his attention on Ashley. 'It's relevant to realise why so many have a problem with this amazing treat. Plebs have a downmarket variant on special occasions. They call it "Pâté",' he remarked, with some distain. 'After all, Foie gras is just fattened goose liver. It's the execution which makes people so upset. The geese are force fed fat, corn and grain, using a metal pipe placed down their throats.'

Damian smiled. He was having the desired effect on Ashley. She was a little unnerved by his graphic description. 'People have a real problem with that,' he continued. 'Thing is, my dear, those birds are very much like you. Just as I have seen you demonstrate in your movies, the goose has no gag reflex, thus feels no pain. And never pronounce it "foys grays" or "fozz grass". It's "fwah-grrah". Down the hatch!'

Damian munched a cracker with the glorified pâté on it. Ashley took her cue to do the same, now looking just a little bit concerned about having accepted the invitation. Then she thought of the money, and turned her attention to the champagne.

He then made his excuses. 'If you'll entertain yourself for a few moments, my dear, I really must take this call.' With that, he bowed out and went to his office, a short walk into the depths of the castle. Pleasantness was soon swamped by unmitigated anger.

'How on Earth did you blow it?' he shouted down the receiver. 'You told me you were a crack shot.' He listened to several excuses, and the faint hopes from the caller that Ray Grady was still going to be a corpse by the weekend. Damian had heard differently. 'Of course he's going to survive! Can't you read between the lines of the news coverage?'

Suggestions were put Damian's way. He was still not impressed. 'No, leave it for now. Doing anything else will attract even more attention.' Damian hated it when people tried to persuade him to change his mind. 'No, you'd only mess it up.' The caller then tried to keep themselves in consideration for any further contracts which might come up. Damian realised the nature of the pitch. 'I am sure another chance will present itself.'

With that, he terminated the call, realising he would probably also have to arrange to terminate the caller, too. His mood soon changed, when he thought of what was waiting for him in the lounge. It had been quite a few weeks since he'd last treated an actress to being fed like a goose.

8

ANSWERS IN A CAPSULE

The Prime Minister's Office was upstairs from the "Ops" room. Ray had his own ideas about which room he should occupy during his tenure, and how it should be decorated. As much as it was for private chats, it was also his bolthole. Whilst he was comfortable being in the public eye, there were moments when he needed to gather his thoughts, put a little fresh air between him and everyone else.

For obvious reasons, it was currently unoccupied. Such vacancy didn't suit it. The stately but confined area was dark, shadows cast across its interior by the intruding beams of street lights. A particular object in the spotlight was on the corner of Ray's imposing, imperious desk. It was of a much-younger Ray, a wedding shot with his bride the first time around, Anna. Their smiles were huge and genuine. He really couldn't keep that picture at home, and Alicia made it a rule never to come to Number 10, unless she couldn't avoid it.

The photo frame suddenly had another beam range across it. A torch, carried by a neutral indistinctive silhouette, scanned the room. The light was searching for something in particular as it panned and scanned. It stopped at an alcove in the wall, behind the historic mantelpiece. The figure made its way across, an outstretched hand then darted around the ledge behind, and attempted to locate something it must have known was there. Into view of the torchlight came a standalone hard drive computing attachment, about the size of a small box of chocolates. It was unlikely this was someone who did it all because the lady loved "Milk Tray".

The box was disconnected from a USB cable anchoring it to its secret location. Out of a satchel, the figure substituted it for another, exactly the same model. It was carefully plugged back in, put back in place, and covered once more. The figure placed the original hard drive in the satchel, and again the torch scanned around to check nothing had been disturbed. As quietly as it had made its entrance, the figure carefully headed back to the door, and left the room.

For just a moment, you almost had the sense that the picture of Anna on the desk had broken its smile to form a scowl.

Back in the "Ops" room, at some point Tony, Georgie and Dawn had pulled some office lounge chairs around, in order to continue to watch the television more comfortably. There was something remarkably draining about viewing variants of the same coverage again and again on the twenty-four-hour rolling news channels.

The office had thinned out its occupancy, the early hours rolling by and overwhelming many. Most of the interns had long since gone, but those still there were finding plenty to do. These included Emily, whose gothic-redhead look took on an air of even greater sultriness in the twilight. She approached with a selection of papers for Dawn, who began to skip through them. There was little of interest that caught her eye. Emily scuttled away, and got ready to leave for the night. Her fellow interns, noting the time, and the fact that Emily was calling quits, decided to do the same. She was very much seen as their "Mother Superior", a casting which very much went with her Northern Irish accent.

Tony looked at the rather naff litre-and-a-half bottle of blended whisky on offer, forlorn on a side table, with only the most desperate in the room being drawn to its contents. He dropped it into the waste paper bin with a loud clunk, which raised no objections from anyone. He pulled a bottle of twenty-five-year-old Chivas Regal Scotch Whisky from a nearby drawer. It made a perfect partner to the soda siphon, ice bucket, tongs, and a trio of crystal glasses on the desk. Georgie took on pouring and distribution duties for the medication.

'You know as a rule I don't,' said a frail Dawn. 'However, I think Ray would insist,' she clarified, as she took the well-stacked glass from Georgie.

Tony wasn't really paying attention, although the appearance of his own allocation of alcohol brought him into focus. He indicated to Georgie that the soda should be squirted in it right to the top. 'Damned if we do, damned if we don't,' he concluded.

Dawn was again trying to be practical. 'The sooner we come clean, the greater the chance we turn this around.'

Georgie had prepared her glass, and interrupted her first gulp. 'Into what? Play the "martyr card"? Show that we're carrying the torch? Doing what he would have wanted?'

Tony rubbed the bridge of his nose with his unoccupied thumb and index finger in frustration. 'Ladies. Remember John Smith's demise and the Labour Party.'

Dawn was trying to comprehend Tony's meaning. 'The best leader with the shortest term?' she enquired.

Tony brought his comment into focus. 'Only takes some smartie to note that, when Smith died, Labour ended up with "Mister Teeth".'

Georgie looked down into the bottom of her whisky glass. 'They did get thirteen years' rule from that.'

'And a life sentence for the rest of us,' Tony guffawed. He found his serious face again. 'Any comparison like that will blow us out of the water. Especially with Blair's trial due anytime soon. Besides, after what happened to UKIP, this will be the final straw for new parties trying to "break the mould".'

Georgie tried to get a handle on recent history. 'Farage must have known that was coming.'

Tony filled up his glass again with soda water. 'Infiltration. They'd had it with Kilroy-Silk. Doubt they thought it would happen again.'

Dawn didn't see the relevance of talking about the other parties and their problems. 'Ray is dead. We can't carry on as before.'

Silence fell, everyone lost for words. As they stared at the grim television pictures again, the sound thankfully still off, Georgie rifled through a series of documents, comparing one back with another. Her expression was half-frown, half-exhilaration. Tony caught her eye, and raised an inquisitive eyebrow.

'Perhaps we can,' she said. Tony and Dawn looked at each other, as Georgie had left it just a little bit too long to answer Tony's question. He had to be cynical to her for doing that.

'What do you suggest?' he sneered. 'Summon up the ghost of Jim Henson to work the body? Frank Oz to provide the voice?'

Georgie missed the edge in Tony's enquiry. 'Not quite. Right lines, though,' she said, encouragingly, which only annoyed Tony. 'Have you ever heard of the Pentagram Consortium?' she pitched.

'Bunch of astrologers?' mooted Tony, who obviously hadn't.

'No,' said Georgie, in her best pub-quiz-host mode. Dawn got up and looked over Georgie's shoulder at the document causing the interest, trying to speed-read the contents. Tony wasn't giving up yet.

'Devil worshippers?' he suggested.

Georgie explained. 'They issued a supportive press release. They liked our plan for the country.' Tony pretended to have a "Eureka" moment.

'They can form our fan club,' he proclaimed, in mock excitement. Dawn summed up the couple of pages being presented.

'That's a thinly disguised attempt to get funding,' she concluded, unhappy that hopes had been raised. Georgie was way ahead of both of them as to the possibilities.

'Do you know what they do?' she enquired. Dawn and Tony looked at each other, puzzled. They stared at Georgie in unison, collectively shrugging their shoulders.

'It's part nanotechnology, part quantum mechanics,' Georgie revealed. As blank stares surrounded her, she expanded. 'A bit of holographics thrown in.' She made the interjection almost apologetic. Tony realised Georgie might be on to something.

'You finally found a use for that physics degree,' he chuckled. 'You were wasted as Ray's talent agent.' Georgie continued giving some background.

'A couple of big corporates were backing them. Until recently. A matter of ethics got in the way.'

Tony again found this a source of amusement. 'Scientists with ethics? My ears deceive me!'

Brusquely, Meddings entered the room, and was clearly concerned with the trio still being around.

'Eye, eye,' Tony quietly whispered, just out of Meddings' earshot.

119

'If you thought this was a long day, it'll be even worse tomorrow,' advised the security chief.

Georgie explained, 'You know us. Twenty-four seven.'

Dawn also felt the need to state the obvious. 'Doubt if any of us could sleep. You get off. We'll need someone still sharp tomorrow to catch us.'

Meddings took this as an order. 'Will do. The late shift can contact me if needed.'

'Count on it,' Dawn confirmed. With that, Meddings turned on his heels and left, shutting the door behind him.

Tony picked up a vibe and spoke to Dawn. 'I can tell. You really hate his guts.'

Georgie felt a firm steer was needed with Dawn concerning this particular observation. 'Keep him out of the loop on this. If this has legs, we'll have to be very selective as to who knows.' With that, Georgie took out her mobile phone and began to make a call.

Tony had seen this sort of steel in Georgie before. 'Your little black book?' he enquired.

'My little sister won't be best pleased,' she warned. With that Georgie got up to get some privacy. 'Back shortly.'

Georgie gave Dawn and Tony a short wave as she left the room. Tony picked up the remote, and turned the volume up on the television again. Dawn took the opportunity to refill her glass.

'You go steady there, gal,' he teased, and was met by one of Dawn's patent saucer-eyed stares of disapproval. Having made her point, she offered to fill up Tony's glass, which he gladly accepted.

The screen was still tuned in to the mainstream news, still in its perpetual repeat cycle. Tony unilaterally decided it was time to change channel.

'I've had enough of mainstream spin,' he declared. 'Let's go rogue.'

The onscreen logo, top left, announced that this was Truth Media TV. Their friend Tina Truth was fronting this version of non-stop coverage of the decaying situation, in a way only low-budget guerrilla broadcasting could do. She was always to be relied upon to tell it how it really was.

'The establishment hit out at our best chance of ongoing peace and prosperity today, with their attempted execution of new Prime Minister Ray Grady,' she spat, almost growling. 'He remains in critical condition at an undisclosed location. Truth Media Television is proud to have backed Ray's election campaign, the only broadcaster to have done so. We now look back on his amazing story…'

Tony shook his head. He didn't think this was going to do either himself or Dawn any good. 'Something else?' he enquired of her.

'Please,' she pleaded, not wanting to have a replay of what they had lost. They would be forced to recall how irreplaceable Ray was, and that none of them had the level of natural charisma needed to fill his shoes. Tony changed channel.

The images moved from revellers painted as hooligans on Election Day, to the "riots" which were apparently gaining so much momentum across the country. He changed the channel again, and again, looking for anything to provide hope. Dawn was annoyed.

'Tampered footage then, agent provocateurs now,' she declared, unhappy that the mainstream was finding the worst examples to fill up their airtime. Tony was as amazed as Dawn was.

'Does anyone still take this crap at face value?' he asked, rhetorically.

'Plenty,' Dawn confirmed, knowing that so many of the general public still wanted to be told what their opinion was.

Tony couldn't help being sarcastic. 'They certainly have gone for greater accuracy in their footage this time,' noting that the very worst of the scenes around the country were being selected. A look at social media websites, and the various still images and videos being distributed by "citizen journalists" was showing a different story. Peaceful protest, devoid of violence, those creating disturbances being rounded on by those wanting to illustrate the very best of humanity.

Dawn wanted to put things in perspective. 'Research indicates our supporters are annoyed at being painted as thugs and anarchists.'

Tony was cynical yet pragmatic. 'They could always stop watching the bloody stuff.'

Dawn smiled. She did also have some good news. 'Ratings for mainstream news down 20% since before the election.' With that, the pair of them toasted the research with a clink of their glasses.

Realising that they were going to be around for the long haul that night, Meddings had been busy. He appeared again, which immediately was cause for concern. Sloping in behind him was Duncan Hurst, the Opposition Leader.

Tony was aghast. 'Bloody hell. Who let you in?' he enquired of Hurst.

Meddings jumped in and tried to explain, 'I thought he might be able to help.' For once, Tony was speechless.

Hurst, full of himself as usual, turned it up to eleven on the condescending scale. 'In times like these, a bit of experience comes in very handy.'

Dawn stepped in, using her years of experience of how to handle this type of career politician. 'From the Leader of the Opposition? We can do without your type of interventions.' It was enough to drive anyone to drink, which is why Dawn poured herself another whisky. She was going to know only too well about such excess in the morning.

Hurst forced a smile, in the way parents do to children who have failed to master potty training. 'Not according to reports.' He commandeered the television remote control, changed channels, and turned the volume up. Tony immediately folded his arms when he realised it was Zena Carsley.

'Police have identified the lone gunman as twenty-four-year-old Chris Bowden,' Zena announced gleefully to her viewers. 'A British national, and a mature student who had worked at the Stock Exchange ever since his graduation last year.'

'They've got that wrong,' Tony interjected. Zena continued.

'Bowden had no previous criminal convictions, but was believed to be under psychiatric evaluation.'

Hurst was ready to give his own evaluation. 'That settles it. A nut. Working on his own.'

Tony's sarcasm was about to go off the Richter scale. 'Oh, of course, just like Oswald. As in Lee Harvey.'

Hurst was genuinely shocked. 'You're not suggesting some sort of conspiracy?'

Dawn thought Hurst's responses were almost scripted. 'Wondered how long it would be until someone used that word.'

'Two shots hit the Prime Minister. Through his head and chest. Mafia style,' Hurst informed. He cut to the chase. 'He's not going to recover from that, now is he?'

Dawn's PR training hit centre stage. 'Ray's incredibly resilient. Hadn't you noticed?'

Tony was already bored with this intrusion on their grieving. 'You've had your chance to gloat,' he sneered, thrusting his nose up at Hurst's chin. 'Go back to your primordial ooze.'

Duncan was unconvinced. 'You need me,' he declared.

'Only as target practice,' Tony retorted, almost giving his tongue whiplash. He looked at the cause of this intrusion. 'Meddings?' The glare was unmistakable, and the unsubtle hint on a fast track. As Dawn turned down the TV volume, Meddings finally turned humble.

'Oh. Right,' he almost whispered. He gently grabbed Hurst's forearm to lead him out. Hurst spluttered at his offer being turned down.

'You should be declaring a national emergency!' he shouted back at Tony and Dawn. She found the drink was helping her to do the talking.

'Take a hint, Hurst,' she growled, and ushered the two of them out, a victorious push seeing them over the threshold. She slammed the door with such force behind Hurst and Meddings that she was sure she felt the building shake.

The pair sat down together, pleased with the outcome. Something then bothered Tony. 'How did he know where the bullets hit?'

Dawn frowned. 'Lucky guess?'

Tony found himself running his index finger around the rim of his glass. 'I thought we'd clamped down on that information. No close-up footage made its way out into the media.'

Dawn couldn't see a conspiracy. 'This is why people think governments can never keep secrets.'

Tony despaired. 'If they only knew,' he huffed.

Dawn was running back through what Hurst had said. Several things were bothering her, but one in particular. 'Why was he so keen to instigate martial law?'

It was Tony's turn to try and disarm any trails of potential wrongdoing. 'Probably knows what's coming. Even more civil unrest.' And then, in his best movie-trailer voice he boomed, 'A Duncan Hurst production in glorious "patsy-scope".' Tony regretted even considering what Hurst had suggested. 'No… We're not doing it. Only criminals benefit from a state of emergency.'

Dawn looked around. 'That's quite a long phone call that Georgie's gone on.'

Tony started looking through some files again. 'Well, you know what she's like. If she gets a lead, she does tend to get straight on with following it up.'

The pair continued to mull things over, interspersing their chatter with taking in more news coverage on the television. The "vox pops" were coming in thick and fast, tending to avoid the general public at all costs. Politicians past and present were giving their views, as well as international statesmen and ambassadors. British celebrities were, on the whole, given a wide berth, most having shown sympathies for the "We the People" cause. That is, except for reality show contestants stretching back over a decade, all desperate for whatever exposure they could get, their agents telling them what to say to get on-air.

Just under an hour later, the door opened and Georgie reappeared. She ushered Vernon Snow into the room. He had made a genuine effort to tidy himself up. The attaché case by his side was sleek matt silver, and a magnet to everyone's eyes. Tony looked at Vernon, raising an eyebrow. Everything suggested to him this was "Joe 90" fast approaching his fortieth birthday, perhaps having experimented with Ayahuasca to expand his creativity and understanding of the universe.

Seeing him in person, Tony was suddenly aware who Vernon was, but more importantly his less-than-distinguished track record.

'You've got to be kidding!' Tony exhaled, far from happy.

Georgie was amazed that Vernon had been recognised. 'You know each other?'

Tony harrumphed. 'Only by reputation. That's enough.'

Dawn was never someone who wanted to be left out of a conversation. 'Care to fill me in?'

Georgie did some introductions. 'Dawn, this is Vernon Snow.' Dawn went to shake Vernon's hand, and he happily obliged. She was perplexed at her own ignorance.

'I should know that name?'

Vernon had got used to having to be defensive. He managed to have a disarmingly dismissive tone about his history. 'Some people question my ethics, I'm afraid to say.'

This was a red rag to the bull that Tony had become. 'Ethics? This is the one-time boy genius, whose tainted research permanently set back the study of links between M.M.R vaccines and autism.'

Vernon tried to empathise with his prosecutor. 'There was a lot at stake.' Regrettably, no choice of words could have disarmed the situation.

'Tell my niece that,' Tony spluttered, 'if you can ever get through to her.'

Dawn had to move things along. 'We're wasting time. Decisions to be made.'

Georgie found herself thinking of song lyrics again. She always did that when under pressure. The Human League was having something of a renaissance on her iPod, and she could even hear Phil Oakey's voice in her mind. She found herself humming along to the song. The gathering all turned to Georgie and looked blankly at her. Sheepishly, she revealed the source. '"Keep Feeling Fascination". Reached number two in 1983.'

None of this helped Tony with his agitation, as he kicked an imaginary can across the floor. Dawn revealed her "Paddington Bear hard stare", which quickly pulled Tony to attention. She needed to get to the business end of matters.

'Vernon, what have you in mind?' she enquired. Knowing what was coming, Georgie went and locked the door. Vernon set his attaché case down on the main desk, with Dawn clearing some of the clutter caused by their communal drinking.

As if he had just heard a fanfare, Vernon opened the case and pulled out a pile of papers. Amongst them were x-rays.

He held them up to the available light. 'Your Prime Minister was hit directly by two bullets.' Tony looked at Georgie inquisitively as to how the guy had got hold of such materials. Georgie just shook her head and put her finger to her lips. 'Narrowly grazed by a third. Definitely more than one gunman… according to our computer reconstruction.'

Dawn looked at Tony, rewardingly. 'As you suspected.' Vernon then held up one of the x-ray plates of Ray's body cavity to the light, at an angle so everyone could see.

'The body shot is easy enough to sort. The heart can be repaired. Just needs a new aortic valve.' He then held up another x-ray plate, this time of Ray's head. 'However, this isn't so good.'

Georgie explained her actions for the benefit of everyone else in the room. 'Which is why I called you in, Vernon.' He smiled, not something he found easy, and then focused again.

'The shot went clean through the left hemisphere of the brain,' Vernon noted, and then looked directly at Tony, inquisitively. 'Do I need to explain the significance?'

Tony wasn't sure why he was now taking part in a "pop quiz". Academically, he replied, 'The left brain does logic… facts and analysis. The right brain is the creative side of things.'

Vernon was impressed. If he had one handy, he would have given Tony a cookie. 'Very good. And we made a lot of progress on which side does what, through my autism research.' Tony scowled at this. For once Vernon wasn't being antagonistic by design. Defensively, he said 'Just saying. Some good can come, out of everything.' Usually, Vernon had other people to do sales pitches for him.

He put the x-rays down, and turned his attention to a pile of files. From within it, Vernon handed out copies of an explanatory sheet. Tony and Dawn read it with disbelief. Georgie smiled at their reaction. What was in front of them was exactly the salvation she thought it would be.

Vernon cleared something up which had been disturbing Tony. 'Judging by the medical data Georgie supplied me, I think we have a solution to your problem.'

Tony wasn't going to be keen on anything medical that Vernon was likely to come up with. 'You've got to be joking,' he said again, dismissively.

Vernon realised he was going to have to make this simple. 'Let me explain,' he urged, and pulled out an "Action Man" doll from his case. It looked like a very run-of-the-mill version of the toy, until Vernon revealed that it had a flip-top cranium. Clicking it open, inside its head everyone could see the two halves of the brain within. 'We know the majority of tissue is still in the brain cavity,' he noted, pointing out the various areas. 'In time, the remaining segments of the brain, given proper stimulation, will rewire themselves to relearn what it's now missing.' Looking at his attentive students, he advised, 'Until then, we have to provide some guidance.'

Tony was playing catch-up, quickly reading from the sheet he had been given. 'This says you're going to place a capsule in Ray's head.'

Vernon was trying to not sound so smug in his plotting. He was failing. 'A mini-submarine, if you like. In the area removed by the gunshot.' He was met with silence and unease. 'Yes. From there, they will control movement, speech, bodily functions.' Tony grimaced. His mind was racing away with what that entailed.

'They?' Tony stuttered. 'People?' he emphasised, such suggestions now going way beyond his levels of comprehension.

Dawn was getting her thoughts straight on the plan. 'You'd put a crew in that capsule to do this?'

Vernon nodded. 'Yes.'

Tony was thinking of a clutch of decades-old science fiction movies. *Fantastic Voyage* was coming to mind. In his slightly hazy drunken state he had to stop his mind wandering off, to visualise a shapely Raquel Welch encased in body-hugging white rubber. He managed to get back to practicalities. 'How's that possible?'

Vernon realised some would never embrace what was actually within reach, and too fantastical to assimilate. 'Do you really think the technology you see in high street stores is "cutting edge"?' He could see he was beginning to get through. 'Behind the scenes, we're at least fifty years ahead,' he announced, far too pompously.

Tony took umbrage. 'Don't treat me like a monkey-boy.'

Vernon realised to take extra care with Tony. 'Not my intention. What you have to realise is your view of what's possible is limited by what you've been told cannot be done.'

Tony was on the edge of being convinced. Georgie tried to be supportive. 'What do we always say? Don't believe what you read in the papers.'

Tony went back to reading the crib sheet. Dawn was still trying to run through the scenario. 'Let's say we go along with this. We have very little time to bring Ray back into action, or we'll lose control of the country.'

Vernon reassured her, 'We could have things sorted as early as tomorrow.'

Tony smelled a rat. 'How's that possible?'

Vernon was coy in his response. 'The Prime Minister would not be our first patient.'

This worried Dawn. Not wanting to hear the answer, she asked, 'With what degree of success?'

Vernon was a little evasive. 'Some better than others. Lots of variables.'

Tony had given up. 'This is totally barking,' he sighed. He looked around at everyone. 'Sorry, did I say that out loud?' The lack of reaction said it all. He elected it was time for another swig of whisky.

Dawn knew her principles were getting in the way. 'What about wanting to always tell the truth to the electorate?'

This was something Georgie had already addressed in her own mind. 'Think of the bigger picture,' she insisted.

Tony, Dawn and Georgie all looked over to the muted television screen, still showing images of civil unrest, marches, and roadblocks. Whatever the truth of those pictures, it wouldn't be long before many would believe the predictive programming they were being subjected to, and go out themselves and be part of the skirmishes nationwide.

It was Tony's turn to be practical. 'Why miniaturise people? If your technology is so good, you could operate him by remote control.'

Vernon took hold of the "Action Man" and put it under a clear Perspex cover, which had previously been keeping some sandwiches relatively fresh. 'This dome could be a thousand and one things which could stop reception. Deliberate jamming is a possibility… especially in classified areas.' He knew he had to paint the picture for his audience. 'Or on foreign soil.' He took the "Action Man" out from under the cover, and swept it in front of his body, left to right, right to left. 'Then there's the possibility of interference. Even, God forbid, someone else taking over the controls.' Seeing the light bulbs going on in the heads of those in front of him, Vernon embellished. 'You know how it is. If you're a pilot, and want to ensure terrorists don't take over your flight… Bring it in on manual.'

Tony and Dawn still had their reservations. Georgie again decided to help Vernon out. 'There aren't any alternatives. We need Ray, even if he's just a figurehead. The technology is sitting there, waiting for another guinea pig. It's not as if we have anything to lose.'

Tony was a tad annoyed that Georgie felt it necessary to restate their predicament. 'Thank you, Basil Exposition,' he huffed.

Dawn, as was her want, decided to think of the budget. 'This will be expensive,' she concluded.

Vernon was used to the interrogation of the "bottom line". 'Do what every other government does with its "Black Ops" spend. Put it through a subhead that won't get cut.' An idea popped into Vernon's head. 'Would fit with health.'

Tony despaired. 'Oh, spiffing!' he retorted.

Vernon remained a fountain of ideas. 'Maybe education. Most popular one is defence.'

Dawn was working through the plan. 'What about Ray's personal knowledge? Stuff none of us could know?'

Vernon was aghast that such a question would be asked. 'Put it down to memory loss,' he said dismissively.

It was at this point that Tony began to buy into the hair-brained scheme. 'I've got a better idea,' he offered, taking his mobile phone out of his pocket. He looked through its address book, and dialled a number. 'Did anyone know that Ray had a daughter from his first marriage?' He was met with a sea of blankness. Georgie and Dawn began to realise there was very little they actually knew about Ray's private life. It had never seemed important to ask.

Georgie was intrigued. 'No,' came her inquisitive answer. What Tony was suggesting was just about coming into focus for her.

'She's mad enough to go for this,' Tony informed, before turning to Vernon. 'I assume you can make space on your team?'

'I had sort-of got that all arranged.' Vernon didn't like the idea of anyone meddling in his carefully constructed plans so early in proceedings, and became tense.

Tony knew the immediate solution, and whispered, 'Think of the money.'

Vernon, surprisingly, didn't take offence at the suggestion that he was so shallow. 'Oh. Okay,' he replied, meekly. Tony put the phone to his ear and walked away from the gathering, choosing a far corner just out of earshot.

The call tone suggested the recipient was somewhere overseas. Not that Tony was paying the bill, but there was something reassuring that their new law reducing the tariffs on inter-country calls had been welcomed in particular by business users. Those, that is, who didn't have "We the People" as top of the pile of what they considered enemies of "free trade". Another manifesto pledge they had kept. Tony couldn't help but keep thinking of news anchor Zena Carsley's claims before the election that they had no workable policies.

Dawn took the opportunity to offer Vernon a drink. He looked at the label. Seeing it was such a highly-regarded single malt, he could hardly refuse.

In Los Angeles, the crowded departure lounge of LAX airport had a mobile phone's chimes cut through the buzz of anticipation like a cheese-wire through a fine Gouda. It was a distinctive ring, a classical piece of music that many thought they recognised, but couldn't actually name.

Bonnie Chase had been born with the surname Grady. She changed it to be able to make it on her own. Not that it was much of a handicap Stateside, as Ray was a virtual unknown until his splash into politics. His television fame was very UK-centric, but the alternative media had loved his speeches, his debating triumphs, all of which had become sensations on the likes of YouTube, and on both side of the Atlantic. Before they were taken down for "copyright violations", that is. No matter, armchair anarchists would re-upload the clips time and again, to such an extent it was difficult for the powers-that-be to keep up.

Bonnie looked at the phone screen. An international call. Bonnie clicked the "accept" button and cautiously said, 'Hello?'

'Hello, is that Bonnie? It's Tony Pearce,' the voice on the other end of the line announced. Ray had put them in touch a few months ago, as he wanted her to be considered as much next-of-kin as Alicia and the children. Although she had never met Tony in person, they had talked in the past, just to have some sort of formal introduction.

'I got your text. I'm on my way,' she advised. Tony had earlier made time to inform her that things were not good with Ray. She had kept up with the sparse coverage on American television cable news channels right from that moment on. It was difficult to get out of her commitments at the David Geffen School of Medicine, particularly as they didn't know of any connection between her and the British Prime Minister. It wasn't something she was prepared to reveal, so she had simply quit, on the spot.

'Where are you now?' Tony enquired.

'At the airport,' she replied, puzzled as to why Tony couldn't have guessed by the soundscape behind her voice. Her full-bodied red hair betrayed her trigger-happy temper, something that she had inherited from her mother.

'I'll have a driver at Gatwick to pick you up. I need your help,' Tony confided. 'In fact, Ray needs your help.'

This was the first positive thing about Ray's condition Bonnie had heard all day. 'Just name it. Whatever I can do.'

Tony had to broach the nitty-gritty. 'Is there anything which will draw you back to America in the near future?' Tony had got his head around the plan enough to appreciate that, if successful, this was going to be a full-time commitment he was asking Bonnie to take on.

She didn't think it necessary to establish her current state of employment. Or that she simply hadn't found any Californian men, or women for that matter, to bond with. It had been a pretty quick five-year stretch. 'Don't you worry your little head on that score,' she confided in Tony. 'You, and Ray, will have my full undivided attention.'

With that, they said farewell to each other. Bonnie looked at the departure board again. She felt a little violated, having refused to go through the body scanners earlier. As a medical practitioner, having looked at their effects on people, she knew only too well about all the dangers they presented to human health.

The pat-down and body search, offered as an alternative, was equally concerning. She could not believe the attitude of the female "officer" who had subjected her to inspection. Bonnie had to ask her to put on a new set of rubber gloves. It beggared belief. It was always those employees who looked like dykes who took the chance to pat her down. Her looks followed those of her mother. Glistening long hair, eyes big and blue, and at her thirty-two years of age she still looked like she was in her mid-twenties.

One of the reasons Ray had kept the mainstream media at arm's length from both of them was the sordid little tabloid story which suggested that Bonnie was some sort of "mystery woman". She had been seen out-and-about with Ray. It was theorised he must be having an affair with her. Ray didn't want to reveal the family connection, which meant he never took the newspaper to court, so the tabloid got away with it. They did get a very curt "cease and desist" which they surprisingly abided by.

That helped make up Bonnie's mind to get out of England. Now, here she was, possibly going back to put herself in the firing line once more. No matter. If her father needed her, she was going to be there for him. It might help in making research on his biography somewhat easier. Bonnie wanted to make sure her father's story was told, regardless of how closely he guarded his family life. She'd already talked Ray around to her way of thinking, and the first draft was near completion.

The confirmation came up on the departure boards, revealing her flight was now ready for boarding. She was filled with relief that this was likely to be the next chapter for her to write, rather than an epitaph on a publication that would be released posthumously.

She hadn't enquired more of Tony to ensure she didn't have any further doubts about returning to Britain. Ray had absolute trust in Tony. Something she was only too aware of. And whatever he had in mind, she would back in its entirety. It's not as if she would be recognised by anyone, having changed her hair colour and style since the tabloid debacle.

For some reason she thought how easily she could now be made to disappear. It was with some degree of trepidation that, in the reality of the situation, she entered the plane. She didn't know whether to laugh or cry in the knowledge that, at this particular moment, only Tony and Ray would miss her…

9

DAMNED DATA RECOVERY

For several weeks, the atmosphere at the London Stock Exchange had been subdued. It had soured ever since election night. For human beings whose reputations lived or died by their gambling on the rise and fall of share prices, none of them had put money on the formulation of the current government. It was a shock, caused by a disbelief in the ability of people to vote with their hearts rather than their heads. For once, the right side of the brain had over-ridden the left side. Logic had gone out of the window, to be replaced entirely by emotion.

Nowhere had this been more evident than above the market floor, within a network of open-plan offices, the main one of which was known as the "bull pen". Around the sides of this matrix of cubicles were the more traditional segregated rooms, the home for staff that at some point needed a barrier for confidentiality. Usually, the most money was made by huge movements in company prices, and it didn't really matter whether this was up or down. As no-one saw the election of a party hostile to the financial sector coming to pass, there had been nothing but losses when the share values collapsed. Many individual investors had lost their shirts.

And for weeks it had looked like there would never be an upward swing ever again. Until the gunning-down of the Prime Minister, that is. Despite the huge number of Members of Parliament under the "We the People" flag, as far as this hive mentality was concerned, only one man was the driving force behind the destruction of their gravy train. As Ray Grady looked to be out of the way for at least a few weeks, perhaps even permanently, it was a beam of daylight for the gamblers. Prices rallied, every piece of bad news about the Prime Minister's condition was met with another market hike. In particular amongst industries related to weapons, pharmaceuticals, and big agricultural corporations.

Informed investors had sucked up huge waves of stocks in the companies involved in the alternative and new energy businesses, and were now reaping the benefits. Ray Grady had made no secret that he didn't believe in the climate change mantra. He was convinced about pollution, sure, but not that it was connected with rises in carbon dioxide. He had told the electorate this was a distraction from the polluting of rivers and land by chemical run-offs from factories, and the desecration of the air by noxious non-natural emissions. And those types of polluters were going to pay. At the time, it was yet more bad news for the associated shares.

Ray also took a dim view of the fracking industry, citing the appalling experiences of those in Australia and the USA. The boring for natural gas was an industry based on underground shockwaves. The derogatory evidence of massive problems had been dismissed by the corporate "spinners", who simply had no shame. Or, indeed, any worry about the permanent pollution of the UK's water table, or the seismic activity which came with the massive web of drilling. These had led to earthquakes, even from the first test bores in the northwest of England.

Ray had even demonstrated that this would not lead to the "cheap fuel" bonanza fracking had been heralded as providing. The desire for short-term profits was just one of the factors which pulled the rug from under the industry's projections.

With Ray Grady having been downed, investors were optimistic that fracking would have to come back to the fore. They also expected that, in turn, there would be a reversal in the re-opening of coal-fired power stations which Ray had insisted on. If you knew what you were doing on the stock markets, there was a lot of money to be made simply by understanding how the majority of players in the game would see things panning out.

The wind farm businesses had also made a substantial recovery, having taken a hammering after Ray had declared all financial incentives for building them to be removed with immediate effect. The prospect that a new election would see a party returned to power that believed in climate change had been a big cause for optimism in the city.

Not that Ray had ever denied climate change was happening. He simply pointed out that changes in the environment never stopped. It only looked bad if you took your baseline as the Little Ice Age, which had its last hurrah during the Victorian era of the 1850s. This had been depicted in fancy pictures of ice fairs on the Thames, when the river had frozen over. It was something which had never been explained by the defenders of the official line with any degree of lucidity. If you start from a very low temperature baseline, Ray argued, of course the temperature surges of recent times would look drastic.

If you had a train to catch, you should never get Ray started on the Medieval Warm Period of 950 AD to 1250 AD, when grapes were a common crop across the southern half of England. He never tired of saying this was something substantiated in the Domesday Book of 1087 AD. It was an "inconvenient truth" which the International Panel on Climate Change simply decided to ignore, or almost laugh off with scientific explanations which, to most, came over as little more than quackery.

The financial sectors weren't interested in any sort of scientific analysis, just how they could profit from it. Unfortunately, "We the People" simply weren't good for business. Now, the atmosphere was like a meadow after a thunder storm. The clouds had dissipated, and there was a cause for just a little optimism.

Into this sea of positivity, reporter Phil Conway walked down a thin corridor on one side of the matrix, and with purpose. It made him look as if he belonged there. A visitor badge was stuck to his jacket pocket. A secretary passed by, Phil nodded and smiled at her, hoping this would somehow reinforce his credentials. He realised they didn't get many strangers in the offices these days, such was the risk associated with being anywhere connected with the financial sector.

Phil was chewing gum today, giving away that he was currently losing out in his addiction to cigarettes. Even though he knew the habit didn't reduce his stress levels, there was some comfort to be had in the equivalent of sucking on a long, thin teat. He had promised he would give up for good at the age of forty, but that was still the best part of five years away. But just for now, the long nights and the foreboding of the last few hours were taking their toll.

Phil reached a door, ordained with a brass plaque marked "Pippa Flynn, Head of Personnel". Straightening his tie, he knocked twice, firmly.

From within, he heard a syrupy voice command, 'Come in!' Phil realised that these would, to most, sound like the tones of a consummate professional. If only they knew her as well as he did, well, their opinions would be transformed.

Stepping inside, behind the ornate desk and dominating the room was his old friend, Pippa. Her face was a shade of thunder. She didn't look up from her computer keyboard.

Outside work, her outlook was as jolly and round as her figure. Phil had always joked she had the perfect stature for a *Carry On* movie. She would always let the world turn of its own accord, never forcing anything, which meant that as far as the marketplace of work was concerned, she was often described as being "not big on systems". Piles of paperwork filled her in-tray and every other space on the desk. Via her keyboard, she was wrestling with something that was long overdue.

Phil pretended to be aghast at the state of her filing. 'Can I buy you a sign that says "One Day I'll Get Organised"?' Pippa finally looked up, and her mood lightened. She was glad to see him. Her staggered reaction was due to her being used to trouble being created by every visitor. Phil was probably bringing more trouble of his own, she surmised, but at least it would be "fun" trouble. She jumped up and almost skidded over the desk to greet him.

'Philip Aloysius Conway!' she declared, before demanding, 'who the hell let you in?' She bear-hugged the man who was several inches taller than her. Phil had no problem in reciprocating.

'If I told you, you'd only fire them,' Phil replied. A slight pause before they giggled together.

'I'm afraid that's my job,' she insisted. 'What about you? Still digging the dirt?'

'Making "The Mole" from *Thunderbirds* look like a toothpick. Not in showbiz pap though. Afraid to say it's more the political stuff.' Phil realised that was a bit of a deal-breaker to the flow of the conversation. He changed topics. 'A little disruption here, I take it?'

Pippa went over to a filter coffee machine at the side of the room, took two large mugs from the shelf underneath it, and poured out two generous portions.

'We could do without protests outside our front door,' she said, as she brought the mug over to Phil. She remembered that he drank it black.

'Yes,' he said awkwardly as he took the mug from her. 'I saw them.'

If this was going to be a political conversation, Pippa wanted to be on the front foot. 'Morning, noon and night. Just because he was shot under our roof doesn't mean we were responsible.'

Phil repositioned his hands to other areas on the side of the mug, trying to dissipate the heat. 'Financiers. Just one of many targets. Ray is a very popular guy.'

'Is or was?' she enquired, on her very own little fishing expedition. Phil didn't answer. 'He'd better survive,' Pippa offered, sternly. 'Then we might be able to get on with our work… in peace.' Phil took a sip of the coffee. Still far too hot. Pippa decided to lighten the mood. 'So, come on. You don't just appear out of the blue. Ever. Last time it was help with your thesis!'

Phil knew when he had to cut to the chase. 'Three guesses who I need background on.' Pippa didn't need to. She realised there had to be an ulterior motive for his visit, but was still glad he had dropped by. A space was cleared in front of her computer, papers thrown on to the floor, so she could drive the keyboard properly.

'It was so out of character,' she stated, revealing how well she knew Chris Bowden, the assassin. 'Gentle chap. Didn't socialise much.' Pippa spoke with just a tinge of regret. Phil went around to her side of the desk, to look over her shoulder at the computer screen. Within seconds, Pippa had called up Bowden's file. She was a consummate professional, even if that didn't include adhering to the Data Protection Act. The choice of passport photo was as unflattering as it could possibly be. The background information gave up a veritable hoard of leads. Phil frowned in amazement as he read what was in front of him.

'Could this stuff find its way to my e-mail inbox?' Phil enquired, at the same time handing her one of his business cards. Pippa stared in disbelief at the card, and did a double-take, the proverbial penny dropping. In dandified lettering was the name "Monty Cristoe", complete with a cartoon of a masked Phil in full 18th Century adventurer outfit. It had the subheading "Truth, Justice, and Political Insight". Beneath that was the email address "monty@cristoe.com". She stared deeply at Phil, looking back and forth between his face and the caricature. She raised an eyebrow.

'You're him?' Pippa whispered.

'I could tell you…' began Phil, 'but then I would have to kill you.'

Pippa giggled. 'But you've…" she paused to correct herself. 'He… has done more to uncover political corruption than anyone.' She felt the need to qualify herself. 'With that blog thing.'

'Monty just has good sources…' Phil stated, offhand. 'Like you, for instance,' he continued, before beaming widely at her. Pippa, understandably, was not convinced by his flattery. She typed the email address from the card.

'I hope this is worth it,' Pippa suggested.

'I always protect my stringers,' Phil replied officiously.

'Do you buy them dinner as well?' she said, obviously fishing.

'Inevitably,' said Phil, with just a little mock scorn in his voice. He looked again at the information on the screen. 'I see he has a brother,' he noted.

'Been in Australia for years,' she replied.

Phil smiled. 'I think that titbit could come in very useful.'

* * *

Alicia Grady was in her lounge, peering out through the curtains. The press contingent was still outside, staking out the house. She'd seen bigger mobs, but these snoopers were the most committed types. To prove that everything was always a business opportunity, the dozen-or-so journalists and photographers now had their own sandwich van serving them. The way the dowdy girl inside the travelling tuck shop was frowning, it was obvious they had expected more hacks to have been in residence.

It wasn't the best of weather for Dougan and Kindon to be on the front steps of the house, ensuring that none of the mob got too close. Dougan turned up the collar of his waterproof jacket, and jogged on the spot for a few seconds. Kindon preferred to bury his hands further into his equivalent coat pockets.

Alicia tried to be pragmatic. 'I know this is their job, but what do they think is going to happen?' She was getting very annoyed. 'He's not here. He's not going to be. So, their target is me. And Alison. And Ryan. Pictures that relay human suffering.'

Alicia turned away from the window and faced into the room. Even after all these years, the lounge was still something to behold. The plush surroundings dripped of affluence, with a round fireplace in the centre of the area, its silver sheen lifting the glow of the flame up a few more notches.

Standing around, with mugs of coffee in hand, were Tony and Georgie. They decided to sit down again. The mood of the room, entirely influenced by Alicia's mindset, meant they had been getting up and down for almost the entire twenty minutes they had been there.

'Run this by me again?' demanded Alicia, who came over and sat between them on the expansive sofa.

It was Georgie's turn to try and explain, while at the same time not giving too much away. 'As Tony said, it's a kick-start of Ray's system. The doctors are quite optimistic.'

Alicia could always read between the lines. 'But it's still experimental?'

Tony was losing his patience, but tried not to show it. 'There aren't any other viable alternatives. It's the only church in town.'

Alicia really wanted there to be a "Plan B". She gulped. 'He won't recover without it?'

Georgie looked at Tony for permission. He wasn't very helpful, staring blankly into the heart of the fire. 'Whilst his body will make a full recovery…' she began again, 'he is… at this time… effectively brain dead.'

Alicia picked up her own mug of coffee, thought of taking a sip, but instead stared into the liquid inside the mug.

Tony tried to inject some hope. 'This process will change that.'

Alicia thought she knew Ray best of all. She didn't realise that one of his biggest charms was that everyone could read him like an open book. 'Ray wouldn't want to live…' Alicia paused, giving what followed a variety of meanings, 'if he couldn't be the man he was.'

Georgie got several of the nuances. Tony didn't. 'That's our thoughts entirely,' he oozed.

'I know the consultant's work,' reassured Georgie, telling a blatant lie. 'He's honest enough to say this will…' She stopped, not wanting to be insensitive.

'If you won't say it…' stepped in Alicia. 'I will. Kill or cure.'

'Precisely,' Tony almost whispered.

This was too difficult a decision for someone like Alicia. She had to find another level of justification. 'I know how important he is to you.'

'And everyone else,' Georgie qualified. She didn't think Alicia quite had a handle on the size of powder keg the whole country was sitting on, should Ray's death actually be confirmed.

Alicia took on a frumpy tone. 'It had better work, then.' Such a delivery didn't suit her age, putting her thirty years closer to the pearly gates than she actually was.

Tony jumped up. 'Excellent,' he enthused. Trying to be offhand, he then asked, 'By the way, I just wondered if you knew where Bonnie was these days?'

Alicia was always annoyed when it came to mention of her rival for Ray's affections. 'No. And I don't care to, either.'

Tony decided to state the obvious. 'She is your step-daughter…'

'Who frowns on being older than me,' Alicia hissed. 'She can stay abroad for all I care.' She looked as if a bad smell had been put under her nose.

'Understood,' Tony noted apologetically. He stared at Georgie, wanting her to provide an escape route. All she could offer was bemusement. The tension was released when Meddings entered the room.

'Sorry to interrupt,' the head of security intoned. 'We're needed back at Downing Street. Urgently.'

Georgie and Tony didn't need to stand on ceremony. They prepared to leave. Alicia stood up to bid them farewell.

Georgie handled the pleasantries. 'Thanks. We'll be in touch.' She suddenly realised some introductions might be necessary. 'By the way, Alicia, have you met Meddings?'

Alicia became uncomfortable. 'Don't think we've ever met in person,' she said hazily. Perhaps it was his good looks. Georgie had seen the effect he had on some women before.

Meddings was more in command of the facts. 'I think we may have spoken on the phone. Once or twice.' Addressing Alicia directly, he said, 'Dougan and Kindon are your main security detail,' as if this information would come as a surprise to her. All that did was spark Alicia's most finely-honed sarcasm.

'Yes. They were so pleased when you were put in charge…' she chagrined, before adding, 'above their heads.'

Tony drew an almost-silent sharp intake of breath, and ushered Georgie away, out of the door. Meddings gave Alicia a forced smile, and also took his cue to depart.

Outside the house, Tony and Georgie walked towards their own black limousine, a monstrosity of a four-by-four. Dougan and Kindon were already walking down the drive ahead, ready to grant them safe passage through the media melee.

'Bit of a frosty reception about the step-daughter,' Georgie concluded.

'Rivalries for affection,' Tony concluded. 'You know how these things are.'

Georgie was still confused. 'I thought you'd already located her?' she asked, looking round to check Meddings was way behind them. He was being shown out of the front door by Alicia.

'Bonnie? Yes, I have, and she's in.' Tony could see that Georgie needed more. 'I wanted to be sure that Alicia doesn't know where she is.'

Georgie was still a beat behind. 'Why?'

He spread his hand out in front of himself, checking his nails again. 'Makes it easier for her to disappear.' With that, Tony jumped into the back of the limo, swiftly followed by Georgie. Meddings ran over to take the seat behind the driver's wheel, before zooming off towards the press pack that stood in between them and a clear road ahead.

* * *

They called it Pentagram. Vernon Snow, when engaged in scientific cogitation, always did so in a matrix-fashion. In three dimensions. When it came to anything artistic, including all aspects of the English language, he was very linear. When people suggested to him the satanic overtones of the choice of moniker, he first dismissed their concerns. Then, he was worried what his peers might think, before having a chuckle as to why the hell he was thinking about what others would construe. Let them believe it was something to do with the "Dark Lord". Perhaps it was edgy enough a title to make people pay attention. And perhaps the devil worshippers in positions of power would give his work a second glance.

It was called Pentagram as it took five people to operate. It required the greatest levels of teamwork, which meant the personality metrics employed in selection of the quintet had to be precision-perfect. This process was made even harder as Vernon insisted he was one of the five picked. It meant there had to be a degree of give-and-take in who was selected. Vernon was not an easy person to factor into the equations.

They had initially achieved the necessary investments. An admirable feat, as Vernon was never one to cut corners. As such, his office was huge, with a high ceiling and a running theme of fine-brushed aluminium for the decor. When describing it to the architects, he said it had to feel part hospital, part prototype testing station. The room also served as the front office to the real hub of the operation, hidden behind a pair of bay doors which took up a whole side of the room.

The centre of the area was dominated by what could only be described as an elaborate hospital trolley. To the uninitiated, the mass of wires and gadgets all over it seemed to suggest a lack of cohesion in the design. They could have been right. Vernon was always adding elements, and taking others away, as his research took him off in different directions. Vernon sat at his ornate desk, tapping a pencil for inspiration. Notice boards seemed to surround him, all occupied by a selection of rusty-yellow "Post-It" notes, vintage photographs, and scribbled mathematical formulae on old-style punch cards. Problems would arise if it was ever necessary to pin anything else up.

Vernon looked over to the trolley. Propped up was the remarkably well-preserved body of Ray Grady, at an angle of forty-five degrees to the horizontal. Many of the wires and couplings were directly attached to this corpse. He might be glad to be dead, as without anaesthetic some of those additions would be really painful.

The gunshot to Ray's head was intriguing. It had been well cleaned up, but was still a very obvious disfigurement. Vernon, in almost stereotypical white coat daubed with a Pentagram identity card on the breast pocket, got up and went to an elaborate control desk. The keyboard and monitor in the middle of the maze were the only recognisable pieces of the bank of technology before him. He began flicking switches, although anyone watching would not be convinced he knew what he was doing.

Those with a medical background would surmise, from some of the desk's readouts, that it was only these systems which were keeping Ray breathing. Did it mean he was alive? Those same medical experts would have said not.

To one end of the desk was a pair of gloves. As big as those used by welders, but with lines of wires leading to all the fingers and thumbs. Vernon slipped them on, and pressed an activation button. Suddenly, Ray's arm raised itself, apparently on its own, in perfect motion with Vernon's movements.

Using the gloves, Vernon went through a movement pattern for hand-shaking with Ray's right hand.

'Okay, try that now.' No-one else was present. The words weren't for Ray's benefit, this was just Vernon's habit of talking out loud. Ray's hand repeated the motion being described by Vernon via the gloves, but it wasn't instantaneous, and happened far too slowly.

Vernon frowned, and twisted a couple of dials. Still wearing the gloves, he pressed the activation button again. Ray made the handshake motion, but now it was ludicrously quick. Vernon could hear the theme to *The Benny Hill Show* in his head. He amended the settings on the dials again.

'And now somewhere in-between,' he mumbled to himself. With another press of the activation button, Ray's handshake was perfect. Vernon decided the best thing to do was smile.

At which point, Tony strolled into the room, a little uncomfortable about the cerise vanity case in his left hand. Following on his heels was Bonnie Chase, dragging a huge suitcase on wheels behind her. Reception had been good enough to clip Pentagram visitor cards to them. Top secret project or not, Vernon liked the idea of everyone having to be carded in the building. Besides, it was a great logo, and it would be a shame not to use it as often as possible.

'Vernon,' said Tony, curtly. 'Let me introduce Bonnie Chase.' Vernon jumped up to shake Bonnie's hand. For some reason he was not expecting someone so elegant.

'I expected you to be a "Grady"?' he said, immediately picking up on the different surname.

'I use my Mother's maiden name,' said Bonnie, every syllable laced with a smile.

'Not married, then?' Vernon questioned, not realising that it sounded like he was in some run-down bar "on the pull".

Bonnie just about resisted being curt. 'No.'

Vernon had to interrogate further. 'You changed it to piss someone off?'

Bonnie looked at Tony, who shrugged his shoulders and smiled. 'My step-mother,' she replied.

Vernon was joining the dots. 'Ah. That would make her the same age as you.'

Bonnie realised this was just a misguided version of scientific curiosity. 'Younger. By two years.'

'Did it work?'

'What do you think?'

Vernon looked at Tony, and smiled. 'I like her,' he concluded.

Considering the scientific rigour demonstrated so far, Tony was puzzled. 'You don't want to see her CV, then?' he asked.

Vernon went and sat down at the control desk before answering. 'Being in the capsule is as much about getting on, as what you bring to the party. We could do all the psychometrics, but there would be little point.' Bonnie was taking an interest in the control desk. 'What's he told you?' he asked of her.

'Somewhere between Frankenstein and Stephen Hawking,' she summarised. Vernon frowned at Tony, who felt the uncomfortable need to defend himself.

'Not my exact words. Bit difficult to summarise. Perhaps you could suggest a suitable, shorthand way?'

'I doubt it,' huffed Vernon.

'Try,' Tony demanded. Vernon looked around to one of the notice boards, seeking out something in particular. His target jumped into his eye-line. It was a holographic postcard of Albert Einstein. Vernon went and unpinned it, with a little regret that he'd had to make a hole in it in the first place. Still, he could get another pristine one quite easily. He waved it mysteriously at Tony, almost in little circles, as Bonnie looked on.

'This is just a single hologram of Einstein,' Vernon explained. 'Agreed?' Bonnie and Tony nodded, just a little perplexed. He picked out a huge pair of scissors from a desk drawer. 'Now, if I cut it in half...' he explained, as he made a single slice right down the middle of his Einstein. Holding up both halves, his audience saw that there were now two versions of Einstein's image, both exactly the same as the original, but now just half the size.

Vernon enjoyed these sorts of magic tricks. He was a little too condescending when he said 'See? The same hologram is now on each of the two smaller cards.' He put down one of the cards, and cut the other one in half again. Tony and Bonnie were half stunned and half amused at what they saw before them. The same thing had happened. Vernon was now holding up two identical images once more, and again at half the size of the parent card. He gave the two halves to Tony, who was still bemused.

Bonnie was a little more on-the-ball. 'The blueprint is maintained, just in half the space.'

'Precisely,' Vernon confirmed.

It was still a little bit much for Tony's brain. He needed further clarification. 'So, you keep cutting yourself in half, again and again, and end up really small?'

'About the size of a pinhead,' said Vernon, with just a little too much emphasis on that final word. Tony pretended not to pick up on the thinly-veiled insult, letting it pass by.

Bonnie had her own questions. 'You can reverse the process?'

Vernon was a little uncomfortable when asked for such specifics. 'That's been the sticking point. But we've ironed out the issues.' Tony grimaced at what was the equivalent of a grenade being thrown into the room. 'No, really. Like conservation of energy, this is just a question of conservation of mass. We're left with husks to later reconstitute with. Those have to remain stable and secure.' Vernon tried another analogy. 'It's just like pushing blobs of Blu-Tack back together.'

'Lord help us,' Tony remarked, not quite managing to say it under his breath.

Bonnie had a little housekeeping to quiz Tony about. 'Have you told the vampire what you're up to?'

'Alicia?'

'Who else?' blurted Bonnie, wondering what other characters Tony might have thought she was talking about.

Tony saw a *Star Trek* metaphor as being useful. 'As Ray used to describe it, I applied some Vulcan philosophy.'

Bonnie revealed her own "Trekker" tendencies. 'You didn't lie. You merely exaggerated.'

Tony snorted. 'In a manner of speaking.'

Vernon felt he should contribute to this conversation. 'We don't necessarily need the consent of next of kin,' he advised.

Bonnie had daggers drawn. 'You can have my consent, and be done with it. I'm related to him by blood.' She took a deep breath and wrestled with the ethics of the situation. 'Still, Alicia ought to know what's going on.'

This was another touchy subject for Vernon, who never actually seemed to run out of things which made him tetchy. 'Until we get the hang of things, it's always the close relatives who rumble that something's up.'

Tony was still not happy to give Alicia the whole story. 'Which is where you're going to be so important,' he advised Bonnie. 'We particularly need your inside knowledge of Ray's background. Stuff that wouldn't be written down.'

Bonnie felt the need to state the obvious. 'You do know we didn't end up on the best of terms?'

Tony was puzzled. 'You? Ray? I thought you were working with him on his autobiography?'

Bonnie dropped her gaze down to the floor. 'I was. But sometimes there's stuff a daughter would rather not know.' She then warmed to the idea of being the "good cop" in the scenario. 'Either way, Alicia should be told.'

Tony tried to bring it back to basics. 'We have to consider security.'

Bonnie hadn't detected the undertow before. 'You suspect my stepmother?'

'Darling, I wouldn't even trust my grandmother,' replied Tony, making it sound like he was ending a relationship by saying, "it's not you, it's me." Bonnie bit her bottom lip, and looked at the control desk.

'How long will we have to keep up this charade?'

Vernon went over to a medical x-ray wall lamp, and pinned up the chart of Ray's brain. He pointed at various parts of the image. 'The brain will try and rewire itself. There is so much we don't understand. Experiments suggest that, in many cases, the nodes will find a way to reconnect the memories. Perhaps many of the essential brain functions.'

Bonnie found facetiousness helped to combat her fears. 'Toilet training included in that?'

Tony decided to follow this riff. 'I hope so. Been clearing up after Ray for long enough.'

Vernon decided to raise the stakes. 'There is some response from the right side of the brain. Not as useful as the left, from a practical point of view. But you never can tell when Ray's creativity and imagination, even his perception of a situation, can help us.'

Tony picked up on the inference. 'Hang on. You've been able to have a conversation with Ray?'

Vernon cleared his throat and walked back to the control desk. 'Not as such. And you really shouldn't think of him as Ray. Any chat won't be grounded in our understanding of reality.'

'A little off-the-wall, then?' asked Bonnie, demanding clarity.

'An understatement,' he huffed, and took a microphone in hand, mounted on a bendable tube on the control desk. He placed it near his mouth, and turned a dial. 'Wrighty? Are you there?'

'Wrighty?' Tony whispered to Bonnie. She looked at Tony and pointed to the right side of her head.

'Right brain,' she whispered. Vernon looked daggers at both of them for daring to converse at such a delicate time. He went back to the microphone.

'We've got visitors.' With that, a dense crackle came over the sound system, and like everything else present was state-of-the-art. The trio heard attempts at shifting some phlegm. If it wasn't such a serious situation, it would have been funny. Bonnie looked over at Ray's body, just in time to see the eyes of the corpse dance to life. She took in a short, sharp breath at seeing movement in her father once more. Her instinct was to put her hand over her mouth.

'That's it, that's it,' encouraged Vernon. 'How are you feeling today?'

'I see shapes,' revealed the disconnected voice. It sounded like Ray's dulcet tones, only an octave higher and very staccato. 'Ovals. Pyramids,' he belched, 'boxes shaped like Monarch Butterflies.' Vernon looked at Tony, almost for approval.

Tony seized the initiative. 'Hello? Do you know who this is?'

'Another traveller,' came the confident reply. 'A long journey, but it feels like we're there already.'

'Oh boy,' grunted Tony, under his breath. Vernon was keen to explore this connection.

'Wrighty,' Vernon said, demanding the ghostly voice pay attention. 'Who can you see?' With that request, Ray's eyes started to dart around the room, without him moving his head. He had the same sort of expression you would see when someone was awoken from a deep R.E.M. sleep. The corpse saw Bonnie, and smiled.

'Hello Bonnie,' came the reply. Bonnie was having trouble coming to terms with hearing her father's voice, and then not seeing his lips move in accompaniment. She found herself smiling. Tony was not so taken, probably due to not being recognised by his old friend. 'That's strange,' said a perplexed Wrighty, 'I thought you'd only just been born?'

Vernon was beginning to understand what was happening. 'Perception of time. This is why your life flashes before you, just before death. You're everywhere and nowhere, "no when", all at the same moment.'

'Hi-ho, silver lining,' suggested Tony, half-singing. Bonnie intercepted Vernon's gaze, pointed to the microphone and then to herself. Vernon nodded approval. She spoke into the device.

'Hello...' she paused, "Dad."

The response was upbeat and very normal. 'I loved that picture you drew of me presenting the sport last Saturday.'

'That's right,' Bonnie replied. 'I remember, too. I drew it when I was seven.'

Wrighty was confused. 'You're seven already?' There was the sound of lips being licked, and with a tad of confusion the disembodied voice lamented. 'It only seems like yesterday that you were born.'

With that, Vernon turned off the controls, and secured the microphone back in its mooring. 'As you can see, we're dealing with fragments,' he said, tetchily. 'Unconnected ones. Not factually based, mainly feelings.'

Tony looked at his watch. 'You do know we're against the clock on this. When are your team arriving?'

Vernon laughed. 'I thought you wanted to approve them all first?'

'As long as there are no serial killers, war criminals or former TV chefs involved, I think we can live with just about anyone.' Tony looked to Bonnie for support. All she could do was shrug her shoulders.

Vernon rubbed his hands together with glee. 'In which case, I have a little presentation to show you.' He jogged over to his office desk, almost skipping. 'I'm glad you've given me a free hand on this, as they are already on their way.' Grabbing a remote control, he dimmed the lights.

Tony took a long sniff. Relaxation on staffing matters had suddenly turned into stomach-churning dread...

10

INSIDE TRACK

Phil Conway had been working on his Australian accent all through the journey. His destination was the high security prison at Belmarsh. It had been described as "Britain's Guantanamo Bay", due to the number of prisoners who had been held there over the years without charge or trial. Phil wondered if Chris Bowden, the only suspect in the assassination of Prime Minister Ray Grady, was going to be the latest in such an undistinguished roll call.

He pulled up at the main gates in his flame-red Nissan Juke. The letter of introduction was enough to gain access. The guard had to check with his superiors, such was the unusual nature of the request. The flunkie was almost impressed with what he had been told. 'You can go through now, Mister Bowden. Parking is one hundred yards down on the right.'

'Cheers, Harold,' replied Phil, with a faint undercurrent of Aussie twang. The guard looked bemused as he raised the gate barrier. His name wasn't Harold. He would find out later the name was slang, in Perth, for a police officer.

Phil could have just asked Georgie Harvey, as Home Office Minister, to get him an audience with the prisoner, but that wouldn't have been half as fun, or as covert. You tend to get more out of people if they don't know who you are working for. A family member will tend to be treated differently by jail staff than someone flying the colours of government.

The personnel files for Chris Bowden, secured from Pippa, had enough information to give the necessary flannel required to get past the majority of

149

local queries. A couple of phone calls had secured him right of access to Bowden from higher up the chain, not bad for an incumbent surrounded by so much red tape. Then again, this was the guy implicated in the first assassination of a Prime Minister since Spencer Perceval's death in 1812, from the gun of John Bellingham. So, in retrospect it was quite frankly shocking he was progressing so far on such a thin ruse.

Phil was convinced of the veracity of the theory that Bowden was a Manchurian Candidate. Acting outside his own will, and programmed to kill. Phil didn't believe that such brainwashing could not be broken down. A college professor had once described to him how the brain unties itself from such inflicted knots eventually, given the right stimulation. Phil was glad this was one of the tools in his own armoury.

In the Belmarsh reception office, he enquired of Bowden's location. His cover as brother Alan was holding up well. As was his accent. It nearly dropped when he was told that Bowden, for security reasons, was being held in the Isis wing. Phil tried not to dash over to that area's reception, simply as the logic of keeping Bowden in what was a young offenders' training centre, for those up to the age of twenty-five, didn't add up. In its early days, the wing had numerous issues to deal with, including the likes of poor staff morale, bullying, and even some prisoners being too frightened to leave their cells.

Arriving at this next reception, Phil was pleased to find out that at least Bowden had been placed in the Segregation Unit. Ray Grady even had support behind bars, particularly after "We the People" made good on their election promise to de-criminalise marijuana, as well as relax prison attitudes to both these and traditional cigarettes. Any one of those banged-up would, like as not, take a dim view of an attempt to assassinate a politician who was actually doing what he said he would, and for their benefit.

Of course, there was also a downside – the mafia-type sects within the jails were annoyed that one of their main currencies of trade had been completely devalued in a single stroke of legislation. So, Phil reckoned the reaction to Bowden, from behind bars, was likely to be mixed.

The officer in charge, Morris, decided to escort Phil personally to Bowden's cell. Morris was full-bearded, and as broad as he was very tall. If anyone was built to be a prison guard, it was him, although his altruistic temperament could have been taken to mean he was a "pussy cat". He wasn't.

There would be no right of privacy, Morris noted, despite Phil's protestations. Morris would be with them both, all the time. Phil had figured that the situation where Bowden would not recognise him, despite supposedly being his brother, could be put down to Bowden having been brainwashed. There was already enough currency in that rumour for such a scenario to be taken as a given.

Inside the Segregation Unit, both men immediately realised something was amiss. Bowden's cell door was open. Morris dashed inside and looked around, checking every nook and cranny, the look of panic permeating his entire face.

'Morris to control. Bowden's not in his cell. What's going on?' he barked into his walkie-talkie. There was a short silence on the other end.

'Should be there, Chief. Nothing scheduled,' came the faltering voice at the other end.

Phil was looking around the rest of the corridor, and was drawn to a doorway a little along and to the left. It was open to his push. Phil flung himself through it. Morris looked out of the cell upon hearing the loud clang and followed, his heavy boots accentuating the urgency.

Phil didn't need to go far along that next corridor to have his worst fears confirmed. In a crumpled heap, on the floor, a small pool of blood leaking from beneath was a body. He stopped in his tracks, waiting for Morris to catch up. Phil dropped his Australian twang.

'If I turn him over, am I going to find that it's Chris Bowden?' Morris did a slight double-take at the change of accent, but realised there were greater problems to address. He stepped forward, and rolled one shoulder of the corpse over. They were both met with the features that had become unmistakeable on the national news.

The face was badly beaten, the blackened bruises already well-formed. There were long scratches on both cheeks, making it look like some big cat had savaged him. Blood was running from one of the ears.

'Someone really did a number on him,' said Phil, bleakly. 'More importantly, how did he get out of his cell?'

Morris tried to not knee-jerk into being on the defensive. The short deep breath he allowed himself gave him enough time to get his bearings. 'No. More importantly, who the hell are you? You've certainly come from nowhere near Australia!'

151

Three guards appeared from the other direction, giving Phil a full court press. He held his hands up, and then indicated the imminent use of his phone. 'Let me put you on to someone to explain.'

At the Pentagram Centre, Tony was trying to get comfortable, ready for Vernon's audio-visual extravaganza, which he had been reliably informed would "blow your mind". A large projection screen was lowering itself from the ceiling, steadily and methodically. The lights were dimmed.

Tony's phone bellowed its ringtone, something which caused Vernon to tut with indignation. Tony looked to see who was calling. 'Sorry, must take this.'

Back at Belmarsh, the guards were uncomfortable with allowing this intruder to make a call. They had collectively remembered a training course, which had told them to proceed with caution so far as the use of phones was concerned. They could be used to remotely detonate explosives. As a consequence they were ever so slowly closing in on Phil.

'Hello Phil, what is it?' asked Tony on the other end of the line.

'Tony, I'm at Belmarsh. Can you have a word with the maitre d' and vouch for me?' Without waiting for the reply, Phil offered the phone to Morris, who took hold of it very timidly. Morris admired the receiver before putting it to his ear.

'Hello?' he said, with some hesitation. Phil watched the look on the guard's face change as he realised who he was listening to. 'Yes, Deputy Prime Minister,' he began, managing to get a word in edgeways. He clearly accepted he was speaking to the second in command of the UK. 'Oh no, Sir, not at all,' he offered, deciding the credentials were legitimate. 'Yes, we will of course offer Mister Conway every assistance. And thank you, sir.'

Morris handed the phone back to Phil, who looked at Morris with disdain. 'Are you sure you don't want to call him back at Downing Street, to make sure he is who he says he is?' Phil enquired. He gambled there would be no such action taken, as there might be a problem in getting the support staff to forward the call to Tony. Morris sheepishly shook his head.

'Afraid it's bad news,' informed Phil to Tony. 'Looks like our assassin has been murdered.' There was silence at the other end of the line. 'Something doesn't add up, so I'll be here a while.' Phil explained the problem to his crowd of onlookers. 'He was out of his cell, no-one around, looks like at least three of them took him out.' Phil frowned at all four prison officers now lined up in front of him. They weren't exactly pro-active. He spoke again to Tony. 'Yes, leave it with me.' With that he concluded the call. 'Well gentlemen, and lady,' he addressed his audience, 'this is going to be a long night.'

* * *

At the Pentagram Centre, Tony informed Bonnie of what had gone down. Vernon was too pre-occupied in amending his presentation to make sure it was sufficiently persuasive. Tony turned to Vernon, time at a premium, knowing he had much to do back at base.

'Okay Vernon, who's in the team?' he asked, knowing his day couldn't get much worse. Vernon pushed a button on the control desk, and a large projection screen lowered itself from the ceiling. From within a control desk drawer, Vernon pulled out a set of folders, just as the projector on the ceiling above their heads powered up. He picked up the first folder on the pile, paused, and dramatically threw it over his shoulder. He then presented the contents of the other three to Tony.

'Well, these are my remaining three choices,' Vernon stated, hesitantly. Both of his audience were surprised to hear the hint of him being on the back foot.

Tony realised what the significance of the discarded folder was. 'Bonnie is critical to our success,' he noted, realising Vernon was effectively throwing a crew member out of his pram.

Vernon looked at Bonnie in inquisition mode. 'I take it you're comfortable with replacing the top neurosurgeon outside of mainstream medicine?'

Bonnie wasn't daunted. 'I specialised more on natural medicines than specific organs.'

'Good. Means you haven't been compromised by pharmaceutical "quackery".'

Tony opened the top folder on the pile in front of him. He sniffed, unimpressed. 'You've got to be kidding.'

'Not known for it,' chided Vernon, at which point he handed Tony and Bonnie their own pairs of 3D-glasses, before putting a pair on himself. Vernon waved his arm towards the screen, demanding undivided attention. In front of the onlookers was a full length image of a petite, lithe, dark-skinned lady, encased in a jumpsuit and sensible ankle boots, the look crowned with a bubble-perm. She placed her hands on her hips and looked down on those watching. Tony was hoping what followed was not going to be accompanied by a deep-toned Hollywood promo voiceover. He was underwhelmed when that was exactly what they got.

'Meet Solange Morrison,' the voice implored. 'Twenty-nine years old, empathic, a strategist and motivator.' Illustrating these words was a series of television clips, the first with her on the sofa of a breakfast television set, illustrating her powers of "healing with hands" on a middle-aged spinster in a wheelchair. Shaking ever so slightly, the patient suddenly rises, and walks, to the applause of the presenters sitting next to Solange.

The voice boomed out again. 'Her natural empathy means she can work out what is on the minds of those around her.' The showreel then projected a scene of her holding hands with participants, around a faded Ouija board in a darkened room. As the camera pulled out, the image was revealed to be a set on a large stage, with an expectant audience looking on. 'She can second-guess and advise what is best,' explained the narrator. 'At one time a medium, she worked in the media, and on tours designed to connect the living with those who had passed over.'

Backing music rose to a crescendo and pounded out, like an expectant heartbeat, as a frail woman in the audience stood up to ask about a recently departed relative. Solange frowned and was shaking as if this was a particularly difficult connection to the spirit world.

The image on screen crackled and smashed, to be replaced by a newspaper headline: "Fraud on a Ouija Board".

'A crank!' bawled Tony, as the screen filled with images of Solange defending herself against irate presenters on a daytime television show.

Vernon gave Tony what he hoped was good news. 'Having been so discredited, no-one is likely to miss her.' Tony and Bonnie were still staring at the screen. Bonnie was circumspect about her potential fellow team member. Tony folded his arms in unguarded annoyance. Vernon had another go at overcoming objections. 'Take into account who called her a crank. The very same mainstream media which tried to deflect the rise of "We The People".'

Bonnie realised only too well why this was a tough sell. 'That TV special where she tried to contact the spirit of Michael Jackson. It was a little bit…'

'Over the top?' jumped in Tony.

'Yes. That'll do,' Bonnie declared, unable to stifle a giggle.

Vernon was now even more tetchy. 'Moving on, or we'll be here all night,' he suggested. Tony turned to the second folder, and the contents caused him to very gently shake his head.

The booming narration began again. 'Walton Valentine, fifty-four years old, a former political party leader, gracious and engendering trust in all those around him.' The dialogue was accompanied by images of the slight, 5' 8" tall Walton on an election campaign trail, pressing-the-flesh at a factory, with a bright yellow and green rosette on his heavy coat, all topped off with a slightly oversized hard hat.

The incidental music heightened, as the politician was seen to be put on the spot, sweating profusely in a television interview, a gratuitous grilling by a much younger Zena Carsley. She decried him enough to build his rage so much that he unplugged his microphone from his tie, and stormed out. The screen then crashed into another set of images, where he was being interviewed outside the Houses of Parliament, before getting a bucket of Monopoly board game money poured over his head by a protestor. The music turned morose as Walton made his resignation speech in the House of Commons.

Tony tried to be speechless, but instead found himself despairing. 'You've picked these clowns just to wind me up!'

Vernon again made light of the situation. 'You ought to have seen my first choices.'

Bonnie wasn't sure what the fuss was about. 'Who's this?'

'Walton Valentine. A disgraced ex-politician,' explained Vernon.

The information helped Bonnie enormously, as the penny then dropped. 'That's what he looks like!'

Tony filled in the picture. 'Changed sides. Could have been a strong force in the independent movement. Got completely wrapped up in the left-right paradigm.'

'My father told me Walton was infiltrating both sides,' Bonnie informed. 'He would then be in a position to reveal both camps were working for the same master.'

Tony lifted up his 3D-glasses so they rested on his brow, and looked at Bonnie. 'Material for his biography?'

'You bet'cha,' she beamed.

Tony wondered if there was more to tell. 'And the expenses scandal?'

'Yes,' she confirmed, 'he was set up.'

Vernon doted as if Bonnie had become his star pupil, and turned his chutzpah to Tony. 'Not as tainted as you thought. If you want political finesse, Walton's your man.' Tony frowned, which acted as the cue for Vernon to press a button to move on to the final presentation.

'Jack Callahan…' chimed the Hollywood voiceover. 'Thirty-three years old, a persuasive ex-union leader.' The footage revealed the buzz-cut square jawed six-footer marching at the front of a group of workers on strike, all carrying a mix of home-made signs: "save our pensions"; "cutbacks lead to more cutbacks"; "you don't know what you're doing"; "after you with the austerity".

The narration played out again. 'A firebrand in his days of power, most renowned for his passion and fairness. He has the ability to do the right thing in tough situations.' The images changed to those of a union meeting, with Jack on stage at a lectern, middle aged women as his audience, showing them passion without anger. Another image sequence revealed him shaking hands with foreign dignitaries, in the fastest roll call ever seen. Amongst those that were made out in their split seconds of exposure were the likes of Kofi Annan, Ron Paul, and Vladimir Putin.

'Just what we need,' concluded Tony, now getting like a vinyl record stuck in a groove. 'Leon Trotsky's bastard child.'

This was easy pickings for Vernon. 'You're still believing the mainstream press, aren't you?'

The comment made Tony double-back. 'Thought he disappeared off the face of the Earth? Tail between his legs?' In response, Vernon took off his 3D-glasses, which was the cue for Bonnie and Tony to do the same.

'He retired from public life to look after his terminally ill wife,' Vernon informed. That was the cue for Tony to look sheepish.

'I didn't know that.' He nervously checked his finger nails.

Bonnie needed some detail. 'What was it?'

'Massive stroke,' Vernon advised. 'That's the one proviso to secure Jack's involvement.'

'Someone with his charm doesn't come cheap,' concluded Tony, picking up the wrong end of the stick.

'That's not it,' Vernon squawked. 'He wants "Ray" to visit his wife once a week. Jack's, that is. Until we're in-the-clear.'

'Not too demanding,' thought Bonnie, who couldn't see this being a deal-breaker.

Tony was convinced by Bonnie being convinced. 'Fair enough.'

Bonnie was thinking through the necessary back story. 'Bound to be reasons we can use for those visits.'

Tony smelled the cooking of principles once more. 'Here we go again,' he barked. 'I was trying to keep us from concealing stuff from the public.'

Vernon laughed at the hypocrisy. 'You're way down that slippery slope now, chap.' Tony didn't really want this to be pointed out. Again, Bonnie saw it necessary to bring Tony to heel and get him to focus.

'Can you cope with this team?' she asked.

Tony had to stop himself biting his nails. 'None of them will be missed much,' he concluded. Turning to Vernon, he asked what he hoped was a stupid question. 'I assume team profiling suggests they will work well together?'

'Like a dream,' Vernon almost whispered, in as reassuring a way as he could.

Slapping his hands together, Tony jumped out of his chair and declared, 'I'm in. You'll make arrangements?' he enquired, realising time was of the essence.

'Sorted,' Vernon confirmed. 'They're on their way.'

Tony should have realised there was no way to stop what had become inevitable. 'Cocky little bugger, aren't you?'

Vernon felt the need to describe his strategy. 'It's a game of chess. I sort-of had you down as the Queen…' he lushed, half-pretending he hadn't meant a double-meaning, 'but in a good way.'

* * *

The mainstream media were desperate for news of Ray's condition. As they weren't on speaking teams with the government, and Ray had taken a hatchet to the cosy relationship between the Westminster media contacts and government officials, they were effectively starved of information, and their audiences had shrunk as a result.

The only ones now tuning in to them were those who were not "internet savvy". And those who preferred to be told how they should interpret the stories put in front of them. Plus those poor souls who were still in a state of denial, that the hundreds of years-old two and three party system had betrayed them.

Georgie had talked through with Ray how they would feed out the truth. The preference for this new administration was to channel their messages directly to the world via the Number 10 website, and their own internet television channel. ATVOD, some self-serving "Authority" put in place to shield the world from a spate of unregulated "Video On Demand" services wanted to get in on the act. As soon as this "Authority" heard of the service getting up and running, they sent a letter to Number 10 demanding a licence fee. Ray had them shut down immediately. For several months, ATVOD had been demanding unreasonable chunks of cash from anyone daring to put out alternative points of view on YouTube and other video services, suggesting they were making "television-like programming". In one swift flick of the pen on a fast-track Act of Parliament, they were no more. Ray saw ATVOD for what it was – just another foundation stone in the censorship agenda.

The space freed up in Downing Street, by letting so many of the spin doctors go, allowed such broadcast facilities to become very much "in house". A sleight-of-hand had helped them get a channel number allocated to them on the Sky television network, too. Of course, the big problem was how the mainstream news media portrayed this, attempting to demonise the service as nothing more than propaganda.

This was why those in Ray's inner circle were keen to work with Truth Media Television. Within days of the election victory, the station had been the subject of a buy-out attempt. No-one was quite sure who the consortium was behind the bid, but the money being tabled was almost off-the-scale. Luckily, behind the scenes of the station, there was an anonymous figurehead, independently wealthy and no fan of the previous political parties who had no need, or desire, to sell. They had famously stood up against ATVOD months previously, which is what had brought the nefarious "Authority" to Ray's attention.

Ray knew who their anonymous benefactor was, but insisted on keeping it confidential from everyone. What they didn't know wouldn't hurt them. Georgie had decided to feed them an exclusive, which would no doubt be picked up and distorted by the dinosaur press. Luckily, enough people were discerning in their interpretations to ensure the party line would float to the surface of the mud created by those now in the gutter.

In the Operations Room at 10 Downing Street, Georgie decided to tune in and see how they pitched the information. She saw the news credits roll, supplemented by a bombastic news jingle. She would have a polite word about that music, it made them seem far too mainstream, and their unique selling point was that they didn't handle things the same way as the more established channels. It was advice only, best intentions and all that, but she hoped they would take it on-board.

The image switched to Truth TV's newsroom set, now in more spacious premises. Success had brought more advertisers and sponsors to the channel. Previously, that had been a difficult task, as Ofcom had been very hostile to alternative news and current affairs shows getting such support. That was another plank of legislation which was quickly amended in the "We the People" first hundred days in power.

Thankfully, Tina hadn't changed. She was still the queen of the goths, although Georgie wondered if she realised how much she was a fantasy for the sadomasochists in her viewing audience. Georgie admired her ability to memorise scripts, never needing an autocue, despite one always rolling through her words in the studio beneath her main close-up camera.

'Ray Grady regained consciousness last night, after the attempt on his life.' Tina's expression was a mix of relief and ongoing concern. 'He is expected to make a complete recovery. The nation can breathe a sigh of relief.' Tina decided to get a little stern with her viewers. 'He will ensure all his manifesto plans continue to be taken forward, although it will be a couple of weeks before he is fully back in harness.'

She switched her gaze to another camera, to her side, and the vision mixer followed her cue. 'Later on we will be looking at some foreign news, as new American President Harry Stanton has succeeded in overturning The Patriot Act, the legal statute which was as much about patriotism as Tony Blair was suitable to be a peace envoy.'

Tina put a finger to her ear to ensure she heard the message from the programme director correctly. 'We now have some live pictures from outside the hospital where Ray Grady is recuperating.'

The monitor in front of Tina revealed the scene to her, and was soon being piped through to those watching the show. Alicia, and children Alison and Ryan, were seen to be turned away by two policemen from the gated hospital doors. Back in the Operations Room, Georgie nodded her approval.

It was a covert masterstroke to have everyone thinking Ray was in one place when he was actually somewhere else. It was a little bit of a cheek to ask Alicia and the kids to be nothing more than props, enhancing the storyline, but luckily they pulled off looking pragmatic and jovial. Alicia understood why this was necessary for Ray's security, so was happy to go along with it.

'As a precaution, to avoid infection, the family and other visitors are being kept away,' Tina informed over the images being played out. 'Doctors do not deny that this was very much a life-threatening incident, and the risk of subsequent infection cannot be underplayed.'

The images quickly changed again, as the audience was whisked away to outside the Houses of Parliament. Tony, accompanied by Dawn, was seen waving to photographers and an assembled crowd, as they made their way into the Westminster hub. 'In the meantime, we will be in the capable hands of Chancellor Tony Pearce,' Tina enthused, 'who also has the role of Deputy Prime Minister.'

Tina was back at the centre of the picture being broadcast, and had a wry smile on her face. 'But there's no need to fear another "Tony" being in charge of the UK!'

* * *

The other outlet which was onside to the government, and getting the oxygen of inside tracks and scoops, was *News First*, surprisingly still in the hands of old-school newspaper baron Leonard White. Its circulation in the last one hundred days had recovered considerably. Not only did its base of loyal readers expand, as it was the only paper which had nailed its colours to the "We the People" mast, but everyone else who wanted to know what was really going on knew they had to pick up a copy off the newsstands.

White had always aggressively opposed putting the contents of his newspaper online, and their web presence simply acted as a shop window for the hard-copy version. With advertising revenues going through the roof, White even cut the price of the paper. Getting people to pay 20p a copy was simply tokenism, but was very much in line with his philosophy that people didn't value anything that they were given for nothing. On the London Underground, the free papers were no longer picked up, and those wanting their news "fix" preferred to contribute towards the *News First* empire.

It was a matter of just over a month before a second title *News Final* was launched, and cleaned up in the evening market for the capital. Leonard White had taken a gamble, by betting on the people of Britain no longer being content to vote for the parties that had become the political "Punch and Judy" show. The fact "We the People" echoed his own beliefs about the party system having become a cartel, where nothing would ever change, was a bonus.

Ray's aggressive manifesto towards reinstating freedom of the press was actually seen by many in the mainstream as counter-productive. Leveson's "enquiry" had been revealed by "We the People" as the Trojan-horse it had long been suspected of being.

The mainstream struggled to comprehend why the new government would once again give them the power to say what they wanted, about whoever they wanted, when many of their principal targets were going to be the "We the People" movement and anyone who supported it. It was a crazy stance to be taken by these hacks, as if they really liked being neutered. Ray had pointed this out in an exclusive interview given to *News First*, also noting that if any news story was proven to be wrong, then the paper's apology and retraction would have to be as big and as prominent as the original splash. No more hiding the "mistake" within the adult phone line classifieds and the horse racing results.

Ray also slammed into the recent statute where journalists and bloggers, when taken to court for the tort of libel, and regardless of the outcome, would see the defending author have to pay both the prosecution costs and their own defence costs. That recent legislation was immediately over-turned for being "nonsense", as Ray described it.

This exclusive was pure gold for *News First*, and the veil was removed as to the truth of how the world worked for some of the most hardened Labour and Tory supporters. Even Liberal Democrats, who were desperate to paint "We the People" as a tool of the far right, simply couldn't get any traction for their views. Adding to their toothless performance in the coalition government the almost total disappearance of their card-carrying membership, and the entire party was left on the verge of bankruptcy.

The Westminster press corps was starved of their exclusives, provided by the spin doctors who were no longer in residence, and as a consequence had nothing to write about. They had to rely entirely on the very thin groove of opposition MPs who would try and feed their mutual need to stay relevant, with allegations of what might be going on behind-the-scenes.

Aside from this meagre bunch of withered vines, they could only report on the scorecard of legislation and angles as provided to them by the government themselves. It would all come direct from Georgie, on a mass briefing given to all outlets at the same time, two mornings a week, once on a Monday, and once on a Friday. The technique came from best practice initiatives as were the norm in big companies. Everyone got to hear the information at the same time, and all the journalists came away with the same party line.

The job of the journalists was to put their own emphasis on the news stories, meaning they only succeeded by finding a way to add value to what they had already been given. "Acting like proper journalists for once" was how Ray cynically described it. If they told a lie, then their opposition titles would be briefed as to what they had got wrong by Georgie, and they themselves would become the targets, and admonished for not being any good at their jobs.

It instantly became a very pragmatic way for the media to police themselves. They kept each other in order, knowing that Georgie the sheepdog's role was to act as whistleblower, giving rival titles the dirt on the paper which had tried to ferment a slur.

If it didn't come from Georgie, it wasn't official, and any alternative lines were easily exploded by showing that it came from someone with an axe to grind. And that was usually from an opposing party or a corporate interest unhappy with the way their lobbying work had been excised with the change of government. And with all sorts of Acts of Parliament happening so quickly, and others being repealed, they had no time to complain or mount any rearguard action.

The only chance the mainstream seemed to have to generate anything news-worthy that would sell papers, or gain listeners or viewers, was to try and target those supportive of "We the People", one by one. It should have come as no surprise that Leonard White was someone who would be in their cross-hairs.

Without Ray intervening, White's extradition to the United States had been cancelled. Others had been returned to British soil that had "disappeared" from the public eye for some time. There were pardons for the likes of Gary McKinnon, who had Asberger's syndrome, once well-known as the computer geek who hacked into the Pentagon's systems and had found their secret reports on UFOs.

The official line from Georgie was that this was heralding a new era in pan-Atlantic relations. The mainstream media assumed Ray must have been involved in the decision. They never took into account this was an action by the new American President, with a different way of doing things and his own supporters to please. There was no doubt he was determined to put the "special relationship" on a more equal footing.

After all, as Ray had famously noted in what was a front-page splash, American had seen the UK as its "bitch" for far too long.

When Leonard White received a personal summons from reporter Zena Carsley, he was of course intrigued. She insisted it would be in his best interests to speak to her before the following morning.

White chose the Punch Tavern on Fleet Street as a venue. It appealed to his sense of humour, and also gave him an excuse to sample some of their prized fish and chips once more. The dark oak panelling, ornate fireplace and marble bar gave the place a sense of history. A series of original Punch-and-Judy themed paintings from 1897 ratcheted up the irony which he wanted to get across to his inquisitor.

White was on his final mouthful of beer-battered haddock when Zena appeared. Dark glasses, a 1960's cloche hat and leather jacket unfortunately had the opposite effect to what she was looking for. She was readily drawing attention to herself.

White stood up and offered her his hand, which she ignored. She sat down, and he retook his place at the table opposite her.

'I hear you're going to be off to America soon?' she gloated.

White picked up one of the remaining thick-cut chips and bit through it with relish. 'Why on Earth would you think that,' he said, almost slurping on the chip, 'my dear,' he added with a smack of his lips.

'Your friend, the American President, might be watching your back but his Attorney General sees things differently.'

White chuckled. 'And what makes you think I know the President? He was virtually unknown until about a year ago.'

Zena was concerned her opening gambit didn't seem to be worrying White at all. 'You cannot expect Ray Grady to protect you now. He will have other priorities, even if he does continue as Prime Minister.'

White signalled a waitress to get the bill. 'First off, as Ray hasn't done anything to protect me, you're going to be very foolish making baseless accusations. Secondly, even if the UK has an about-turn on not deporting me, such possibilities will soon change.' He could tell Zena wasn't following his line. 'Surely you've looked at the scorecard from Number 10 for the next week?'

Zena stared blankly. She let other people look at such minutiae for her. The scorecard was a grid which Ray and Georgie used to plan which news would be their main focus each day, allowing messages on every area of policy to be clearly communicated. It would mean the public knew exactly how the "We the People" manifesto was being enacted. It came from an idea introduced by a previous Labour Government, except back then what took a year to roll out was now done in a week.

'Okay, let me tell you what happens in the next few days,' said White, as if he was a teacher who had caught a pupil staring out of the window. 'The government will overturn The Extradition Act of 2003. At that point, anyone in the UK who finds proceedings taken up against them by the Americans, or anyone else for that matter, will have recourse. They will be able to have their lawyers cross-examine the alleged evidence or allegations made against them by the authorities.' The waitress arrived with the bill. 'Now that's what I call fairness, and you really cannot build any sort of story around that.'

White gave his full attention to paying the bill. As part of the "We the People" initiative to get people off credit and back to paying with cash, there was now an incentive to use paper money, in the shape of a credit tax applied to all card payments. White was fishing around in his pocket for his wallet to unleash the relevant folded notes. He wasn't going to be searching for coinage, as he considered it poor form not to give a reasonable tip.

While White was distracted by this housekeeping, Zena had just the necessary few seconds to drop a colourless capsule into his three-quarter-downed pint of real ale. Her deception was assisted by White insisting on drinking from an opaque pewter tankard, which he left at the pub for safe keeping.

The waitress left the table with a smile, finished plate in hand, enough money for her own meal later squirreled away in her pocket. 'Anything else?' White enquired. By Zena's non-response, he concluded all potential rugs had been pulled from under her. He got up to leave.

'Aren't you going to finish your drink?' she urgently begged.

'I'm afraid the atmosphere in here has gone very chilly,' he remarked. 'Besides, whilst the Old Speckled Hen is remarkable, I'm afraid it's not good for my digestion.' He put his coat on, which had been over the back of his chair. 'However, if you are stopping, don't miss the chance to try their fish and chips. Award winning, you know.'

The irony of an American recommending a British national dish to her, well, that thundered through her head all the way home. She'd been dismissed like an intern, and started to wonder how far she would have got in her journalism career without considerable help.

She had wanted to be famous, but couldn't lower herself to appearing on "reality" television. She traded off having been used by men, and the odd woman, with how they had assisted her in climbing the ladder of celebrity. As she admired her queen-sized water bed in her generous apartment, covered in the finest black silk sheets, she decided her playground of choice was far better than the tried-and-trusted casting couch.

Part of her really admired those who had got to the top of their chosen careers just with their own talent and skills. But the evil spirit on the other shoulder reminded her of those who were much better than her and had to take on dead-end jobs to survive. Any of them really deserved to be where she was now. But doubts about her sometimes-demeaning necessity for progress, and often parasitic behaviour, soon evaporated as she admired her home.

Later that night, after her partner of the evening had satisfied his desires, clinging on grimly beneath her vigorous impaled body, she rolled off, staring across his torso at the window.

For once, the Leader of the Opposition, Duncan Hurst, sensed just a little remorse within her. He frowned at the potential for trouble this might signal. 'Don't worry, there'll be other stories.'

Zena laughed scornfully. 'What? From you? You can't even get into their inner circle when Grady's out of the way!'

Hurst didn't want to be defensive, but had little choice. 'With or without Grady, they can't control the policy narrative like this for much longer.'

'You twat,' hectored Zena. 'You will not catch them out as they are telling the truth about everything.'

'I'm sure that will change,' begged Hurst. 'At some point, something will happen which will see them have to tell a little lie. They are still in their honeymoon period. It's just unfortunate Grady's little accident had the reverse effect to what we expected.'

Zena gulped as she appreciated the type of people her success relied on. If she had ever thought of it before, she had put it to the back of her mind. 'What was in that capsule tonight?'

'I genuinely have no idea,' Hurst replied, holding eye contact with her to emphasise his point.

'And you had something to do with Grady getting a bullet?' Zena asked, albeit uncomfortably. Sometimes, things are better left unsaid.

Hurst bounced up from the bed and began to dress. 'Of course not,' he raged. 'That would be the equivalent of staging a coup. They might have got away with that in the States, when they took out Kennedy in 1963, but this is Britain. The people here tend to see through contract killings, even if they aren't in broad daylight with the entire country looking on.'

He had got to the point in dressing where he was straightening his tie. 'Take that royal murder. They could only keep the lid on that for just over fifteen years, before the majority of Brits realised the truth.' He slipped his shoes on. 'I am sure they had no idea the size of the genie they were letting out of the bottle.'

With that, Hurst put on his jacket and stormed out, the front door flapping on its hinges as he slammed it behind him. Suddenly, Zena's mobile phone rang, and she looked at the caller I.D. on the screen. She gazed upwards to the top left corner of the ceiling in her bedroom, and waved a greeting.

Damian always liked her "floor shows", and appreciated the blackmail value of her dalliances. He would no doubt say to her that he looked forward to entertaining her when she was next on a holiday break. Some things about his priorities were disturbingly predictable. She knew only too well how that would pan out, and what she would need to do to keep her job and the accompanying high profile.

Things were once again going to get very painful for her. Quite literally.

11

INSERTION DAY

Bonnie still couldn't help being in awe. Who wouldn't be with the technology Pentagram had at its fingertips? Vernon might well be a card-carrying genius, but she couldn't fathom why he had problems being likable with it. Driven by a desire to succeed, it wasn't fame he was after, which was the only note of humbleness that chimed with Bonnie. He wanted to build his achievements ever-higher, just for the surprise of what might then follow.

She had switched off during Vernon's latest briefing about the mechanics of what she was embroiled with. It was a merciful break when the lesson was interrupted by the arrival of the other recruits.

Jack, Solange, and Walton entered the room from the entrance corridor. Bonnie had memorised first names from the copious notes she had been supplied with, alongside a general idea of their roles on the mission. Jack looked like he'd been airlifted off a mountaintop, windswept hair and a cumbersome backpack in hand.

Solange had gone for a trouser-suit, her black perm looking like it was welded to its collar. That walk of hers betrayed the strength in her lower body; the suitcase on wheels in the wake behind her simply glided over the floor. Walton, however, was put to shame; the travel bag over his shoulder weighed heavily on his frame. As he took in the harmonic motion of the lady in front, he made a note to make more of that gym membership he had been bullied into taking up.

'Vernon Snow!' The exclamation from Jack was unnecessarily bombastic, instantly breaking up any hope of further tutorage for Bonnie. 'Have you been getting in people's heads again?' he quizzed, almost chiding the scientist. Vernon got up resolutely to shake Jack's hand.

'And now you're going to get in someone else's,' Vernon sniggered. Bonnie joined the gathering, and Walton found himself smitten for the second time in a minute.

'Walton Valentine,' he gushed, introducing himself, shaking Bonnie's hand for a little bit too long. 'You must be our replacement team member?'

Bonnie had a piece of the jigsaw missing. 'You've worked together before?'

Walton was a little puzzled by such a statement, and nervously looked Vernon in the eye. 'You've not told her?'

'Need-to-know basis,' he replied, quickly trying to move the conversation forward. Solange provided the much-needed distraction when she looked across the room, recognising who it was on the treatment table. It broke up the formalities of further introductions. She hurried over, her attention caught by the rigid plaster now covering the head-shot wound. Jack and Vernon followed her, almost skipping with enthusiasm.

'That's not who I think it is?' Solange enquired, knowing full well that it was.

'Almost certainly,' Vernon guessed.

Jack let out a short, staccato whistle. 'No wonder you had the backing to try this again.'

Bonnie was still not keen to let Vernon off the hook. 'What is it you're not telling me?'

'Prototypes,' Vernon confirmed brusquely. 'Helped us fine-tune things.'

Bonnie was unimpressed by the down-selling of what had gone on before. 'It didn't have a happy ending?'

Vernon squirmed. 'Well, I wouldn't say that... necessarily.'

Jack, Walton and Solange remained transfixed by Ray's motionless body. Walton was first to break the silence. 'I thought it might have been him.'

Jack was completing the puzzle in his head, one ever-present since he had the call from Vernon. 'Who else would be important enough to fast-track us back into action?'

Walton could always make a crisis out of a diversion. 'Makes things a bit difficult. Not sure I agree with his politics.'

Solange was surprised at his short-sightedness. 'Now's your chance to have an influence on that.' She couldn't believe that Walton was unable to see the bigger picture.

'Literally,' commended Vernon, 'you can be the man on-the-inside.'

Bonnie wasn't keen on what she was hearing. 'Be aware I'll be defending my father's ideology.'

'Your father?' muttered Walton, feeling the need to look down at his feet. 'I didn't know.' He tried to commiserate and back-track simultaneously, which just made him sound feeble.

'And you…' Jack intoned to Bonnie, 'literally, our inside-track.'

Bonnie felt the need to state her agenda. 'I'm doing this to keep his dream alive.'

'Creepy,' blurted Solange, immediately realising her comment might be taken the wrong way. 'Don't you find this all a little bit… Oedipal?'

Bonnie wondered how someone with a talent for empathy would come up with such a blunt question. 'Never entered my mind,' she snapped, before it dawned on her that perhaps she was being tested, 'until now.'

'The gang's all here,' Vernon enthused, a sense of urgency now pervading the room. 'Let's suit-up.'

* * *

Zena Carsley's ratings had taken another hammering. Despite her public relations people working overtime to get some "upbeat profiling" as they described it, the more they tried the more they lost ground. The latest features about her in women's magazines had come across badly. The readership didn't buy that she had worked hard to get to where she was. The tales of privileged upbringing, leaked by Number 10, had put her in her place.

"Her" show was being starved of exclusives of any kind, and the production team found themselves having to do their own take on stories covered elsewhere. Pressure to perform was beginning to show, and the studio was not a nice place to be. The lights seemed to be brighter than usual. Hotter. As the music of the opening titles faded, she felt her throat dry up.

'Ray Grady is still fighting for his life,' she began, worry lines forming to the side of her eyes. 'Although recent reports suggest that he has managed a few words to his inner circle of overpaid civil service consultants.'

Having been unable to get usable footage at the dummy hospital, let alone even know about the real one, the news team had raided the archives. They had plundered stock footage from a couple of years previously. Zena spoke over grainy images of a younger Alicia Grady walking up a London street to the front door of a salubrious building. Her hair styling was a lot different to the here-and-now, much more cascading and bubbly. She was looking concerned at the attentions of a small band of paparazzi, even back then trying to secure a scoop of a picture. Daughter Alison, then just aged five, walked as petulantly as her frame allowed, and baby Ryan, aged three, was confined to Alicia's arms.

The glimpses were brief, but anyone paying any sort of attention would have realised the archive nature of the pictures. The trio were upset at something, and were not in the mood to be harangued. Zena then tried to add a new context to these old images. 'However, Grady's situation remains grave. The Prime Minister's wife, Alicia, and their children, are deliberately being kept away from seeing their husband and father.'

Zena pulled on her metaphorical hobnail boots. 'This almost-fascistic approach, in excluding close family members from visiting a relative, raises concerns about those handling such matters.'

Without giving her viewers enough time to process what was being manufactured before them, the studio gallery moved the show on, and Zena now had a picture of Tony Pearce behind her, yet another shot from the archives. It showed him with a champagne saucer-glass in-hand.

'Questions remain as to the suitability of Tony Pearce, currently filling in as Prime Minister.' The picture behind Zena then changed to one of Tony with unbridled anger warping his face. 'A failed parliamentary lobbyist, he dropped out to become a farmer. Many doubted his sanity when he took a violent confrontational stand against G.M. Crops. His attitude to such super-foods raises serious doubts as to his ability to govern.'

Audience research over the subsequent days was not something which was going to be beneficial to Zena's future prospects. It confirmed none of those watching took anything she said seriously. She had been relegated to nothing more than "eye candy" for the older man, and a study in fashion misfires for the younger woman. If she was a man, she would be described as impotent. Even her regular studio "talking heads" began distancing themselves from her.

She was going to need serious help to recapture the credentials needed to stand in the limelight again.

* * *

At mission control, the Pentagram quintet had changed into matching apparel. Vernon wasn't sure whether he'd taken the clothing influences from the movie *Forbidden Planet* or the original version of *The Italian Job*. Either way, the light blue material was a halfway point between the shade of blue-gray and navy blue which the outfits in those films were known for. All the team would have preferred something a little less regimented, but they decided to humour the man who had brought them together. The men referred to them as "boiler overalls", the ladies as "jump suits". Everyone agreed they were both lightweight and hard wearing. Luckily, Jack had talked Vernon out of his desire for them to have matching baseball caps.

Vernon did get his way on the matching travel bags. Space was at a premium in the capsule, and weight was an issue in his overall calculations. He'd chuckled at the architects who had built new shopping complexes on flood plains, but hadn't accounted for the weight of stock and human beings into their equations. They'd eventually been hit by as big a sinking feeling as their own colossal structures.

Vernon wasn't all authoritarian. The team would be allowed to relax in some of their own clothing of choice, as long as they had it high-tech dry-cleaned before going aboard, to avoid possible infection risks.

The less said about the steam showers they had to endure before suiting-up the better. It was a way of removing their entire outer layer of skin, a process masochists would no doubt have enjoyed.

Even Ray, despite his circumstances, had been given the once-over. He was in white coveralls, and his head-wound had been once more exposed to the air, bandage removed with no signs of further bleeding, despite the gaping hole. The air's oxygen content had been increased within the room.

Bonnie looked around to see a trio of anonymous masked surgeons going through their preliminaries at the control desk. For some reason she thought better of asking who they were.

With a nod from Vernon, Jack stepped up to the plate. 'Ready, team?'

Bonnie suddenly clicked in terms of the roles that had been assigned. 'You're in charge, then?'

Jack nodded. 'Vernon just presses the buttons. Someone has to make the final decisions.'

Vernon could understand Bonnie being confused, even though she actually wasn't. 'Team dynamics. You'll listen to Jack in a crisis, but not necessarily me.'

Solange had heard it all before. 'As you're so keen to remind us.' With that, Jack gave a casual salute to the masked surgeons, who proceeded to run the control desk like Kraftwerk on speed. Jack ushered Vernon, Solange, Bonnie and Walton towards the huge bay doors on the opposite side of the room, which began to make a deafening hum.

The gap being created was large enough to drive half a dozen double-decker buses through, side by side. Only Bonnie was awestruck by the sight that was befalling them. She saw this was "business as usual" for the others, and as a consequence tried to act cool. She didn't succeed, due to the scale of what was being presented to her.

Vernon caught Bonnie's eye, attempting to show how blasé he was as to what lay within the aircraft hanger beyond. Bonnie winked at him to catch him out of his stride.

Taking up the centre stage was a rounded-cornered flying saucer of a craft, bristling in chrome, as roving travel spots picked up its contours. Bonnie had to admire Vernon's stage-manager-ship – he obviously liked to impress. Even for five people, this was a generous-sized vehicle.

Bonnie counted the lighting arrays, and smiled when she saw there were five of them. They were effectively in the middle of a pentagram. Satanic symbolism indeed, but she wasn't concerned, as Vernon wasn't the sort of person who would be governed by any such belief systems, positive or negative. That simply wouldn't meld with his scientific sensibilities.

The quintet approached the craft. Away to one side in the hanger, a glass-walled control booth was now occupied by the three masked surgeons. Bonnie was impressed by their stealth in changing their vantage points unnoticed.

'Say hello to our new inclusion-capsule,' Jack enthused to Bonnie.

'Couldn't you have got one in red?' she replied, still trying to underplay her awe.

'Is chrome too clinical?' Vernon asked, having made the mistake of taking her comment seriously. Jack ushered Solange, Bonnie, Walton and Vernon to a podium, directly beneath the middle of the capsule. Within the control booth, the masked surgeons took their Kraftwerk homage into overdrive.

172

The podium elevated up into the belly of the capsule, its floor vibrating in its ascent, a purr of mechanical certainty filling the air. Bonnie shut her eyes for a few seconds, not wanting to admit to her fear of heights. She felt much better when the podium clicked into place in the floor of the capsule, allowing her to open one eye to observe her new surroundings.

They found themselves in the equivalent of an elevator. With perfect timing, the single door in front of them revealed what was beyond. They were at the centre of the back wall of the cockpit of the craft. The five positions were in an arc, so everyone could see each other at the same time, whilst also being able to view a panoramic screen towards the front of the arena. Vernon, Solange and Walton knew which seats were theirs, while Jack took on his command role by pointing Bonnie at the station which was furthest to the left.

'If I were an estate agent, I'd describe this as compact bijou,' Bonnie commented to Jack, who beamed in response. She could see why they were so keen on team dynamics in this set-up, given the cramped work environment. She just hoped her late addition was not going to cause too many issues.

'280 degrees of vision,' Vernon noted to the screen. 'We'll see everything which is captured by Ray's eyes.' Every inch of the layout had been occupied by one piece of kit or another, all with a vital role in what was going to unfold.

'Better than the schematics,' Bonnie remarked.

Jack smirked. 'Technical drawing was never one of Vernon's strong points.' Vernon stared at Jack, who winked in return. Jack took the captain's chair, in the centre of the array. Walton was between Jack and Bonnie, Vernon the other side of Jack, with Solange furthest from Bonnie. A laptop on a podium began to rise in front of Jack from his console, and he logged himself in via the keypad.

'Everyone set?' Vernon enquired, an action deemed not to be a command duty. Everyone nodded in approval. Vernon in turn looked at Jack, who spoke into a microphone attachment on the top of the laptop podium.

'Inclusion capsule ready,' he advised those listening. 'Commence holographic separation.' Outside in the hanger, the five lighting arrays were gradually building up to full power.

They beamed their glow onto the capsule, which began to emit a fluorescent violet luminescence. The masked surgeons looked on, as they watched the bizarre spectacle of the capsule beginning to fold, and fold, and fold in again on itself, shrinking down in size at every action.

Inside the capsule, Bonnie was starting to fray around the edges, her nerves jangling as the viewing screen was filled with an ever-magnifying image of what lay outside. Just like being on a train, when you are aware you are moving but everything remains fairly stable within, the jostling that was felt by the five was of the same magnitude.

Vernon was keeping up with his own personal on-screen data on the miniaturisation, and making corrections as the process began to accelerate. A faint hum, with a little underscore of a kettle whistle reached a crescendo, and then began to claw its way back to normality.

Solange was monitoring the team's stress levels via her screen. She was aware that Bonnie was getting near to hyper-ventilating. Her fellow "old timers" were much more in their stride. Jack was gripping the arms of his seat, as his calmness still didn't stretch to completely trusting this step of the operation.

Walton, meanwhile, had his arms crossed and was looking bored. He was very fatalistic in his view of life these days, and wasn't going to let any new-fangled technology get in the way of that new mantra.

The violet glow was getting more intense as the capsule became smaller and smaller. Hundreds of gradually-shrinking versions of the capsule were seen dancing away from the main beam, into a large silo marked "Holographic Subject Matter". This was a conservation of energy. Matter wasn't being destroyed, it was simply changing form.

And then, suddenly, silence. The original capsule had shrunk so much a casual onlooker might have thought it had completely disappeared. The lighting arrays receded in brightness, and the masked surgeons walked towards what was the centre of the area previously occupied by the full-sized craft.

This was a meticulous operation. The craft rested at the centre of a small, round, golden plate, the type which was no doubt found in ancient Rome at the centre of a banquet table. The ship had become the size of a paracetamol caplet. One of the masked surgeons, the slimmest of the trio, picked the plate up and walked back towards the Recovery Room. He, or she, was careful not to shake or spill the capsule. This was a little over-zealous caution, as the craft had gravitational compensators so that the contents would never be shaken or stirred.

Flanked by the other surgeons, it was now the duty of the head surgeon to insert the capsule into Ray's head wound. The surgeons would then seal them in with some handy "stitching", achieved by some of the finest in laser technology.

At that point, the tricky part of the mechanics of the job would be concluded. It would then be a question of how successful the links with the host brain would be. From past experience, they knew that would be more down to luck than judgement.

* * *

Phil Conway put his foot hard down on the accelerator pedal of the Nissan Juke. He hadn't expected to be occupied for so long at Belmarsh the previous evening. He never had trouble sleeping, regardless of what was occupying his mind, so he had stayed under the covers as long as his morning schedule would allow. He never skipped breakfast. Such a fissure in routine would always catch up with him by early afternoon.

Phil's mind went back to the Pont de l'Alma tunnel in Paris, August 1997. The same thing had happened there. CCTV systems failed, suddenly, in unison. And now, checking the tapes around the time of the murder of Chris Bowden, exactly the same thing had happened at Belmarsh.

Of course, he knew he would be labelled a conspiracy theorist to suggest this "failure" was anything more than coincidence. At best, luck was on the side of the three murderers who had disposed of the "Bowden" problem. Forensics had deemed it was three "perps" to be on the lookout for. It seemed easier to blame it on other prisoners than dig deeper. Phil was more for keeping an open mind as to whom the assassins really were. He wasn't even sold on the idea that there needed to be more than one.

Morris and his superiors at the prison were at a loss to explain how their technology had failed them. This was precisely the sort of incident which the cameras were there to document. When it really mattered, they had all gone missing.

Phil had asked if there was any way to work out who had been near the control systems, especially as recordings started again several minutes after the time the incriminating images should have been captured. The visitor logs revealed nothing suspicious, and none of the prisoners had the means and opportunity to have been involved. Not by the evidence that was to hand, anyhow. Phil always went with his gut instinct in matters such as this. It had to have been an "inside job".

Phil pulled up in one of the official car parks for the House of Commons. It was a perk Ray had sorted for him, and Phil couldn't work out how it hadn't come to the attention of the bloodhounds in the mainstream media. Surely they could easily paint it as a "conflict of interest?" It would be like shooting fish in a barrel. He could only surmise they were too busy hiding their own previous "conflicts of interest" to take shots at those now benefiting in the way they used to.

Phil looked at the range of vehicles on display. Under the previous governments, they would have been far more conformist, sober black or grey colours, functional rather than showing any flair. Now it was a different aspect. The colours were bright, models ranging from vintage to sporty, all a reflection of the more creative mindsets of those who were now running the country.

He made his way along the corridors of power, leather document pouch in hand, passing by various administrators who were dressed in the same style as the cars he'd just been enamoured with. Phil was seeking out one of the House of Commons bars, and eventually found the one he was looking for.

The "Sports and Social" felt more like a traditional pub. A very homely carpet on the floor, real ales from around the country to savour, and there was even a dart board. Luckily this wasn't a Thursday night, as at that point a rather embarrassing karaoke evening was a regular occurrence. Phil, for some reason, straightened himself up before entering, as if he was about to go onstage.

He scanned around the room and eventually saw his quarry, squirreled away in a discrete alcove. Duncan Hurst was trying to hide behind a broadsheet newspaper, its headline: "Grady approval rating soars". Regrettably, the top of Hurst's head was almost unique, and Phil marched over to him. Phil knew this wasn't Hurst's regular haunt, but was grateful for the tip-off. Hurst usually preferred the Pugin Room, with its tea and croissants. However, this way he hoped to hide in plain sight. Not to be.

'Nothing like a good shooting to improve your position in the polls,' Phil remarked. Hurst looked over his paper and grimaced, not so much at what was on the front of his broadsheet, but as to who was reminding him of the bad news.

'So it would seem,' the politician replied.

'You should try it sometime,' Phil suggested, as he sat down.

Hurst was already annoyed at the interruption. 'Is there a point to your visit?'

Phil removed some paper from the file pouch under his arm, and passed it across to Hurst for inspection.

'Some interesting data,' commented Phil, as Hurst tried not to raise an eyebrow at what had been presented. 'Donations that have been coming your way.'

'This is nothing new,' Hurst scoffed, 'as well you know.'

'The allegations are old. The background is new.' Phil pointed Hurst to a particular line on the paper currently at the top of the pile. 'This chunk of dough, as a for-instance. Just a front company. Doesn't exist.'

Hurst pretended to be dense. 'Your point being?'

Phil wasn't keen on this merry dance. 'These days, taking backhanders from pharmaceutical companies is a definite no-no.'

Hurst gave a forced smile of victory. 'I think media interest in that sort of thing is on the wane.'

Phil reclined back in the high-sided armchair. 'They will lose billions when "We the People" removes their ability to patent variants of naturally-based products.' The pause was met with silence. 'Don't say you didn't know that?'

Hurst was sure that playing it cool was still the way to go. 'I may have made representations. The public knows most of the people involved in alternative natural health are nothing more that snake-oil salesmen.'

'That's not the case,' squealed Phil, suddenly on the back foot. It was why he was a journalist, not a politician.

'Tell your mates at Wapping that,' offered Hurst, offhandedly looking for more revelations in Phil's paperwork. 'Besides, "We the People" will soon be ripped apart at the seams, with or without Grady.'

'The party isn't just Ray, as you well know. It's a set of ideas that create a philosophy.' Phil knew that Hurst was well aware of this, but it was time to place him in the cross-hairs of victory. 'You know our Chancellor has brought back The Bradbury Pound.' Phil's words were like garlic to a vampire. 'Just like 1914 all over again. Done in forty-eight hours. Legal tender being printed by the government, not by the banks. Immediately snuffing out all the chaos caused by fractional reserve banking. Money actually backed by something again, even if it is just the credit of the state. And you people have said it was an insoluble problem ever since it came to a head in 2008.' Hurst just shrugged his shoulders. 'Did you like the nice little touch in the design of the notes? Borrowed from the 1914 inspiration. George slaying the dragon. What was the main symbol of the City of London again?'

'It's just another way of cranking up the national debt. They've changed nothing,' balked Hurst.

'But the major difference is that we no longer have bankers raking in loads of interest from their notes. 0% interest on the Bradbury Pound to the economy. And soon, these will be the only notes that remain in circulation. National credit. Issued exclusively for physical production. A promise to society itself, and a fuel to productivity that is not borrowed from private sources.'

'This is New World Order you are fighting,' warned Hurst. 'You have no idea how big the backlash will be around the world. It won't come from governments. It will come from corporations, themselves with their strings pulled by the most powerful families on the planet.' Hurst was suddenly aware there was genuine fear in his tone. 'There's still time to turn back. There really is a better way.'

'For those of you still putting yourselves ahead of the general population, then you have your lifestyles to defend. And no doubt your lives, too. But the tipping point has been reached. Can't you see that? People have had their hypnotic spell broken. They can see you all for what you really are.' There was a hush following Phil's assertive defence of the party. He wasn't being a proper journalist anymore. He was simply unable to try and take in views from both sides, as there was no defence for what had happened in the UK and around the world for centuries.

'People won't be patient enough during the time this is going to take. As soon as there is no food on the table, no water in the tap, no power to keep their lights on, they'll be demanding change again. On the streets. They will take survival over ideology every time.' Hurst had rehearsed that diatribe well. He would no doubt use it the next time he was invited back on television.

Phil was learning not to take these verbal attacks personally. 'Nice speech, but already out of date. All your chums in the energy, water and transport networks, those foreign companies who threatened to withdraw from our shores when "We the People" got into power, funny that none of them have.'

Hurst was beginning to fidget quite chaotically. 'And you know only too well why they haven't. It was outrageous. If any of them had done so, their infrastructure would have been seized, and with no compensation. That's communism,' remarked a very offended Hurst.

'Is it really?' queried Phil. 'I think Ray called it a breach of contract, with a legitimate consideration for such unwillingness to continue to deliver on their obligations. He knew how to appeal to their base instincts. They'll still get their profits, only not so big and with a lawful chunk going back into updating the infrastructure. As it all should have been, right from the beginning.'

'Just you wait until you have to introduce food rationing,' countered Hurst. 'Then you'll see how loyal your population is to an ideology.'

'That's where being British will really come to the fore,' Phil beamed. 'This is a war. A war, as you said, against the corporations. The veil has been lifted, and the population can see what's really going on.' Hurst looked at Phil, an expression which betrayed seeing the reporter as naive. 'Besides which,' Phil continued, not distracted by Hurst's gurning, 'we can get virtually all the food we need from the Commonwealth. We don't need anything from Europe. And just wait until the financial incentives for getting into organic farming kick in.'

Hurst was suddenly keen to change the subject. 'Do you want a tip-off or not?'

'Depends if what you've got is true or not,' Phil scoffed.

Hurst offered up a proverb, 'It doesn't take long for new political forces to be compromised.'

'I think they're doing pretty well at stopping that happening.'

'You've heard of The Bilderberg Group?' Hurst beamed, like a child with a secret.

Phil gave him the equivalent of a Wikipedia entry. 'Diplomats and business leaders. They get together once a year for a jolly.'

Hurst laughed. 'So we're told. Check out their official delegate list for last year. There might be one or two surprises.' Hurst then imperiously threw the paper evidence back at Phil, and got up to leave. 'If you'll excuse me,' he said, as he departed the room.

Phil stared at his documents, miffed that they did not seem to have had any impact. Time would tell as to whether they lit any blue touch-papers or not. With that thought he smiled, and collected the items together. There was money to be lost, and much more to be made, and it would be too magnetic for a player like Hurst. Phil could almost guarantee that.

12

TEST DRIVERS

Walton hated all the waiting. There was little he could do in advance as part of the team. So much of his role was all about reacting to their ever-changing situations. He looked up from his screen to check on the activity around him. Bonnie, Solange and Jack seemed to be in a similar predicament. Everyone was waiting on Vernon.

As was to be expected, Vernon was shifting his attention frenetically, from one control panel to another. Walton was always tempted to suggest to him that he should delegate more, but realised that would be a fruitless pursuit. And Vernon was probably right, so much to teach before even pressing a single button. Maybe in time there would be more trust for the rest of them. As it was, Vernon was indispensable. Walton would find that unacceptable in any other circumstance. He was comforted by having Jack around; he knew that Vernon had the best possible protection.

Walton went back to his internet surfing. He was looking at the patterns of stock prices, between having munches out of a "Marathon" bar. He looked at the wrapper and smiled. That was one of Ray's more eccentric policies, encouraging big manufacturers to turn back to the original British branding on products, with tax incentives to do so. All moving away from the "global-friendly" revisionism they had adopted. The incentive was back-handed, as you might have expected from Ray. If they didn't revise the name, then the government would add Value Added Tax to the items at some 30%. No more "Snickers" bars then. Walton had stashed some "Opal Fruits" for the mission, too.

He was still amazed at how the abolition of Value Added Tax on virtually everything had managed to work. The adoption of the Bradbury Pound principle had improved the balance sheets at a stroke. No more issuing of money by the Bank of England, charged at interest to Corporation UK. With the government now issuing the currency, and not charging itself interest, the figures had temporarily looked very impressive.

That was until the stock markets did their best to rig their barometers against the move. The graphs were now showing that, after a big rise in share values, prices were beginning to slump again.

Walton alerted anyone who might want a distraction. 'Stock rises are beginning to tail off.' This was really important, he thought. 'That will be the leak about Ray making a recovery.'

Walton frowned at the dichotomy. A Prime Minister is elected, stock prices fall. Bradbury Pound implemented, the stock prices rise. World markets gang-up on the London Stock Exchange, prices heavily slump. The Prime Minister is gunned down, stock prices rise.

It was then announced that Ray was making a recovery, and stock prices began to fall back again. The irony wasn't lost on Walton that this was the complete opposite to the situation when such a person in high office normally meets a tragedy. But in most of those cases, it was known the victim was in the pocket of the finance fraternity.

Jack was beginning to get impatient. 'Are we on?' he enquired of Vernon.

'Don't try and rush genius,' he snapped back, his tetchy gene coming to the surface.

'And I cannot rush *you*, either,' muttered Jack, under his breath. Vernon grimaced a false smile, not being quite sure what Jack had said, and flicked the main switch on his systems. In front of them all, the panoramic screen sparked into life again, this time fully calibrated.

Jack was always impressed at the first time they all got to see through the eyes of their host. 'Vernon, if you ever want another trade, installing these in people's homes will go down a storm. Just think what it would be like watching a Roland Emmerich film on one of these!'

Vernon snorted in derision. The mere thought of using such high-calibre resources, just for a popcorn-riddled exercise in witnessing lots of things exploding.

As they all looked to the screen, this was the ultimate in reality gaming.

They were looking at the ceiling above Ray Grady's body. Vernon contacted the team outside. 'Okay boys, time to initiate vertical take-off.'

With that, the view slowly but surely changed. The trolley elevated the body to a standing position. There was a reassuring mechanical whirr, like a food processor crushing bananas. For the masked surgeons looking on, there was an eerie resemblance to Hannibal Lecter in what they were watching unfold.

One of the masked surgeons stepped forward, and placed a prosthetic patch over the hole in Ray's brow. This wasn't any standard hospital gauze, but a sophisticated piece of nanotechnology. Little ultraviolet sparks danced around the edges of the wound, now unseen beneath the material. After a few seconds, the sparks mapped the border of the area that had been missing from Ray's skull. The coastline then started to pulse, initially slowly, but then reaching a crescendo at pace, and then faded away.

The masked surgeon taking the lead on this part of the procedure pulled away the gauze. There remained signs of a small scar, although not by any means revealing the extent of the original wound. The effect was that it made the bullet entry point not look as critical as it actually had been.

Automatically, Ray fidgeted to life. Vernon smiled, as this was how intrinsic he had made the programmed reactions within the control systems. Just a little shakily, the Prime Minister began making a few small, calculated steps across the room.

Vernon was concentrating on navigating Ray around, using a similar pair of wired gloves to those he had used earlier outside the body. In keyboard terms, he already had shortcuts programmed in, so he was arrogantly making the movement look effortless.

As part of this settling-in process, by design the room was far from empty. There were enough pieces of furniture scattered around to create a fairly challenging obstacle course. It was the sort of setting that we all take for granted, but are more conscious of when we are helping a baby take its first steps.

Jack was convinced. 'Looking good,' he declared. Suddenly there was an almighty crash. Vernon looked sheepish, biting his bottom lip.

'Sorry,' he said brusquely, 'low table.'

'I could have told you that was there.' The five crew members looked around to discover where those words had come from. Vernon cottoned on first, realising they were again hearing Wrighty, Ray's inner voice.

'Wrighty!' he gushed, almost like greeting an old friend. 'I wonder if you could help out with this.'

Solange was excited, staying seated but still managing to look like she was jumping around. 'We're actually hearing from his right brain,' she giggled, feeling the need to explain what had happened, even if it was just for her own benefit.

'Better than last time,' Walton noted dryly.

Solange was only too aware of the significance of the development. 'This will give us a fighting chance.'

'Wrighty,' Vernon addressed, 'I'm going to put you live on motion sensing. Can you avoid bumping into things?'

'Only if I want to,' the disconnected voice announced coyly.

'I'll take that as a yes,' Vernon assumed, looking around at the others for confirmation. They weren't very helpful.

A few buttons pressed, a few settings changed, and Vernon stepped back, very much in hope of another breakthrough. And with that, Ray began to walk around the room, hesitantly, but steadily.

Bonnie was impressed. The terrain was something they were going to have to tackle during Ray's every waking moment of the day. 'Looking the part,' she bubbled. 'How about sitting down?'

Vernon nodded. 'Wrighty, let's sit down.' With that, Ray turned himself in the direction of the office control desk's chair. One of Ray's arms came out to steady himself in the manoeuvre.

'Did you extend his arm?' Bonnie asked, hoping that she knew the answer.

'No,' Vernon confirmed. 'Must be Wrighty lending a helping hand,' he quipped.

Jack looked to the craft's inner ceiling. 'Welcome to Vernon's painful pun emporium.'

Solange decided it was time to mark out some territory with Vernon. 'I assume you'll want me to take over with Wrighty from here?'

Jack felt some extra affirmation was needed. 'Vern, you're not supposed to do everything.' Vernon shook his head in disbelief that he was being reminded about the nature of the team dynamics, and pressed a few switches.

'Comms with Wrighty now over to your desk, Solange.'

She smiled, perhaps a little too widely. She spoke into her microphone, not exactly sure of where she should be looking when she did so. 'Hello Wrighty. My name is Solange and I'll be your flight attendant for our journey.'

'What a lovely voice,' marvelled the disconnected vocals. 'Plenty of colourful tones. I like it!'

'I can tell we're going to get on,' Solange cooed. All this without having to resort to her usual manoeuvres, which often included staring widely at the person in question, flickering her eyelids.

Walton had been looking through some information at his station, and decided to make his way over to Vernon. 'Looks like the assassin was a Manchurian candidate,' he advised.

'Someone from the North West?' mocked Vernon.

'*Not* Mancunian,' Walton dryly corrected.

Jack decided to rescue Walton from Vernon's frivolity. 'Programmed for the task. M.K. Ultra at work again?'

Bonnie saw a way to expose some of her specialism. 'Altars. Compartmentalised separate personalities.'

Not to be outdone, Solange added 'The handler would know exactly what buttons to press, so to speak.'

With everyone grasping the relevance, Walton continued. 'The bullet trajectories are all wrong. He wasn't acting alone. Unless he could jump twenty feet in the air.'

Jack concentrated on what the major issue was for him within this discovery. 'More importantly, we have no idea who they were working for.'

'The answer is always close to home,' the voice of Wrighty said mysteriously, the team still not quite up to speed how his outputs could integrate with theirs. It was Solange who took on the task.

'Wrighty, is there someone who can help us?'

'Someone?' the disconnected voice asked quizzically. 'Some… thing. I always watch my back. Be somewhere when you aren't.'

While this sort of thing appealed to Walton's love of crosswords, this was beyond him. Solange jabbed further. 'Can you elaborate?'

Wrighty began to become more eloquent. 'Harness the sounds of emotion. Of betrayal. Safe from the elements, where I will feel safe.' Solange shrugged her shoulders. Walton stepped up to the plate.

'Cryptic,' he said, unhelpfully.

Bonnie explored the background of what was being said. 'The right brain doesn't anchor itself down to facts. People, trivia, or places.'

Walton could use this. 'Places. Where would Ray feel safe?'

Jack was again practical in his evaluation. 'You'd imagine his home. We'll need some detective work.'

* * *

Night had fallen. Dawn moved away from the window, which afforded a view of the busy street below. She didn't have time for the "great outdoors" in any sense of the description. She never saw the purpose of having a window box, let alone a garden. A studio apartment in the hub of the city was all she needed. Perhaps she wasn't the best person to be the Foreign Office Minister, as she only saw travel as a functional necessity, rather than a joy in itself.

No need for a car or any other form of personal transport. She had been able to take the Tube without any fuss right up until the start of the election campaign. It was taxis for a time. Now, she could hail a diplomatic limo with a simple text message. Ray afforded his inner circle the luxury, although he knew that keeping such fringe benefits would always be a stick that someone or other might use to beat them with.

She sat down at an incredibly expensive vanity table with matching cushioned stool. It had been everywhere with her, the one piece of furniture that she'd never left behind. She'd bought it with money she'd been left in her aunt's will. Every time Dawn looked at it, happy memories came into sharp focus within her mind's eye. If the vanity table didn't get through the doors of a prospective apartment, she'd carry on searching for another new place.

Dawn got it at an auction. She spent all of the £5,000 she had been left in one go. She even had to chip in, out of her own pocket, for the auction fees and delivery on top. It had been a good investment, though. The insurers now valued it at £12,000. Mahogany with a satin birch interior and silver gilt tops. Manufactured in 1907 by Mark H.J. Linton of Paris, although it was proud to announce it was built in London via engravings on some of its silver components. Even the mirror folded down, which was useful for its frequent trips here and there.

She concentrated on combing through her long afro hair with a suitably sturdy brush. The classical music playing quietly in the background, a Vaughan Williams compilation, didn't quite mask the sound of the en-suite shower on the other side of the room. The steam was creating clouds which seeped out, heading in her direction. She frowned at the possibility that such a mist might not be the best of environments for her beloved vanity table.

Dawn continued combing through her hair. She had reached the necessary effect, but carried on anyway. 'I don't know how to turn this around,' she shouted, to make herself heard in the en-suite. 'Ray is not going to be the man he was. How can one man make so much of a difference?' The shower stopped, to be replaced by just the concluding drips. She didn't feel these were the sort of comments she could make elsewhere. 'I feel like we're all playing on a stage.' Still no response. 'One that's far too big for us.'

Meddings came into the room, long white towel around his waist, and drying his hair with another. 'There will always be people fighting the government,' he calmly reassured. 'Don't underestimate your role in keeping this ship afloat.' With that, he threw the hair towel across the room and put his hands on Dawn's shoulders. Dawn closed her eyes, a brief shiver running right down her spine. As Meddings kissed her neck, she had to focus to stop herself lusting after what was beneath the other towel.

'I know it's a team, but we'll only be average without our star player,' she breathed heavily, having to force herself from letting her eyes close.

'I wish you'd talk about me like that,' he joked. That was the last bastion of resistance. Dawn stood up to face him and the passion of their mouths connecting accelerated, as she tugged his other towel away. Her now-naked lover was in front of her, and the mirror of her prized antique would again witness her distaste for being made to wait.

* * *

Phil Conway had only set foot inside Downing Street once. It had been many years ago, when just a junior reporter, standing in for a senior colleague when she was ill. With the illness having been a drunken stupor, his excuse for being an understudy had been met with a knowing breeziness by the information officer in charge that day.

All was set up for a TV interview. Phil had dressed in his smart conventional suit, sitting in a plush leather chair, next to the Drawing Room's fireplace. Sitting next to him was Ray, looking relaxed. Phil wondered if perhaps he was a little "spaced out". The twinkle he'd always known in Ray's eyes was still there, but he looked like his thoughts were somewhere else. As the director counted him in, Phil subconsciously adjusted his tie one more time, before a final consultation of his notes, via a clipboard nestled on his lap. He closed his eyes briefly, then raised his head and smiled, beaming directly down the camera lens.

'Welcome to the first in a new series of *The PM's Fireside Chats* with me, Phil Conway.' The vision mixer began to switch swiftly from camera to camera, setting on a two-shot that accommodated both Phil and Ray. 'Prime Minister Grady, great to see you've recovered.'

'Ray, please,' came the reply, removing the boundaries of formality.

'It must have been harrowing,' Phil suggested. 'How much do you remember of the shooting?'

Ray paused momentarily, and then licked his lips before proceeding. It was a tick which Bonnie had noticed over the years, and took the chance to implement. 'Very little. They tell me that I have lost a lot of short-term memories.'

Phil thought it worthwhile to follow up on this avenue. 'Do you remember your election win?'

Ray jumped straight back, a bounce in his voice. 'How could I forget that?'

'And that you're Prime Minister?' Phil jested.

'Prime Minister? I thought I was a TV host!' There was a brief, uncomfortable pause, before Ray laughed. 'Of course I know! Granted, it was never a job I expected to have. But I still relish it.'

Phil decided the pleasantries had gone on long enough. 'Turning now to the unemployment figures…'

'Oh hell,' came Ray's spontaneous reply.

Inside the capsule cockpit, Walton realised what he had said had been echoed by his host's mouth. He rolled his eyes skywards and backed away from his microphone. No doubt the Young Turks on the team would be a little too unforgiving. He tried to rescue the situation. 'By that, I mean that it must be hell, for those who have recently lost their jobs.'

Phil raised an eyebrow, but continued. 'With so many corporations withdrawing their operations from the country, there could be an additional two million people on the dole by Christmas.'

'A temporary situation,' came the reply from Ray, via Walton. 'It will take a few months to set up new manufacturing and farming operations to make the UK self sufficient again.'

Phil sensed blood. 'But what will happen to people in the meantime?' The vision mixer chose a camera angle in the process of doing a slow zoom in on Ray's face.

'Who do you think is going to be building these facilities?' Ray replied, soothingly.

Phil wasn't convinced. 'But where's the money coming from?'

Walton was sure he had this all covered with what would be Ray's reply. 'The hundreds of billions all saved by withdrawing from Europe, and cancelling our debt with the I.M.F.'

Phil checked his notes. He decided to change tack. 'How are your family coping with your recovery?'

It was Bonnie's turn to choose Ray's words. How often, as a teenager, would she have longed to have had this level of control over her father. 'You know my wife, she'd rather I got a job with regular hours for once.' Must mention the children. 'The kids are glad I'm back on the telly again.'

The vision mixer chose a close-up of Phil. 'There was talk that your relationship had hit some problems?' Ray's reaction was to look slightly stumped. Inside the capsule, Bonnie was speechless.

Solange decided to jump in. 'What marriage doesn't have ups and downs? You just find ways to pay attention to each other's needs.' Ray's close-up showed him looking very earnest. 'We're ordinary people, not a disconnected elite.'

Conscious of the time, Phil decided to go to his wrap-up question. 'Finally, what have you to say to your critics?'

Within the capsule, Jack decided to field this one. 'Closed minds are the enemies of forward thinking.' The vision mixer was now tight in on Ray. 'I have been given an opportunity to lead this country back to true independence. And just like this great nation, I have the chance, not to "Die Another Day", but to "Live Another Life".'

With that there was a communal sigh of relief. Looking around beyond the confines of the fireplace, the chairs, and the backdrop, this was not

Downing Street, but a mocked-up studio in the Pentagram Hospital. Phil was sure he'd get another chance to visit the real place again soon, maybe today. Dawn had been acting as director, as Georgie operated the camera. Tony had a hand over his face, not exactly thrilled by what he had witnessed.

'Thanks team. That's all for now,' shouted Dawn. The small band of technicians, quite possibly the same people who were behind the veils of the masked surgeons, began to crash-down the equipment. Phil approached Georgie.

'So much for the dress rehearsal,' he sighed. 'Thanks for letting me in on this.'

'Phil, you're not daft enough to jeopardise the best set of leads you'll ever have,' she crowed.

'Which reminds me,' said the journalist. 'I'm okay to use your office?'

Georgie was amazed that Phil thought he had to ask. 'You know where it is. Take a limo back to Downing Street.'

Phil grinned. 'Cheers,' he said, with a staccato wave as he walked away. Georgie wasn't quite finished yet.

'Oh, and Phil, what was that about marital disharmony?' she enquired. 'Did you make that up?'

Phil took in a deep breath. 'I never make things up.' With that he winked and left.

Tony had made his way to Dawn, and was wiping his hands in a very O.C.D. manner. 'A bloody disaster.'

As usual, Dawn was more pragmatic. 'Bad dress rehearsal, good first night.'

At that point, one of Ray's incumbents joined the conversation. 'Jack here. This is mainly a problem with the updated technology.' In the capsule, Jack was giving Vernon one of those stares which were normally confined to schoolchildren who hadn't done the homework they'd promised.

'Sure, blame the tech,' Vernon bleated. 'Couldn't possibly have been user error.'

Jack was himself defensive. 'I'm not blaming anyone.'

Outside, Tony and Dawn were treated to seeing Ray looking positively schizophrenic.

'It didn't sound like that to me,' snapped Vernon.

'You could take it as praise for having upgraded the systems,' Jack barked.

'I know your sort,' accused Vernon. 'They just hate change.'

'We will get the hang of it,' Jack commented, becoming his own peacemaker. 'We just need to relax.'

Watching Ray's internal monologue played out in front of her, Dawn could feel the first inklings of a headache. 'Yes, chill out, why don't you, guys?' Ray came to order, as silence echoed both inside and out of the carcass. 'And next time you have a spat, is there any chance you could turn your microphones off?'

'Five ventriloquists sharing the one dummy,' Tony commented, as he walked off to wherever he might be able to get a drink.

Inside Ray, Jack and Vernon were staring at each other. Jack broke the deadlock. 'It won't happen again,' he seethed. Vernon harrumphed, and went back to his station.

'Records,' uttered the disconnected voice of Wrighty. 'Not those round things. Stay off the pills.' Solange, bemused, looked at Jack. Jack looked at Vernon, hoping for guidance. Vernon shrugged his shoulders, with just a hint of petulance.

* * *

Georgie's office at Downing Street was compact but tidy. In one corner, a computer terminal, and Phil occupied the chair in front of it. He was staring intently at the screen. He had gained access to materials he really shouldn't. The words were cold but revealing. "Information on Chris Bowden. September 2011 – July 2013: Applied Economics, University of Cambridge". It was an intriguing background for a Prime Ministerial assassin. Checking connections and facts again saw Phil raise an eyebrow. In November 2004, the Faculty of Applied Economics ceased to exist at Cambridge, merging to form the Faculty of Economics and Politics.

Why the inconsistency in titles, Phil wondered. Not wanting to admit to having the word Politics in his degree, perhaps? He'd let that information brew in his mind. Next on the list on screen was "August 2013 – April 2014: Westgard Pharmaceuticals. May 2014 – August 2014: Unknown". Most employers were suspicious of any gaps in a CV, and this was definite cause for concern.Far more detail than from his previous employers. "September 2014 – Present: Floor Broker, London Stock Exchange".

Phil paused, drumming his fingers on the desk by the right-hand side of the keyboard. Inspiration returned and he began to type away. He was using the "StartRight" search engine, one of several which now made a virtue of not tracking or recording the enquiries you made of it. In the query box he entered "Bilderberg Attendees 2014".

With just a brief pause, the list of participants came up in front of Phil, and he began to scroll down it. Momentarily, he stopped in his tracks. There was a name there, and he was shocked to see it included. It was a revelation he simply had to circulate as quickly as possible. He fished out his mobile phone from within the inner breast pocket of his jacket, and quickly made a call.

The line was engaged. He banged the desk in frustration.

***

Tony liked the atmosphere in the Prime Minister's private office. Part of him wished that the job could be his on a permanent basis, although the morbid foreboding of the accompanying responsibility soon jolted him from his daydream. He was being made to wait on the red phone, the "hot line".

With his free hand, he was pointing a remote control at a TV monitor, where he was fast-forwarding and rewinding through a recording of the earlier dry-run Prime Ministerial interview. Tony could not help his grimace at what he witnessed. He was relieved when he was addressed on the phone again.

'Yes, I'm still here,' he confirmed. He listened intently, and took in a very silent but sharp intake of breath. 'He'd like to visit... when?' he said awkwardly, hoping in some way he had misheard the request. It was now time to stall. 'Obviously Prime Minister Grady would be delighted at such visible support from the President. However...' he paused, only to be the victim of a gattling-gun's-worth of clarifications.

'I understand, Madame Secretary,' Tony conceded. 'Obviously, we would be foolish to turn such an opportunity down...'

Tony wondered who had taught her how to be condescending, and whether it was something he could perfect through a distance learning course. 'Yes, I'll get my people to talk to your people.' He paused to listen further. 'Thank you.' He was just about to round off the conversation, when he realised the call had been cut off at the other end.

Tony replaced the receiver, and then bit his bottom lip, a subconscious action which hurt just a little bit. He took his mobile phone out of his pocket, and pressed a choice on the speed-dial.

Within the capsule cockpit, the call went through to Jack. He pressed the side of his headset microphone to receive the call. 'Tony? What's up?'

Tony decided to try and bluff his way through the call, although how that would influence the final outcome he had little idea. 'I seem to have just given out an invitation.'

Jack pretended not to be concerned. 'That's nice. Can anyone come?'

It was no good. Tony just had to lay his cards on the table. 'It's the American President.'

Jack paused. The enormity of the problem that had just been dropped on him came into sharp focus. 'How soon?'

Tony blurted out, 'Next week.' He was met with a stony silence. 'Wants to strike while the iron is hot,' was the next gambit, hoping that this would explain why they had all just been dropped in it.

It was at this point Jack wished he'd not amplified both ends of the conversation throughout the entire control room of the capsule. There was visible panic on the faces of Vernon, Solange, Bonnie and particularly Walton, who broke ranks by taking off his headset microphone and throwing it against the wall.

Jack looked at the outside view from the capsule screen. As Ray was horizontal, resting up, all they could see was the cold silver ceiling above them.

Vernon voiced everyone's concerns succinctly. 'You've got to be joking.'

Ever the optimist, Solange chipped in, 'We have the get-out-of-jail card.' Everyone looked at her, with a wish that this was a straw they could clutch. 'The brain injury.'

It was up to Bonnie to warn of the dragons ahead. 'Don't want to play on that too much. The opposition will say Ray's not fit to govern.'

Surprisingly, the ever-cautious Walton brought hope to the table. 'Not all bad news. As we know, their guy is new at this, too. He'll be as cautious as we are.'

Despite the fact it was he who had created this awkward appointment, Tony was the most pessimistic. 'Aside from the fact he hasn't recently been shot in the head.' Tony looked around for the drinks cabinet.

Walton looked uncomfortable at the reaction, and decided to returns to his work. Guess he'd chosen the wrong day to stay off the "Opal Fruits".

Tony's distress was put on hold by a sharp knock on the door. Summoning the caller to enter, Phil came in, carrying an information folder. Tony beckoned Phil over, who was quietly beaming at finally getting inside Number 10 again. Tony put his mobile phone on speaker.

Jack continued, 'While we're here, I need to throw something else into the mix.'

Tony thoroughly expected the bad to get worse. 'Tell me some good news!'

Jack shared the musings of his team. 'We think Ray may have recorded some conversations. Wrighty hinted as much.' Phil looked at Tony in confusion, and raised an eyebrow.

'The erratic murmurings of Ray's right brain,' Tony explained.

'But of course,' Phil replied, not really understanding at all. He then addressed Jack. 'Alicia would have been told about things like that?'

Jack cottoned on to who he was speaking to, 'Oh, hi Phil. You'd certainly tell someone, wouldn't you?'

'I think he'd have told me before her,' Tony barked, trying to establish the pecking order as he saw it. 'And she's certainly not mentioned anything.'

Jack had a plan. 'We'll just have to search the house when we get back.'

Phil's enquiring journalistic mind cut across the trains of thought. 'Why do you think it'll be there?'

'Wrighty said it would be somewhere where Ray felt safe,' Jack revealed.

Phil saw things differently. 'He's not going to have the most important meetings at home.'

Tony was right-on with Phil on this. 'It would be here,' he concluded. 'In this room. Jack, we'll get back to you.' With that, Tony terminated the call and put his mobile back in his pocket. He looked around the room. 'Where to begin?' he asked, thinking a journalist would be more savvy to this sort of activity. He was correct with the assumption, as Phil had already started looking around the walls.

Ineptly, Tony tried to follow suit, looking more like Basil Fawlty trying to locate suspect masonry than acting as a dedicated sleuth. Phil concentrated on the mantelpiece, as Tony looked through the bookcase, checking each book carefully.

Tony then heard a sound like a lock being turned. Phil summoned him over. Tony put down the current book he was looking at, and walked across the room to see what the fuss was about. Phil had found a hidden alcove behind the mantelpiece.

Phil applied some leverage and was then able to negotiate the inside of the cubby hole. He pulled out a grey-coloured compact box of tricks.

'Hard drive,' Phil confirmed. Tony's face beamed, as Phil handed it over to him. As Tony rotated the gadget in his hands, Phil walked over and picked up the information folder he had brought in with him. 'I hope that softens you up for what's coming. You aren't going to like what I've found…'

13

ENEMY WITHIN

Zena Carsley was thankful for her make-up lady. The bags under her eyes would have looked even more pronounced without the careful application of the right amount of "slap". Last week's viewing figures for her shows had been atrocious, and her usual defenders were no longer interested in continuing to protect her.

The network had decided to throw its might behind the Conservative Party. While the polls showed an increase in the appreciation index for the grouping itself, the leader Duncan Hurst still wasn't considered trustworthy. Despite "We the People" having warned that there was no easy road from the abyss which the country had fallen into, the harsh realities were beginning to sway the less-committed of their supporters. The problem was the majority of these people were shifting to being "don't knows" rather than actually changing allegiances.

Zena looked across the desk at Hurst. The news studio seemed much hotter than usual. For both of them. She became momentarily distracted by the beads of sweat on his brow. As usual his answers were succinct, but dripped with non-specific platitudes. Getting answers of substance was like juggling with jelly.

'Mister Hurst, what you seem to be suggesting is a vote of no-confidence in the Prime Minister?' *Go on, Mister Leader of the Opposition, try and be non-specific with that*, she thought.

Hurst licked his lips. 'The public voted for Grady, who is not in power, for obvious reasons.' Zena couldn't believe that Hurst would think making such a quip about an attempted assassination would be a winning move. Hurst noticed her annoyance. 'Currently, we have Tony Pearce standing in. Now, Tony's a nice chap, but hardly the diplomat that this country needs.'

The insincerity just annoyed Zena. How could she actually make this public school nanny's-boy seem endearing? 'But Grady is due back soon. And he has made no secret that his priority is putting matters at home in order.'

Duncan was taken aback by Zena's aggressive commentary. He began to realise why his backroom team were not favouring her for exclusive interviews. 'Precisely my point. That will be seen as a sign of weakness on the global stage.' Hurst decided to give Zena something specific to work with. 'We need another general election right now, so we can put matters in order, before it is too late.'

Zena wasn't going to play ball. 'Aren't people going to be electioned-out?' As Hurst continued, he noticed Zena was getting a message from the production gallery via her earpiece. Hurst pondered if she was any good at her job he would not have noticed the interaction.

'The public wanted to give the major parties a good-old kick up the backside. We understand that. We've listened. Now we can get on with instigating the type of change that people want to see.' Hurst might as well have been talking to the potted plants which littered the stage set, added in a ridiculous attempt to soften Zena's image.

'Mister Hurst, we're getting unconfirmed reports that the new President of the United States will be making an official visit to Britain next week.' Zena had loaded the statement in such a way so Duncan appreciated this would be seen as a vote of confidence in the government. Hurst was ruffled.

'Well, yes, there you go. Grady will not be back at the helm by then.'

'Apparently he will be,' Zena replied, pleased that she had the benefit of better intelligence than her prey.

'I see,' stumbled Hurst.

He didn't expect Zena to come to his rescue, but that was exactly what she did. 'If anything, it might help prove your point, in that Grady simply isn't up to the task of global diplomacy.'

Hurst guessed correctly. Zena had heard in her earpiece not to step out of line. Perhaps there was still hope for her, if it wasn't for those lousy ratings.

In the Prime Minister's Private Office, Georgie was thumbing through an information folder, gazing at every part of the paperwork inside, and totally aghast. Phil was standing over her, hands on hips, and just a little impatient.

Across the room, Tony was sprawled in Ray's office desk chair, whisky tumbler in hand, tapping it against the desk, frowning.

Phil tried to add some perspective. 'There are much darker forces at play.' He received no response. 'Everywhere.'

Tony stared into his tumbler, hoping that the various refractions of light would illuminate the situation for him. 'But the Bilderberg Group.' Even the mention of its name had previously lined him, or anyone else mentioning it, up for ridicule. 'A talking shop for heavyweight has-beens.'

'I thought that, too,' sympathised Phil, 'but that's precisely what they want you to think.' He handed Tony a few pages stapled together. It clearly noted on its front that this was an attendance list. 'Look at who was there.' Tony scanned the contents quickly, flicking the pages back and forth. 'Captains of industry. Presidents and Prime Ministers. Major media moguls. No has-beens.' The credentials were not open to debate. 'You really think they'd just attend a navel-gazing jamboree?' Georgie moved behind Tony and looked over his shoulder at the list.

Tony looked back at her. He noted the frown lines on her face. 'Busy people,' he confirmed.

Phil qualified the situation. 'They go there to be given the agenda for the next twelve months.'

Georgie was up to speed on the Bilderbergers. 'And beyond.' She made a few pointing movements to names on the list. 'There are people new to the scene on here. The up-and-comings.'

'Those on the cusp of power,' Phil confirmed. 'Sit down if you think Presidents and Prime Ministers are voted for by the public. They're chosen. Outside of any democratic process.'

In years gone by, Tony would have baulked at such comments, labelling them as the rantings of tin-foil-hatted conspiracy theorists. With what he had witnessed in the last few months, the reality was all too real.

* * *

As they anticipated, the Presidential visit came around far too quickly. The Pillared Room at Downing Street had been chosen as the venue, keeping everything in-house, and a place which Ray's workers could practice in away from the prying eyes of any onlookers.

Tony had decided to play the "Commonwealth" card as a backdrop to the reception for the American President. With formal relations with all members of the European Union officially having been curtailed, it was reassuring that Britain's far-flung "stomping grounds" welcomed their partnerships being highly-regarded once more.

Around the room, relevant mid-sized flags were unfurled on sturdy poles. Australia, Cameroon, Ghana, India, Jamaica, New Zealand, Nigeria, Pakistan, South Africa, all intermixed with Union Jacks. Representatives from these states were helping create a terrific buzz in the room, so much so that the string quartet, playing gently on a small raised stage in a corner, struggled to make themselves heard.

A focal point for many, his mere presence enough to reflect the importance of the occasion, was Conrad Connelly. The American Ambassador was a sprightly sixty-two years old, with the demeanour of a silver fox, and the Stars-and-Stripes pin badge on his lapel enhanced his patriotism. The Indian Ambassador and his wife had taken the opportunity to hog his attentions and detail possible areas of future interaction between their two countries.

More surreptitious was Georgie, who was able to enter the room unheralded. Her evening ball-gown had a flavour of the 1980s, helpful considering the era had come back into style somewhat, mainly due to some of the music chosen by Ray for the post-election celebrations. The irony that this era was beginning to reflect the "loads-a-money" decade and its Champagne Charlies was not lost on Georgie. It didn't take her long to spot Conrad, her target, and she headed straight over to him.

'Sorry to interrupt,' she said to the Indian husband and wife. 'Nice to see you again, Mister Ambassador.'

Conrad beamed in recognition, then relief. 'Georgie! I thought you'd be here.' He turned to his guests. 'If you'll excuse me.' With that, he whisked Georgie away to a quiet corner.

199

In the meantime, the Indian Ambassador and his wife recognised Dawn, who was talking to a waiter, and made their way over to her. Dawn was initially taken aback to be approached by such dignitaries, but was soon demonstrating how pleased she was to see them. The waiter moved on his way, leaving the trio to make their small talk.

In a quiet corner, Conrad was at his most charming with Georgie. 'Quite a step-up from a talent agent,' he noted.

'And for you,' Georgie chuckled, 'quite a step-up from Hollywood.'

Conrad took a sip of champagne. 'It's like your guy, Ray. You have to know how to work an audience.' He looked around. 'Where is he?'

Georgie made the excuses. 'You know how it is. Calls and meetings never stop.' She decided to turn the tables. 'How's your man taking Britain's new-found independence?'

'He's quite progressive, too,' noted Conrad, before becoming circumspect. 'Happy that Ray survived. Should stop folk getting the same idea again on our side of the pond.'

As if that was the cue, the string quartet stopped playing, mid-song. The room hushed in recognition of the change in atmosphere. Tony stepped up on the raised stage area, adjusted his jacket and went up to the microphone.

'M'Lords, Ladies and Gentlemen, it is my honour to present to you the Prime Minister of the United Kingdom, Ray Grady!' This was greeted with gentle, respectful applause, as one might expect from those assembled, as Ray entered the room with Alicia on his arm. It was a show of unity, and many thought a sensible act, given what Ray had been through. The string quartet played the relevant bars from the concluding section of "The William Tell Overture".

Ray waved to all corners of the room, and then began to shake hands with selected individuals within the crowd along his route towards the stage. Alicia took a step back, always someone who was a little uncomfortable with such crowds, but stayed close enough to Ray to catch him, if necessary.

Conrad peered over his clapping hands, skilfully working the movement around the wine glass he was holding, to eyeball Georgie. 'Looking good,' he smiled, but was also intrigued. 'How serious was it?'

Georgie was necessarily reserved. 'About as serious as it can get.' She then realised that the two men had never met. 'Do you want an introduction?'

Conrad was keen. 'Sure!'

As the music chimed up again, inside Ray's head the team had finally got their act together. The viewing screen gave the quintet Ray's point of view as he shook hands with various dignitaries.

Jack noticed an external signal. 'Right flank. Georgie's trying to attract our attention.'

Vernon was beginning to treat the whole project like a computer game. 'Roger that,' and with that he steered Ray towards Georgie and Conrad.

Georgie offered out an arm for Ray to steady himself on his left flank. 'Prime Minister,' she flustered, 'may I introduce Conrad Connelly, the American Ambassador?'

'A pleasure,' Conrad cheerily drooled, offering out his right hand. Automatically, Ray raised his arm and the pair shook hands.

Vernon took on the greetings. 'Conrad Connelly! Loved you as that spy on the original *Battlestar Galactica*.' Jack stared at him. He wasn't sure if Ray would have known such televisual minutiae.

'Not a lot of people remember that,' Conrad replied, not too sure whether to be impressed or a tad concerned.

Jack jumped in to reply. 'Just call it the geek in me.' Jack turned to scowl at Vernon, who rolled his eyes in reply. Why was it that certain areas of trivia seemed to garner such a poor reputation?

Conrad moved things along. 'Is there anything you'd like from the President's visit?'

'A big fuss about a trade agreement,' noted Walton, taking his turn to lead Ray's agenda. 'Always popular,' he suggested.

'Especially as Europe has banned us from exporting to them,' said Georgie, with a little sour thrown into her sweetness. 'Although a few will break ranks on that sooner rather than later.'

Conrad grunted, half with humour, half with scorn. 'Most only follow the dictats when it suits them.' He took a measured sip from his glass. 'I'm sure something newsworthy can be arranged.'

Tony came over to the group, conscious of the time. 'Prime Minister. Your speech.'

Ray nodded, again a reflex action which Vernon had programmed in. 'Yes. Excuse me.' With a parting wave, Tony led Ray to a lectern on the little stage, over to the side where the string quartet were playing. The musicians, who were used to being second fiddle to those paying them, reached a suitable juncture and stopped playing. The well-behaved audience at once took this as the cue to come to attention, and gather around their host.

Ray cleared his throat. Rousing openings to speeches were Jack's domain. 'Thank you all for coming tonight. I apologise for not recalling all your names.' Jack realised Ray wouldn't want too much sympathy. 'It's difficult at the best of times. Even worse when a bullet grazes past your brain!' The comment garnered polite laughter from some of the audience, still finding it difficult to judge the mood of the evening. 'Anyway, I hope you will not be too offended.' Ray looked around the room, a gulp coming from nowhere. 'Now, business at hand.'

Walton took on the next step of the briefing. '"We the People" is not a political party. It is a meeting of minds. Our opinions represent those of our constituents.' Those who knew Ray expected there to be a little quip to follow. 'It used to be called a grass-roots movement, but we're different because we've got rid of the weeds!'

The laughter was a little less forced now. Every person in the room was listening intently. Ray continued, 'We take our lead from the cornerstones of the American Constitution. A fine document, recently undermined by the very politicians who were supposed to protect it.' A dramatic pause. 'But not anymore.'

Ray stared directly at Conrad, who stood tall and proud. 'I know from speaking to Conrad Connelly that his new President takes on much of our philosophy. As they would say over there, it was the act of "taking the trash out".' Conrad smiled, and began a round of applause which snaked through the audience.

Walton was getting into full-swing. 'This may not come as a surprise to you, thanks to our chums in the media...' the pause that followed allowed Jack enough time to look at Solange, and mouth the word "chums", questioning its use with something of disdain. Solange tutted her disapproval of the use of the word, and also for Jack pulling Walton up on it.

'I am happy to confirm that the President will be paying an official visit next week, over various matters of mutual interest,' Ray glowed, which was greeted with solid applause. Those present were only too aware of the significance.

The statuesque waiter came out of the audience with a tray of filled champagne flutes, and went out of his way to pass one up to Ray. Solange jumped on the impromptu happening. 'I would like to propose a toast.' Vernon followed Solange's thinking, and he made Ray raise his champagne flute accordingly. 'To new friendships, new partnerships!'

The waiting staff had very quickly ensured everyone had some liquid in their glasses. The audience raised them in unison, and a crescendo of clinking reverberated around the room, a mumbling approval in accompaniment. Ray looked at the string quartet, and winked. With that, they started to play again as Ray left the stage, taking his leave behind a partition screen.

Tony sidled up to Georgie. 'Nice touch with the champagne,' he remarked.

'Not my idea,' she chortled. Tony bit his lip, as he stared at the waiter who had delivered Ray his glass. Over recent receptions, he had begun to know most of the staff for these types of functions. Tony carefully directed Georgie's attention towards him.

'Have you seen him before?' he enquired.

Georgie did her best to have a good look without staring directly at the hired help. 'Don't think so.'

Tony was catching on, albeit slowly. 'I vetted all the staff personally.' Within an instant there was panic on both their faces. They looked around for Ray, getting ever more fractious as they simply could not see him.

But behind the partition, Ray was catching his breath. Within the Prime Minister, Jack was concerned. 'What's going on?' he asked of Vernon.

'Systems have gone offline,' was the reply, not exactly what anyone wanted to hear. From out of the ether, Wrighty spoke again.

'Don't worry. Everything will be fine.' Vernon shrugged his shoulders, but for some reason both of the ladies within Ray were relieved to hear this intervention.

Outside, and independent of the crew's control, Ray looked around, although his befuddled expression was not within his programming. A mist began to fill the area where he stood, the blocky nature of the partition ensuring that the billows were not seen beyond, in the main room. Gaining form, Anna, Ray's deceased wife, materialised in front of him. Within the capsule, the sensors did not pick up any signs of the spectre-like apparition.

'I thought I'd dreamt you before,' Ray said, the words heard by the Pentagram team. All of them were puzzled upon hearing this one-sided conversation. 'Why are you back here now?' Ray enquired.

Anna smiled, cheekily. 'What's the point of having a guardian angel if you're not going to let me help out?'

'I suppose you're going to tell me to go easy on the champagne,' Ray mocked.

Bonnie seized on to what was happening. 'This must be Wrighty having a conversation with someone.'

Jack looked at her quizzically. 'Real or imaginary?'

Bonnie doubted her reply was going to be considered helpful, but tried anyway. 'Ever wondered exactly what ghosts are?' she asked.

Jack raised an eyebrow. Vernon snorted. Solange pondered the possibilities. Walton found something else to pretend to be doing.

Outside, Anna was now fully formed in front of Ray. 'You make me sound like a right nag,' she said with a huff.

Solange decided to ask the question. 'Wrighty! What's going on? Is that you talking?'

'It's part of me,' the right-brain jovially replied. 'But not all of me. Go figure.'

Wrighty continued his conversation with Anna via Ray. 'They are going to have problems understanding what's going on here.'

Anna stroked Ray's chest. 'Quantum physics is always seen as a bizarre sideshow.' More for the benefit of those who might be listening, she continued. 'Wavelengths. Life after death. Alternative realities.' She took the opportunity to kiss Ray slowly on the lips. 'The fact is your deceased wife is standing right before you.'

'And despite me being brain dead,' Ray provided further exposition, 'I'm managing to have a conversation with you.'

Anna looked Ray directly in the face. 'All in the blink of an eye.' She gave a wink to the crew within Ray's brain, knowing they couldn't see her, before giggling mischievously.

Ray realised Anna appearing to him must be something of a necessity. 'I take it this is something urgent?'

Anna gently patted him on the top of his arm. 'You guessed it already.' She pointed at the glass. 'Don't drink the champagne.'

Ray was deflated. 'That's it?'

'It's enough,' Anna harrumphed. Sensing they were about to be disturbed, she disappeared just as quickly as she had materialised. A half-second later and Georgie poked her head around the end of the partition screen, and was relieved to see Ray standing there.

Near the entrance to the hall, Tony was walking stealthily towards the mysterious unknown waiter.

Georgie saw that Ray still had the champagne flute in hand, but it remained stationary by his lips. Realising what was about to happen, she initiated a flying tackle on him, somehow causing Ray to clatter into the partition, knocking it over with a loud crash.

Ray stumbled about as the champagne flute cascaded into the air, before it began falling towards the polished wooden floor within the main hall. The commotion attracted attention, and onlookers watched events in a mixture of surprise and just a little fear. The flute seemed to take forever in its predestined motion. The crash made an especially loud noise considering the size of the object. The liquid from within splashed onto the polished wood. Ordinarily that would have been the end of it, but in this case smoke began to billow, as smouldering with an accompanying faint mist of smoke took place wherever the champagne had struck.

As the audience was distracted, Tony knocked the tray out of the suspicious waiter's hands and quickly toppled him to the floor. Again, the glassware became a centre of attention, but this time without any wood smoking. The commotion alerted Dougan and Kindon, who had been milling around incognito, and they dashed to assist Tony. The handcuffing of the waiter was so swift and graceful it was almost like watching ballet.

Two of the proper guard detail appeared, and readily dragged the waiter away. Seeing that Ray was a little shell-shocked by the happenstance, and Georgie was quietly escorting him out of a side entrance, Tony stepped in to cover. He looked around, straightened his tie, hopped onstage and addressed the audience.

'Apologies for that. Unfortunately British sparkling wine is no match for champagne!' The laughter from those assembled was polite and more a sign of relief than anything else.

As Georgie directed Ray towards his office, the team within him carried out a debrief. 'What happened there?' asked Bonnie.

Jack almost subconsciously found himself taking one of Walton's "Opal Fruits" from the packet left on his console. A lime one. 'Once again, I don't think we're in as much control of events as we should be.'

Later, in the Prime Minister's Office, Tony, Georgie and Phil were standing around, looking tense, and waiting. A television monitor was paused on a black screen, and gave out the feeling of being particularly ominous in a corner. The door opened, and Dawn entered, immediately sensing an atmosphere.

'Problem?' she enquired. Tony picked up the remote control, and the DVD player kicked into life, its image filling the screen, keen to play its part.

'You could say that,' remarked Tony, very offhand. The images began to flicker across the screen, all recorded from earlier at the reception. All of them were security camera images, with four of them in view at a time. The one that was particularly unfolding the narrative came from the device positioned high in the ceiling of the venue.

Dawn watched intently. The others shared their time between looking at what they had already seen again, and surreptitiously keeping track of Dawn's reactions. In the centre of the frame the Indian Ambassador and his wife, who made their way over to Dawn and the waiter. Everyone's attention was then switched to another angle.

Tony realised he had goofed. 'Hang on,' he gulped, 'I didn't rewind.' The image moved backwards, to a time before what they had all just seen. The waiter was shown to approach Dawn, who took one of the champagne flutes off the tray. The waiter gave her a furtive nod, and Dawn placed the flute back on the tray, taking another one instead.

Dawn was conscious that all eyes in the room were now on her. 'What? He told me that was some of the non-alcoholic fizz.'

Tony was not convinced. He fast-forwarded through the recording again. The images passed through the various incidents of the occasion. The waiter moved away from Dawn, the Indian Ambassador and his wife. Continuing to balance the tray in his right hand, the waiter lifted his arm up, and said something to the face of his wristwatch, which was on the palm-side of his wrist. Once more all eyes were on Dawn, who still didn't understand the implication.

Tony shook his head very gently. He went to rewind again. 'Phil, can you oblige?' Everyone watched the footage of the waiter and his watch again. At which point, Phil demonstrated his lip-reading skills.

'Ops Leader has approved. Getting into position now.' All eyes again moved back to Dawn, who was wide-eyed in disbelief. She cleared her throat.

'Ops Leader? What? Me?' She took a pause and decided they had all lost their collective minds. 'Ridiculous.'

Tony was prepared for this moment. He had hoped this would be something Dawn would have made easy for him. He guessed this was another sign he was a really bad judge of character. He picked up an information folder, consulting one of the sheets within. 'Where were you at the end of May last year?' He was speaking the words without looking up.

Dawn couldn't believe the question. 'I don't know,' she said incredulously. Who would be able to answer such a query given how much time had passed?

Georgie helped fill in the blanks. 'You were on holiday.'

Dawn was still at a loss. 'Quite possibly.'

Tony still couldn't look up from the file. 'The Marriott Hotel. Copenhagen.'

'Never been to Denmark,' Dawn emphasised, confident that such an error would get her off the hook.

Phil's journalistic contacts would beg to differ. 'That's not what passport control says.'

Dawn was sure she could now clear up this error. 'One country I've never visited.' The only further corroboration she could manage was a faint bleating of, 'Honestly.'

Tony passed Dawn a couple of sheets from the file, clearly marked "Bilderberg Attendee List 2014".

Tony gave a narration to the paperwork. 'This is the guest list for the Bilderberg Group last year. Granted, the most senior of people there don't tend to be on it, but the foot soldiers and the up-and-comings definitely are. Your surname is Blunt.' Dawn could not believe what she was reading.

'That's not me. Must be someone with the same name.'

Phil chipped in, 'It lists this "Dawn Blunt" as being an official with the European Parliament.'

Georgie tried to play good-cop. 'What was your job last year?'

'This is ridiculous. I have never been to a Bilderberg meeting.' She suddenly remembered something important. 'Besides which, didn't they meet in Watford last year? At the Grove Hotel?'

Tony scoffed. 'Now you're just playing dumb. That was 2013.' He gave a heavy sigh. 'In some countries, attendance by national officials is considered treason.'

Phil smiled. 'Got to love the way some of our foreign friends approach things.'

Tony played along with the false joviality. 'Was a good time to go. Excellent agenda items, apparently. Amazing they got to their 62nd anniversary and still maintain that fog of almost total secrecy as to what they get up to.'

Georgie was right into Dawn's face. 'What did they have you down for? An even more cushy job in Brussels?'

Dawn was sticking to her story. 'I wasn't there.'

Tony called time on the intricate dance they were all stomping through. 'I'll need your door cards. Consider yourself suspended.'

Dawn saw there really was no point in arguing further. She hurled her door entry pass card onto the desk.

'And your smartphone,' Tony added, coldly. Dawn looked quizzically at Tony. 'Government issue.' There was going to be no respite on this, so Dawn took the device out of her pocket. A swift knock on the door temporarily broke the tension.

'Come in!' barked Tony, at which point Meddings joined them. Despite his hardened background, even he sensed the heady atmosphere.

'You called?' Meddings addressed Tony.

'Escort Ms Blunt from the building.' A brief pause as Meddings took in what was going on. 'She won't be coming back,' said Tony, clarifying what was going on. The security man was now even more puzzled.

'Irreconcilable differences,' Georgie explained to him.

Meddings pretended to understand. 'Okay.'

As Dawn made her way towards Meddings and the door, Tony acidly chirped, 'Oh, and don't try to leave the country.' Dawn was struggling to hold things together, not helped by Meddings beckoning her to leave the room, and then looking to console her by trying to put his arm around her, in what was an inappropriate way. She wriggled clear of his clutches and stormed out. Meddings scurried off behind her, trying to keep up. Ray passed him on his way into the room, and was given a cursory acknowledgement from Meddings.

Ray closed the door, and looked at those in the room with curiosity. 'Have I missed the party?'

Georgie summed it up for everyone. 'Sometimes traitors are right under your nose.'

14

STRANGE BEDFELLOWS

Ray Grady was back at home. It was late in the evening, with the team inside his head now a little thinned out. Some were taking the chance to get some downtime. Walton was at the controls, with Vernon catching up on some diagnostics.

The room was dominated by the fireplace, being one of those you can walk around, its place in the centre of the room creating a level of opulence a little more than perhaps the frugal size of the house deserved. It was roaring away nicely.

Away on one of the couches, Alicia was knitting. The creation was going to become something bright and bulky. Alison and Ryan were transfixed quietly by the television. They weren't normal children by any stretch of the imagination – no iPads for them past six o'clock in the evening.

Ray was looking along his extremely eclectic bookcase shelves. He wasn't searching for anything in particular. That was, until, Wrighty chipped in.

'*That* one,' the disconnected voice said. Walton was taken aback to see the front screen of the capsule zoom in on one particular book. The incident was significant enough to catch Vernon's attention.

'You do that?' he enquired of Walton, who shook his head in response. Vernon found himself subconsciously tapping his bottom teeth with his pen, as both of them looked at the book now in sharp focus. "The Bilderberg Group, by Daniel Estulin".

Walton controlled Ray to take the book off the shelf, and to sit down with it on the long sofa. He began to flick through the pages, Walton taking great note of the contents.

Alicia spoke. 'Ray, I've been thinking,' she mused, trying to sound offhand. 'Wouldn't it be easier for you if we actually moved into Number 10?'

'No, your earlier logic was right,' Ray replied, although Walton was a little concerned, as the answer hadn't come from him. Vernon looked up from his work once more and frowned. Wrighty was intervening again.

'What was that?' Alicia replied, as if confused by the reply.

Walton decided to busk it, in terms of giving the background to the answer. 'Keep the domains of work and home separate. We're only twenty minutes away when Kindon or Meddings is driving!'

The mention of the Meddings name seemed to trigger Alicia to look at her watch. 'Time,' she announced curtly. In turn, Ray looked at his watch.

Within the capsule, Solange and Bonnie returned to their stations. They looked at Walton, who shook his head. 'Still need to do a little research,' he noted, confirming he was going to delay his break.

Bonnie had just put on her headset microphone when she looked over to Solange, checking her transmit button was set to "off" before speaking to her. 'Bedtime for the kids.'

Solange nodded, and spoke into her headset microphone. 'Seven o'clock already?' Outside, Ray spontaneously smiled. 'You are a taskmaster!' Ray put his book down, bounced off the sofa and moved to Alison and Ryan, who were still stretched on the floor in front of the television. They were watching *Thunderbirds* on Blu-ray. The original from the 1960s, not one of the remakes. 'Come on, gang! Upstairs.'

Alison and Ryan reluctantly stirred. Alison looked like she was quietly heading for the door, before turning on her heels and jumping into Ray's arms. 'It's nice to have you back,' she whispered in his ear.

Ray returned the whisper. 'I'm really happy to be back.'

'We're really glad you and Mommy are being nice to each other again.'

In the capsule, the words from the young girl were the equivalent of someone pulling a pin on a grenade. Solange quickly turned around to see

Jack was back on the bridge. If ever there was a time to ask him for guidance, it was now. Jack rotated his hand to suggest Solange did some fishing. She took her cue.

'It wasn't that bad, was it?' she said through Ray's lips.

The team could see Alison's face on the screen in front of them, in huge Imax-style close-up. 'I was okay. But Ryan was very upset.'

Solange decided to rely on platitudes. 'No need to worry now. We know how important we are to each other.' That was enough for the time being, and seemed to do the trick. 'Now come on, up you go.'

Ray put Alison back on the ground. Alison took Ryan by the hand and together they headed out of the room. Ray watched them go up the stairs, and then closed the lounge door. He went to sit on Alicia's sofa, rather than return to his book.

'Okay?' questioned Alicia. Solange continued her fishing expedition.

'Just a shock how much is still fuzzy in my memory.' Ray stared at Alicia, hoping to get a reaction. Nothing. 'You and I, for instance.' Alicia realised she was being asked for some reassurance.

'I'm here now. That's all you need to know.' She decided that a little vitriol was needed. 'And at least you haven't called me Anna.'

Jack decided to step in with a response. 'Having my first wife die isn't something that's easy to forget.' Point made. 'Believe you me, if I could, I would.'

Alicia was keen to re-establish the parameters of what had gone on between them previously. 'You've never fallen out of love with her, have you?'

Jack asked what needed to be known. 'Tony tells me you didn't know about my office recorder.' The query definitely put Alicia on the defensive.

'I'd have told him eventually.' She realised more of an explanation was required. 'While there was a chance you'd recover, why involve him?'

Bonnie took her turn. 'Tony is my best friend.'

'You say that now,' reminded Alicia. 'Don't you remember all those spats?'

This was heading into Walton's area of specialism. 'Politics. Never an exact science,' he mused via Ray. 'Especially when we were starting from scratch.' Walton couldn't believe he was going to be the one defending Tony. 'He's certainly proved his worth in the last couple of weeks.'

'Given what's happened, you'll understand why trust isn't something I have much of,' said Alicia, sniffily.

Ray nodded, but Walton's attention was suddenly grabbed by the television. Alicia saw Ray's distraction, and let out a sigh. She just knew that was all the serious chat she was going to get for the evening, and went back to her knitting. Vernon navigated Ray closer to the set, for a better view of what was of interest.

Walton couldn't understand why the channel was tuned into Zena Carsley's show. Surely Alicia wasn't a fan? The public relations people had obviously been paying attention, as her make-up and fashions had been toned down, now more businesswoman that hooker. She was in deadly-serious mode, and as Ray turned up the volume a still picture of the entrance to the Channel Tunnel appeared next to her. Across the bottom of the screen a scrolling text bar announced "Breaking News".

'That top story once again,' she chirruped. 'The Channel Tunnel's Dover entrance is under attack. We have confirmation that a bomb has been detonated. Trains inside are being turned back to the French end of the tunnel. A group of fanatical pro-Europeans have declared responsibility for the attacks.'

Ray shook his head. 'How convenient,' noted Walton through Ray.

'The style of the bombing has all the hallmarks of left-wing extremist Reginald Dorrans.'

For some reason Walton found himself providing Alicia with some exposition. 'He's never been linked to a bombing before!'

Alicia was puzzled. 'Why would pro-Europeans bomb the Channel Tunnel?' Before Ray could answer, the front doorbell rang.

'Sorry Ali, they're playing my song,' Ray joked.

As he rushed out towards the front door, Alicia noted, 'Don't you remember you are never supposed to call me Ali.'

'Ah. Right,' Jack meekly replied, quickly pointing to his temple to explain his faulty memory, punctuated with a sharp smile followed by a grimace.

* * *

The black limousine had its pair of motorcycle outriders ahead of it setting the pace. The convoy of five vehicles – two bikes, the limo, and two more bikes, dashed through the streets of London. The traffic lights all played their part in making their journey as swift as possible.

Inside Ray's head, any thought of catching up on sleep was put to one side. Jack was annoyed they were still getting caught out by social trivia. 'Still no intel on their marital problems?' he enquired of anyone who would listen.

Solange stepped forward to take the bullet. 'Some couples keep everything well under wraps.'

Bonnie tried to give the benefit of her inside track. 'Staying together would have been for the benefit of the children. One of Ray's priorities.'

Vernon showed his generic suspicion towards women. 'Can we believe her?'

'I'm biased,' conceded Bonnie. 'Equally, I don't think she's that good a liar.'

Walton tried to be practical. 'Flowers and chocolates tomorrow.'

Solange smiled. 'Walton, you fuzzy old romantic.'

The minutes seemed like hours before Ray arrived at the Downing Street Operations Room. The interns were back already, keen for some overtime. Meddings, Dougan and Kindon were busy on the phones, seeing what their security contacts had to offer them on what had happened. Tony and Georgie were rifling through incoming information. It had to be serious, as Ray's entrance was not greeted by anyone.

'Charming,' mocked Walton, before on the outside Ray made his way over to Tony, who looked the most likely to talk to him. 'What have we got?'

'It's all a bit too tidy,' Tony mused.

Georgie shared what she had found. 'Thanks to Vue-Vid, we've had some very interesting sightings.' She turned the flat screen of her computer towards Ray. On it was a Vue-Vid clip of a "black ops" man, wearing a baseball cap. Those watching could see him leaving the scene at the Channel Tunnel.

Tony recognised the stealthy swagger. 'Need I say M.I.6.?'

'Another false flag. Self-inflicted wound,' commented Jack via Ray.

Tony stopped chomping on his biro. 'We've found clips of a whole bunch of them. Some eastern European operatives in the mix.'

'A lot of videos disappeared very quickly,' informed Georgie. 'Apparently removed due to "rights violations".'

'We captured them before they went to the trash tab in the sky,' Tony added, smugly.

Georgie was keen to give credit where credit was due. 'Kudos to citizen journalists. We're doing our bit by re-uploading them.' The team might have consigned ATVOD to be an "Authority" of the past, no longer closing down accounts on YouTube for being too "television-like" or raking in huge mounds of licence fees from individuals and small companies, but still videos were being regularly censored. Tony thought this would be another legislation priority when everything had calmed down.

Jack realised the identification process had been lightning-fast. 'How did you I.D. the perps so quickly?'

Georgie looked at the back of her hand, fingers spread. 'Harry over at "5" has been very helpful,' she informed with a wink. 'I think we may have turned him!'

Jack realised speed was of the essence. 'Footage ready to roll?'

'Sure,' said Georgie.

Jack had a plan. 'Put it on a laptop for me.'

A few minutes passed, and Ray made his way to the front door at Downing Street. Outside, the floodlit steps of Number 10 beckoned. The press contingent were out in force, but huddled behind their safety barriers. The door to Number 10 was opened for Ray by a police officer on sentry duty within, and Ray skipped out. His iPad was clutched carefully under his arm as he walked up to the lectern to address the crowd.

'Good evening,' he bellowed into the microphone. He realised the audio equipment was sensitive enough for him not to have to project his voice to the other side of the street. He was a little annoyed not to hear anything back from those assembled. 'I said good evening,' he said slowly in a very low voice.

Taking their cue, the press contingent gave him a very mumbled "good evening" back.

'You have been reporting an incident in Dover,' Ray observed, looking at as many of the hacks in the eyes as possible. 'You are telling everyone that the Channel Tunnel has been bombed by left-wingers, whose objective is to undermine the government.' A few camera flashes went off, but Jack, via Ray, was not going to be put off. 'First off, step back from this. Take a deep breath. Look at it again.' He added a dramatic pause, which was the cue for Walton to take over from Jack.

'Such left-wingers would not carry out actions like this.' The lesson in politics began. 'They want us back in Europe, and this wouldn't achieve that. Ask yourself… who *would* do this, and why?' Ray held up the iPad, screen facing the contingent. The camera crews and photographers all zoomed in on the moving images they could see on the device. The reporters might have been at a loss to see in fine detail what those with the lenses could see from a distance, but they would be brought up-to-speed by their colleagues later.

The images were of the agent provocateurs making their way from the Channel Tunnel entrance. Ray, looking from the side so that he didn't block anyone's angle, pointed at a "black ops" agent on the iPad screen. 'See this guy here? Someone explain to me why an M.I.6. agent is involved in bombing the Channel Tunnel?'

The accusation certainly had the attention of those in attendance, the shock was immediately followed by murmurs of disbelief. 'And here's more of them,' Ray continued, with Walton's help. 'Tell your readers and viewers about false-flag operations!'

It was clear this would need explaining for the majority present, these mushrooms which continued to inhabit the mainstream media. 'Covert sections of your own side commit atrocities to be blamed on your rivals or enemies.' Walton couldn't believe he really had to explain further. 'Think Germany. 1933. Hitler's fire at the Reichstag. Set by his own people, which led to a huge removal of civil liberties.' Walton was now into his stride. 'A phoney incident in the Gulf of Tonkin gave a reason to escalate the Vietnam War.' No-one present wanted to make eye contact with Ray. 'Look them up.'

Ray pointed to the iPad again, still streaming images of the "black ops" men at work. 'We'll be making this footage available to all media outlets,' Ray advised. 'And to those responsible, a personal message for you.' Ray gave his down-the-lens stare to the camera front and centre. 'We know who you are. We know where you live. Give yourselves up and we'll protect you.' Ray gave out a marked, heavy sigh. 'Those pulling your strings would like nothing better than to "dispose" of you.'

Ray hardly had time to catch his breath from seizing the moment, when the first question came from one of the reporters. 'Prime Minister! Can you comment on the suspension of the Foreign Office Minister, Dawn Blunt?'

Ray was annoyed. Jack voiced his concerns, perhaps too bluntly. 'Here we go again. You don't concentrate on the real story, even when it's handed to you on a plate.' Ray tucked the iPad back under his arm. 'No more questions,' he snapped, as he turned on his heels and stormed back inside Number 10.

Ray promptly returned home, and with no real need to switch off, save for the sensibilities of those who inhabited him, he was once again in the lounge. Walton was using his host's eyes to get back to perusing the book on the Bilderberg Group. Yes, he could no doubt download the title to his computer, and read it from there, but this was far more fun. Flicking through the appendices at the back, Walton took notice of a section headed "Bilderberg Group – Attendees 2014". He was looking for Dawn Blunt's name, knowing that it should be there.

But nothing. Automatically, Ray started shaking his head. Walton was getting used to these auto-pilot functions. He would never say to Vernon this was all very impressive. Trying to put it into perspective, he did wonder if this had more to do with the activity of the right brain, which they seemed to have been able to tap into.

It was at that point something else on the pages caught his eye. Another name. "Duncan Hurst – Environment Minister, UK". Walton summoned Jack over to him, and pointed at the name, now zoomed in and filling the centre of the capsule's main viewing screen.

'That's strange,' said a bemused Jack. 'Walton, pull up the list that Phil gave us.' A few keystrokes and Walton did so, splitting the content of the main screen. One side revealed the computer printout, a still shot taken from Ray's earlier point of view. Next to this was the current book page, the one that Ray was now looking at.

Where "Duncan Hurst, Environment Minister, UK" sat on the list in the book, the view of the printout read "Dawn Blunt – Adviser, European Parliament."

'Should have seen that before. In the internet print-out, the entries are generally in alphabetical order by surname. Except that "Blunt" appears in the list within the "H" section,' Walton observed. Jack shook his head. 'I think apologies are in order.'

On auto-pilot again, Ray stared at the book in disbelief. His pause for contemplation was interrupted by hearing the words 'Ray! Visitor!' They came from Alicia's mouth, standing there in the doorway, with Phil standing behind her. He had a computer hard drive under his arm. The team revved back up for action.

'Evening Phil. Late shift?'

Before Phil could reply, Alicia brusquely said 'I'll check how the new child minder is getting on,' leaving the two of them to their business, closing the door behind her.

'Just got the hard drive back,' Phil advised. Ray got up to make an inspection.

'I've got something for you, too,' Ray replied. They swapped the hard drive for the book, already neatly tabbed at the relevant page. Phil opened the publication where it was marked. 'See there?' Ray guided, pointing at the relevant section. 'No Dawn Blunt.'

'But Duncan Hurst instead,' Phil confirmed. 'Perhaps they changed the online information?'

'I'll leave you to double check,' Ray cajoled. 'What about the drive?' he enquired, waving the box around.

'It's blank. Not just that, it's never been used.'

Ray's crew was perplexed. Jack stepped in. 'What are you saying?'

'It's been replaced. It's not the original.' Inside Ray's head, the team were collectively puzzled.

* * *

The American Embassy, or at least one of them in London, was located in Grosvenor Square in Mayfair. Despite its high profile, those using G.P.S. to find it were often perplexed by being directed to a Royal Mail sorting office. It was obviously someone's little joke when post codes had been allocated to the area back in 1917. Hardly top-line espionage; it might just have been a pedant being extra-careful at the time.

In the Ambassador's office, Conrad Connelly was tense. He realised he was being considered a fool. Threats of exposure of his own secrets didn't gain much traction with him. He had always been seen as a rogue, and in essence people would expect nothing less of him. Whatever dirt came out about him, very few people would be surprised. He knew there was nothing true which would harm his audience-appreciation figures. He slowly took his glasses off, and cleaned them with a handy optician's cloth. Why did they insist on imprinting the name of their business on them these days?

That was what it was like being a former actor. His characters had been anti-heroes, and a great many people very easily confused fiction and reality. On the other side of the coin, he was equipped with a penchant for extracting information from people, at times when they should have been keeping things to themselves.

He wasn't someone who held any particular political beliefs, but was keen to be seen to represent the views of whoever happened to be in the Whitehouse. As a musician, too, at this very moment one song was playing over and over in his head. "T'aint what you do (it's the way that you do it)", with Ella Fitzgerald on lead vocals.

He stared over the desk at Duncan Hurst. He was fascinated with his black skin, which was looking especially shiny thanks to Conrad having cranked up the heating. He was used to such temperatures. Had been all his life. Hurst wasn't, and the beads of sweat made him look more nefarious than usual. Conrad couldn't understand why his constituents kept voting for this man across the desk from him. An empathy bypass on legs.

Conrad decided that his self-inflicted pause to think had gone on long enough. 'So, Mister Hurst, let me see if I've got this.' He leaned over towards him, as if betraying a confidence. 'You want us to interfere in your affairs of State?'

Hurst licked his lips. 'You know how this will pan out.' He inadvertently shook his head. 'Blood on the streets…' he raised his eyebrows, 'if there isn't a coup.'

Conrad felt he really had to explain some basics to this jumped-up interloper. 'You forget. Ray Grady's approach has many similarities to the reconstituted "Tea Party" which brought our President to power.'

Hurst couldn't control his smugness. 'That grouping emerged out of your Republican Party.'

Conrad shook his head. 'So the media would have you believe. It eventually carved its own niche, smashing through the left-right political paradigm. The right tried to absorb it. Use the energy for its own devices. But they eventually failed. And next to that, we had an unprecedented early election, following Mr Obama's impeachment.'

Hurst was catching on that the viewpoints Conrad had picked up in Britain's mainstream media may have been amended to a distorted agenda. 'What are you saying?'

Conrad tried to make the conversation practical. 'We can learn from "We the People", and they can learn from us.' He stared through his heavy glasses at his prey. 'Your politics are from a bygone era.'

Hurst picked up the message loud and clear, and got up to leave. 'You may live to regret this,' he threatened.

Conrad recognised a ruse when he heard one. 'If we trace any "manufactured terror" back to you, guess who we'll be coming after?' The reply almost stopped Hurst in his tracks. He wasn't expecting such a direct and assertive response.

* * *

Phil really did like Georgie's office in Downing Street. There was a latent energy within it. Almost as if the spirits from days-gone-by were riding on his shoulders, sticking their collective feet into his ribs, urging him to dig ever-deeper into what was really going on.

Next to him was Ray's copy of "The Bilderberg Group" book, placed to the right of the keyboard and screen. He had propped it open at the page which read "62nd Bilderberg Group Meeting, 29th May to 1st June 2014, Copenhagen, Denmark". He began to tap away, keying in "Dawn Blunt May 2014" into the search bar on the Vue-Vid website. Within the time of a heartbeat, the search results came up. A little way down the list was one video described as "Dawn Blunt Interview – EU accounts unaudited for 20th year. 30th May 2014, Brussels". Phil clicked on the link, and after a short time to buffer, he saw a younger Dawn on the screen. It was a head-and-shoulders shot, clearly within the European Parliament reception. A European Flag, resplendent with its twelve satanic stars, somehow fluttered in the background. Dawn had the microphones of several broadcasters almost pushed under her nose as she navigated through the prepared statement in her hand.

'I regret to report that, for the 20th year in a row, we have not been able to sign off a fully audited set of accounts for the European Parliament. The discrepancies continue to remain, without being addressed.'

Phil paused the video, and checked his notes. 'You can't be in two places at once,' he said aloud. Slightly embarrassed, he cleared his throat. Talking to one's self is always the first sign of madness, despite any evidence to the contrary.

Later, in the Prime Minister's Private Office, Ray was sitting in his desk chair, with Tony standing by his side. Both looked very uncomfortable, but were trying not to. Any onlooker who had been following the press stories would have been surprised to see Dawn sitting in the chair across the desk from Tony. She was hurriedly processing the contents of "The Bilderberg Group" book.

Tony broke the silence. 'Someone was trying to set you up.'

'Substituting your name for Hurst's in the online records,' noted Jack via Ray.

Dawn was aware now of the chain of events, and was annoyed. 'If it hadn't been for that book, you'd have never twigged.'

'I know,' Ray confirmed. 'Making you guilty until proven innocent. The European Napoleonic Law way of doing things. Should never be ours.'

Tony decided to try and find a positive in all of the happenings. 'It could have been worse. At least we didn't have you arrested.' From Dawn's reaction, he realised this wasn't the best choice of scenario.

'You want thanks for small mercies?' she shrieked.

Ray went on the attack. 'Probably too soon for you to be taking the high ground.'

Dawn was now very prickly. 'Meaning what?' Tony took his cue, and handed over a folder containing papers for inspection.

'I'm not ashamed, given our suspicions, that we've had you followed,' he revealed. Dawn looked at the contents, and was shocked.

Ray looked for her to confide in them. 'Perhaps there's something you want to tell us?' Dawn gave out a heavy sigh. She realised the time had passed for her to carry on holding secrets.

* * *

For a man with such a record of military service, Meddings had a very fashion-conscious apartment. It was far plusher than his salary would underwrite, all white and chrome. His soundtrack for the evening included Gustav Holst, with "Jupiter – The Bringer of Jollity" doing its best to drown out the rain lashing against his windows. A past fiancé had bought him that particular CD as an ironic joke, one that he didn't understand at the time, and to be frank still didn't.

Wearing a silk dressing gown over a pair of designer boxer shorts, he was working on his laptop, perched on a creamy-coloured sofa. It was obviously something important to him, as he was not best-pleased to have the doorbell interrupt his train of thought.

After a deep sigh, he put the laptop on the coffee table in front of him and got up. He thought twice about putting his slippers on, which were tidily arranged along his path to the front door, but thought better of it. He rattled free the security chain before turning the catch on the lock.

As close to the door as she could get, he was surprised to see Alicia standing there in front of him. Wrapped tightly around her was a black latex raincoat, her hair soaked from the storms lashing down outside. The Prime Minister's wife was the last person he expected to see on a night like this. Meddings was slightly panicked, and pulled Alicia through the door, quickly slamming it behind her.

'What are you doing?' he spat, through gritted teeth. Alicia responded with purposeful playfulness.

'Renewing acquaintances,' she whispered at volume, stroking his chest through the gap in his gown. Meddings looked around, as if he could see through walls and doors.

'Where's your security?' he queried, knowing only too well what the protocols for her excursions anywhere were. Alicia put her arms around his neck. Meddings was getting more and more uncomfortable.

'I told Dougan and Kindon the truth,' she coyly revealed. This did nothing for his nerves. 'I'm catching up with an old university pal,' she said, with mock indignation.

Meddings continued with the practicalities. 'This is very dangerous,' he noted, although now not with so much conviction.

'Turns you on, doesn't it?' she hissed. From exploring for chest hairs to curl with her fingers, Alicia's hands moved very deliberately downwards. Slowly. Confidently. 'You'd be surprised how little people talk. How things can be brushed off.'

Any remaining resistance was beginning to melt away. 'No-one suspects?' he enquired, desperate for one final reassurance. Taking his head in both hands, Alicia pulled him down to her so that their lips met. A little peck, followed by them taking turns to respond to the passion, their tongues eagerly darting back and forth between their mouths.

'Does that answer your question?' she purred breathlessly, coming up for air. Their feet began to respond to the matador-style dance that both were now getting into the rhythm with.

Had Meddings been paying attention to his surroundings, as any good soldier would, he might have been more aware of the accidental flash which went off in the woods across the road from the side of his apartment block.

The heavy rain also helped to shield his senses from being alert enough to sense his home being under observation. Phil was wrapped up well, hiding in a tree, with his faithful telephoto-lens camera clutched in both hands. He had the unit set to silent, rattling off dozens of images to be stored in the high capacity memory card.

From his point of view, right down and through the lens, he had a dynamic view of Meddings and Alicia through the nearest window. He had been doing this stuff long enough to be able to know which angle would give him the most compromising telephoto snaps. He also smiled at how observant he could be, when he noticed Alicia arrive outside the apartment block. There were tell-tale signs he had picked up, the same as when he had caught other celebrities with their lovers and mistresses.

His hunch that this was the place to be tonight was correct. His other hunch about the attire of one of his targets was also confirmed.

Alicia had nothing on under that raincoat.

15

TRUST NO-ONE

The House of Commons was a very unbalanced chamber since the election. The opposition benches were thinly populated, allowing those from Plaid Cymru and the Scottish National Party to be more front-and-centre than they had ever been.

Plaid were glad they could use "Cymru" again in their name. The Scottish National Party was proudly saying their name in full. Having found they could only call themselves "SNP" without falling foul of European directives, which did not allow them to either specify their country or their policy of nationalism, now they wore their badge with pride.

"We the People" getting into power had been a masterstroke for them. They were getting a greater degree of autonomy than ever before, and without having to be answerable to Eurocrats across the English Channel. Those within the SNP ranks who had simply wanted to use independence as a gravy-train to Brussels, swapping Westminster for being ruled from even further away, had been banished from their party once their true intentions had become known, post referendum failure.

Prime Minister's Question Time was always something of a spectacle, but previously just a very stage-managed affair where point-scoring was the order of the day. Having it at noon gave it the flavour of a Wild West showdown, the sheriff trying to uphold the law, the speaker playing the judge. Since coming to power, Ray had made the opposition look more like criminals on trial, a role they had found very difficult to shake free of.

Tony was stationed at the dispatch box. Whereas without Ray about he had gripped it for dear life, now he was far more relaxed and enjoying the experience. It helped that Ray was sat down behind him, flanked by Dawn and Georgie. Tony's focus was Duncan Hurst across the divide, a leader in name only for the rag-tag groups which now filled the opposition benches.

'To answer the honourable gentleman's question,' Tony brusquely replied, trying not to grin too widely. 'The balance of cash at the Treasury looks glorious, following our refusal to pay the I.M.F. any more interest.' He savoured the cheers from the government benches, and such was the imbalance in numbers, these drowned out the gutsy negative reaction from the collected opposition.

'I looked at the figures, and the UK is now in a position to cancel the debts owed to it by all third world countries,' Tony semi-chortled. He stopped short of gloating, never good for one's image. 'Free at last from crippling repayments. Let's hope other countries follow our lead.' The further cheers showed how well this was going down with his allies. 'At this point, I would like to welcome back my honourable colleague, the Prime Minister!'

Tony picked his briefing folder up and went to sit down in one smooth move. Loud applause rang out, even amongst some on the opposite side of the venue, as Ray took his place at the box. For some it had felt like forever since the last time he was there. For others, it was something they never expected to see again, and for them it had come around far too soon.

'As Mark Twain said, "reports of my death have been greatly exaggerated".' An excellent opening gambit, which generated belly laughs from the government benches. 'I welcome my Chancellor's work, which has gone a long way to establish the new Commonwealth!' Ray looked daggers at Hurst. 'The Leader of the Opposition's banking buddies may not be happy with this.' A sea of different tones of jeers accompanied his statement. 'Or, indeed, with my forthcoming frank and meaningful trade discussions to be held with the new American President.'

Some of the Opposition started to boo with such gusto that the few of them generated an impressive wall of sound. Those on the government benches couldn't help but laugh. Anyone would think the general public weren't going to see this, and understand the back story of their reactions as a consequence.

Ray played on this. 'What are you booing for?' he demanded. 'Afraid we'll further upset your European paymasters, *n'est pas?*'

And so it went on, for a solid ninety minutes of banter. Duncan Hurst tried to get a few sound-bite jabs in, but he could tell his political currency was in default. He knew those who financed his adventures would be looking on, and they would be very unimpressed with their investment. He may be a psychopath, but he knew only too well there would be repercussions if he couldn't turn things around.

Ray Grady was back, and there was no sign of any weaknesses for him to exploit. In fact, if Hurst didn't know any better, he would swear the patter was stronger than ever. The choice of words more biting. The background knowledge and grasp of the facts taking on a greater incisiveness. The recovery was almost too good to be true.

* * *

Back in Georgie's office in Downing Street, Phil was continuing to use his journalistic training to best effect. On the computer screen was a member list for "The Fabian Appreciation Society, University of Cambridge".

Attention to detail had given him many breaks, or "good fortune" as those who didn't work as hard as he did would put it. Able to join together facts that didn't seem to sit together at all, but digging deeper would garner unexpected results. This was going to be one of those occasions.

Two names. One big clue. Carl Meddings. Alicia Stone. A security officer. And an unusual christian name shared with the Prime Minister's wife. Buried within an alphabetical listing. Two people who claimed they had no history, but Phil had an uneasy feeling. He knew to always trust such thoughts.

What if they were one and the same? It would be more unusual that they didn't know each other if that was the case. After all, in that group's year, there were just a couple dozen names in that society. It wasn't as if this was a student union club with more than 300 members, such as the same year's "Cult TV" society.

Looking deeper into the website, Phil clicked on the group's "About Us" link. He had a vague idea of their objectives, but it was a little disturbing to see it written down. "The Fabian Society advances the principles of socialism via gradualist and reformist, rather than revolutionary, means".

The "totalitarian tiptoe" technique rather than an all-out bloody battle. The "boiling frog" approach. Turn up the heat ever so slowly, so that the poor creature doesn't realise it's being poached to death. Before anyone could realise what had happened, these "change agents" would have created a post-democratic era. Phil wished for a cigarette, but settled for shaking his head, and grinding his teeth together.

Broadening the canvas of research, Phil called up Downing Street's personnel records, and did a search on "Carl Meddings". The CV, complete with photo, highlighted a packed career, which was nothing unusual for this sort of person. Phil's attention was drawn to more recent entries. "May – August 2014: Unknown. October 2014 – Present: Devene Security Services".

Phil thinned his eyes in a beam of recognition. He called up Chris Bowden's CV again, which Pippa had sent on to him from the Stock Exchange. Comparing the two files on screen, side by side, he saw a point of congruence. The Prime Minister's assassin also had the entry "May – August 2014: Unknown".

In his line of work, he realised years ago there was no such thing as coincidence, except in the most mundane of circumstances. And this certainly wasn't one of them. He picked up his mobile and initiated a call. After a little longer than he was comfortable with, finally the call was picked up.

'It's me. What was Alicia's maiden name?'

* * *

Damian was soaking his feet in a Garra Rufa Fish Foot Spa. The surroundings were all metallic black, not quite enough to reflect the objects next to the walls, but enough to give the space a feeling of depth. He was wearing a pair of outrageous sun glasses as he "caught some rays". He looked like Trevor Horn in his "Buggles" era, but the specs were bigger and with a bolder purple frame.

A sleek mobile phone was in his hand, pressed to his ear. Considering this was normally an experience that relaxed him, he was very agitated. Noting his seeming displeasure, the female "treatment operative" took this as a cue to stir the fish in the tank. This annoyed Damian further, who waved her away, and pointed her to the exit.

'I want no more excuses,' he confided with the caller. 'Finish the job. Tonight.' He listened for a short time, but was not keen on what he was hearing. 'This guy is denting our profits far too much.'

With that, he terminated the call, and stared down at the fish cajoling his feet. He shook his head, and began to see how many he could squash under foot.

* * *

Ray Grady was in his lounge, which allowed him a recharge and some contemplation. His body might not need this so much anymore, but for the five people buried in his skull, they needed to get their bearings. This wasn't a nine-to-five for any of them. Vernon knew at some point he would have to look at a secondary crew to alternate with his current colleagues. He had a list, ready to be contacted. There were even the names of back-ups to the back-ups which would have to be contacted in due course.

He didn't even want to think about who was going to understudy for himself. He knew he was virtually irreplaceable. This was going to be a job for life. Well, Ray's lifetime anyway. Walton would soon be looking for enigmatic characters that would be able to continue Ray's legacy. The assassination had come far too early in Ray's term of office for such stars of the future to make themselves known.

The one good thing was that success begets success. The vision of the future under "We the People" was now beginning to firm up in people's minds. Those wanting to play their part would foment their views and rise to the top of the party structure. And all the time they had to look for the "controlled opposition" who would be put in the mix to divert the party from its ideals. None of this was going to be easy, but they really couldn't extend Ray's sell-by date by more than a couple of years.

They'd have to put the new leader in place before the next general election. But that was a task for another time.

Ray's party of five was watching the television. Activity which sharpened their reactions and team working. Watching quiz shows. This was *Mastermind* with John Humphreys in the chair, although no-one was too sure if this was a new edition or a repeat from one of those game-show channels. Someone could have checked, but it was a distraction from the fun at hand. It was a general knowledge round. The level of concentration was such that no-one was paying attention to Alicia, who was fiddling with her Blackberry, sitting on an armchair in the corner.

Humphreys was as gruff as ever. 'And now our next contestant,' he said with his usual bombastic demeanour. Inside Ray's head, the quintet of Jack, Vernon, Bonnie, Solange and Walton were ready to roll. 'Your general knowledge round starts… now. What modern term derives from the Czechoslovakian word for "forced labour"?'

'Robot,' barked Vernon.

"Correct. *Exophthalmic Goitre* is the medical term for which condition?'

'Graves' Disease,' shouted Bonnie.

'In which year was the Suez Canal opened?'

'1869,' informed Walton.

'Used in cause-and-effect analysis, what is the Ishikawa diagram more commonly known as?'

'Fishbone,' advised Solange.

'What number is between nine and eleven on a regulation dartboard?'

'Fourteen,' said Jack, clearly on home soil.

'Which artist produced drawings depicting shelter in London Underground railway stations during World War Two's Blitz bombings?'

'Henry Moore,' said Wrighty laconically, coming out of left field. The team looked around to the walls of the capsule in amazement.

'Nice one, Wrighty!' beamed Solange, as the end of the round was signalled. Outside, Alicia was amazed by Ray's performance, and was just a little suspicious.

'How did you do that?' she asked.

'Getting more of my memory back,' Ray replied feebly, thanks to Vernon. The interrogation was cut short by a knock at the door.

'Come in!' jumped in Jack, via Ray, glad of the interruption. Tony, Georgie and Dawn entered, escorted by Meddings just behind them.

Tony had an information folder under his arm. He looked around to Meddings. 'Thanks. Might as well check on your team.'

Meddings wasn't keen on the brush-off. 'They've got the night off,' he said, bemused.

'Oh. Okay,' said Tony. 'Check something else,' he barked. Meddings finally grasped the hint and left the room. With that, Tony's face turned to the worst aspect of grim.

Before he could say anything, a mobile phone beeped. It was Ray's. He held his hand up to stop proceedings, and took out the device, quickly reading a text message.

'One second,' he advised, before quickly keying in a reply. 'Sorry about that. What's going on?' Tony, Georgie and Dawn fidgeted, failing to decide who would tell Ray, who was rightly now concerned. 'Tony? Got a Kermit in your throat?'

'You might want to sit down,' said Tony, realising that this was an unnecessary comment, given that five people in Ray's head weren't likely to need to do so. They took their cue, however, and Ray did so. Alicia, expecting this to be parliamentary business, took this as a cue to leave.

'No,' Dawn pointedly said to Alicia. 'This concerns you, too.' Alicia sheepishly returned to her armchair.

'You sure?' Ray queried, the quintet within him all wondering what was coming next.

'Ask *her*,' suggested Georgie, pointing at Alicia, who tried not to look guilty.

'What's this about?' she enquired.

Tony wanted the horse to open its mouth. 'Guess.' With nothing forthcoming, he thrust the information folder into Alicia's hands. She opened it with some reticence and saw Phil's snaps from the previous evening. They were in glorious colour, 10" x 8" prints, all taken outside the Meddings flat. They'd probably fetch a good price in Soho, and even better returns from mud-flinging tabloids. Alicia bowed her head, realising her game was up. She looked straight into Ray's eyes, and inadvertently those of the five people within.

'You were working day and night,' she offered, sheepishly.

'Sure, I knew it would be my fault,' said Jack via Ray.

Tony wasn't going to let her off the hook. 'You've known him since university.'

Dawn joined the dots. 'Being part of the Fabian Society doesn't really go down well when you have connections to "We the People".'

'Alicia,' pleaded Solange via Ray. 'The children. We can build something up together again.'

'That will be your feminine side influencing your words,' sneered Tony, knowing that his dialogue would be understood by the team within. That annoyed Solange.

Jack looked at his team, and said to them, discretely, 'This really is the "long game".'

Georgie stepped in to give the necessary exposition. 'You met at university. You,' she said pointedly to Alicia, 'or your handlers more precisely, had this in mind right from the start.'

Dawn decided to take away any hope of a soft landing. 'And don't go thinking you and him have any sort of future.'

'What?' replied Alicia with her best air of acting puzzled.

'You weren't the only one he was having an affair with,' Dawn qualified aggressively. Georgie caught Dawn's eye, doing her best to crank up some empathy with her.

'You're lying,' queried Alicia, not realising she had missed the stage where she could have gone into some sort of denial phase.

'Why would she?' said an annoyed Georgie. 'What would she gain?'

Dawn gave both barrels. 'How would I know about his birthmark?' She pointed to her left side. Alicia sharply looked around to try and find an ally. When none were forthcoming, she broke down, and crashed back into her armchair, both her hands over her mouth so as to speak no further evil. The pupils of her eyes were wide open, and tears welled up.

Meddings had been listening to everything from the other side of the door. Now was the time for action. He smashed into the room, right hand clasping a Soviet Patparine, nine-point-two millimetre revolver. One by one he covered everyone in the room, taking turns to point it at those in front of him. Tony, Dawn and Georgie all thought it best to put their hands up.

Ray looked at them, all with their hands raised. Jack ensured that Ray shrugged, and then approached Meddings.

'Careful,' began Tony, before stressing the name 'Ray.' Ray stopped, as if a second thought was required. It was enough for Meddings to beckon Alicia with his hand, to join him. To stand next to him. Still tearful, but not sure why, Alicia did so.

Jack was piecing it together. 'I see. You know my wife. And you know the would-be assassin from the Stock Exchange.' Meddings raised an eyebrow, but within Ray's head, it was time to review the surveillance tapes of the incident that began their latest adventure. Vernon began to look through the footage.

The camera he chose first was from the control room, up high and at the back of the auditorium. What had they all missed? Vernon found the action where the shots were fired by Chris Bowden, from the floor at the front of the auditorium. There was a little bit of a shake to the image from the camera. Not what would have been expected from that vantage point.

Vernon checked other camera angles, and found one in the general direction of the control room, from the front left of the auditorium. He zoomed in on the control booth. Flashes of light from an opening in the glass. The same slot where projector beams came out from. The flashes weren't part of the picture which was filling the screen on the stage.

Vernon zoomed in further. He smiled at the power of the technology at his finger tips. Looking directly through the aperture he had the inside of the control booth in extreme close-up. Applying image filters, the darkness within was suddenly exposed. And there was Meddings, slipping a powerful revolver, complete with silencer, away into a holster beneath his jacket. Vernon rubbed his hands, with the glee of a gamer that had just got the top score.

'You were the other trigger, weren't you?' Vernon voiced via Ray. The husk of the Prime Minister stared right at Meddings. But Vernon wasn't finished. He located another camera angle, this time of the stage, but again at a considerable distance. Review of this would have been discounted on first sift for its lack of detail. Vernon was able to zoom in on some side doors. As clear as a confession, the quintet saw Meddings as he stormed into the room. And that was via the quickest entrance to use to get into the auditorium from the control booth.

Keeping the image nice and tight on Meddings, Vernon followed him as he went over to join Dougan and Kindon in helping to pin Chris the assassin down. Following the movement of the hands of Meddings, the crew saw him palm the revolver belonging to Chris from its landing point by where his two operatives and the shooter were struggling. No wonder they couldn't find it. Again tracing his movements, Meddings dashed over to join the medics who were working on Ray's slain body. Tony and Georgie were looking on in close proximity, but when Georgie averted her gaze and Tony grasped her head to his neck, it was all the chance Meddings needed.

Meddings slipped both revolvers into one of the medic's kit bags. Ray revealed the course of actions to all those in the room. The magician's trick had been exposed. Initially, Meddings was baffled as to how all the details had come out. He put it down to how bright a man Ray was.

'You got me,' Meddings conceded. 'I had both guns smuggled out.'

'Just enough to create a doubt in a jury's mind,' appreciated Dawn. 'And no murder weapons found makes for doubt in a court case.'

'Can't even trust the ambulance service these days,' sighed Tony. 'The N.H.S. obviously doesn't pay them enough.'

'I wondered why they weren't on the delegate list,' reasoned Georgie. 'The medics,' she qualified.

As they were still at gunpoint, Georgie decided they might as well fill in the entire picture. 'What happened last year?' he asked of Meddings. 'You and Chris disappeared off the face of the Earth. At the same time.' Meddings looked confused at this.

'You don't remember, do you?' Dawn concluded.

'Funny, that,' Tony continued. 'Neither did your fellow shooter.'

'Seems like the pair of you disappeared in Eastern Europe,' Georgie suggested.

As if she had clicked a replay button on an answering machine, Meddings stared ahead and began to repeat himself, over and over. 'Stop these madmen. Stop these corrupt politicians. Stop these madmen. Stop these corrupt politicians.'

'Thought so,' Georgie concluded.

'No doubt the handiwork of an M.K. Ultra program,' Jack said, adding to the mix.

Dawn was confused by the revelations. 'But "We the People" didn't exist last year.'

'Didn't need to,' Georgie replied. 'Anyone could have been made their target. Plenty more dupes who volunteered are still out there. Their existing connections just made them the obvious choice.'

Via Ray, Jack upped the stakes. 'Your mate Chris. He won't be getting off on an insanity plea. Been taken out of the picture already.'

Meddings smiled. 'Someone has to know what really happened first.' Inside the capsule, Vernon finished hastily striking his keyboard.

'Have you seen one of these before?' he enquired. Ray pulled out his mobile phone and clicked a button.

The recording was perfect. 'You got me. I had his gun smuggled out,' confessed Meddings from earlier. Dawn was heard to reply 'Just enough to create a doubt in a jury's mind. No murder weapons found makes for doubt in a court case.'

'Can't even trust medics these days,' said Tony on the audio replay. 'The N.H.S. doesn't pay them enough.'

'Already up on Vue-Vid?' Georgie enquired.

Ray grinned. 'Oh yes. Technology. Marvellous.'

'Just cannon fodder,' added Dawn, putting matters into perspective. She turned to Alicia. 'As *you* will be.'

'My brother died in Afghanistan,' Meddings snapped. 'And what did you politicians care?' He stared at Ray, who seemed to be only half-listening, being far too pre-occupied with fiddling with his mobile.

'That wasn't on our watch,' Jack said via Ray, who had quickly jumped back into a focus on the matters at hand.

'But you're pulling our troops out,' Meddings sneered. 'I don't want his death to be in vain,' he pleaded.

Tony again indulged in his annoying habit of staring at his finger nails with his palm stretched out in front of him. 'It already has been.'

Dawn thought it time to try and reason with the mercenary in front of her. 'Blame the corporations who benefit from wars. It's their money which ensures their weapons have a use.'

Georgie opted to provide more background. 'Did we mention we know those who trained you worked for the very same corporations?'

Meddings was annoyed, partly because the memories of that training simply weren't in sharp focus. It was like he could sense the edge of the relevant memories, but couldn't see the content within the boundaries. He gripped his revolver tightly in response, clenching his teeth, unsure who to gun down first.

Ray sighed. 'Thing is, you've shown your hand far too early.'

'Sorry?' replied Meddings, not quite understanding.

'Giving Dougan and Kindon the night off,' Ray qualified. 'Dead giveaway.'

Tony immediately realised the significance. 'Withdrawal of standard security procedures?'

'Like clockwork on all such operations,' Ray said, going into history mode, thanks to Walton. 'J.F.K.; Bobby Kennedy; Martin Luther King. Recognised it straight away.'

Ray held up the screen of his mobile so that Meddings could see it. An incoming text message simply advised, "Been given the night off".

Jack couldn't resist giving Ray's voice the demeanour of a game show host. 'Our researchers asked Dougan and Kindon: "where are you this evening"?' Meddings raised his revolver, pointing it directly at Ray.

There was a brief pause. Like an elastic band snapping, Alicia suddenly slapped Meddings' arm. A single shot discharged, but was diverted from its target. A high-pitched yelp from Tony was enough to signal the projectile had hit him in the shoulder. Squealing in a way that was part young child after being given a Chinese burn, part distressed sow, Tony flopped to the floor, banging his feet like drums on the carpet beneath. Georgie dived down to see if she could help him out, and without any thought for her own safety Dawn scuttled across to assist.

Ray was standing by one of the expansive windows, which took up around a third of two of the walls of the room. Something came into view in the corner of his eye. It was Anna, seen by no-one else, and beckoning him to quickly move to the centre of the room. He could never resist an invitation from her, and much to the disbelief of the quintet inside his head, Ray did so.

As if that was a cue, an eruption of noise and commotion followed. The windows of the room, from both sides, were suddenly and simultaneously smashed in. Two special-ops-issued gas canisters spiralled into the arena, creating a curtain of billowing smoke in just a couple of seconds.

Recollections of images of the storming of embassies flashed through the minds of the musketeers. And so it came to pass. Dark figures in full combat gear, resplendent in gas masks, high-tech helmets, bullet-proof vests, and armed with M-16 assault rifles, the strike force on their high wires crashed into the room. Shards of glass cascaded everywhere. A pair of the troopers went immediately to shield Tony, Georgie and Dawn.

Meddings blinked involuntarily at Alicia, and struck her with the butt of the revolver, sending her flying across the carpet. The coverage from the smoke was now complete, and Meddings struggled to see enough of the room to be able to accurately point the gun at Ray.

'Oh no, not again,' an outburst from Ray which came via Wrighty. The right brain, in particular, always gets sick of constant repetition.

But there was yet another roll of the dice. The inner door burst open, and Phil unexpectedly stormed in, satchel over shoulder, with a large handkerchief wrapped around his mouth, spaghetti-western style. It didn't look quite right that he had a revolver in his hand.

Jack realised the smoke presently gave everyone a disadvantage. Luckily, such a moment had been prepared for. 'Convert to infra-red!' he barked at Vernon. With that, the image seen on the main screen within the capsule took on scarlet hues. As if they had escaped to the planet Mars, the team could see Phil standing at the door, struggling to make out who was who.

Meddings aimed his gun in the direction of the door, unclear as to the exact co-ordinates he needed to take down Phil.

'Phil! Left left, thirty degrees!' Jack shouted out, via Ray. Phil adjusted his aim in response, and the shot hit Meddings in the shoulder. The target dropped his revolver and recoiled, with the gun bouncing across the floor in Alicia's direction. The hiss of the smoke canisters had been replaced by a chorus of coughing and spluttering.

Meddings staggered, then had a moment of clarity, and jumped at Phil. He knocked Phil out cold, and seized his revolver.

Alicia crawled for Meddings' piece, sobbing under her breath. She collected it, and struggled to her feet before taking aim at Meddings. The reality was she could not see clearly enough through the smoke and her tears to be brave enough to pull the trigger.

The lack of visibility worked both ways. Meddings was having difficulty dragging himself to his feet, the tear gas was really painful. The smoke cleared enough for two of the commandos to acquire their target. They quickly took aim and made the shot, their co-ordination took out a leg each. Meddings flopped in a heap, movement only now possible by dragging himself via the strength in his arms.

Alicia surveyed the situation and slowly moved towards Meddings. With Georgie in command of Tony's situation, Dawn looked up to realise what Alicia was about to do. She sprang to her feet and dashed over, a flying leap allowing her the time to seize the revolver from Meddings, just as he was straightening up his aim on Alicia.

The two commandos who had incapacitated Meddings took their cue to then take hold of one of his arms each, and dragged him towards the back of the house, through the luxurious conservatory, where they broke down its pair of external doors. They knew to expect them to be locked.

When clear of the house, the commandos threw off their gas marks. It was Dougan and Kindon, clearly not having had a night off. They looked around the early evening vista, their view having been made easier by the movement sensors which activated the floodlights in the garden. They continued to drag Meddings well clear of the house, the billows of smoke eventually giving up chasing them from the building.

Next out was Alicia, still carrying a revolver, coughing and trying to dry her eyes with a handkerchief. Just behind were Phil and Dawn, who were helping Tony escape from the premises. They sat Tony down on a low garden wall, which isolated an area of garden patio, raised a little and usually put to use for gatherings involving barbecues. Phil pulled his scarf down from his mouth, unavoidably coughing from the smoke.

Dawn looked at the revolver in her hand, and expertly checked that it was loaded.

At the rear of the pack was Ray, flanked by the three other commandos with Georgie just behind. The smoke was clearly having no effect on him, and far too nonchalantly he walked out with his hands in his pockets.

He looked back at Georgie, the smoke causing her to cough heartily, but not enough to stop her getting out her mobile to call for help. She looked up to see Ray heading back to her, at which point she raised a questioning eyebrow. The team inside Ray suddenly understood the cause for her concern. He started to half-heartedly cough for the benefit of the onlookers, before providing an arm for Georgie to rely on in getting away from the house and the smoke.

Elsewhere at the scene, Dougan and Kindon now stood over Meddings, rifles poised. Despite his incapacity, they weren't going to take any chances. Phil approached them, and took the opportunity to "high five" with Dougan. Ray spotted this and scuttled over to Phil.

'You really do know all sorts of people,' Ray observed.

'They mentioned they had been stood down without replacement cover in place. It was obvious what was coming next.'

'Thanks for your text,' Ray enthused. 'Made all the difference.' Ray then grinned at Dougan and Kindon. 'Nice job, guys.' With that, Dougan and Kindon saluted Ray, who laughed as he shook his head at their formality.

Alicia made her way over and crouched down next to Meddings. She simply wasn't sure which emotions were the ones to allow to surface, given what had just happened.

Meddings himself was breathless. He needed to clarify his situation. 'Alicia, I used Dawn. For the sake of the mission. She meant nothing to me.'

Next to the two of them, as they crouched on the floor, Dawn stood over both of them with revolver in hand.

'Mother warned me about toy-boys,' she hissed at Meddings. 'I had to fake it every time.' With that, she handed the weapon to Kindon, and Dougan took that as a cue to apply handcuffs to Alicia.

Georgie was still attending to Tony. For whatever reason, he was making a meal of his injury. Far off in the distance, and getting louder by the second, were the unmistakeable warbles of police and ambulance vehicles approaching the scene.

Alicia was frogmarched away from the scene by Dougan. They passed Ray and Phil on the way, and the reporter held his hand up to suggest a temporary pause was in order. Even though he was revelling in Georgie's attentions, Tony was near enough to want to ensure he paid attention to what happened next, and sat up to watch.

Dougan applied the necessary pressure to Alicia's arm. Phil fumbled in his satchel, and pulled out a computer hard drive, which he waved erratically in front of her. 'Look what I found at your boyfriend's gaff,' he taunted.

Such baiting only brought out Alicia's coldest persona. 'How do you think he got access to the private office?' she mocked.

That was exactly what Phil needed to complete the picture. 'Thought so.'

Tony wanted to ensure he was on the same page as everyone else. 'The original hard drive?' he enquired.

'Got it in one,' Phil beamed. He then decided to mock Alicia, as he wasn't keen that there seemed to be an overly sentimental amount of pity for her. 'You and James Bond won't be sailing off into the sunset.'

'Don't tell me he worked for "Six" as well?' Jack enquired via Ray, wanting to nail exactly what had happened.

'I wish it was that simple,' Phil remarked, still aware all was not yet crystal clear. 'On the books, but not on this case.'

'House cleaning in the morning,' Ray ordered to his staff.

Phil decided to walk away from the uncomfortable pauses that followed, and saw Dawn a good distance away from everyone. She was still standing over Meddings. Almost unseen, she gave him a kick. Phil smiled, knowing exactly what it was like to realise that someone you gave your unconditional love to wasn't the person you had thought them to be.

The police arrived, and were brought up to speed. They were finding it hard going trying to work out who they should be arresting, until Phil stepped in with the necessary background.

Bonnie, meanwhile, was providing the words for Ray as he interrogated Alicia. 'Our entire marriage was a sham?' he asked.

'At first,' she qualified. 'Even in your TV career you had influence. That attracted interest.'

'Whose?' Ray demanded. Alicia laughed nervously.

'I'd be dead by tomorrow if I told you,' she said with genuine fear. She pointed at Meddings. 'Same for him.'

'Shadow people?'

'Another puppet will be along soon,' Alicia confided. 'Those behind this have plenty. You'll never know who they are. They are united by a common purpose.'

Ray shrugged his shoulders. 'Despite all this, I think I owe you an apology.'

It was Alicia's turn to be confused. 'For what?'

Ray took a deep breath. 'For never stopping loving Anna.'

'Sometimes it was like she was right there with us,' said Alicia, finally confident enough to speak of her long-held anxieties. 'Spooky.'

The ambulances arrived. Slowly approaching what they believed to be a happily married husband and wife, the medics had an intense debate with the police as to which of them should take custody of Alicia. Ray realised his time was running out.

'Yeah. 'Til death do us part,' he mumbled, before being decisive with Alicia. 'We could stay together for the children,' he mused. 'Family is forever.' He looked at Alicia, who frowned. A different tack needed, then. 'Or you could disappear,' said with a superior level of disconnection. 'A tragic accident. A new life. Whatever.' As if needing a reason for such altruism, he added, 'You did try to save my life.'

There was an uncomfortable pause. Ray looked up to see Dawn and Georgie helping Tony to his feet, and trying to take him to the front of the house, almost as if they needed to get him to jump any sort of queue for ambulance attention.

Alicia realised she had to address Ray's suggestions. 'It would be easy to stay with you.' She also needed to tell him what, for her, was an inconvenient truth. 'It wasn't just a job by the end.'

Ray had a sudden epiphany. One moment of clarity changed everything. 'I was kidding myself with you.' His thoughts now meant he was striking through all his previous suggestions. 'My first wife was my soulmate. And that was never fair on you.'

No further words needed to be said. Alicia was taken away, with ambulance men arguing with a pair of police women as to who had first-dibs on the patient/suspect.

Ray looked away, then looked up, and peered down to the far end of his garden. He looked around to see if anyone else was aware of the swirling mist he saw there. It reminded him of one chilly morning in the Scottish highlands. Like most of his most treasured memories, of course he was with Anna at the time.

As if that memory had summoned her, he could see Anna standing there. He again looked around to see if anyone else was taking notice, looking his way, or saw what was out there in front of him. Wishful thinking, or curved ball reality, Anna then waved and blew him a kiss. He smiled.

Ray strolled down the garden to where Anna was standing in what was now a disconcertingly thick fog.

'Where's he going?' enquired Jack. 'Who's navigating?' was the more important question.

It was a cue for the remnants of what remained of Ray to share time with his first wife. 'That went well,' chirped Anna, as she hugged Ray, only too glad to be able to reciprocate.

'Remind me next time some young strumpet takes my fancy,' he said sternly. 'I hereby give you permission to slap me into the middle of next week.'

Solange was looking at her control desk. 'Who's he speaking to?' she questioned, totally bemused. 'Where's this stuff coming from?'

Part of her hoped Wrighty would chip in with some information, no matter how obtuse its content might have been.

But he didn't. Instead Vernon chipped in. 'Damned if I know. Just another one of those unexplainable glitches.'

He thought it best to not make mention to the rest of the crew that he was presently unable to wrestle back control of Ray's navigation systems.

After all, he was supposed to be completely in command of such things. And you never admit anything that gets in the way of your "genius" tag.

16

RENDEZVOUS REWIND

Back in the Prime Minister's Private Office, there was an immediate sign that things were never truly going to be back to what they had been. To the outside world, everyone saw a leader who had cheated death. His occasional stumble on a step could be forgiven. And even the unusual choice of words, which now and then seemed ever so out of character. The majority of the population were just glad that they still had someone they could believe in.

What they would have made of the spectacle that was unfolding in the most inner of sanctums was something not to dwell upon. Ray was sat down in his cream-leather executive chair, with a cable running down from the back of his head to a black box on the desk in front of him. It acted as a buffer to the recovered hard drive. Ray had his eyes shut, and was smiling.

'This is excellent,' Vernon sighed, via Ray. 'It really fills in the background to a lot of his, ah, my, meetings and memories.'

Georgie was standing by the door, checking through the in-tray for any urgent incoming messages. Tony, arm in a sling, was sitting opposite Ray, a puzzled frown over his face, trying to interpret every facial gesture that his boss was making.

'Surely he hadn't planned for this?' remarked Georgie.

'Plenty of incriminating stuff,' Ray noted, obviously happy to speak in the third person about "himself". He pointed at the back of his neck. 'Don't expect he thought it would be used like this.'

Georgie wondered. 'Why trust only his wife with the knowledge it existed?'

'Always the optimist.'

Within the inclusion capsule, Vernon was totally fascinated by the process of downloading the contents of the hard drive. It was now Solange who was speaking for Ray.

'Love conquers all,' she chimed. 'Etcetera.'

Walton was still trying to put recent events into perspective. 'When those in the shadows play the long-game, you don't expect them to be pointing women in your direction. Having them marry you. Having kids. Then doing their bit to ensure you don't achieve your goals.' Despite his age, Walton really was very naive about the nature of relationships.

'Download complete,' informed Vernon, slapping his hands together. Outside, Ray unplugged the cable from the back of his head.

'I think it might be time for some engine oil,' Jack suggested, via Ray. Their vessel moved over to the drinks cabinet to distribute a fine Tomintoul Speyside Glenlivet whisky.

Tony was the first to be handed a glass. 'Our party. A success before the establishment had time to infiltrate and corrupt it. And they still had traps laid.' He shuddered at the cloud of depression he was bringing to the room. 'Who would have ever suspected Alicia?'

Jack took up the riff, a little dismayed. 'No system left to save. It's broken. We have to start again. No more donations. With such cash comes obligations tied to apron strings. Those debts are never of benefit to the majority. The payback can never be worth it.'

Tony stared at Ray, considering his words. 'Is that Jack or Walton?' he enquired.

'That was Jack,' came the indignant reply. 'This is Walton.'

Vernon had been keenly analysing the downloaded information, and was keen to share. 'Wonder if this is what they didn't want us to find?' Vernon pressed a button, and an archive recording began. Inside and out, everyone was listening attentively.

'Look, it's like this, you don't want to upset the pharmaceutical industries.'

'Duncan Hurst,' said Walton, identifying one of his long-term political thorns. The voice continued.

'This is a fight which will make you some powerful enemies.'

'Duncan, this is simple,' the voice of Ray replied. 'Big Pharma makes a fortune from reconstituting natural remedies, but without most of the benefit of the originals. As well as adding extra little traps which ensure further business. After all, healthy people aren't good for profits. Patent the knock-offs, and sell them at a whopping profit. You want to ban everything natural, and not allow people to know what the fruits of nature can do. It's madness.' The voice got very assertive. 'I will not be threatened by Big Pharma, Big Mamma, or Big Daddy. We're only just getting rid of Big Brother!'

Tony took a long swig from his tumbler. 'I assume our Pharmaceutical Corporate Control Act gets pushed up the agenda?'

'Take that as a given,' Ray replied.

The entrance door was clicked open, and Dawn came into the room. 'It's time. Ray, are you sure you're up to seeing visitors?'

The meeting set between Ray and the American President had come around very quickly. The location for their public discussions had been perfectly choreographed. The White State Drawing Room had become the location of choice for the media to get their images of high profile visitors in conversation with the Prime Minister. A Downing Street fireplace was the centrepiece, with a comfortable armchair on either side of it. A highly ornamental coffee table was between them, useful for any props or talking points which might be required.

Until the 1940s, it had been a private area for the exclusive use of the Prime Minister and his family. Any ghosts from before that time would no doubt be mortified with the heavy level of traffic it now endured.

Cameramen from all wings of the media were busy getting their shots lined up to capture those who would be sitting in front of the fireplace. Truth Media TV was there, Tina and her trusty cameraman, now reaching far more people after having been granted a community television broadcasting licence. The Freeview spectrum was now opened up to them, so they were widely seen in their own area. What didn't change was how they looked. Being any part of the establishment was never going to rub off on them.

If nothing else, Ray's term of office was to become synonymous with the speed of its actions. No pontificating or prevaricating. If something had to be done, it was done at pace.

Ray entered the room first, his entourage in tow. Flashbulbs were sparse at that moment, the "money shot" would be the two leaders of their respective parts of the world meeting for the first time.

'Good morning,' Ray boomed at the media. 'Thanks for coming. Hope we live up to your expectations.' A murmur of polite laughter followed. 'Without further ado, here's someone I have come to know on the phone simply as Harry. You might get away with calling him Mr Stanton, but for your less appraised readers, listeners and viewers, I would like to welcome "POTUS", the President of the United States of America.'

Harry Stanton bounded into the room, arm raised in deference to the assembled, respectful and solid applause greeting him. This was someone who knew how to give the press what they wanted. He paused long enough for everyone to get their viewfinder lines inch-perfect, and then shook Ray's hand.

The handshake carried on as the flashbulbs ignited for a good half-minute. It was a firm grip from both men, but even Ray had trouble keeping up with Harry's enthusiasm to milk the moment for all he could.

Ray ushered Harry to sit down. They both made themselves comfortable, as the room settled. The men had decided to give top value to those networks which had sent their crews to the event. This wasn't just going to be a photo opportunity.

'Mr President, it has been a delight to consult with you on matters of common interest which we can take forward together,' Ray began.

Harry beamed. 'Here's me, coming from a libertarian Republican background, and I have to admit I have no idea where the heck you guys have come from!' The media hacks laughed, warming to him right away, in just the same way as their transatlantic counterparts had done so.

'Oh, come on Harry, how can anyone take seriously a political labelling system where, if you go far enough to the left you meet the extreme right?' The American President chuckled in response, lifted a cup, and took a sip of coffee. 'We're all about doing the right thing, not what colour our rosettes happen to be.'

'These folks want to know what we are going to sort out together,' Harry suggested, moving the dialogue forward. 'Shall we start with food and food supplements?'

'You have made great progress on that front for quite some time,' noted

Ray. 'Loved that advert by Mel Gibson showing that defining vitamins and other supplements as drugs was nonsense.'

'Loved that you repealed everything the European Commission had insisted upon as soon as you left the EU.'

'All that was at the beckon call of the Codex Alimentarius group,' Ray noted. 'The pharmaceutical corporations were having a field day.'

'So now, people can sell what they want, and buy what they want. The only thing we insist on is honesty in the labelling. Give the exact constituents of all these pills and potions, if not going so far as the balance of them in the recipe.' Harry smiled and raised his eyebrows. 'Oh, and all patents connected to food and drink are to be revoked.'

'You know what they'll say, Harry? All the conmen will be able to sell their "snake oils" without restriction.'

Harry leaned over towards Ray. 'That's why I want to suggest our two nations set up an independent body to check out all claims made on packaging, and in advertising. If the claims are validated, then there's no charge.' He then settled back in his armchair. 'If we find out these cowboys are ripping people off and telling lies, we serve them with a fine. Second time it happens, things get even worse for them.'

Ray nodded. 'Mind you, we're going to have quite a few objections to what we're doing about sugar, salt and flour.'

Harry grunted. 'Yeah, you know people just hate more taxes.' The room fell into an expectant hush.

'Well, the bad news is that we are going to tax all the refined white sugars, white salt and white flour in the marketplace.' Some of the newspaper reporters couldn't help but gasp. 'The good news is that for unrefined sugars, salts and flours, we'll be using the tax raised on the refined versions to subsidise the prices of these more natural products. The ones that retain the trace nutrients which nature intended us to have in our diets.'

'We'll be accused with giving with one hand and taking with the other,' Harry mocked.

'Just think how much colour we'll be adding to people's lives,' Ray replied assertively. 'The glorious pink and reddish hues of natural Himalayan salt for instance. Courtesy of the eighty-four trace minerals in it. Oh, and I should say we'll be eliminating sell-by dates from such salts. They've been locked in the Earth for thousands of years. They aren't going to go off in a geological blink of an eye, just because they've been extracted for use on our food!'

'And to help with the obesity problem, you know we have it bad in the USA, Ray, we're going to get manufacturers out of the habit of using glucose-fructose syrup. So, let's tax the substance back to the Stone Age!'

'I'll certainly join you in that one,' confirmed Ray. 'Terrible stuff. All calories, no benefits. Tell you what, let's add Monosodium Glutamate to that list. If people can't cook well enough without it, they ought to stay out of the kitchen.' Hacks in the room were madly scribbling. The mainstream news sources were working out how they could spin all this to the benefit of the status quo. Without banning things, they certainly couldn't be accused of double standards on urging people to make different food choices.

'Okay, as we're playing a bizarre game of poker here,' Harry teased, 'I'll take your Monosodium Glutamate and raise you with a total blanket ban on forced medication by the use of Sodium Fluoride in water supplies.'

'Oh, come on Harry, catch up, that's one of the first things we did when we got into office,' Ray replied with mock indignation.

'But did you make the water companies liable for the damage caused to the human body? Imagine the size of those class action lawsuits.'

Ray laughed. 'No, no we didn't. Obviously there are some things we can learn from you Americans.' The room was warming to the adversarial banter, despite the fact that beneath the rehearsed show in front of them, the leaders were agreed on everything.

'And another thing, what are you doing about those smart meters?' enquired Harry.

'You mean those command-and-control units which will lead to higher energy prices, and higher water prices, as well as frying everyone near them with huge doses of RF radiation?' Ray countered.

'That will be them. Yes.'

'Charge the energy companies monthly for each unit installed, until they are all removed at their own cost. No passing the bottom line on to the customers, either, or we'll revoke their rights to continue trading.'

'I think that's called a full court press,' joked Harry.

'Now, I don't want to be rude, but Harry, I think you've been fracking around far too much!' Ray chided.

'I wondered how long it would be until you accused me of fracking all over the place,' gushed Harry, deliberately sounding like he was a serial Lothario.

'It's got to stop Harry,' urged Ray, sounding like a concerned mother. 'You're poisoning your water supply, as well as using up billions of gallons of the keys to life itself.'

Harry looked sheepish in reply, 'And the way you are decimating the farming land by the nasty seepage into the soil. I mean, I ask you, it's almost like you want to do everything to put up the prices of food and water!'

'But Mom,' Harry said in a childlike voice, 'I can't rely on wind, wave or solar. What am I to do?'

'Bring back online your coal-fired stations, young man,' suggested Ray, waving his index finger at the world leader opposite. 'There's no pollution from them anymore, due to the better air filtration systems that are in service.' The American President nodded in mock fear. 'And stop any further investment in nuclear plants. We can rely on fossil fuels for the time being, especially as it appears that inactive mines are now replenishing themselves, and that the concept of "peak oil" is a complete hoax.'

Harry smiled. 'Yes, we're onboard with all that. I also offer my commitment to extract the patents that the big oil companies have removed from the public domain, and get our scientists to work on them.'

Ray could tell there was something of a "knowledge gap" within the assembled media representatives. 'Tesla technologies. Zero Point energies. There's a lot more at stake now than profits. All these amazing discoveries are going to be brought into mainstream research, whether they like it or not.' The journalists taking note had another couple of terms to look up later.

'Ray, I like your style,' gushed the President. 'I think you will find a use for this.' From behind his chair, Harry passed Ray a framed A3-sized facsimile of the American Constitution. Those reporters in the room who recognised it just had to laugh.

'The American Constitution,' Ray confirmed, filling in the blanks for those in the room who were falling behind. 'I'll have fun comparing this to the documents that make up our own British Constitution. Which you based it on.'

'Didn't know there was such a thing,' said Harry, exactly to script.

'Put that down to these reporters and their ancestors not doing their research.' Ray rolled out his best withering look. 'It's not all in one place, you see. Your lot just pulled all the elements together.'

That was the cue for Ray to reach around the back of his own chair. He pulled out a copy of Estulin's book on "The Bilderberg Group".

'And since like me you have not, and never will be, a member of the Bilderberg Group, I thought you could benefit from a copy of this.' Ray handed over the tome, and Harry smiled widely.

'Well, at least it's not a DVD box set!' he quipped. 'Know your enemy, I take it?'

'I'm not keen on world government,' Ray emphasised.

'Neither am I. Strangely enough, I prefer to be able to trade with whoever I like.'

'Which brings me to my next point. For those of us who recognise that owners of large corporations and members of specific bloodlines have a very "Burger King" attitude to the affairs of our planet…"

'Sorry, Ray, don't quite follow,' interjected Harry.

'You know. "Burger King". "Have it *their* way",' confirmed Ray. Harry laughed. 'I believe it is time for two of our universities to pool resources on the creation of a faculty that will look at how events have been manipulated over the centuries for the benefit of a chosen few. The thirteen clans. The elite. This transatlantic initiative should go under the banner of "The Department of False Flag Terrorism".'

The atmosphere in the room reflected that this term perplexed many of those present. Harry explained, 'I'll give you the benefit of doubt, that you may know it under its more traditional term of "black flag". These are covert operations designed to appear as though they are being carried out by groups other than those who actually planned and executed them. In particular, in the 21st Century they refer to acts carried out by military or security force personnel, which are then blamed on terrorists.' Harry looked around the room. 'Lesson over.'

'Our University of St Andrews does a course on Terrorism Studies,' noted Ray. 'I think it would be perfect for them to take this on and expand the relevant department.'

'I think this is one for our Department of Justice, Law and Society at the American University, Washington DC,' suggested Harry.

What they didn't reveal to the room was that both departments had already been approached. The offer of financial support for the new courses was all that had been needed for rapid agreement to be reached.

It had been a whirlwind of policy revelations, co-ordinated for maximum effect on both sides of the Atlantic. Both men were happy to take questions, and the session began to run out of steam half an hour later. With the more poisonous sections of the press not finding any areas of disagreement to harvest, or flaws in logic to reveal, there would be very little their news bulletins or column inches could make a fuss about.

Suddenly, "We the People" had one of the strongest business partners of all. Together, the UK and USA made a trading block which no country or union would want to ignore. The long-term survival of the party was secure. Now, it was just a question of keeping all the citizens onside through any manufactured problems ahead.

***

There was a certain irony to Duncan Hurst finding himself in Strangers' Bar at the House of Commons. He sat at the service bar, on one of its high stools, staring at the bottle optics and beer pumps in front of him. Any bar, anywhere, can easily become a lonely place to find yourself. Especially when friends were thin on the ground.

On a single, medium sized flat-screen TV, there was a relay of Ray Grady and the President of the United States of America. Their double-act would please everyone from small social clubs in northern England, to the Las Vegas Boulevard. Hurst was surprised that so much of their meeting was being broadcast. It wasn't the sort of thinking which should be encouraged.

He was making the large brandy last. The glass was disproportionately huge, all the better for smelling the fumes coming off the liquid within.

Phil entered the venue. He'd been told where to find Hurst. He took the chance to just stare at the solitary figure, size him up, not aware he was nowhere near realising the many heavy weights that Hurst's shoulders now had to accommodate. He approached the bar, and stood next to Hurst. No-one was around to serve him.

'Cheer up,' Phil suggested. 'I'm sure you'll soon get the credit you deserve.' Duncan scowled. 'Your pals at "6" are being pressured.' Duncan continued to stare ahead, trying to ignore the reporter next to him. 'And guess who they'll drop in it first?'

Duncan looked around at Phil with disdain. 'What do you want?'

'In an ideal world, the details of who you really work for.' Duncan gulped down half of the remaining brandy, very slowly turning his gaze back to straight in front of himself.

Phil smiled, message definitely received, and left. A barman then appeared, and came up to Duncan to request his requirements. 'A double. Two of them.'

* * *

At times like this, Damian found solace in a game of poker. His personal poker table, that is, part of the expansive gaming room on the island. It was almost like he was playing a character in the game, wearing a poker visor to add to the atmosphere.

He didn't want to be troubled by having to play with real people, though. Most poker players annoyed him intensely. No self-control, no ability to control their little tics and giveaways that simply spoiled a game. Around the table with him were three animatronic robots. Technology within them was a little hush-hush, and some people may have needed a double-take to appreciate the precise nature of these players. They really did look so human. The washed-out actress robot. The old huckster robot. The Young Turk robot. All with their own way of approaching the game.

A flashing blue light made itself known on Damian's Bluetooth earpiece. He tapped it to establish a connection. One day he was going to speak to someone on the phone with good news for him. Today was not going to be that day.

'Shoddy workmanship,' he said with exasperation, before checking his cards again for some sign of potential progress. 'And they wonder why the world is going to the dogs.' He tapped his cards on the table, for no apparent reason. 'I mean, how difficult is it to extinguish someone these days?'

He listened to the feeble excuses coming down the phone line at him. His masters at the Bilderberg Group could potentially sideline him for putting his faith in such withered incompetents. And as for Duncan Hurst, well, he had been right all along how third-rate that sycophant really was. Maybe it was time to spill all the dirt he had on him. Take him out of the picture for good. And then have him "suicided". He was sure his operatives would make it an honourable death, behind the scenes.

He felt the need to turn away from the table before answering the latest bleatings he was having to endure from his caller. 'We need to sort this out sharp. Other countries will start getting ideas.' Again, the magnitude of the problem was not being appreciated. 'Leave it with you?'

It was as if he was expected to forget the mistakes and accompanying ridicule he had endured to date. 'Tell you what, how about if I, just for fun, bankrupt your country?'

A sharp tap on the earpiece finished the call, and Damian looked at his cards once more. He scowled, then hyperventilated, and threw his hand into the middle of the table. Sometimes the odds are always against you.

'Fold!'

* * *

Someone had once told Ray it was not the etiquette to take leaders of other countries back to the Prime Minister's Private Office. Ray had thought that ridiculous, and had broken the code almost from day one. It was a piece of information that the hard drive had confirmed for the Pentagram Team. As such, it would have been churlish not to follow established patterns of behaviour.

Ray opened the door and beckoned the President, or Harry as he could now call him, into his inner sanctum. 'I assume you are a whisky man?' he enquired of his visitor, as he headed over to the drinks cabinet and started preparations.

'I limit myself to only the finest,' Harry replied. 'Has to be from Scotland.'

'From a continent that gave us bourbon, I'm happy to hear it.' Ray filled a pair of tumblers with shots of Laphroaig Triple Wood single malt, famous for being bottled at 48% ABV, and handed one to the President, who sniffed it approvingly.

'Very peaty. Neat.'

'I'm glad we see eye to eye on so many things. I think our little show earlier went very well.'

'Let's just see what the editors do with it. So much to cover in one go. Will be interesting what ignites their ire the most.'

Ray went to the large side window, and looked out. Harry joined him.

The two leaders looked to the heavens, seeing a sky that was clear blue, with the sunshine making for a warm, balmy day.

'It's the simple things in life which people will begin to appreciate again,' said Ray, waxing lyrical. 'Able to look up without a sea of fog above our heads.'

Harry cooed appreciation. 'Glad to see you've got rid of those chemtrails, too.'

'Makes a huge difference in defusing tensions in the Isles by not poisoning our own people,' Ray confirmed.

'Population reduction by the back door.'

'Whilst cooling the planet to fight global warming,' Ray scorned. 'Which wasn't happening in the first place! No wonder everywhere has actually been getting colder.'

'Corporate profits being put above everything else.'

'Hopefully, this is the beginning of the end for the New World Order.'

Harry gazed into his tumbler, realising he had to address realities. 'With such a quiet revolution in both our countries, we'll both be short of allies.'

Ray nodded sagely, and offered up his glass. 'To the future.'

'The future,' the President confirmed, and they clinked tumblers.

Inside Ray's head, the team were realising that, when Ray was relaxing, they could also take it easy. Vernon, however, was never off-duty. Something had caught his eye on the instrument settings, causing him to rub his temples.

Jack looked over, concerned at Vernon's concern. 'Everything okay?' he enquired.

'Not sure. Almost getting what I might describe as cross-channel interference.'

'Any immediate danger?' asked Jack.

'That's the whole point of us being within Ray, so these sorts of things aren't a problem,' Vernon reassured. 'But this is like a "ghosting" on an old analogue TV picture. Like when two transmitters are broadcasting on the same wavelength. Except that's almost impossible in this digital age.'

Vernon stared at the front view-screen, which was filled with a close-up of the American President's face as Ray was standing right in front of him. Vernon was concentrating on the world leader's eyes. They seemed both empty and alive at the same time. The rest of the team tried to see what it was he was staring at so avidly.

Over Ray's heartbeat, a second heartbeat now drummed its own tune.

Definitely interference of some sort. Vernon zoomed in on the iris of the President's right eye, and suddenly they found themselves zooming in right to the centre of the President's head.

The bizarre refractive properties of the human eye let them see far more than they ever should have done. Inside the President's head, but in a different position to their own, was an almost identical insertion capsule.

And for those inside the President's capsule, they were making the same revelation. The technology of discovery was working both ways. They too were a crew of five. They too had similar boiler suits, but theirs were red, white and blue in colour. With some stars braided on to them. And with baseball caps on each of their heads.

Different sides of the Atlantic. Same objective. Same sort of enigmatic leader. Same problem to solve.

Jack looked around at his team. 'It appears we are not the only ones on a mission.'

Vernon let out a scream. 'Bastards! Who gave them permission to pirate my technology?'

TO BE CONTINUED

ACKNOWLEDGEMENTS

My thanks to my late parents, Harold and Eunice, for always encouraging me to write, even getting me an enormous electric typewriter at a very young age. I'm only sorry neither of you saw this first novel make the bookshelves.

This concept started out as a film script, but the reactions my agent, Daisy Jones, got to it from production companies were baffling. Producers were scared of the content. No-one wanted to tackle the story of a peaceful political revolution. Certainly not one set within the boundaries of the United Kingdom.

Thanks to Daisy, between us we decided that a novel was the way to go. Considering it first came to life in late 2010, fuelled by the coalition that came from that year's general election, the time for its publication is most certainly now. There are no political parties that can be trusted, and deep down the majority of the switched-on population knows this. As geopolitical expert Ian R Crane notes, they are all "controlled opposition" and it is he I must thank for lighting the blue touch-paper of devising the British public a new political option.

Without the unflinching and continuing support of my wife, Sarah, I simply wouldn't have been able to devote the necessary time to expand the original script into what you are now holding in your hands. Meanwhile, Johnnie P was always at the end of the phone to provide extra knowledge and context to flesh out what has, in effect, become an alternative universe. He also made the connection for me to Jason of Liquorice, who came up with the cover designs that hopefully added to your temptation to pick this novel up, either via virtual or actual bookshelves.

Special thanks to the Edge Media Television team who helped make *On The Edge* (series three) such a special a time in my life – particularly Keith, David, Steve and Mark. Major kudos to those who have helped out on *Doomwatch®*, and its predecessor "Red Alert Radio" on Peterborough FM – name-checks for Tom, Lexy, Steph, Matthew, Sabrina, Shelley and Pedro. And of course to all our guests and correspondents who provided so much of the content which finds itself encapsulated and adopted in this novel. Gold stars for Brian and Mike of the UK Column who helped take *Doomwatch®* to the next level.

I'd also like to thank the defenders of mainstream opinion who provided the final motivation to cross the finish line on writing this tome. They did this inadvertently, but their almost-unrelenting support of official lines on so many subjects was something I couldn't ignore. They will no doubt dismiss much of what is mentioned herein, currently happening in the world around us, as pure hokum. So be it, but the lack of documentary proof doesn't mean it isn't a reality.

It is now twenty years since I met Harlan Ellison, while I was running the very first Cult TV Festival. His essays on both life and the media have long inspired me in my writing, and now his unparalleled speculative fiction finally comes into play. I hope he sees what's in front of you here as being something more than gibberish.

My wife and I even had the pleasure to meet the iconic Patrick McGoohan back in 2008. Lunch at Spago Beverly Hills. His kind words about an earlier script of mine remain stapled to the wall in my studio here at Cult TV Towers. Every time I need a kick to keep things moving, I look at that letter.

Finally, I'd like to thank *you* for getting hold of this work of speculative fiction. I readily admit that, for us to enter this world of alternatives, the majority of the UK population will have to change. First, as noted in the text, they must take on-board that all political parties start with the same number of votes on Election Day: zero. Secondly, they'll have to stop wanting to back a winner and actually vote for policies they believe in. And finally, those who don't vote at all will need to realise that making their mark really can make a difference to their lives.

Even above the likes of quantum physics, holographic universes, and hologram science contained herein, believing in those three changes is the

255

largest leap of logic of all. I hope that, at a general election in the near future, my cynicism is proven as unjustified.

Alex J Geairns (aka alex:g)
Cult TV Towers, Whittlesey, Peterborough, UK
August 2014